Black Mischief

BOOK TWO OF THE AFRICAN TRILOGY

CARL HANCOCK

Carl Hancock was born in Aberdare, then a mining valley town in South Wales. After seven years in the local grammar school, he moved on to university where he studied for degrees in Classics and in English and became a teacher. His career took him to secondary schools in Britain, Cyprus and Malta. Latterly, he enjoyed six years in Pembroke House, a preparatory school up-country in the Kenya part of the Great Rift Valley, sometimes known as the White Highlands. He has two grown-up children and currently lives on a small farm in the Adelaide Hills.

Published in Australia by Sid Harta Publishers Pty Ltd,
ABN: 46 119 415 842
23 Stirling Crescent, Glen Waverley, Victoria
3150 Australia
Telephone: +61 3 9560 9920, Facsimile: +61 3 9545 1742
E-mail: author@sidharta.com.au

First published in Australia July 2011
This edition published July 2011

Cover design, typesetting: Chameleon Print Design

Hancock, Carl
Black Mischief
ISBN: 1-921829-29-X
EAN13: 978-1-921829-29-1
pp364

Glossary

askari	guard
dawa	medicine
duka	shop
fundi	expert
Hakuna matata	no worries
jua kali	improvised
kwaheri	goodbye
matatu	minibus taxi
matumba	market
mbati	corrugated iron
mbaye	thief
mzee	old man
mzungo	stranger
posho	milled and boiled maize
shamba	small farm
wananchi	ordinary people
tackies (local usage)	trainers

To the 'wananchi' of Kenya. You are the talented but undervalued heartbeat of your country. You are the hope that someday soon your country will have the leadership you need and deserve.

Chapter One

It was the biggest party seen at Muthaiga in years. That was no surprise. After all, Abel Rubai was the richest man in the country and he wanted something extra special to celebrate his oldest boy's engagement. One thing still puzzled him. As he watched his future daughter-in-law make her entrance into the L-shaped dining room with her family, he could see again what a prize Julius had won himself. Only, how had his boy managed to snare this girl? Why had she suddenly broken off her engagement to Tom McCall, the cocky farmer boy from Naivasha? Abel had always believed that there wasn't a woman in Kenya who didn't have her price, but this Rebecca was different. She was a beauty and the people loved her. She was a wealthy girl in her own right after her singing successes in the United States of America. She would bring a lot to the family. Maybe, from now on, the wananchi would be a bit less suspicious of him. And, just maybe, she would help turn Julius around from being the self-centred brat he had been for most of his adult life into the kind of son and heir he had planned for, one who would make the many advantages he had been gifted with pay off in a big way.

Simon Liwatt, the head porter at the club, was having a quiet night. He was at his desk close to the normally popular back entrance to the club. For this special night the guests had come through the front entrance and for the hour that the party had been going, he had not had a single visitor. He could hear the fun and frolicking going on in the room next door, but he was indifferent to the noise, the laughter of the rich folks having a jolly good time. But at last his lonely haven was invaded. A door from the dining room was opened. Before he could look up from the ledger where he was checking some lists, a voice from the figure whose large shape was casting its shadow across his desk addressed him curtly.

'Keys. Drinks room. Now!'

There was no need for Simon to look up to find out who was trying to break a strict club rule and forcing him to do the same. He recognised the voice and the manner. He reached across to a row of keys and placed the relevant one on the counter. It was no hard task for the head porter to mask the anger he felt for Julius Rubai under a bland, submissive exterior. He was a master of hiding his true feelings when need be.

'Here we are, sir.'

The most unpopular member of the club strode out of sight, muttering to himself, only to return within a minute clutching a glass and a bottle of Jack Daniels. He broke the seal, poured himself a large measure and gulped it down.

'Ahh! Now that's a man's drink, not like that wine and champagne muck they're serving in there.'

He poured a refill and set the tumbler on the desk counter.

'You should get yourself one of these,' he snorted. 'Must be boring as hell in here.' His tone had shifted to patronising, the closest Julius Rubai came to friendly when addressing one of the servants.

Simon squirmed inwardly. He preferred Julius's arrogant tone. At least that was more honest. None of the club staff enjoyed dealing with this rich man's son. He was demanding, rude and did not seem to understand the concept of respect.

The sound of footsteps hurrying up the steps from the car park drifted in through the open door. Julius moved to check on the newcomer. Simon was not unpleasantly amazed to see a lightning change of expression show on Julius's face. Tortured rage might have been his description, if he had had time to reflect. Before he could, he picked up the unmistakable voice of the young farmer from the flower farm on the shores of Lake Naivasha. Simon had known three generations of the McCall family and liked them all.

Julius had been shocked to see coming up the steps towards the entrance that muscular, rolling gait he had been familiar with since he was seven years old. He was seething with a mixture of anger and panic. Since his school days up in Pembroke House, the name McCall had always spelt danger.

'You bastard, what are you doing here?'

'Charming! Excuse me, Mr Rubai, I want to check the family pigeonhole.'

Tom had long understood the unnerving effect his presence seemed to have on his old school colleague. He did not glory in the fact, but it had always been hard to resist the little digs that would send Julius's temper soaring.

'The club is out of bounds tonight and you know it!'

'Oh, not again! Look, Phil will be along in a minute. You must remember Phil. He's got a letter signed by the committee. Says we can come in. Trust a lawyer to find a way around a problem.'

Simon smiled and nodded his head. The McCall boy had got it right. There was the copy of the docket on his desk, given to him by the club secretary.

'Why have you come here tonight?'

'It's our night for squash. Friday night.'

'Liar!'

'I beg your pardon.'

'You won't leave her alone, will you?'

Tom hesitated and looked away. Julius, aware that Simon would be tuned in to every word they said, motioned for Tom to move back from the door. For his own reasons, Tom was happy to comply, but having withdrawn no more than ten metres, turned on Julius.

'Listen, Mr Rubai and get this straight. I wouldn't do anything to spoil this night for her. God knows why she has gone for a loser like you. But it's her choice and I respect it. Have you bloody well got that?'

'And you can keep your foul tongue for the likes of your friend Coulson.'

'Foul tongue? You're losing it, old chap!'

'Don't you "old chap" me! This isn't one of your colonies any more. We do the bossing about now!'

'Yeah, tell me about it, but you don't own this club, yet!'

'And you have to prove what a clever little chap you are, so you come here to try to spoil our evening.'

'Pure bullshit! How could I spoil your night by collecting our mail just as I do every time I come to this club? Am I going to piss in the drinks or something?'

'Typical! Rebecca should see you now.'

'You're right, Rubai. Coarse and crude, but why is it that just being in your company brings out the worst in me?'

'So, will you leave now?'

'Of course I will, when I'm good and ready. First, I'm going in there …'

'I forbid you!'

'You haven't got your heavy boys around you now. You wouldn't want to mess up that smart white coat rolling about in the dust with scum like me!'

'Don't worry about my coat. We'll sort this for once and for all.'

Simon had left his desk and watched the exchanges of the two angry men with dismay. It crossed his mind that he might save the day by offering to check on the McCall pigeonhole, but fear overruled the possibility, fear for himself and his job. He would be in dangerous territory. Everyone in the club knew some version of how this Rebecca Kamau had suddenly ditched Tom McCall for Julius Rubai.

That evening, for the first time Simon had been close to her as she entered the club. She was the most beautiful woman he had ever seen and he understood why two men might fight hard to get her. In his eyes, she had made a crazy choice, but what did he know about women? He had never married, never really got on with any of his five sisters. But he saw clearly that all these angry words would do no good.

'Too late, Bwana McCall, too late! Better go down into town with your friend and find a quiet bar.'

Simon hoped that this wild talk of fighting would come to nothing. There was a brief silence. Perhaps he should speak up, let them know that someone was watching, be a distraction. Once again fear got the better of him. And Julius, for one, was finished with words. Without warning, he strode off past Tom and down the grassy bank to a gap in the hedge that opened out onto the golf course. Tom followed him into the semidarkness.

In mounting panic, Simon hurried across the empty lounge and peeped into the party room. As he had hoped, there was a Rubai man on the door. His whispered message was soon transmitted into the ears of the Big Man. The result was immediate. The broad smile on the host's face changed briefly to a frown, but, regaining his composure, he rose from his chair and crossed the room towards the open door. His progress was swift but measured.

In seconds he was hurrying down the steps in the company of half a dozen of his best boys. Simon stood at the door and watched the beams of torches as they haphazardly searched the darkness for the two young men. The first shot rang out from somewhere deep into the course. By the time the second shot was heard only seconds later, Simon was reaching out for his phone, barely conscious of the shouts coming from the Rubai group out on the course and the uproar close by as the scores of guests rushed out of the dining room to follow where the now focused beams of light drew them on.

Simon's call to Nairobi Hospital for assistance was soon done. Afterwards he sat riveted to his chair, trembling, with his eyes closed. Two more shots, a surge of noise and then sudden silence increased his fear and his anger with himself for being such a coward. There might be someone dead out there and minutes ago he had had the opportunity to have prevented whatever had happened. In the middle of his deep anxiety, there was one thing he knew for certain. He would never willingly share the story of the events that had unfolded since Julius Rubai had left his engagement party to demand the keys to the club drinks room.

The long silence outside was finally broken. There were voices in the car park. He hurried to the door and looked out. He was stunned by what he saw. Rebecca Kamau was unmistakable, but why was her dress torn? Why was she crying? One other member of her family he recognised for sure. Her father was moving with slow, powerful strides following lawyer Coulson to the bwana's car. In his arms he carried the limp shape of a man's body. Simon bit his clenched fist and let the tears flow. In his cowardice he had allowed the good young farmer of Londiani to lose his life.

Chapter Two

Two mothers were united in grief. Two eldest sons had been in mortal danger. Twice in four months Tom McCall had come close to death. Julius Rubai lost his life to a bullet from his own gun on what should have been the happiest day of his life. On the evening of May twenty-fifth on the fourth green of the Muthaiga Golf Club two shots rang out. Guests at the engagement party in the dining room rushed out to find two young men lying on the clipped, damp grass. Tom was bleeding from a wound in his thigh. Julius was dying after an attempt by a bodyguard of Julius's father to seize the gun had gone badly wrong.

The young men had been boys together at Pembroke House, a boarding prep school in up-country Gilgil, and had never got on. Julius, son of a rich and powerful father, was used to getting his way and hated the farmer's son's popularity. Fair-haired Tom had an easy charm and was happy with his life. Julius was never really at ease with the very English ways of the school. He could not understand why no one made a fuss of him or saw him as something special.

One evening towards the end of Julius's last term there had been a clash over house rules in the shower queue. Julius tried to show Tom up in front of the boys standing in line with their towels draped around their naked bodies. When Tom refused to cooperate, Julius tried to grab his shoulder but only managed to scratch the flesh and draw blood. The fight was short but vicious. Ben Boyd, the duty master, had managed to pull them apart and gave them a severe warning. Within two hours the anger and hate bubbled over again and, while the rest of the senior school were working quietly at their prep, they were tearing into each other under cover of darkness down on the playing fields.

Twelve years later, their two lives slammed into each other on a deadly collision course. Traditional Kenyan wisdom would have described what happened as a fate sent by the gods. Rebecca and Tom were deeply in love and over all prejudices and objections, save one. Five years before, Julius had chanced to see Rebecca performing at a concert at the Bomas Centre and lusted after her ever since. In a fury of frustration that he could not persuade her out of this stupid infatuation for the arrogant, little white bwana, he made barely veiled threats about the consequences of what she was getting herself into. Rebecca, terrified and unable to share her fears, realised that to save Tom she must sacrifice herself. It was a secret she must keep to herself. Her desperate action would be misunderstood by those whom she loved most. She would not be able to tell them the truth and she would hurt them. But as long as Tom was safe, she would be content and there would be a kind of peace. She was ready to become the wife of Julius. The shedding of Rubai blood did not bring closure.

Two mothers were united in grief, but the pain was not equally shared. Both struggled to stay afloat in a whirlpool of emotions. Maura McCall could not hide her joy that her son had survived, nor could she shake off a sense of guilt for this blessing. For Sally Rubai the passing of the days did not bring healing for her loss. She simply became more used to the merciless reality.

It was five months later when Maura finally persuaded Sally to leave her Karen home to travel to take tea on the veranda of Londiani. The two women had not been out of contact in the time since that fateful May night. There had been letters, mostly from Maura's side, but it was in the telephone calls where the bond began to grow strong. At first, the conversations were punctuated by long silences and focused on the May night, but gradually they were able to talk about other things. The silences became shorter and the range of topics wider. There was more and more of what Alex, Maura's husband, described as 'woman talk' and moments of uninhibited hilarity when Sally's gravelly, sexy chuckle rang down the line and brought tears to Maura's eyes.

It was a balmy afternoon when Sally's chauffeur-driven Mercedes pulled up on the driveway close to the three steps leading up to the veranda of Londiani. Soon four women were sitting around the table spread with a blue cloth laden with silver and the Royal Worcester tea set. There was a fifth woman present who should have been seated, too, but Angela Kamau could not yet bring herself to accept that she was more than an ordinary servant in the McCall household. Rebecca had managed to talk her mother into swapping her Big House clothes for a pair of pink slacks and a close fitting white blouse. As Maura watched Angela returning to the kitchen after delivering milk and sugar to the table, she remembered for the umpteenth time the words of their neighbour, Bertie Briggs, about the smart sexiness of Somali women, 'the best lookers in Africa'. It was obvious from where Rebecca inherited her looks, the tall, full figure, the well-sculpted almost oriental facial features and one song from her father, Stephen, would have told anyone that his rich bass-baritone voice was special and that his genes would have had a big part in creating the extraordinary soprano sound of his firstborn.

The coming together of these women had been an awkward one. The scars of violence ensured that this would be so, in spite of the warmth they all felt for each other. It had been the men in the Rubai family who had brought Tom McCall close to death twice, but it was Julius, Sally's firstborn, her special boy, who had lost his life on that May evening.

Rafaella, the good-looking, Italian born matriarch of the McCalls of Londiani, had also been plunged down into the depths of grief of loss two years before when her husband, Don, had died not a hundred metres from that veranda when his small white aircraft had been forced just the smallest fraction too far right as it came in to land on the slippery dirt runway on Crescent Island. On the eve of Christmas, joy turned to despair in a single moment. The wildebeest that had forced Don off course then skipped away to nibble at a patch of grass under a nearby acacia tree.

It was Rafaella who had been first down the steps to embrace the portly Sally. The hug was long and the two became four, five even when Sally insisted that Angela, hovering in the background, come down the steps to join them. Before the women separated, Sally was into a burst of that throaty, chuckling laughter that made the little group rock gently.

'Ladies, can you see that I have put on a little weight in the belly region?'

None of the four was willing to acknowledge what they had all noticed as soon as she stepped down from her car.

'I have some news. A little one is on his way. Yes, I know that I am a bit older than usual for having a child. But it is a wonderful gift to us. I said to Abel that if God has granted us the ability to do this thing, then we should accept the chance. Glory be, Abel said that he totally agreed! I have to admit I enjoyed the process of, what shall we say, procreation! I feel like an eighteen year old again.' She rounded off her announcement with another sexy chuckle.

All awkwardness was gone. The exchanges were open and no subject was taboo. Maura was intrigued by one word of Sally's.

'"His", Sally. How do you know it will be a boy?'

'Ah, yes, it's true. The wonders of science. One little scan and the mystery is gone. And I am not unhappy. For one thing I can talk to him. Yes, we have had many conversations. They are all a bit one-sided just now, of course. And our son-to-be has a name. It is Abel's choice.'

Rebecca looked across at her mother who was standing behind Maura's chair and winced briefly. Sally alone of the company did not notice the tiny gesture. Rebecca had guessed a name and it set off a stream of unpleasant memories.

'The boy will be called Julius. I must tell you that this child is already bringing new life to this family in more ways than one!'

There was a brief silence. None of Sally's companions could think of anything to say to keep the flow of the conversation from breaking. Sally understood.

'Julius, God bless his soul, brought bad things to this family. I know it. He brought many bad things to himself also. I failed him. I could not lead him out of his darkness. Perhaps no one can do that in somebody else's life. Rebecca, I had a big hope that with you he would find himself. God forgive me, on that day when you came to our house drenched in the rain and said that your engagement to Thomas was over, I pushed away the truth that was so clear. You gave me hope for the first time in years. I thought you could grow to love him, bring him back to us. After that terrible night, our lives fell apart for a time. It was hard for us all but especially for his father. His heart was broken. Maura, thank God for your letters! If only I could have persuaded Abel to read them, but so many things reminded him of his special boy. Glory be to God, every day I pray that a healing will begin for Abel. I think that this new child will help him.'

Rebecca reached across to take Sally's hand. 'Sally, it's all right, Mama, I'm not being disrespectful.' Her tone was firmly controlled at first and the words came slowly as if they were being carved out of some hard substance. 'Many things have happened to us all in this last year. There has been much danger. For me the biggest danger is that I have learned to deceive, sometimes by telling lies and sometimes by just not telling the truth. If I wanted to give an excuse for myself, I would say I did all this not for myself but to protect another person. I was afraid for Thomas. I became a clever liar and I became less tender for being so. Sally, I was not honest when I came to your home in Karen. Did my lies help to kill Julius? Yes, they did. When I started out on this dangerous path I thought I was being strong. Julius was too strong for me. I was weak and in a panic.'

'Child, when you came to me, I saw these things and my weakness was that I was a deceiver too, hiding away from the truth. I hoped you would come to love Julius. Darling, these wounds will be with us to the end, but the blood has dried and we must wash it away, together. But, you know, part of the problem is that we are little people and we think that happiness is our birthright. On very good days I have a little chuckle about this. It's true! It always helps. One time I was alone in the bedroom and I took off all my clothes and stood in front of my long mirror. It still makes me smile when I remember it. I moved about a bit. In seconds I was laughing out loud and talking to that woman wobbling back at me. That's a pretty face, Sal, but with all that blubber, don't think of entering any races! Picture it!'

Without rising from her chair, she gently shook the upper part of her body. 'Isn't it hilarious? Our dog can do it much better!'

The chuckle was back, and the broad smile. She kept the movement going, raised her bent arms and swayed sinuously as though she was dancing. A burst of coarse laughter was infectious and all her companions, almost in spite of themselves, were smiling, with Rebecca and even Angela bending over and happily losing control.

Sally stopped her moving and gradually the laughter subsided. The solemnity returned, at a deeper level than before the change of mood. There followed a long, relaxed silence broken by a subdued Sally.

'I want to ask you a favour. Abel wants to visit.' Another silence with Maura and Rafaella, and Angela and Rebecca exchanging puzzled looks. 'I can see you are shocked. He needs to talk with Alex and Thomas.'

'But why, Sally? It's not six months ago that he wanted to kill Tom. If it's anything to do with that horrible night, why don't you include Stephen? He would have been the first to die if Abel had pulled the trigger.'

'Maura, when I cooled his anger just enough to prevent him pulling the trigger, that was the greatest achievement of my life and I thank God for it every day. And I beg you to let him come. Try to see him for what he is today. Rafaella, Angela, Rebecca and you, Maura, you are the dearest women in the world to me. You do not judge me. I am not the big man's wife here. Talk to your men. See what they say. Let me know.'

Chapter Three

Reuben Rubai was the second son of Sally and Abel and quite different from his elder brother. While Julius was tall and muscular, Reuben was shorter and wiry. Julius was proud of his close crop of tight, curly hair. Reuben worked hard to look after his thick, flowing locks which his brother often told him was a sign that he was not a proper Rubai. 'They make you look like a whitey with black skin. Get them shaved off. I'll do the job. No charge.'

Reuben's reply was to smile and shake his head as he pushed the hair back from his forehead. 'Uh,uh. This mop will come in handy one day. Just you wait.'

Julius was a loner with no close friends. Reuben loved mixed company and could call on a dozen or more people to help him when he found himself in trouble. Julius was spoilt and Reuben scorned him for grovelling to their father to make sure he was well stocked with funds. He resented his father for not recognising or not caring that it was his second son who was the political animal, the one he should be supporting and encouraging. Reuben knew that his father did not approve of what he liked to call his social failings, letting the family down for the sake of his stupid ideas.

As a boy, he rarely came home in the car sent out to pick up the Rubai children from their city schools. He preferred to find his way down into town. He was constantly sharing with street kids money, food even clothes. He insisted on travelling on matatus, anytime he could. This infuriated his father and stirred the scorn of Julius.

'Listen, little brother, you got to stop this crap way of living. You may not look like a Rubai, but you better try acting like one.'

Reuben had a sharp answer ready but did not want to risk another thump in the head for crossing his touchy bully of a brother.

But it was at a matatu stop in Tom Mboya Street in Nairobi where Reuben met Lydia. She asked him for a light. His response was to snatch the cigarette from her lips, stamp it into the pavement and invite her for a cup of coffee. When he discovered that she lived in Kibera, one of the three large slum townships scattered around the city, his interest was roused. It was a place he wanted to visit, but it was a place he was wary of entering alone.

'What's a good looker like you doing living in that dump?'

'Well, for one thing it is not a dump and for another you're wasting my time unless you are looking for a bit of fun. Not expensive, just two thousand an hour.'

'Mucho cheapo! That's way below the going rate even for an old banger who's been on the game for yonks.'

'Why do you talk so funny?'

'I read a lot of books.'

'I can read. But I don't get much books. My brother can read, too. He's in America.'

'Does he approve of you doing this?'

'Approve?'

'Does he mind you going to bed with strangers?'

'He don't know. Anyway, it's my first day. You could be my first customer. But I don't have no bed. I have a friend who will rent me a room in her hotel. Not far from here. You pay for the room. No bedbugs, no cockroaches.'

Reuben was about to make the big moral statement, but no words came from his mouth, only a sad groan. His eyes welled up. It was part pity but mostly anger. Even in this thin, poor quality dress and the plastic shoes she was an attractive girl, a child forced to grow up too quickly who would not be short of customers out on the streets. Her limbs were well formed and smooth as carved brown ivory. Her lips were thin, her trusting, dark eyes were calm and inquisitive, her body lithe. And she was shorter than Reuben. He liked that. He pondered for a moment, taken up with a piece of mental arithmetic. Then, his mind made up, his tone became businesslike.

'Listen. Don't do this. Come here every week at about this time and there'll be an envelope waiting with five thousand shillings inside, six if I can raise it. I'll come myself if I can. You just stay off the streets. I know people. I can help to get you into a good school near home. You can learn to talk funny like me. What do you think?'

There was a long silence. Lydia was staring over Reuben's shoulder at passers-by in the street outside as if she was making some calculations of her own.

Fearing that she might turn him down, he pushed in another argument.

'I know that a girl like you, fresh on the streets, could make a lot more than five thousand a week, but for sure sooner or later someone will give you a dose. You'll be sick or you could die. Now then?'

'Who are you? Have you got the religion or something? Just like those who come 'round Kibera every day. They talk a lot but nothing changes. Except the nuns in those crazy uniforms. They live in there with us. I like to talk with them.'

'But you haven't talked to them about this stuff.'

'I have. Sister Caroline thinks it might be a good idea. Do it for a year, make some money and get out of that place.'

'Now I've heard everything! Nuns telling girls to go on the game!'

'No game. Business.'

'Business! You crazy kid! Look, I'll make it ten thousand. My mother will give me the extra when I tell her about you.'

He pulled out his wallet and counted off five thousand. 'No envelope. Next time there'll be fifteen thousand. Promise.'

'You very rich boy. You don't live in Kibera.'

'No, but some day you could invite me to your house or something.'

'Better have a strong nose!'

'Yeah. Just take the money. Then we can get a matatu. I can go home that way.'

The deal was struck and Reuben never failed to keep his promise of payment. And within weeks he had found her a new school. To her surprise, she liked the place and after a time became a boarder. It was easier that way and her family approved. One less mouth to feed.

Over the next few years they built up a strong but strictly non-romantic relationship. Once, during a noisy night out at the Carnivore with a dozen or so members of what was known around town as the Reuben set, he had put his arm around her shoulder and declared her to be his blood brother. The whoop of mocking delight sent the decibels soaring around that corner table, to the annoyance of fellow diners and to the distress of Angelo, the young Italian manager. He dreaded seeing this mob of well-off Nairobi youth enter his restaurant but knew that he would not take them on, tell them to cut down the noise or throw them out. He was too sensible, too worried for his job, too anxious about his wellbeing.

'Reuben, take your hands off me. You know I'm not a girl like that!' Lydia patted his face gently and rocked with laughter. It was four years on since they had met on Tom Mboya Street. Lydia was a much-changed young lady. She had put on a little weight to round out her figure, learned a lot about the art of make-up and dress, realised that men found her very attractive and revelled in their attention. In the last months they had seen a lot less of each other mostly because of her new job somewhere out on the big industrial estate off the Mombasa Road. So, she was taken aback when she was invited to Julius's engagement party on May twenty-fifth. When Reuben met her at the main gate of the Muthaiga, she had just stepped down from a taxi. It was the first time he had seen her dressed formally and he was impressed.

'Man, look at us, you in that cool get-up and me in my Che Guevara outfit. Yellow suits you. You are going to be a star in there. Hey, that dress must have cost you.'

'No, no, just the material. My mother and her sister have a machine and they are very good at the dressmaking.'

He was still shaking his head in wonder as he followed her up the steps and into the party. She soon showed that she was at ease in this company as she smiled her way around the crowded room. After a time he began to take a different slant on her social ease. It dawned on him that she was especially familiar to some of the guests, all of them middle-aged men. He only knew them as wealthy owners of big, city businesses. Each took Lydia aside for a few moments and greeted her animatedly and each time this happened she looked over her shoulder as if she were trying to locate someone in the crowd. When he realised that the someone was himself, he decided to move in. He crossed the room casually until he was close behind her and in the few seconds when she was between conversations, took her by the elbow and guided her into an empty side room.

'So, Miss Nairobi, you forgot about your side of our little agreement!'

'I never missed once coming to the coffee shop, even after you started sending delivery boys with the envelope. Anyway that was a long time ago now.'

'Mmn. How come you know those jerks in there? You know the ones, all shiny faces and expensive suits? More important, how do they know you?'

'Business associates?' Lydia fluttered her eyes hopefully.

'Flat on your back, legs open wide kind of business.'

'Anyone ever tell you that you have a dirty mouth?'

'Lots of times, but it only happens when I'm angry. I'm angry now, mostly with myself for not seeing what was going on, more like what was coming off! Go on, tell me, how much?'

Lydia looked down at the carpet and pouted. 'I didn't want to hurt you. I owe you … so many things.'

'How much?' A burst of laughter in the main room fuelled his mounting anger.

'Okay, Okay! I want to buy a house on the Ngong Road. You know my brother, Simon, is sick. I think it's the TB. He needs a dry house. I could raise the money with seven thousand a week, but it would take such a long time. Houses like this are very expensive.'

'Don't tell me. I know.'

'That's just it. You don't know. Money flows through your house like a river. You don't need a proper job. How much is this party costing? Mostly these men are very kind. Perhaps you won't believe this, but every time I undress and get ready, I think of us meeting on Tom Mboya Street all that time ago …'

There was a long pause when Reuben sighed and stared down at the carpet. When he looked up again, he had a wry smile on his face. He raised his arms dramatically as if in surrender.

'Stop! Stop! Anagnorisis. No, it's not a dirty word. Look it up. I like to read Greek plays. Very old ones. Suddenly coming to see things that you didn't see before though they were there all the time.'

'Have you been drinking?'

'You know better than that.'

'But it's your brother's engagement party.'

'I apologise. You have every right. We're all at it, this selling game. Nyama Choma, underwear. You have a very good product.'

'You make it sound disgusting.'

'Well, isn't it? A man and a woman, naked in bed, at it like a couple of randy dogs. But a lot of people obviously get a lot out of it, so. Caught me by surprise. That's all. Shall I still send the envelopes? No, sorry. Stupid question. I want to send them. Use the money to get a good doctor for Simon.'

Uproar broke out in the next room. There were screams and the sound of people on the move.

By the time Reuben reached the fourth fairway his brother was dead and in the light of the torches he saw his father unsteadily pointing a gun at a big man carrying the body of a white man. Then his mother was moving very gently towards her husband's shoulder. Words were spoken and the gun fell to the ground. In a few moments the main drama was over and the shock waves began to eddy out from the surreal epicentre of shock and death.

Reuben watched but felt no compulsion to move out of the darkness to join his parents who were surrounded by a wide circle of party guests. Their silence had changed to a low murmuring. He was stunned but frightened, too. His father's head was bowed towards his chest and he was sobbing, and to go near him now was to risk one of his outbursts of rage, this time probably for being the son who was still alive. All the while the big man and his little group was moving closer towards him. He recognised the body. It was that show-off farmer from some place up in the wilds of the Rift Valley bush. But Reuben's eyes were drawn and fixed on something else. The lower part of a woman's green dress had been torn away to reveal a pair of shapely thighs and part of a white undergarment. His numbed mind was, briefly, empty of thoughts. The sight of those thighs had struck him without warning. His bowels went into a sweet meltdown and a warm excitement filled his mind. He pulled himself behind the slender trunk of the acacia and, hidden from view, stared wide-eyed as Rebecca Kamau walked solemnly by.

Chapter Four

Ruthless Abel Rubai was a fine actor, but his performances were never seen in any theatre. His role playing was strictly for real life situations. In high school he had never gone near any of the plays or musicals that often starred his own beautiful girlfriend, Sally Molan. He was too busy working at his books, mostly on mathematics.

The work paid off in a big way and, with one outrageous piece of luck, he found himself, at the age of twenty, appointed financial adviser to a new president. Mister President had been principal of Kakamega High in Abel's early days at the school and been impressed with the handsome Kalenjin boy with the smart brain and the keenness to get on.

President and protégé flourished together. They learned quickly how to use their privileged positions for their personal advancement. Mister President was delighted to discover that his boy possessed a very special gift. In the privacy of his quarters in State House, when Abel reported that another big stash of money had been salted away in one of a growing number of foreign banks, his boss would whoop with delight.

'Mister Midas, what would this poor, humble schoolteacher do without you? God has truly blessed you with a wonderful gift!'

Abel's reply was usually a modest smile and a gentle nod. He did not mention his gratitude for the gift he had received from the leader of the nation. So many times he had watched how the big man played the role of the 'man with two faces'. This was one of his mama's many colourful phrases to describe people and life in the village.

'Abel, boy, you be very careful if you ever meet one of these kind of folks. They'll steal the posho off your plate when you not looking.'

So, when there was a meeting with a smart talking Western ambassador or the chief of some big multinational, interested in investing in Kenya, Abel would stand by in amazement and admiration as he listened to his old headmaster spinning his yarns.

'Mama, this old fellow is a man with four faces, maybe more. Who knows?'

But, for sure, Abel never lost a single spoonful of posho.

As the months and years passed, Abel honed his acting skills until they were pretty well perfect not only in matters of money. He enjoyed being a very private man, to the point where no one, not even Sally, knew the truth of his thoughts. He had become very wealthy, solely by his own efforts. The money had helped him to develop his own power base. He had gathered around him a group of men, powerful in their own minor ways. He had become Mr Big, the shadowy figure without whose consent nothing of any importance in the country moved forward. He would not tolerate opposition. He had his methods of making sure that the country was run in the proper way, the Rubai way. These methods sometimes involved the disappearance of people who did not understand what was best for the country.

His equilibrium had been shattered by the death of Julius. His beloved son had been snatched from him just when it seemed that the boy was emerging from his wild period and ready to become the true heir to the Rubai fortune and the Rubai way. For a time his senses had been numbed and he suffered bouts of deep depression. A worse stage was to follow. More and more he became convinced that Julius's death was a judgment, a punishment. So there was something in this mumbo jumbo bible stuff that dominated Sally's life. And the bastard who gave out the punishments had chosen his moment carefully, to hit him when he was at his most vulnerable.

He had known that Sally had been in contact with the McCalls, specifically the mother of the man whom he saw as his son's real murderer, even though the cocky runt of a farmer had not actually pulled the trigger. If talking and writing to this woman helped Sally, he would have to put up with it.

But it was not enough for Sally just to get on with dealing with her problem. She had to be looking around for something or someone who could take away his own pain.

Chapter Five

Within a week of Sally's visit, the Rubai family descended en masse on Londiani. Eddie and Rollo were back in Oundle School, but the rest of the McCalls were waiting on the veranda to greet them. Rebecca had her left hand in Tom's right, so making her prominent engagement ring invisible. It had been arranged that everyone would dress informally, mainly to ensure that Abel would not appear wearing one of his dozens of dark, London tailored suits. Reuben Rubai had gone his own way and turned up in a black suit and polo shirt, in spite of his mother's pleading. This and the defiant scowl in his expression caused Tom and his father to exchange quick glances of mild amusement. Sally's extra dose of exuberance and the enthusiasm and noise of the younger Rubai children quenched any gloom that Reuben hoped to create with his melodramatic entrance. When the handshakes and hugs were done, coffee, cold sodas and beer were brought out and the polite but strained conversation began.

Maura, happy survivor of a thousand parties of every description, would make sure that there would be no uncomfortable silences to endure. Her skills were never put to the test. Sally, with her natural warmth and good humour, enjoyed social contact and was always ready to talk children, even more so because she was carrying her 'miracle' baby, her new son.

'The children are so happy to come to Naivasha. They know about the hippos and they are hoping they will see one. It's half term and I love having them home all day. After having Julius in Eton and so far away I vowed that none of the others would go to boarding school.'

Maura smiled and looked across at Tom. 'Our three all went to Oundle. Eddie and Rollo are in their last year. I think they enjoy getting away from home for a while. Right, Tom?'

'I didn't think the weather was too flash. Made me appreciate home, but there were plenty of fun times.'

Everyone could see that the Rubai men were not enjoying this visit. Abel was sinking his beers too quickly and Reuben succeeded in making it clear that he was bored and did not want to hang around in this bush backwater. Maura had also made plans for the afternoon's activities. Sally went with Rafaella and Maura on a visit to Naivasha Hospital to see how the staff had spent the hundred thousand shilling gift donated by the Rubai family for the previous Christmas. Rebecca and her sisters, Martha and Jane, led the younger Rubais through a herd of grazing waterbuck down to the lake, confident that a few hippos would do them the courtesy of rising to the surface to wiggle their little ears in greeting.

So to the business on the veranda where four men sat uneasily, waiting. Abel looked towards Reuben whose expression had shifted from surly to scornful. The Rubais were not used to humility. The McCalls were looking out over the grassy plain that led down to the yacht club, composed, sipping their sodas.

The silence was broken by a rush of words from Abel. He was in a hurry.

'Let's get something straight here. I loved Julius, probably too much. In my head I've been back on that golf course a hundred times a day and every time I hope I'm not going to lose him. I even allowed myself to be conned by Sally into praying. A waste of time, of course.' He paused briefly. 'I never realised before how deep pain can go.

'One night I arrived home and there was this stranger in the sitting room, a friend of Sally's. She'd come over from London, a psycho something. She stayed for a week and we … talked every evening. At the end of her stay, the pain was less. She kept on about bringing closure. I only half understood what she meant. Forgiveness, she used that word so many times, how I must forgive myself, forgive Julius even. Yes, there were times when I felt angry with him, too! I could cope with all that, but I must also ask for forgiveness. Now that was an idea that churned my insides. I don't ask for anything. The killer was when she said I must ask forgiveness from you, McCall, forgiveness for being ready to kill you. I had my finger on the trigger.'

Tom broke in. 'I remembered none of that. I was out cold. Philip Coulson told me about how Stephen was carrying me.'

Reuben moved to the edge of his chair. For the first time that afternoon he was ready to give up the incomprehensible mumbling and speak up, but Alex was in before him. He looked directly into Abel's eyes.

'Tom mentions Stephen. You know he's our foreman. He'll be here shortly.'

Abel narrowed his gaze. 'Why so? What's he got to do with this?'

'In case you've forgotten, you were pointing your gun at Stephen.'

'I'm not hearing this! You are telling me to ask forgiveness from the man who beat up my son till he was unconscious and carried him over here like a slab of meat?' Abel was struggling to hold his temper.

Tom could not hold back, but his voice remained calm. 'Mr Rubai, Julius had just tried to rape Stephen's daughter.'

Reuben moved across the room and in three long strides launched himself onto a startled Tom.

'I will not let you say filthy lies about my brother.'

Tom pushed Reuben to the floor. 'What time does your keeper arrive?'

From his position on one knee, Reuben launched another verbal assault on Tom. 'You murdered Julius. You didn't pull any trigger, but you knew exactly what you were doing when you turned up at the club. You knew what that would do to him on the happiest night of his life! Papa, you should have pulled that trigger and you know it!'

Abel rose to his feet and stood looking down on Reuben. 'That's enough!' His nostrils flared with anger and he sucked in long, heavy breaths. 'Do not disgrace your brother's memory with your stupid words!'

Reuben backed away until he collided with his chair. He raised his right arm and pointed towards his father. After a brief hesitation he launched out. 'My brother's sacred memory! Julius was a first-class shit! The only person he ever cared for was Julius Rubai. You and Mama spoilt him rotten. In the last five years he hardly spent a night at home. Most times he was out shagging a piece, as he called it. He had a dick for a brain! He disgusted me!'

'Have you finished?!' his father screamed.

'Now you and Mama are having another child and you are calling him Julius already! Do you hate me so much? Okay, some people say I don't look like a proper Rubai. But I've kept myself clean and I do care for others. Sometimes I wish we were a poor family. There's a lot more love going 'round in Kibera than there is in Karen!'

Reuben was spent. He was sitting on the floor, head down and sobbing. Tom and Alex were so bewildered that they could not bring themselves to move, to say a single word. Abel had sat down and, for a time, was silent.

When the words came they were quietly spoken and took a lot of effort.

'So, I'm asking for forgiveness, after all. If Sally was here she'd be praying for us.' He managed a weak smile. 'It can take a lifetime to learn some things, but sometimes understanding comes in one second. You McCalls must despise us.'

Reuben interrupted his father. 'Papa, it is wrong for us to be here. You are right. These white people despise us. The old hatreds are still there.'

It was Alex's turn to interrupt. 'Not true. We don't despise, don't hate you, anybody. I believe that a part of you fears us. Yes, fears. Sounds crazy?'

'Not so crazy perhaps, not so crazy.' Abel closed his eyes and seemed about to doze off. A beaming smile lit up his face and his eyes popped open and completed a picture of contentment. He leaned forward in his seat and pointed his finger in the general direction of Tom and Alex. There was no malice in the gesture.

'And then again we are learning from you. But soon, I think, the days of fearing and learning will be over.' He raised himself to his feet and walked slowly towards Reuben. Reuben, standing now, looked warily at his father as he came closer. When Abel raised his arm Reuben ducked to avoid the blow that never came. Instead Abel closed his arm around his son's shoulders and led the pair of them down the steps off the veranda towards the nearest of the two Mercedes, turned and took a step back towards the veranda and fired his parting shot to Tom.

'Thomas McCall, the girl is yours again now. But my son did not have to die for this. Yes, he was headstrong and you knew this, too. There was no need for you to be in that place. Julius's quick temper cost him dearly that night.'

There was no smile now. He spoke the words in the solemn, neutral way of a judge pronouncing sentence on a criminal. Moments later the dust raised by the car speeding up the dirt track leading up to South Lake Road was settling back to earth.

Tom and Alex did not move, did not speak. Tom looked down towards the lake and watched Rebecca and her sister leading the Rubai children back to Londiani. They were skylarking and in the still air the sound of their laughter was clear to the two serious faced men waiting up at Big House.

The voices of Angela and Stephen Kamau could be heard in the sitting room. Stephen was first to join them on the veranda. He was surprised to find no Rubais present.

'Bwana, sorry to be late. There was a little bit of trouble with a machine in the loading bay. It is fixed. But where is the Rubai family? Angela told me I must hurry.'

'Sit down, Stephen. Please, Angela, this time.' Reluctantly she obeyed. 'Angela, I don't know if you heard any of that row that was going on here just now.'

'Mr Alex, when my girls left to take the Rubai children to see the lake, I borrowed the bicycle to go down to the fields to fetch Stephen.'

Stephen was scrutinising his bosses' faces. 'Thomas, are you well? You are very pale.'

'Stephen, someone has just let me know that he thinks that

I'm a murderer! Not very pleasant. But if I am as pale as all that, it's because I think that person may have a point.'

Tom was trembling. 'Sorry about all this.' He was trying to gather himself. 'It's almost five months since it happened and every day it's been the same question: did I need to be at the club that night? I've wrestled and wrestled with this and my best answer is that I wanted to see her once more before she, well, belonged to him. I never expected to see him, didn't enter my head. There were five seconds when it could have happened and it did, it did.'

Before a shaken Alex could try to console his son, Stephen had moved to Tom's side, put his arm around his shoulders and grasped tightly. Rebecca and the children were almost off the plain and onto the gravel of the driveway.

'Thomas, take a good look at her. What do you see?'

'You know the answer to that.'

'Sure. There was a time when the idea scared me. A long time ago now. You talk about Julius Rubai. Such a mixed up man. He was a headstrong, selfish person. The Bible says that we should not judge others, but it also says that we must be as wise as serpents. That young man did not have to die, but, Thomas, you did not make this thing happen. He had a choice.'

'And so did I, Stephen! I knew that the engagement party was happening. I knew all right! Philip gave me a hammering on the squash court. Couldn't concentrate. Afterwards there was a kind of craving to see her just once more, but I resisted. I went to collect the mail like I always do, but I was desperate to get out and away from that place.'

'Thomas, look at it this way. On the surface what you say is true, but truth is rarely on the surface. Truth, it's a big mystery and it has many, many threads. Fate, I don't believe in it. God's will, but He gave us free will. Guilt, it is easy to take that on board, comfortable, too, in a strange way. Fear, we are getting close here. The human heart has many wounds to bear. The death of that young man is a massive wound for the Rubai family. They have to bear it. We have a wound here, too, a smaller one perhaps, but we have to bear it. And the best dawa? Love ...'

The lake travellers were back, excited, noisy and thirsty. Five minutes later Sally, Maura and Rafaella returned from their visit into town. Sally was shocked to discover that Abel and Reuben had gone home. Alex wanted to explain, but he was forced to delay to allow the children's enthusiasm to run its course. While she was listening to their stories of the adventure of a ride on a boat on the lake where they had seen hippos, five of them, under the boat, about David trailing his hand in the milky, green water and nearly touching the wet, brown back of a baby one, and thank goodness he didn't because that would have made his mother angry and she would have tipped the boat over ... Sally did not have the usual relaxed smile that lit up her whole being when she was in the company of her children. Meanwhile, after a nod in her direction, Stephen took the opportunity to go back to the fields. Alex walked with him to the kitchen where he drew the big man to him in a warm hug.

'Stephen, it was a very lucky day for the McCalls when you walked down our driveway. You're the wisest man I know. What you said to Tom in there. Fantastic! Thank you. I'll be down soon. Don't ever leave us. Well, my turn to explain something. Here I come, Mrs Rubai!'

Alex had not recovered his composure. He felt light-headed after the two assaults on his thinking powers from Abel Rubai and then from his own son. But when an anxious Sally asked what it was that had sent Abel and Reuben home so abruptly, his instinct for quiet diplomacy served him well.

'Sally, it got a little heated here when you ladies were away, but I think it's fair to say that it was, how shall I say, mission accomplished for Abel.'

'You mean he asked forgiveness?'

'Yes, but it was forgiveness from himself for himself.'

'Alex, you're talking in riddles here.' For the first time since he had known her, there was tetchiness in her voice. For a few moments she was the wife of the big man in the country and she wanted straight answers, now!

'Well, in the end you'll have to wait to find out at home. But … but when he left here, he was his old self-assured self. And he and Reuben were good pals, in harmony.'

She narrowed her eyes into a frown. 'Hmm, that's a bit of a puzzle. Those two don't always get along. "Harmony", that's a mighty word.'

Without warning this new abrasiveness in Sally melted away. She shook her head and chuckled to herself. She patted her stomach. 'Julius, my boy, we'll need to talk about this later.'

The children came out of the kitchen carrying glasses of soda and tea plates that could barely contain the huge slices of chocolate cake that Angela had just cut for them. Her children were happy and Sally's good humour was fully restored. She called out to Angela who was still in the kitchen. 'I hope you've got a slice or two of this gorgeous cake left! There's a boy in here says he needs some pretty quick!'

Chapter Six

Sally arrived home just before sunset. All the cars were in, but Abel was nowhere to be seen. Reuben was watching a sports program on the plasma. That was a surprise to his mother.

'Son, what's going on? First the McCalls tell me that you and your daddy were in harmony down at their place and now you're watching little people chasing after a ball on the television. Am I missing something? What did they give you to drink after we left?'

The boy was smiling and eager to explain about his father.

'Never seen him smile so much at one time. Like he just got some big worry off his back. Told me some stories about the old days in the village. He was laughing and joking.

'Then, as we were coming up the Escarpment, he made this one phone call and now there are twelve men sitting around the table in his conference room. Just snaps his fingers and they all come running. He must have some big hold over them!'

Reuben did not explain to his mother about his sudden, new interest in football. In fact, there was still no interest, in any sport. Watching the television was just another attempt to shut out certain troublesome thoughts from his mind. Rebecca Kamau. When he saw her standing on the McCall veranda, it needed a big effort to stop staring at her. In the months since the night in the Muthaiga, he had relived the scene of her coming towards where he was hidden thousands of times. The slow movement of those lovely thighs, the frightened expression in her dark eyes. In his fantasies he had touched her cool flesh, smelt the perfume of her, possessed her willing body, moaned at the overwhelming thrill of their coming together. He had resolved that one day there would be a real coming together. Some day it would happen, even if it cost him his life. But, for now, he must keep his fantasies well hidden.

Alex and Reuben had given Sally an accurate but partial picture of Abel's state of mind. Neither of them could have been aware that a miraculous shift had taken place in his outlook on the world, and so very quickly.

'It only took a few of your words, Mister Alex. Suddenly I could smell the release. Like a white witchdoctor you broke the spell and did not even understand what you had done.'

'I believe part of you fears us.'

'Yes, Bwana McCall, yes, yes! I see it. Fear, guilt, I must have been crazy! Asking forgiveness from you people. Sally, how could I let you persuade me to eat that crap? Well, it's gone now. I don't need your forgiveness, anybody's forgiveness. No part of us fears you or anybody else. Can't you see it in my eyes? I can breathe again.'

'Julius, I should have pulled that trigger. I allowed fear to betray me. I cannot bring you back, but I will make it up to you. But we will bide our time. We will be patient. When the moment comes, we will be ready. We will talk about this. We'll hit them when it will hurt most. I have come back to life. I will live for both of us.'

* * *

This was the first meeting of the Circle as the exclusive group was known around Nairobi since Abel and Sally had returned from England. They had been looking at possible boarding schools for thirteen year old David who was in his last year in the Banda School. Abel found two that he liked, but as with Reuben six years before, and against his better judgement, Sally won her battle to have the boys educated in Nairobi.

Before Abel came in to join them, his colleagues had been in a subdued mood. Most of them had been at the engagement party, watched with horror as a wild-eyed Abel had pointed a gun at a big man carrying what looked like the corpse of a young white man. After that May night, meetings of the Circle had been few and at none of them had any real business been completed. There were rumours of nervous breakdowns and that Abel had taken to the bottle. They were fearful for their own positions. Abel was so dominant a force in the group that they accepted that he could remove any or all of them, replace them with a fresh batch of minions and carry on pulling the strings of government and most of the other institutions of the country. Money was the key and Abel was a magician at creating mountains of the stuff. Not one of them had been in his screen room where he was known to work long hours taking on financial wizards around the globe, usually making impressive profits. It was Abel's version of the sporting life, to outwit marketing giants and yet remain a shadowy figure behind the scenes. He was a man who enjoyed surprises as long as he was the one who was creating them. He was about to spring another one.

He strode into the room exuding energy, power and enthusiasm. His smile was confident and reassuring to his colleagues. Fitter and slimmer than they could remember, he was down to business before he had taken his place at the head of the table.

'Gentlemen, good to be back. Just like old times, I feel. Now then, if there's no objection, let's get to the election.'

There were murmurs of approval and even a short burst of applause. The feeling of relief around the table was palpable and the change of mood instantaneous. They may not have been in charge in the affairs of the country, but they were happy, and lucky, to be the back-up crew to the main man. The spin-offs in terms of money and influence were considerable. They would still have the first and biggest slice of the millions and millions of shillings, dollars, euros floating around. They were grateful that their leader never took a single shilling of the aid money or the pickings of the other scams and schemes that brought spice to the financial life of their great country. Abel continued.

'As you all realise, we must put an end to the reign of our beloved president, who has proved to have been an inspired choice to replace his much lamented predecessor. Joseph Oringa has obeyed our instructions to the letter and has, by the way, not been an expensive item on our balance sheet. Headmasters never are! I am pleased to announce that the elections for parliament and president will take place on the first Saturday of the new year. This will give us plenty of time to prepare our people in every district.'

The cheers from Abel's conference room were heard all 'round the house. Sally, who was in the kitchen with her chef, organising supper, paused to listen. She had become an expert in judging moods from the noises that she heard coming out of that room. Silence was always ominous. This cheering was high on the scale and she was eager to see what kind of Abel would emerge from this meeting. The signs were promising. The family outing to Londiani must have been a success after all.

Chapter Seven

Sally did not have long to wait to have her hope confirmed. Marcel, the French chef, had finished his work and she was alone in the kitchen. Through the open door, she saw Abel sauntering towards her whistling as he conducted an imaginary orchestra.

'Sally, I didn't hear you come in. Mmn, that is one very pleasant smell! I think we both deserve a hug.'

Sally considered herself to be an expert on reading body language. What she saw stunned and thrilled her. The transformation in her husband was miraculous. Her response to his suggestion was to open her arms and issue an excited warning.

'Husband, do not forget that you are hugging two people. Not too tight now. We don't want to give the little one a nasty shock.' She was a very happy lady. For the first time in many months Abel was giving her his complete attention. She sounded him out, hesitantly.

'So it was a success, then?'

'Sure. They all want me to stand for the big one.'

'Abel, are we talking about the same thing?'

'Why don't we have supper in here, just the two of us? The kids ...'

'Have had their supper an hour ago. Not very hungry. You missed out on the chocolate cake.'

'Remember those times in Wiaki Way? No kids. Not much money.'

'When we always shared our secrets.'

'Always told each other the truth. I'm glad you made me go up to the McCall place.'

'Made you? Nobody makes Abel Rubai do anything.'

'I learned more than I expected, 'specially about this forgiveness stuff and about myself.'

'At last, Abel. I knew it could happen. Those people in the meeting are so right. President Abel Rubai! Hey, that means we will get to meet the queen! All this and a new baby. If only our Julius could see this. Oh, forgive me, Abel. But I am so excited to have you back.'

'Julius. See, I can say his name without it bringing on the dark thoughts, the bad temper. The pain is there, but the wound is healing. Anyway, what was that you said about … passing on? Our boy is not far away, just in the next room. I think I'm ready to buy that now.'

To Abel, Sally was the dearest thing in the world. From the very first he had been protective of her. They had met when they were children. They began their working careers together with Neisland, Kapper and Reed, the most successful accountancy firm in the country. When the new president himself invited Abel to join his staff, they shared their new prosperity. At just about the same time Julius was born and things changed. Sally willingly became a full-time mother and wife. Abel was drawn along a new and private path. As financial adviser to the main man, Abel became a power in the land and soon the power. Always he kept his family and public lives separate. In Sally's eyes, Abel continued to be the upright, enthusiastic idealist of their shared youth. But the dreamer had become the realist. It was safer for both of them that she was not invited into his new world. He had been more than ready to embrace the truth that to play a winning game often meant playing a dirty game. She would never have understood that.

The death of Julius knocked him sideways for a time, but he recovered his poise. He came back to the fray more ruthless, more shameless. Get in his way at your peril. Yes, he had spoken the truth about his visit to Londiani. He had learned a lot. Sally believed him and for Abel her innocence, her trust were important. What need was there for her to be bothered about the cauldron of hot anger that burned deep in the hidden places of his being? When the time came, the McCalls would learn the truth the hardest possible way. They would never see it coming.

'Sally, how would you like it if you had a son for an MP? Nakuru South is open this time.'

'You mean Reuben?'

'Yeah, we had a talk on the way home. You know, I don't believe we ever got that close before.'

'Can he win?'

Abel was highly amused. 'I think I can say that the people of the district will be falling over themselves to vote for the son of their president.'

'But isn't the McCall boy …'

'Woman, he would be lucky to get a hundred votes, all from his white farmer friends, Europeans who stole good African soil to make their fortune.'

Chapter Eight

'Thomas, I am afraid.'

A day had passed since the visit to Londiani of the whole Rubai family. Tom McCall had returned to Big House after a morning in the fields. He had been grateful that it had been a busy time for him. Workers came to the young bwana with problems from the moment he had set foot in the farm office. The hours had passed quickly. One of the refrigerated trucks that transported the farm produce down to Jomo Kenyatta Airport needed a service and the foreman mechanic was off sick. In one of the flower tents a fight broke out. Two of his best young apprentices were rolling around on a patch of rich brown earth that was ready for replanting. There was some serious hitting going on and Tom had been forced to march the pair of them down to the lakeside for a stern chat. The hour he spent with those bright eighteen year olds had been the highlight of his morning.

He was home early for lunch. He did not go straight in for a beer with his father on the veranda. Instead he went 'round to the back of the house, intending to spend a few minutes in the laundry garden. It was a favourite place where, sitting on a warm, sunny bank of mown grass he had often watched Rebecca and Angela working at the washing troughs.

On one of those days, when her mother had gone into the

kitchen to help the memsahib to prepare lunch, a delicious thought ran through Rebecca's mind.

'Thomas, when we are married, you won't mind if I want to help out with the laundry sometimes?'

'As long as you don't ask for special pay rates.'

He had not expected her to be there that late morning. It was her day for helping out in Hippo House, the play school on the Buckles' land just beyond the parkland of Sanctuary Farm. He heard her before he saw her. She was singing 'Broken Hearted Mama', a favourite blues song written by Tony Wajiru. Tom waited behind the screen of the cei-apple hedge until she had finished.

'Thomas, I was just thinking about you and suddenly, how does your father say it? "Bob is your uncle."'

'So, thinking about me, you sing a sad song.'

She hesitated before answering, absently squeezing the white piece of washing she held in her hands. 'You know that is not true.'

'But what happened about Hippo House? Are you feeling all right? Usually I can hardly drag you away.'

There was another hesitation before she spoke, longer this time. 'Thomas, I am afraid.'

In a long silence they looked at one another across the sunlit garden until Tom said quietly, 'Something that happened yesterday, isn't it?'

'I wish they did not come.'

Tom smiled wryly and shook his head. 'Big mistake.'

'Sally wants good things. She loves her husband so much. She cannot see any fault in him. Their children loved it by the lake. When the hippos showed their faces above the water, they thought they had come 'specially to say hello to them. They were happy and excited nearly all the way back. We were close to Big House when they heard their father shouting angrily. Straight away the fun went out of them.'

"Becca, there wasn't a whole lot of fun stuff going on back here. Papa Rubai is a scary one, but the son and heir, I think he is crazy, bonkers, nuts, take your pick.'

'Thomas,' she looked down at her washing and sighed, 'that one, Julius's brother, he looks at me so strangely. It makes me shudder. I think he would like me to be dead. He blames me, I am sure of it.'

Tom moved quickly to the washing trough. He put his arm around her shoulder and led her towards the path that took them to the top of the bank. No words were spoken until they were standing under their acacia and looking out over the big waters of the lake. The afternoon haze hung down from the sky like the finest gauze so that Old Longonot and Suswa had lost their sharp edge and taken on a vague, mysterious outline.

'Thomas, how many times did we meet at this tree, when we were afraid to speak? Hiding here in the darkness, those nights seem so far away now. There was hope then and all our little dreams. Fear has come now. I thought the bad things were gone.'

'There is a dawa for all this.'

'Dawa for cleaning the mind?'

'Yep.'

'When we were in New York Monica and the other girls laughed about Freddie, Toni's drummer. He was going to see, I think they called the person a shrunk. Monica said, "No wonder. Banging those drums every night has fried his brains." So, was that a doctor of the mind?'

'Well, sort of. I remember Freddie. We got on really well. He was missing Nyeri. That was his problem. Like I was missing this place when I was over there. New York was too noisy for him. "This crazy place is driving me nuts."'

'I do not think that there are any shrunks in Naivasha.'

'Wrong!'

'Thomas, you are laughing at me. This is serious. You know how it was with Julius and now …'

'I'm not laughing. I'm telling you the truth. Lots of shrinks around this lake. Matter of fact *we* are going to see one this afternoon. Going on the Harley. Bertie's getting her ready. Sometime after three.'

'You say "shrinks". When am I going to learn to speak proper English? Perhaps you will teach me.'

"Becca, There is not a single thing in the world that I could teach you.'

* * *

The washing on the lines was ballooning, puffed out by the warm breeze. Tom arrived early.

'I have to gather in the clothes before we go and I want to change my …'

'Rebecca, I've always wanted to help out here. Your mother would never let me. "No, Bwana, if the mehmsahib saw such a thing." This is my chance.'

'But I will be quicker on my own.'

He compromised. She took the washing down, but he slowed her progress by following along the lines and, every few yards, grasping her around the waist.

'Just checking you haven't strained a muscle or something. All this stretching can be dangerous. And just one more kiss, to keep your spirits up.'

They walked the couple of hundred metres over to Rusinga.

On the way, they paused on a piece of raised ground where they watched builders pouring concrete into the foundations of what would be a large bungalow.

'Won't be long now. Mister Sawyer says in three months we can move in.'

'Then we will start our garden, Thomas.'

'No flowers, please.'

'But we will have a vegetable area, an orchard and I would like a very large English lawn. Can we have jacaranda and a cei-apple hedge like Londiani ...?'

'Don't forget the date palms, the small coffee plantation, the paddling pool!'

'Thomas McCall, if you are not careful ...'

'And if you are not careful, Madam, we will be late for our appointment.'

'You mean there really is a mind doctor ...'

'Would I lie to you? Look over there. I hope you've brought sunglasses. Solomon's been polishing the Harley. Come on.'

* * *

Bertie Briggs was the McCalls' nearest neighbour. He was waiting for them near the gate to his farmhouse. Ewan was almost three and he was perched in front of his father and reaching out for the handlebars of the Harley. The fair-haired boy's birthday was not far away, the anniversary of the day when Bertie had gained a son and lost his soul mate on the same bloodstained bed in Nairobi Hospital. Ewan was Bertie's most precious treasure and his greatest worry.

'Tom, can I come with you? I know how to hang on. Dad and Solomon have been teaching me.'

'Next week. I promise you. Today I have to give Rebecca a lesson. Big ladies have to learn how to hang on, too, you know.'

'But Rebecca is not a big lady. She's my teacher in Hippo House. She knows everything!'

Bertie slid from the saddle and lifted Ewan off with him.

'And we have to go over to Londiani to see another big lady who knows everything as well. We're having tea with Rafaella. Remember? Pizza and chocolate cake. She told me it's your favourite.'

'Yes, but Tom could take me on the bike and you could follow us.'

'Talkative boys don't get chocolate cake for tea. Tom, Solomon filled her up in town this morning.'

Bertie moved in on Tom and hugged him. 'Bless you, boy.'

'That's a new one, Mister Briggs! Why for?'

A flustered Bertie blinked sharply to hold back a tear. 'Oh, lots of things. I just saw you again at Ewan's age. It's the time of year. You two look after each other out there. Don't bother to bring back the bike tonight. Solomon will come over in the morning.'

Within minutes Tom was travelling at a sedate speed down South Lake Road in the direction of Hell's Gate. Clinging close to his back, Rebecca was enjoying her first ride on the Harley. The breeze they created caused her scalp to tingle and played with her long, black hair, making it dance about erratically. Progress was slow and not only because Tom wanted it that way. The workers on the flower farms had finished for the day and on both sides of the road hundreds of them were walking and chatting their way into Naivasha town. There was not a single one of them who did not know the young couple going in the opposite direction. In six months Rebecca had become the most famous woman in the country, an international singing star with the Toni Wajiru band. Tom had miraculously survived two violent attacks on his life. It was not only the local kids who had given him the nicknames of Superman and Lazarus.

So there was a great deal of smiling and waving and calling in their direction. It was Tom's first outing on the bike since the day, nine months before, when he had taken Lucy, a friend visiting from England, on the same route, with almost fatal consequences to himself. He needed to try to regain his equilibrium after the visit of the Rubai family. It was not only Rebecca who needed to see the mind doctor. Abel Rubai who had supposedly come for some kind of reconciliation and his son, Reuben, had caught him unawares and, without realising it, unleashed the demon. Julius was dead. How much guilt did he bear for this death? Stephen, the pastor father of Rebecca, had almost succeeded in leading him out of this dark forest of his own creation. Rebecca could help him take those last few steps.

On the road to Eburu they would pass through a real forest. At the Kingoni police post they left the tarmac and were onto the wide, dusty trail that would bring them to the north side of the lake. One advantage of the late coming of the short rains was that where there normally would have been deep mud, the track was dry and the many potholes easy to see. Tom made brief stops, just as he had done when Lucy was his passenger.

Each time after the sound of the motor died and the dust had fallen to earth, they sat in silence and just looked around. Rebecca was aware that Tom was troubled, had been since that night when the bullet from Julius's gun lodged in his thigh. She knew that something had happened, something was said the day before to make things worse for him. The forgiveness talk had failed.

Since he was a boy Tom had never been one to share his problems, but Rebecca knew that there had been angry words exchanged in the meeting that was meant to bring some kind of peace. Nor was she fooled by the careless light-heartedness in his manner on their journey out.

After travelling along forest trails and over rough, undulating tracks, he parked the bike under a tree at the top end of a grass airstrip. It was wider and longer than the home strip on Crescent Island. On this road to Eburu, much further away from the lake water, big animals were rarely seen. Perhaps only the birds had a home here though. On his many visits, he had sometimes shared his refuge with giraffe or gazelle and others of the diminishing numbers of other creatures of the African plains who were passing through. They sat comfortably, arms interlinked with their backs resting against the smooth trunk of a yellow fever tree. They said nothing. It was enough to be part of the vast, dry landscape, with the sun well down in the western sky. Dusk was not far away. In the cool of the late afternoon, every blade of grass, every leaf seemed unwilling to break the stillness. The loudest noise was the sound of their own breathing until they caught the sudden rush of air from the wing beat of a dozen white cattle egrets moving purposefully up from the lakeside, flying directly above them on their way home after their day's work. Tom looked up.

'I wonder if they're coming from Loldia or the Lang farm next to Karura Tu. I love those creatures. They are hard workers. They don't miss a day on the job. I wonder where they live. Perhaps they are in a hurry in case they'll be late for tea!'

'Papa likes them, too. He always stops to watch them fly over. He thinks they have a special gift, a reward for being the hardest workers in the Garden of Eden.'

"Becca, you know my grandma is a Catholic.'

'She used to talk about the beautiful churches in Verona. And you know she would not approve of the "grandma"!'

'Yes, I know. I like to tease her sometimes. She tried to teach us a bit of Italian when we were kids. Waste of time. She used to call us her figlii moroni, or something like that. Anyway, she goes to confession once a month, an Irish priest in Nakuru. And the happiest boy I knew in Oundle was a left footer, too, Todd Tremlett. Before we went to the pub on Saturday night, he was in the box in Saint Mary's. A dry-clean for the soul he called it. Those egrets don't need any confession. No hang-ups.'

'Lucky egrets. Lucky boy. I must tell Papa. He'll enjoy the story. But Papa teaches a different way. When we were younger, he read to us from a story by a mzungo who lived a long time ago. Every night before bedtime, we all sat 'round the table and listened to a chapter from Pastor Bunyan.'

'*Pilgrim's Progress.* Our scripture teacher read it with us at Pembroke. All I can remember are a few words I still don't understand. Umm, one was "delectable" and a really weird bit, "slough of despond". We had relatives living in Slough, near London. I couldn't figure it out.'

'Despond, despair, Thomas! Papa told us it was a very hurtful thing.'

'And guilt?'

'A bad pain!'

'You make it sound like a sickness. I've got a good dose of whatever it is just now. It hangs around like a heavy cold you can't get rid of.'

'But, Thomas, isn't that why we have come to talk to the mind doctor?' She looked him in the face and arched her eyebrows in a smiling innocence.

He smiled back and pulled her close enough to kiss her lightly on the cheek. "Becca, I'm so looking forward to you wifing me. How can one woman be so beautiful and so clever?'

'Not so clever. Why am I afraid of this brother of Julius?'

In the silence that followed, Tom watched a line of ants moving in procession up the smooth trunk of the tree. She, in her turn, was watching him closely. Her eyes narrowed in curiosity when she saw the solemn expression melt into bemusement and then into a beaming smile.

'Thomas, you must share with me.'

'Stephen Kamau!'

'You are giving me puzzles again.'

'It was about a month ago.' His voice was full of excitement. 'I was in the office with your father when he was warning one of the young planters for being lazy. The kid, Matthias, was scared, thought for sure he was going to lose his job.

'Bwana Kamau, my papa will kill me. You know he's very angry man.'

'Son, you are good church boy?'

'Not so good.'

'Did you ever read this verse? "Go to the ant, thou sluggard. Consider her ways and be wise?"'

'What's a sluggard, Bwana?'

Rebecca was laughing. 'Papa told us that story after he came home from the fields. But, Thomas, what are you talking about?'

'Don't you see? Watching the ants just now.'

'I saw ants. I know they can show us when rain is coming soon. Don't tell me these are the mind doctors!'

'They've been around millions of years longer than us, just like the bees.'

'You will tell wonderful stories to our children, just like Papa did for me and the girls, but …'

His enthusiastic flow was halted for a few seconds as he savoured the thought of having half a dozen mirror images running 'round the house. 'I was watching the leader and for a moment he sort of paused and looked over.'

'Thomas, what is happening with you?' She was pleased to see him enjoying himself.

'Just then he, is it a he? Well, his eyes suddenly became very bright. At that very moment a name came into my head. Guess!'

'The children will love this story. Ants, bees and now?'

'Julius!'

Her jaw dropped and her eyes fluttered in mild shock. 'Thomas!'

He drew her close and wrapped his arms around her shoulders.

'Darling, darling, darling, I didn't mean it to be like this. I can be such a thoughtless prat.'

Words dried up on both sides. They did not attempt to look into each other's eyes. Gradually her deep sighs eased and she moved her head back until she could see his face. She smiled.

'Julius, you are right. He is like a hand reaching out of the grave to grasp our hearts. Perhaps why I am afraid of the look on Reuben's face. I can see his brother's anger.'

'Julius was a spoilt, ruthless … I can't find the right word. He didn't give a damn about anyone except Julius. And yet if I hadn't been in the Muthaiga that night, he would still be alive.'

'And I would be his wife! I should not have led him on, told him untruths, but my heart still tells me that he was ready to kill you. I have talked to Papa about this. He says that the

Rubais are a family crazy for revenge. They must have their own way in everything. Mary calls it karma.'

He felt a surge of emotion. He did not hold back.

'I'm ready to spew him up, pass him out of my guts like a tapeworm!' Tom punched the air defiantly. 'Yeah, get shot of him. Get rid of all the sentimental crap!'

One short outburst and Tom felt weary. He closed his eyes and let his head loll back against the tree. He began again in a low, resigned tone.

'No, I'm not. We're stuck with him. Can't undo the past, can we?'

She shook her head in resignation. 'What can we do, Thomas?'

'Ah, yeah. Sometimes, 'Becca, when you're at the bottom of a deep hole, you can see the sky, the stars better than you can from a mountain top.'

'Did the mind doctor tell you this?'

'Now who's doing the mocking. Only kidding! Todd Tremlett.'

'The Catholic boy in England? I wish I knew him.'

'We'll invite him to the wedding. Grandma would love him.'

'We can live with this. We can share it.'

'It could teach us to know how blest we are.'

'I think we've met the mind doctor. I ...'

Tom was interrupted by a familiar sound. A light aircraft was approaching their end of the airstrip. There were two, both bigger than the McCall Cessna. As the red planes sped past, they could see passengers who were peering out, trying to get their bearings.

'Visitors. The Elliots have four luxury bungalows down by the lake. Expensive. These people are in for a treat. They are about to enter paradise, or as near to it as you could expect on this earth.'

'Perhaps it's the Rubais coming to make an offer.' Rebecca closed her eyes and shook her head vigorously in annoyance with herself. 'Sorry, Thomas, for being a thoughtless, what's that word you like, prat!'

Tom stared gloomily down at the ground for a few seconds. Next moment he had her neck locked in his right arm as he searched for her mouth. Two, three long kisses later, he was up and drawing Rebecca to her feet. 'Let's just check. Whoever they are, they've got plenty of dosh, schoolboy talk for cash.'

'Or dough, not for making bread. You have told me this.'

'Learning to speak English proper.'

'You mean "properly".'

'Only testing. Dong! Ten out of ten!'

The passengers were being helped down onto the ground at the other end of the strip. In the hazy air of late afternoon, Tom and Rebecca peered theatrically along the hundred metres separating them from busy activity. She was the first to reach a conclusion.

'No, I cannot see any pregnant ladies down there.'

'Agreed.' His tone changed from businesslike to wistful. 'I don't think any Rubais will be spending tonight on this lakeside. I told you that the air up here is very special. It can do miracles. Rebecca, sweetheart, where has all the guilt gone?'

'Thomas, I cannot see a pregnant lady down there, but Sally has been in my mind such a lot today. I have this wonderful warm feeling in me for her. I owe her so much.'

Two minibuses drove up to the red planes. All engines were switched off down there. Excited laughter drifted up to them. They could see people moving into the buses and being driven off. Within minutes they were alone again, listening to the sound of their own breathing.

'Thomas, I am ready.' She released her arm and turned him to face her.

'What do you mean?'

He could feel her body being pressed hard against him.

'Perhaps there is a better mind doctor here.'

He understood. 'Rebecca, what are you doing to me?'

'I know what I have said before but …'

'In a few weeks. You are the strong one. Feel my forehead. It's red hot. I'm confused. I mean …'

'You are afraid?' She arched her back and teased him with a smile.

'Rebecca, I …'

'I want you to lie with me. Remember those words so long ago? God will bless us, for sure.'

'But …'

Her reply was to begin unbuttoning her blouse.

'Bloody hell, and I said paradise was down the road …'

Afterwards, they continued to hold each other close on the soft grass. Evening had come and with it the first chill air of the night. The plains around them that had been green and brown were now shadowy with the onset of night. So, when they sat up, there was a great pool of light out on the lake. The dying sun above the jagged darkness of the western shore cast out a bar of molten gold that reached to the edge of the water not far below where they sat.

'Thomas, we are in the Garden of Eden. Our people believe that.'

'And so do I. If you told me at this moment that we were the only human beings on the planet, I'd believe you.'

'So, you are Bwana Adam and I am Memsahib Eve.'

'The Eve part I can understand. God, you're beautiful.'

'And perhaps we have started to make a little one.'

'Let's try again, just to make sure!'

Rebecca crossed her arms and shivered briefly. 'The dew is coming. Papa says it is God's gift to the night animals.'

'I like the freshness of it, but we can't risk you catching a cold. You can shelter behind me on the bike. Put my shirt on over your blouse.'

'So you can catch the cold instead.'

Out on North Road the shelter of the trees and the constant bouncing about on the rough surface kept the shivers at bay. Tom helped out by singing all the way down to the main road. Rebecca grasped his cool, hard body and snuggled under his shoulders. She was glad that he could not see her face. He might have misunderstood what he saw there. They had just shared the most unforgettable experience of their young lives and the bond they shared had never been stronger. But the tightly drawn lips and the sadness in the eyes might have told him that Rebecca was being weighed down by a new guilt. She had allowed herself to be deceived by delicious lust. She had given in to the passion of the moment and was already suffering the pain of regret.

The truth was very different. A deeply felt emotion was troubling her. It was fear. All the comforting words they had exchanged in that beautiful, solitary place, the ecstacy of those minutes when they had melted together under the darkening sky had not managed to reach and wash away the powerful sense of foreboding that had been rooted in her for months like a curse. Twice the Rubais had come close to killing Tom. Next time they would succeed and that time would be soon. This was the pain and she could not share it.

She prayed long and often, but the consolation was short-lived. Now they had become part of each other. They had become man and wife before God.

Chapter Nine

Reuben Rubai was deeply affected by the family visit to the flower farm, disturbed by the new thoughts, the unexpectedly different personal horizons that were invading his consciousness. He would need time to get a handle on what was happening to him.

Sport, he hated the stuff, so why did his mother, when she got home, find him sitting in front of the plasma screen watching a soccer match? Worse still, why was he animated by the kicking, the heading and the running, willing on the team in the red shirts?

Later, stretched out on his bed, he rationalised his way out of this stupid behaviour. It was all bound up in the vivid colours, the graceful movement of young men in the prime of their lives, the passion of the spectators. Yes, of course, he wasn't taken with the idea of a contest but with the theatre of it all. He had never noticed this before. For the first time he could remember he saw drama in the hoofing, the shouting, the tantrums. After spending a tense hour and a half alone in a car with his father, the ordinariness of the match, its unthreatening remoteness was a comfort, a balm, nothing more than a timely antidote, a brief aberration. Yet he wanted to find out if the reds had won the match.

He remembered something else, this time about life in the house when Julius was with them. Julius was a great borrower.

Reuben knew that, unless he went looking, he would never see his stuff again. Almost every time he went searching, he found Julius soaking in a hot bath.

'Planning time! You should try it. Wash the body, clear the thinking processes. Get up, a new man, clean and fresh, ready for anything. It always works. I could teach you a lot if you had the brains to listen.'

He decided to try out his brother's remedy. He would run the water in the hope that he, too, would rise up out of the bath a new man. Lying in the comfort of the hot water, he let his thoughts drift. One memory of his brother triggered another. On the night of the party, Reuben was standing on the golf course watching events from a distance. It took a few minutes to dawn on him that Julius was one of the two shapes lying stretched out on the green surrounded by a crowd of stunned party guests. Dead men, a dead brother.

'Now I'm the son and heir of the Rubai family.'

The words of his instinctive first reaction came out unbidden and startled him. The shock of them was quickly followed by a wave of shame that swept through him like a warm flush. He heard himself apologising to his mother out loud. 'Mama, I don't … No, Mama, it is a thought from the evil one. How often have you told us to be on watch …?'

He smiled at the memory. When the thought came again, as it frequently did in the days and months that followed, there was no blaming this evil one. He was more than ready to live with it.

'It is a fact, the truth. But why does no one else see it this way?'

He did not expect a special family moment to formalise the fact, but in five months of waiting to see if anyone else openly recognised his truth, he was disappointed. Above all, he wanted his father to say something. Just a word would have been enough. Nothing.

He turned on the hot tap again and let the water run until it was up to his neck. He became drowsy and was only roused by the distant sound of water sloshing about.

'What the …!'

In seconds he had switched off the tap and leaped out onto a flood of rapidly cooling water. The floor drains were unable to cope with the unexpected deluge. Like a child stamping through puddles, Reuben splashed up and down the tiled floor.

'Make waves! Make waves!'

His feet were following the rhythm of his words. When weariness got the better of him, he stamped into his bedroom rubbing himself down in a fit of wild laughter. He put on the voice of an angry Phillys, the maid who looked after his room.

'Bwana Rubai, what have you done? Your mama will not be pleased to hear about this!'

He came to a sudden halt. Wrapping the towel around his wet body, he stared blankly.

'Bwana Rubai, what have you done?'

In his own voice this time. 'You, me, yes, I did this thing and someone will notice. Someone out there will have to pay attention.'

He flopped down onto the bottom of his bed. There, less than two metres away was a framed family portrait on his dressing table. It was the only photo he had of Julius. But it was not his brother, not any of his family that caught his attention. They were standing around a gleaming piece of yellow and silver machinery, Julius's new toy, a large BMW motorcycle.

He threw down his towel and took the photo over to his bed, focused his gaze on the bike and began to dream.

Three weeks later the dream began to become a reality. The afternoon was warm and still and as he eased the newly polished bike down the driveway, Reuben was dry-mouthed and nervous. Bernard, the house mechanic, had taught him to handle the superb piece of German engineering, watched over him and built up his confidence. Now he was on his own. He enjoyed the squeak of his new leathers as he moved his arms to steer through the lodge gate and out onto the public road. At least he knew that he looked the part.

When Julius first brought the bike home, Papa had persuaded the Nairobi council to lay a half mile strip of top grade tarmac to replace the murram road right outside the main entrance. This had become a practice track where Julius gradually built up his speed on timed runs. Reuben had it fixed in his mind that his brother had once hit a hundred and ninety for a marked two hundred metre run. But, as usual, Julius became bored with his new toy and never rode the machine on any of the planned long distance safaris to the coast and the Uganda border. And he disliked the sweats he raised under the riding gear. No, a car was a much superior vehicle. For now, Bernard would keep the bike in good order but out of sight.

Reuben's plans for the big, yellow machine were less ambitious. For the first time in his life he was willingly playing the sporty type. The prospect of danger was thrilling. His aim was to tame the powerful beast enough to get himself down into town and tear along Uhuru Highway and any other main road that took his fancy. He would be the mystery rider that turned heads with his speed and daring. If the cops ever managed to pull him over, all the better. *The Nation* and *The*

Standard would enjoy printing stories about the wild son of the Big Man. He would be noticed, perhaps even by his father. For now it would be gentle runs around the block.

For half an hour he rode up and down the stretch of tarmac, shifting through the low gears, weaving and turning and successfully keeping his balance. He wondered if he should try something a little faster, just push it a little harder, test the timing device that Julius had brought over from Germany to make recording speeds easy and reliable, all at the touch of a button. The bike itself seemed to be urging him to be more bold. When Reuben revved the engine enough to suggest he was about to give it free rein, the response was alert and eager.

His first timed run was exciting. One hundred was no great speed, but it gave him a sense of fear, of risk. He wanted more. A hundred and five, a hundred and eight. The faster he went, the easier it was to control the bike. Bernard had warned him that speed was a drug and that he must not push too hard. He would allow himself one more run.

He started on the murram, a hundred metres back from the beginning of the tarmac. Before setting off, he looked down his track imagining that he was at the start of a big race. By the time he passed the lodge gate he knew he must be going at well over a hundred and could not resist pushing much harder, whatever happened. What a way to go!

The crossroad was coming up fast and, with a great effort, he eased back. He had never felt a greater sense of achievement. During the hour and more that he had been out on the road, he had not seen a single other person. This had been a bonus.

When she rounded the corner up ahead, he was caught completely off guard. A big, bay horse was trotting towards him on the edge of the road. The small female rider tried to steer the animal out of the way. All would have been well had he braked calmly and eased gently to a stop. He hesitated, and then panicked. He was too heavy on the brakes and the bike skidded off the tarmac onto the grass verge and came to rest, with the front wheel just touching the boundary wall. Reuben was not physically hurt and the machine was undamaged, even if insulted by smears and smudges of red mud and dust.

Instead of being grateful for a soft landing, he was furious with the person who had dared to ruin his perfect afternoon. As he checked over the BMW, he raged against the young woman sitting on the verge ten metres away, holding the reins of her horse.

'You stupid, stupid cow! Look what you've done! You'll pay for this.'

To have a good look at the bike, Reuben pulled off his helmet. The girl was close enough to recognise a neighbour. She screamed back.

'Oh no! Not another half-wit Rubai allowed out on the road to terrify the neighbourhood! More money than sense. Little boys playing with big man's toys. And you can't even control the bloody thing.'

Even in his anger Reuben saw that the young woman was in pain. She was struggling to get to her feet and he hurried over to help.

Passions were cooling on both sides. She raised her left arm to restrain any possible over enthusiasm. 'My bloody arm has gone. Help me up. That's all I want from you. Then just bugger off before I really lose it!'

He held back. He wanted to help. But that would mean he had to get very close to her, to touch her. The idea created its own panic. *Oh, shit! She's looking at me! Now what do I do?*

Shut my eyes. That would be useless. She probably thinks I'm some kind of weirdo!

Out loud he tried to make up a sensible explanation for his hesitation. 'See, I'm just working out the best way to, sort of, approach this. Don't want to make things worse, you know?'

'No, I don't know. Just grab me around the waist and lift. I don't bite! Not usually.'

Stung by his own stupidity, he obeyed meekly. His ordeal was over in seconds, but the reverberations of the simple act stayed with him much longer.

He stood behind her and grabbed her 'round the waist. Her flesh was firm under his grasp. The flat of his hand touched the sharp bottom of her rib cage then slid up inadvertently. The softer feel of her breasts acted on him like an electric shock. He almost let go. She glared at him, but her grimace was for the pain, not for anger.

'Okay, leave it. Come on, Shadow. Home, boy!

Reuben did not know much about perfume. He could distinguish between Lydia's flowery scents and his mother's musky French and expensive concoctions. But on this female the scent of jasmine mingled with the smell of human perspiration. It intoxicated him.

'Can I carry your hat?'

She paused and looked intently at him.

God, what was happening to him? All his life girls then women, well, he liked them, got on with them. Lydia was one of his best mates. But this was different and made him feel uncomfortable. For a second time a woman was causing confusion in his mind. It was that whore, Rebecca Kamau, who had first disturbed him. When she had been Julius's woman, he had paid her no attention, had hardly noticed her until the night his brother died. Within minutes those smooth thighs under the torn green dress were exciting him in a delicious way. He saw them again countless times in his imagination. The vision created an aching sense of longing.

Yesterday, at the McCall place, he had been forced to be in her presence without daring to say even a single word to her. He had found himself constantly watching her. His frustration had been physically painful. He had not wanted to be on that crazy expedition in the first place, asking for forgiveness from that arrogant bunch of white nobodies. Stupid! Stupid! But when she had taken the kids off on a walk to the lake, he longed to go with them, to be with her to talk, anything. Instead he was forced to stay, he and his father against the slimy toad and his land robbing father.

Within minutes of the start of this private, futile confrontation, rage was boiling up inside him. This son and heir, this whitey bastard had mesmerised, tricked an innocent beauty, taken advantage of her, probably shagged her. Look at him sitting there, typical European in the mzungo uniform, shorts; big brown, scuffed boots; long, thick socks; the confident, muscular pose, who expects to get his way, and pretty damn quick. First they steal the best bits of land and next they grab all the other jewels they set their eyes on. This one had grabbed a diamond and killed his brother in the process.

On the journey home to Karen, his father's long silences had allowed him to follow his drifting thoughts. His rage had subsided. He relived parts of the blazing row with the McCalls and enjoyed, actually enjoyed, allowing pictures from the past to rise from his subconscious, all of this Rebecca. She should have been a part of the family by now. He saw her in the green silk dress at the party in the Muthaiga. There had not been a single smile and the sadness in her expression had, in retrospect, only enhanced its beauty.

And now this horsey one had been looking at him, paying him attention. This pale face, soft blue eyes, crinkly blonde hair, damp from the exercise, these breasts that he had touched just moments before were affecting him in a disturbing way. What the hell was going on?

And now this one was saying nothing.

'What's your name? Should I know you? We're neighbours, then.'

She walked on without a word, hooking her hat from a saddle strap. She looked up and was surprised that he was still with her after she turned the corner off the Rubai road. As she strode along the dusty verge, she was checking her horse for damage. Twenty, thirty metres more they walked on in silence. She stopped, snorted a long breath down her nose and turned to him.

'Look, Mister Rubai, I don't need your help. I'm almost home. Why don't you go and check on that machine of yours! You never know. It looks expensive.'

'How do you know my name?'

'I know the machine. I thought I'd seen the last of it with your brother …'

'Just tell me your name. Not a lot to ask. You see, I'm sorry. I was going too fast. I just got excited. That's all.'

'And I've got a broken arm. That's all right. Our family is stuffed full of doctors. But if there's anything wrong with Shadow …'

'Shadow? That's a weird name for a horse …'

'Sonny Jim, why don't you just … bugger off and let me cross this road in peace.'

'Is that your place with the smart grass and the flowers outside? The English garden my mother called it. We were passing the other day. She loves the stone wall, too. She would like to see inside. Perhaps your family would like to come to tea one day. Then you could invite us back. That's what English neighbours do, isn't it? I'd better hang on for a bit. See you across the road. You could feel faint or something. Delayed shock. But you're all doctors. You'd know that.'

He was finding it hard to find a convincing reason for not going back to check on the bike. It would be just his luck that the wrong person just happened by and saw his chance. Two minutes and the machine could be gone. And the girl was gritting her teeth with the effort of keeping going. She could be down any second. He would help her up and carry her to the gate. There would be no hesitation this time. He craved for a repeat of the electric thrill coursing up and down his body that came by touching her flesh.

She said nothing but plodded on, leading Shadow onto the murram and towards her gate. She focused her mind on the steady, comforting clomp of her big boy's feet and the nod of his head. Her broken arm began to throb heavily and the pain was intensifying. Please God, I won't keel over or do anything that would give this strange person a reason to hang about, to come into the driveway, up to the house. She concentrated harder. She knew the big wooden gates would be left open. They always were when she was out on a ride. She hoped that her father was back from the hospital. He was the best one in the family with broken bones. Perhaps one of the boys would be at the gate, out to look for his baby sister.

Robert, the day askari, sprang up from his seat just inside his little hut and came towards her. She felt safe at last, enough to give a polite goodbye to her companion and send him on his way.

'Thank you for your help. I'm fine now. You really should go back to check on your … Honda.'

'BMW.'

'Yes, I'm sure. But I'm sure, too, that any crooks around won't be fussy. By the way, we're not English. Welsh. Not the same. Goodbye. Robert, I think we could close the gate for a while.'

For the first time in her life Eryl Daniels wished that the driveway of Cartref had been a little shorter.

Reuben Rubai turned the corner onto his own road. In an instant all thoughts of women and their stupid horses were blanked out from his mind. The bike was gone, helmet and all!

'Mbaya! Mbaya!'

He struggled to run along the weedy verge, wished he wasn't wearing those heavy leathers, switched to the road where it was just as hard to move quickly, thought about the hell and damnation he would inflict on the robbers. As he was turning into his own driveway, he heard the sound of a vehicle racing along the road towards him. Amazing, a police car. They were onto the case already! But they sped by with the two boys in blue not even glancing in his direction. He raised his arms and shouted after them. Far too late even to take their number.

He stormed up the drive, cursing furiously. In the garage he found his bike resting upright on its stand and Bernard with a grin on his face and polishing hard.

At the precise moment of this discovery, Sergeant Ezra Kabari was honking the horn of his police Peugeot waiting for Robert, the day askari of Cartref, to open the wooden gates that he had shut less than ten minutes before.

The sergeant and his inspector had bad news for the Daniels family.

Chapter Ten

Paul Miller and Daniel Komar were visiting Londiani. They usually called in when they were travelling north to keep in close contact with their candidates. The founder members of the Serena Party had news for their candidate for Nakuru South.

'Tom, the election is going to be in January. News straight out of the meeting in the Big Man's house. And would you believe, he's putting up Reuben to take you on here. Story is that the kid doesn't know a thing about it.'

'But is he old enough?'

'Tom, he's a Rubai, so he's old enough. Right, Daniel?'

'Fact is Papa Rubai is obsessed with this place. Rebecca, I'm sorry to bring the name up, but Julius is having a big say in this. The wound is still raw. Having another son in the seat here will keep a piece of his memory alive.'

'Julius was a thug, I know, but you knew he was around. I wouldn't recognise this one if he walked up those steps right now.'

'Paul, he was here two days ago, the whole family was. Reconciliation meeting. What a farce! Rebecca was the lucky one, taking the youngest ones down to the lake to see the hippos. Dad and I were left with the angry buffalo and the crazy dik-dik!'

'Tom, we think that this buffalo is taking a big risk. You can win.'

'Yes, Paul, but money will be grabbing the votes for KANU, as usual.'

A fish eagle screeched high overhead as she swooped down onto the lake to pick up her supper. Paul followed her flight, pointing as she dived.

'Good omen! Local girl gets her way and tries to tell us something. Get out there and bring home the big fish!'

The three men chuckled, but a preoccupied Rebecca was staring out beyond the calm waters and the dry plains to the massive bulk of her friend, Old Longonot. Her expression was calm but serious.

'Perhaps not a good omen. A powerful bird has come to steal from our lake.'

'Wrong, love. She is our bird, no stranger, and she only takes what she and her family need.'

'The Rubais will win. We all know it.'

'Rebecca!'

'I am sorry, Paul, Daniel. Thomas knows that this one is no good man. Papa's people down at the coast would say that he has the evil eye.'

'But you know that your father doesn't go for that superstitious stuff.'

'I know it. I know, too, that each time I think I am clear of this family, they are back like a bad smell.'

She wanted to be alone with Tom. Riding home from Eburu, grasping Tom's body, wearing his shirt, she had hope that this time the haunting was over. Now she needed Tom's comforting again and she was ashamed. Please God, I am carrying his child and yet I am a child myself, crying out for help. In her desperate need she was willing to embarrass herself, opening her heart in front of these two highly intelligent, strong men.

'Thomas, you said just now that I was the lucky one taking the Rubai children down to the lake. Not so lucky. Before I took the children, we were having sodas on the veranda. On the surface everything was "civilised".'

'My mother's favourite word!' Tom was smiling, but inwardly, he was apprehensive.

'Inside here I was very confused, very frightened. It was my first time being with that family, the first time since they found out that I was a teller of lies. I think Sally understood but to lose her son because of me.'

'Rebecca, no!'

She picked up the mild irritation in Tom's voice.

'Oh, God, I am making it worse.'

Paul stepped in. He was distressed to see this brave, innocent young woman punishing herself. He positioned himself in front of her and looked into her face. He took a long, slow breath. His tone was compassionate but firm.

'Young lady, Daniel and I have sat in courts of law up and down this country more times than we care to remember. By any legal criteria there is no blame, none attached to the name of Rebecca Kamau, for the death of Mister Julius Rubai, nor to the name of Thomas McCall, for that matter.'

'Paul, on the veranda, that other brother … Three times I turned and he was staring at me. I shuddered then and I've shuddered every time I've remembered that face since. Those eyes were full of hate. "You killed my brother!" Thomas, you are so much stronger. I am failing you again.'

Before Tom could reply, Paul raised his hand and continued.

'Heart law is more important than court law, that's for sure. Hard hearts never see any blame in themselves. That is why

Daniel and I are so busy. But there is a problem with this heart law. The heart and the mind have to be tough. Not hard. Dear Rebecca, you have a choice here. Perfection! Perfection! You are punishing yourself for not being perfect. Crazy! But you can spend the rest of your life with this, punishing Tom, everyone else around you as well.'

Paul saw the cheeks wet with tears but continued.

'Or, yes, or you can carry the wound and give it time to heal. The scar will never disappear completely. And this scar will make you even stronger than you are. The Rubais are not going be carried away on the wind, but see them for what they are. And there are huge wells of love around you. Now, do I make sense?'

A long silence followed. A special moment had been created and no one wanted to be the person to break the spell with a wrong word. Rebecca closed her own eyes, but she felt the focus of her three companions on her. She knew that one of the wells of love was open and offering her its freshness.

She opened her eyes. The heightened emotion present in the air around helped the three men to be aware of a change in Rebecca. The damp cheeks were glowing and the smile radiant. She broke the silence.

'I think we could all do with a coffee. I've brought a flask. No power on yet.'

They were standing in what would be the kitchen of a long, low, single storey house when the builders were finished with their work. While Rebecca busied herself with the drinks, Tom led the two lawyers out onto the grass to get a different perspective on the progress of the new home.

'Wow, Paul, what a view!'

'And you can walk to work!'

A happily subdued Rebecca sat between her two guests. Tom picked up a piece of discarded wood and swung it thoughtfully to and fro. A pleasant calm hung over them all, survivors content to have overcome the squalls of a minor emotional storm. The men failed to light on a topic of conversation to push on with. Rebecca suffered no inhibitions.

'I am thinking a lot about buildings these days. We are lucky to have good men to help us here.'

Tom was taken aback by the assured calmness in her whole manner.

'Don't tell me you're thinking of putting up something else around here!'

'Not quite around here, Thomas, but I've talked to Mister Sawyer about things. He says he has one or two jobs lined up after he finishes with us.'

'Come on! Don't keep us in suspense!'

'All right. What do you think about a ... new hospital in the town?'

A long silence followed while the three men took in the unexpected news. Paul remembered a visit to the maternity ward of the present public hospital at the beginning of the year. His wife, Miriam, and Rebecca had been very upset then by a conversation with the Australian matron of Pembroke House who was finishing off a training stint at the unit.

'"We treat out cattle better in Oz." Miriam reminded me of the visit and those words just last week.'

Rebecca nodded her head several times in solemn confirmation of Paul's speculation. She reached out to touch Tom's shoulder and to look into his eyes. What she saw brought a smile to her face.

'So, you are happy with the idea?'

'Great! Wonderful! But don't hospitals cost a bit more than houses to build? And all the equipment …'

'Sensible, practical Farmer Tom! But this has got to happen. Paul, how many times have I heard you tell us about your dream for Kenya? Dreams here must begin small. There, I've finally got it out of my heart.'

Chapter Eleven

Inspector John Kostas led his sergeant across the gravel driveway to the front door of the home of the Daniels family. His long strides forced his chubby colleague to break into a trot to keep up. Those at home that afternoon were in the kitchen which was doubling up as a temporary surgery. Mother Dorothy, the only Daniels with no medical qualifications, was moving her lips fretfully as she watched her husband bathe away the congealed blood from their daughter's forearm. Their two elder sons, Gareth, gyneacologist, and Rhys, paediatrician, watched their father in admiration as he worked his gentle magic.

'Dad, if your hands were as soft when you're holding your putter, you'd give Tiger Woods a run for his money!'

'Gareth, it was the time I wasted on the rugby field that did for my golf. And, by the way, the big man in my day was Jack Niklaus. Eryl, I need to know exactly what happened out there with you and old Shadow.'

There was a gentle tap on the half open door. Rhys answered and reluctantly led two strangers into this private hub of the Daniels clan.

'You are members of the Daniels family. Correct?'

Father David nodded with a look of puzzled irritation. Before he could put the taller, swarthy intruder in his place, the man was off again in a less abrasive tone.

'This is my sergeant, Ezra Kabari and I am Inspector John Kostas. We are from the CID, Nairobi Hill.'

'So? Look, my daughter here has probably broken her arm. Please wait outside. Your business can surely wait a few minutes. My business is vitally important just now.'

'Regrettably, sir, we cannot afford to waste a single minute.'

Sergeant Ezra was eager to add a few words of his own. He did so with pride.

'Sir, the Inspector is with us for just three months. He's helping with training. From the Athens Police Department. In Greece. He's seen lots …'

A brief widening of the eyes and a tight-lipped smile from his much admired colleague cut the sergeant's flow abruptly. The Inspector continued with some urgency. 'Doctor, Mister Daniels (David Daniels nodded appreciatively that, for the first time a policeman was addressing him correctly) you have a younger sister, Sonya, who is now Sonya Mboya, married to Doctor Simon Mboya.'

'True, but …'

'And can you confirm that she is not presently in the country?'

'Yes. She is in Wales for a friend's wedding. With the three children.'

Dorothy Daniels, who hated the sight of policemen as much as she did the sight of her only daughter's blood, was beginning to show outward signs of the fear that was growing in the minds of all five of the Daniels family present. She pleaded, 'Inspector, we know that policemen who come calling don't normally bring good news.'

'I am afraid you are right on this occasion. We need to contact Mrs Mboya. Her husband has been taken.'

'Taken?' Gareth Daniels wished this elegantly dressed,

handsome man would be less formal and more open. 'Do you mean kidnapped?'

'Sergeant, the report came to you.'

'I'm very sorry. Today the doctor took his weekly clinic at Kibera, starting at seven. He parked outside his mobile surgery in his usual spot close to the little row of dukas, just by the entrance.'

'Sonya usually goes with him. Llewellyn said he was going to try … Oh my God!'

Rhys put his arm around his mother's shoulders as she screwed her face into a mask of pain.

'Llewellyn's our brother. Another doctor.' He smiled wanly.

The inspector took over. 'Yes, we know. A little after noon, a white van pulled up in front of the surgery. Three young men stepped down. Very smartly dressed, dark suits, sunglasses.'

'We have witnesses, so many witnesses!' Sergeant Kabari was wringing his hands in angry agitation.

'Patience, Sergeant. We have to learn that it's important for a policeman to keep his emotions under control when he is working. We have to start with the facts as we have them right now. These young men smashed their way in through the door of the surgery and threw out half a dozen female patients and their children. There was a lot of shouting and screaming and soon people were rushing from all over the place. Two shots sent the crowd scattering. Doctor Simon staggered down the steps, pushed so hard that he went sprawling in the dust. He was bleeding. Someone said it was from his shoulder but could not be sure. The doctor was into the back of the matatu so quickly …

'Doctor Welshman (that's what our old lady witness called him) chased after the third thug with a heavy lump of wood, but a new man, older and heavier, surprised him, grabbed the wood and smashed it into Welshman's neck, knocked him out cold. In seconds the matatu was gone and soon mingling with the traffic on the main road.

'Doctor Welshman was taken to Nairobi Hospital less than an hour ago.'

Without interrupting the Inspector's flow, Dorothy got up and left the room.

'And Doctor Simon, where is he now? You tell me how to find a specific white matatu in this city. But our boys are working on it. I know … I know that policemen are not the most popular people in this country. But most of our people know Doctor Simon and the work he does down there and Muthare and Haruma. And most of them have kids of their own. They are very pissed off. That's not too impolite? Emotional, I know, but sometimes …'

He shrugged and looked around at the faces that were fixed on him.

The silence that followed the Inspector's grim story was short-lived. Gareth Daniels, with a catch in his voice, explained to the policemen. 'Dr Welshman, that's our brother. Nickname. Had it for years. He liked it. So many Doctor Daniels around here. He enjoys being that bit different! You saw our Mam go out. She'll be halfway to the hospital by now!'

The Inspector nodded and smiled. 'Ezra and I will leave you in just a couple of minutes. It's our job to make sure that the family, all the family, know about any bad stuff, good stuff, but …'

'Yeah, we understand. We'll do it.' Rhys, the middle of the three brothers, was the star man in the family when it came to crises and his mind was whirring with practical thoughts and plans.

'Sonya and the children are due back in three days. They

are over in Wales for a friend's wedding. Llewellyn's wife, Kate, will be here later. We'll divert her to the hospital. A lawyer this time. Sorry for being a bit shirty when you arrived. As you can see, things here weren't exactly going swimmingly even before you arrived. And we thought …' Rhys shook his head in disbelief. 'Simon should have been at that wedding. He changed his mind the day before they were due to leave. Sod's law, big time! But there you go. Any ideas? What kind of a demented so-and-so can do shitty things like this? Sorry for going on like this.'

For the first time since the arrival of the policemen, David Daniels interrupted his work on his daughter's arm. He went over to a cupboard and pulled out four tumblers and a large water glass.

'What say to a stiff whisky, to settle the nerves? Water for you, young lady. Just in case you need an anaesthetic later. Care to join us, gentlemen?'

'Another day, perhaps. Just now we have to follow your wife to the hospital. My family will be praying. I just want to check. You will let Ms Mboya know? We can do it, but …'

'Don't worry. It's our job.'

'Thank God for your mother, Gareth. Inspector, my wife's got the gift, and the guts for it. You get on with getting him back.'

Only one glass was used. David took the drink in one gulp, thought about another but instead looked out through the window to watch the police car move sedately down the drive and disappear through the gate. He turned away to follow his family into the sitting room. There was a distant roll of thunder.

Ten minutes later he was alone. Rhys had volunteered to go down to Kibera to check on the state of the clinic. Gareth was on family duty, taking his sister to casualty in Nairobi Hospital.

'Eryl, I'm almost sure that the arm is not broken, but you don't take chances with bone injuries.'

Sitting back in an armchair with his eyes closed, David allowed his mind to drift. Minutes later he was roused from a doze and wondering where he was.

Simon. The harsh reality was soon back in the centre of his mind. Their first meeting had been in that very room. As a seventeen year old, he had come along with his uncle, Tom, who had been making a speech to students at the medical faculty in the university. It was a few days later that David discovered why he had not seen much of the young man that night. He had spent most of his time wandering 'round the garden with Sonya. Their shared passion for the wonders and possibilities of life in the world of medicine began that night and continued until that morning. He and Simon had become best friends.

The world had admired the wonderful gifts of the charismatic Tom. He had been loved too much and paid the price, the president who never was, cut down by his inferiors. In his own field Simon had been as gifted, loved by the masses who saw him as one of their own.

'Where are you, my friend?' The tears were streaming down. 'Captain Cat there in the muffled middle, he's crying all over his nose,' and Sonya not ten miles from the statue of the old fraud tugging on his bell rope on the shores of Swansea Bay, and not knowing, not knowing and no one to tell her but himself. The solution was waiting on a shelf in the room next door.

The golden liquid burned his throat. Two tumblers made him ready. Three would have made him sick. He dialled the number and as he waited for the tone to ring in the hallway of that Llanelli house, he was not sure whether he wanted her to be there to answer.

'Sonya, how was the wedding, love? How was the weather?'

The long pause on the other end put him into a panic. He had been cut off after a single 'hello'.

'David, have you been drinking? You're there on your own, aren't you?' Then came the lightning change of tone from chiding domestic anxiety to terrified recognition as though vibrations had carried the message across the thousands of miles that separated brother and sister. 'It's Simon, isn't it?'

'He was taken from the clinic early this morning. The police have been here. They've got men out searching.'

Listening to his words caused him to feel weak and useless. The sense of shame deepened when Sonya began again.

'David, I'm coming home tonight.'

'But what if they won't change your flight?'

'That'll be no problem. If they try to be difficult, I'll give them the scream treatment.'

'We'll be at the airport. And the boys?'

'David! But I won't tell them anything till we're back. Perhaps there will good news by then.'

He knew well enough that chances were small for a rare happy ending. The only time he could remember when it happened was Tom McCall's miraculous escape from that hut in the Kakamega Forest. 'Rubai.' Maura was certain that he was behind it. She had not wavered from this belief since the moment she heard that he had been taken. Big men in dark suits were a Rubai trademark. The brazen bastard made no effort to hide his handiwork.

There were two possibilities. Simon was already dead or he was being held in a safe hideaway awaiting his fate. It was totally incomprehensible that this could happen to a great healer of the poorest, most disadvantaged people in the country. Big money drew out the brutes and savage bullies.

What could he be going through at that very moment? The pain and the frustration that he was suffering himself was unbearable. What in God's name could he, anyone, do to help? He contemplated finishing the bottle on the table beside him. Stupid idea and a selfish one.

Rubai was probably sitting in that monstrosity of a house around the corner planning his next atrocity on the people he claimed to serve.

'Wait a minute!' David sensed a new thought forming in his befuddled mind. When he and Dorothy had spent the first year of their married life up in the border country at Lokichokio working with refugees Jock Andrews had slipped a pistol into his meagre baggage without telling him. He still had the note it was wrapped in: 'From a sensible Scotsman to a stubborn fellow Celt, no need to shoot it, just wave it *if* the time comes. And don't forget your beautiful wife!'

'The time has come, Jock lad!'

The plan was simple. Take the gun from the locked drawer in his study, walk over to the pink palace to give his head a chance to clear and tell some bullshit story to the askari on the gate. Another story to get him with the lord of the manor.

'Mister Rubai, I believe …' He would think it out on the way over.

He stood up, took a single step and fell down, taking the whisky bottle with him. He lay on the carpet laughing and crying. As he tried to get up, the room started to spin around him. Nausea attacked his gorge. He had a new, pressing problem. Would he throw up before he could escape to the downstairs bathroom?

He crawled towards the door, holding back a new burst of laughter. He pulled down a newspaper from a side table, just in case. He must not vomit onto the newly cleaned carpet. He made to the passageway and gave up. The powerful heaves from his stomach produced a weak stream of phlegm and the smell of whisky. He leaned against a doorpost waiting for possible aftershocks that never came and lamented his pathetic efforts, his general uselessness.

The phone rang and he scooted into the hall like an injured warthog.

'David … David, are you all right?'

'Of course, Dot. Just sitting here … meditating.'

Fortunately, Dorothy was more into passing on information rather than seeking it.

'Llewellyn is going to be okay. Thank God the blow missed his skull. No damage to the vertebrae, but the bruising, the worst I've ever seen. Eryl's having a plaster put on right now. As you said, no break. David, we've been blessed. Just one more thing. I phoned Maura. She's on her way. She'd never have forgiven me if I hadn't let her know.'

'I've phoned Sonya. She'll be here in the morning with the boys.'

'How did she take it?'

He sighed wearily. 'I don't know. She didn't show much. I'll be glad to have her home.'

* * *

That night, supper for eight around the dining table at Cartref began with a silent prayer. Dorothy had asked the girls to bring out candles for the occasion. A visitor joining them late would have been struck by a theatrical quality in the scene. At first, conversation was minimal and subdued and the focus was on eating. The food was something to occupy the mind. For a time there was little sense of sharing fellowship. Each of them was taken up with their own drama.

Outside the ring of light, the shadows provided an apt backdrop for heavy thoughts. Simon was on their minds, but it was Sonya who held the centre of their imaginations. Each of them had their own vision of where she might be, what she might be thinking at any given moment. In less than twelve hours she and the boys would be there with them. Until they arrived, unless there was unexpected news about Simon, the situation would be frozen. Until then there was nothing that they could do to ease the fears and apprehensions. It was a time of uncomfortable waiting.

Imperceptibly there was a shift in the collective mood. The wine flowed more freely than was usual at a party at the Daniels home. Tongues began to loosen. An unexpected change was taking place. Sonya's arrival time was a barrier and, on this side of it, the eight friends around the table were moving back to their normal lives. The anxiety, the compassion for the Mboya family became an overhanging backdrop.

Maura sat across from Bertie. When the call from Dorothy came, Alex and Tom were up in Meru on flower business and Bertie drove her down to Karen without hesitation. He was a charming, lively guest, as usual, and only Maura understood the emotional cost he was paying for coming to her rescue. He was spending the night away from Ewan for the first time since he had brought the tiny baby home to Rusinga. He was missing his son, but there was something else to trouble him. There was another pain which was as raw at the dinner table that night as it had been almost three years before in that same room. Sonya had been Anna's gynaecologist. She was the one who had first brought the little bundle of life to him and with it the cataclysmic shock of news that still reverberated down his life. Anna had insisted that they save the child even at the risk of her own life. Sonya had brought him and his son to 'Cartref' and looked after them until they were ready to travel back to Naivasha when Maura and Alex came to take them home.

Sonya had been with Anna to help her bring Ewan safely into the world. Sonya had cried with him in his grief. Now Sonya would soon be with them with an agony of her own.

Yet the atmosphere in that room was anything but gloomy. He had never known a family who laughed so much. With so many doctors in the family joy and pain were part of their daily work, constant companions which added an emotional richness to their world. Eryl, in her new plaster and sling, told the story of her accident as a hilarious drama. The Daniels family of Karen had the gift of living life with light-hearted seriousness.

None of them misunderstood the prognosis for a prominent man who was snatched off the streets in broad daylight. Maura McCall, the mother of one who had defied the prognosis, wished that Tom had been able to be with them. He would have been a living proof that survival was possible. She had a suggestion.

'Bertie and I passed the pink palace on our way here.'

'The candy floss castle. Belongs on a beach somewhere. Gives this place a bad name.'

'Rhys, you've got no taste. Abel Rubai, man of the future, he knows about these modern trends. "Open Sesame" in Swahili is Abel Rubai!'

Maura took up the point. 'Gareth, I wish we could find

some magic words to get inside that twisted mind and straighten it out. Look, something was working in my mind all the way down.'

'Oh, that explains why you hardly spoke a word to me.'

'Sorry, Bertie. That man scares me stiff. He's so unpredictable. He's vicious, he's … crazy. There's not much going on in this country that he doesn't know about. We all realise that. Deadly as a cobra. Where will he strike next?'

'I met the baby cobra this afternoon. Another nut case. Weirdo. I think a cobra could have controlled that motorbike better.'

'When Tom was taken, the worst thing was not knowing. That was unbearable. You remember Lucy? She could tell us what she had seen, the cars, the big men, Tom being bundled into the boot of a Mercedes. Then, nothing. Simon gets a visit from three big men in smart suits and he vanishes.

'"Rubai." Look at me. I'm still trembling. I know he was behind all that … stuff.'

'But, sweetheart, something puzzles me here. Why would Rubai go through all that trouble with Tom? And then bring him back? Remember, I was in Londiani when the Rubais arrived and then that fantastic phone call that Tom was alive … and the inspector from the Nakuru police. And Alex's speech thanking Rubai for his work behind the scenes.'

'Dot, that was not the way it really happened. I'll tell you another time. Rubai's a snake. He's … he's hard. He can look you in the eye, smile and stab you in the back all in a single second. His warmest emotion is anger. Look, love, I'm sorry for working myself up! But have you ever met Sally, his wife?'

'I think I've seen her passing in the car once or twice.'

'She's a one off and she loves him. And, more to the point, he loves her. And she's pregnant again at forty-three, I think.

And if he's behind this, this stuff, Sally's our best hope, perhaps our only hope. David, you're looking at me as if I've just escaped from the loony bin! The point is we try to put some pressure on her, get her on our side. We have to go over there, and soon.'

Between the sniffles and the tears she was struggling not to break down. 'I'm no brain box. I know you won't laugh at me, but, please God, don't pity me.'

David's expression was grim and startled both at the same time, but there were tears as well. He sighed and when he spoke his voice had a tremble in it.

'No, you're not crazy. We're the stupid ones. Yes, the Daniels family. Stay cool at all times. Even today with all this crap raining down on us! Look at us. My old mam would have been straight down onto her knees. What did she call it? "Pounding on the windows of heaven!" We are much more sophisticated. When trouble comes, we smile, get on with our dinner and tell our stories. Not a lot gets done that way. Tell you the truth, I'm bloody ashamed. Listen. This afternoon, I was in the house on my own, feeling pretty useless. Dot, remember that gun Jock Andrews gave me when we were up north?'

'David! No!'

'Don't be daft. Not me! I was going to go over there and, well, put one between his eyes.'

'And?'

'I fell arse over tip as I tried to get up out of the chair. Some assassin, me.'

After a long silence, a weary Maura croaked a single question before leaving the room.

'What time does Sonya's plane get in tomorrow?'

Chapter Twelve

Next morning at the respectable calling hour of ten o'clock, two women passed through the wooden gates of Cartref, the Daniels' house in the district of Karen, and turned right. Sonya Mboya and Maura McCall were on a mission. It was rare to see two white women out walking on these quiet roads at any time of the day. Three cars had been offered for the short journey, even a couple of volunteer drivers, but all were refused. Walking would give them a chance to get better acquainted and they could work themselves up for the ordeal that lay ahead.

They had met at half a dozen social occasions but never shared a long conversation. On the way back from Jomo Kenyatta, David had mentioned Maura's idea of confronting the Rubais at their home. Sonya's mind was on thoughts of Simon.

'Why would she want to do that?'

'Sonya, we all know who's causing all this strife.'

'I do, too. So, we knock on the door and ask if the man of the house can come out to play! They'd never let us near him.'

'Wrong, sweetheart. Maura can get you in. Listen.'

* * *

The two women drew curious glances from the busload of pupils from Hillcrest School as they passed on their way up-country to play a series of hockey matches against Saint Andrews Turi. The dark one moved with quick, clipped strides that sent her frizzy black hair bobbing attractively. The heavier built Sonya, younger, with the handsome head of thick auburn hair bustled along, swinging her arms across her body and swaying her hips in rhythmic counterpoint.

Maura raised a hand to the bus, guessing where those young, friendly faces might be going. It reminded her of the many times she and Alex travelled to support their boys in their matches with the other prep schools scattered up and down the Central Rift. In eight hours these same children would be returning home on this same road, weary from their matches and the long journey at the end of a good day's sport, a very ordinary day.

Out there with morning air still fresh, the task that lay ahead of them had an awesome menace about it. All the support in the world could not deliver any real help. They turned left at the corner. Up ahead they could see the lodge at the end of the Rubai drive. Inside the fence of the estate, heavy machinery was at work converting scrubby bushland into parkland. They stepped onto the tarmac road and changed their shoes. Each supported the other as they swapped tackies for something more suitable. It was their first physical contact. They paused before going on and made eye contact.

'Last chance to change your mind, Maura.'

'Wouldn't miss this for anything. I'm terrified.'

'You don't have to do this. Out here I can see we haven't got a lot to go on. But I hope and I believe. Not because I have to …'

'I can get us in there. Sally, she's got a good heart. And he loves her. That's our chance.'

'Hold my hand. The power of two.'

They moved on and Sonya dried her tears.

'Maura, I'm still not sure whether I'm in Wales or Nairobi, but I'm so desperate, I'll do anything. But there have been threats, so many.'

'Threats?'

'We talked a lot. Simon was convinced it was the articles and books. He's been writing them since long before the children were born.'

'I know. I read a lot of them. He's got the gift.'

'At first, everyone loved his work: *Down to earth doctoring for today's Kenyans*, *Stories from my casebook*. Those days seem so far away. We were so naïve. Then came the change.'

'He stopped writing.'

'For a long time. It was little Noah's fault. We were on our way home from Nakuru. It was a Sunday evening, the usual heavy traffic. I was still two weeks from my time with him. Suddenly Noah sent the message that he couldn't wait any longer. We were just past the bumps in the road, you know, the old tollgate this side of Gilgil. There was no real pain but I knew. I would, wouldn't I?' She smiled. 'I remember saying I wish Dr Satchwell was here. David calls him the best baby puller in Africa. It's funny to look back now. Simon got more and more agitated. "I am not having my son born on the side of the road! Hang on! Got an idea. We're going into Naivasha. There's a hospital." Those were his last words until he almost crashed the car as we turned into the hospital car park! Maura, he loves life so much. I'm so blessed. Just talking about him. There will be a miracle.'

'I wish Tom was here. He's a proof …'

'Please, God.'

* * *

'No, we don't have an appointment, but if you'll just let Memsahib know that her good friend from Londiani has come to call. You did say that she is in?'

'I will check. One moment, please.'

The tall young man in the dark green uniform disappeared briefly into his office and returned with a pleased smile on his face.

'Ladies, a car will be coming. Two minutes!'

'We can walk.' Maura was already leading Sonya through the gate. 'My friend and I love gardens. We've heard that you have made a new one here. We can have a peep on our way.'

They lingered on that final part of their walk, trying to compose themselves and to think of first words to say. None came.

Sally was at the front door to meet Maura, her only visitor, as she thought. Her smile of welcome froze when she recognised that Maura's companion was Sonya Mboya whose picture she had just seen in *The Nation* in a family portrait alongside the article covering the kidnap of Simon.

'Oh, my God! I have just been reading. Oh, I am so sorry, so sorry! Please, forgive me! Maura, it is good to have you in my home at last! And, Sonya!' Sally reached out to grasp the hands of her guests, but for a few seconds had to struggle to find the right sympathetic words..

'Sonya, words. No use. But, our hearts speak better, clearer. Isn't that so, Maura?'

A gentle pull from Sally and the three bodies were locked tight together in a silent embrace. There was no awkwardness possible in this simple communion. The shared pain was the bond. Maura tightened her grasp and broke the silence.

'Ladies, life can be a complete bastard! But if we can hold on to hope, surely to God there's a chance for us!'

'Who can have done this cruel thing? Ladies, please, come inside. We will take some refreshment.'

They broke apart and soon they were sitting in the same golden chairs where, six months before, Rebecca Kamau had taken afternoon tea on the day she had arrived at the Rubai house, wet and bedraggled, to break the news that her engagement to Tom McCall was over.

Sally was over her initial shock and understood at once why Maura had brought this unfortunate woman here to the house. 'You want to see Abel.'

'Is he at home, Sally? The house seems so quiet.'

'He is in his screen room. When he is here in the morning, we meet together for coffee at eleven. But …'

'Please, don't disturb him.'

'He's never late. I am sure he will try to help. Remember when Thomas was taken …' She broke off.

Straightaway Sally showed signs of distress. Maura had suspected that this would happen but had taken the risk. Tom was alive, Sally believed, because Abel had acted quickly. If Tom had not survived, perhaps her Julius … Once again Sally was fighting off the temptation to blame Tom and, by association, his mother for what had happened to her beloved firstborn. Maura had seen this struggle in Sally before but steadfastly refused to indulge it in the slightest degree. The risk was that this time Sally would take the easier way and see the 'truth' that Abel and Reuben had pressed on her so many times and let the ensuing resentment sour her attitude to Sonya and her distress.

Sally rode the storm of her temptation. She refused to conveniently forget the Rubai family tragedy was a Rubai family creation. Her doggedness cost her. The old wound was as raw as ever. She smiled at Maura through the lens of tears.

Not for the first time the two mothers held each other very tight, each feeling the physical throb of the other's body as the pain took hold again. But Maura was very conscious of the waste of dwelling on the past when there was a vital necessity to try to ward off another possible violent death. She hardened her sensitivity. Perhaps she and Sonya were too late already, but the miracle of her Tom's return still gave her hope. Quickly she got to the reason why she and Sonya were there.

'Sally, do you think Abel will be ready to help?'

Sally did not answer at once. It was taking time for her to journey back to the present.

'Yes, yes. He is a good man. He has not seen *The Nation*, but he has his own ways of knowing. He's in his screen room. He follows the markets. Did I already say that? He will be here soon.'

Abel Rubai was indeed in his screen room. He had enjoyed another profitable night working, competing with unseen friends and rivals all over the world. The screens were dark now and he was leaning forward in the comfort of his favourite red leather armchair. He, too, was involved in a train of thought that had reached out of the past into this present moment. There was the ritual remembering of Julius, snatched away just when he was growing into his true self and, as usual, the pain of this memory triggered the vivid scene of the dying son. The worst of it was the inevitable next picture, the brown-legged, fair-haired features of the always smiling, always mocking scourge of the white rat of Londiani.

'Why did I hesitate? All the work was done. Just a simple "yes" from me. Julius would be here today and that other one ... a forgotten statistic.'

He was conscious that he was again putting his recent

resolve to be his cold, ruthless best self in danger of weakening. Crazy! Stupid! What is going on inside this head of mine? Everything went according to plan yesterday morning. The boys picked up Mboya at the place he had in Kibera. Mboya, he remembered this one's uncle. He often recalled the day when he heard the news that he had been gunned down in Nairobi. 'Good riddance!' had been his father's comment when the sound of the announcer's words filled their shamba home with the shock news. Later, over their supper of posho and beans, Father had gone on, 'Abel, never trust a Luo. They are too clever. This one wanted to be the Big Man. I know it. Bad, all bad!'

This nephew, this Simon, was clever, too, and won a scholarship to study medicine overseas. When Abel read in the papers that he had married a fellow student, Sonya Daniels, he was sure that their next step would be migration from England to the United States. There was big money to be made over there. Good riddance!

But no, they had come back to Kenya. For a time they worked in the practice of her elder brother. It wasn't long before articles in Simon's name appeared in the papers. Abel made a point of reading them. He would have admitted it to no one, but since the evening of the news broadcast announcing his death, the story of Tom Mboya had fascinated him. He had read the books about him, but nowhere could he find the essence of this handsome, charming man, nor how or why, irrespective of tribe, so many Kenyans were attracted to him. His popularity at home and abroad brought him down. He had become too big a threat.

Abel had admired a lot of Simon's writings. There was some envy, too, for the wider horizons he had experienced in those years spent in Europe. The articles were popular for their blend of sound, simple medical advice and the humorous stories he used to illustrate these pieces.

Abel remembered the article where the tone began to change. Gone was the folksy humour. This piece was mostly some sentimental rubbish about an unplanned visit to Naivasha Hospital. His first kid was born there, but not out of choice. There was so much anger in that writing. He was raving like an idiot about the shocking conditions, the inhumanity and the rest of that stuff. After that a long silence.

It was years later when one of his staff dropped a newspaper cutting on Abel's desk. Mboya, the writer, was back in business. By now he had built and equipped the first of his clinics. Simon's articles appeared again nationally and in foreign medical journals. At first, these pieces made Abel feel merely uncomfortable, but it was not long before his anger was roused not so much by the medical contents but the increased amount of politicking in them. There was a ready audience for these open attacks on the government and its 'corrupt' practices. How long would it be before he and his clever pals would be making cocky challenges? We'll see about that.

Abel puzzled over the sources of Mboya's material. Could it be someone in the Inner Twelve who was leaking information? Abel resolved to act when barely veiled threats to his own position appeared. Another Mboya, another threat. The fool was writing his own death warrant. But Abel was a patient man. He would give Mboya the chance to change his ways. His own ways were not subtle. He was not that patient! Abel's team of enforcers knew their business. They enjoyed making sure that the message got through to the little man with the big ideas.

He checked the wall clock. Five minutes to coffee time.

Better be on his way. After his half hour with Sally, he would return to the privacy of his screen room and make a couple of phone calls. He was ready to give the word. He began to whistle, a sure sign that the man of the house was in a happy mood.

Realising that he was coming, Maura fixed her gaze on the open door of the sitting room to watch Abel's immediate reaction when he saw Sonya and herself. It lasted only a moment or two, but that was long enough for her to pick up a hint of shock, even of panic that confirmed her suspicion. The affable smile, the bright wide eyes came too late to hide his secret.

'Ladies, what a pleasant surprise. Four for coffee. It's a long time since we had that, Sally!

His wife's smile was sickly, but neither of the guests could summon up even that gesture. Sonya was looking down, fiddling aimlessly with her fingers. Maura met the challenge of his look. The false charm had vanished and been replaced by a patronising contempt. He suspected what was coming and was preparing his position.

Instinctively Maura knew that the approach that she and Sonya had considered would have to be ditched. Gentle conciliation was not going to work. Abel Rubai would interpret that as begging, grovelling. His ego might swell, but it would not diminish the threat to Simon's life, if there was a life left to threaten.

'You know that you are our only chance. You helped save my Tom.'

Three pairs of female eyes were riveted on Abel Rubai as he looked down into his coffee, taking his time to make sure that he stirred the last speck of cream into the rich brown liquid. When he lifted his head, Sonya caught her breath at the sight of his face. There was a broad smile on his lips, but the eyes were cold, hooded like a cobra about to spit his venom. She had never seen such a frightening combination of features.

Abel, the master builder of tension, sipped his drink once, twice to make sure that the taste and the temperature were satisfactory. He cleared his throat and began.

'Maura, as direct as ever, I see! Well I see I must be direct, too. Seeing you here, Mrs Mboya, tells me everything. I have to say at once that I can do very little to help. Maura, I told you that what happened with your son all those months ago,' he flicked his free hand casually, as if he were pushing away a fly, 'was little more than chance, a piece of good fortune. I telephoned the main police stations around the country, and Inspector Kariuki of Nakuru … came up with the goods. Lightning doesn't strike …' He waited for someone to complete the expression.

Sonya obliged. 'Oh, but it does!' She moved forward in her seat and focused on Abel as if she were a teacher eager to make an important point in a lesson. Her energy levels were rising fast. 'Mr Rubai, what kind of wretched human being could want to punish a man, a doctor, working to help the poorest people in this country, to give them a little hope?'

Sally found the pain of Julius's loss beginning to overwhelm her once more with the usual side effect, a deepened compassion for the suffering of someone who had lost a loved one or was in danger of doing so.

'Sonya, Abel will do anything he can. There are cruel people at work among us. Abel, perhaps if you telephoned the police …'

'Perhaps.' Abel did not try to hide his irritation with his wife. She was trying to invade a world that he meant to keep private, mainly for her own good.

Maura picked up the conflict of vibrations between

husband and wife and her intuition, honed to a sharp edge, told her why it was so. She saw clearly that this wily man who lived by his wits did not give a fig for the lives of those whom he saw as a threat. He was the strong man in the ruling elite. The air of mystery created by his shadowy position fostered awe in friend and foe. Dangerous and ruthless, he was also astute and knew exactly when to hold back. Maura knew what she must do.

'Abel, you are making a mistake here.'

The big man poured himself another coffee, then turned to face Maura full on. He gave her the benefit of an expression of amused contempt before he spoke.

'My dear Maura, please be more specific. Mistake? Of underestimating my powers to be of assistance to this lady? Mistake of … well, you tell me. I'm intrigued.'

She weighed in without hesitation. 'Mistake of thinking that we are idiots! Simon Mboya was becoming a nuisance to certain people in this country.'

'I have to agree with you there but – and listen carefully – I am not one of those people.'

Maura hesitated to look across at Sonya. She was upset to see distress written large in her expression. For a few seconds she hesitated. Perhaps it was she who was making the mistake. No! No! She did not doubt that the man sitting opposite her was the moving force behind the danger to a good man's life, but she had realised that she was a novice in the world of intrigue which was the natural habitat of Mr Abel Rubai. He would make her pay for her wild boldness, but she had to go on.

'Half a dozen young men in smart suits, the Rubai trademark. Anyone with half a brain would recognise that.'

Abel chuckled and he reached out to touch his wife's arm.

He wanted to reassure her that her beloved husband had not turned into an evil scourge of his, the good people of Kenya.

'Maura, you are the one who is mistaken. I can forgive you, but look what you are doing to your friend here! I am sure you are acting in love, but your desperation has temporarily turned your mind.' He raised his hand as a gesture to prevent her from renewing her attack. 'Please, dear lady, just listen. Yes, I give work to a lot of young men. Yes, I like them to look smart and I can afford to buy them good quality clothes. But I don't have a corner on the market of the hundreds of very competent tailors working in this city. Now, something more important. If you come with me to my library, you will find a lot of literature about the Mboya family. I have all the books and articles written about the great Thomas. I have always been a big admirer. I remember the day the news came through about his murder on the streets of this city. You can inspect the boxes where I keep the articles that Simon wrote.

'Why would I want to do any harm to a man who was helping, and will help again, God willing, to fight disease in the most deserving of the wananchi?'

Sally sat back in her chair, relaxed again to have it proved to her that her man still had the upright character that she had seen in him all those years ago when they first met in a youth service in the village branch of the Presbyterian Church of East Africa. Sonya, too, could understand the logic of what he said. Perhaps the shock of almost losing Tom in a kidnapping was still with Maura and caused suspicions to surface where there were none.

Maura refused to let go. 'Right, then, you're too clever for me, and you can see that I'm not very smart with words so, to shut me up, just do one thing and I'll go home. Say – and I'm not asking you to swear – that you had nothing to do with all this, that even now, you'll try your best to get Simon back alive.'

'No!'

The curt reply shocked the room into silence. Abel gave his companions time to draw their conclusions before going on. When he did so, he spoke with quiet assurance.

'No. I cannot satisfy you on this. If you take this to be an unspoken confession of guilt, let that be on your conscience. If you cannot believe what I have said already, if you think I am a liar, then "yes" or "no", what difference would either of these words make?'

'So, we are wasting our time and your time? And, Sonya, it breaks my heart that I have failed you.'

Sally interrupted. 'No, Maura. There is too much love in what you have done for it to be called a failure. Abel, darling, just say that ...'

Sonya was desperate to get away. 'Please, I must get back to the boys. My hope is dying and it terrifies me.'

She rose from her seat and moved unsteadily towards the door, brushing a coffee cup and sending it noisily to the floor. 'I'm so sorry, Mrs Rubai, so sorry! Please ... I promise to pay for the damage, but just now ...' She turned to look towards Sally as she spoke and made an effort to stand tall. After a brief glance towards Abel, she spoke again with a trembling but compassionate voice. 'Mrs Rubai, you are a good lady. Thank you for your kindness. I will pray for your family.'

Maura was afraid that Sonya would fall and grasped her under the shoulders. She hurried her to the sitting room door and out into the fresh air. Sally Rubai clutched her stomach and weeping freely looked across at her husband. There was no emotion showing on his face as first he watched the departing visitors, then stooped to pick up the fallen cup. He checked for damage, found none then placed it meticulously back on its saucer.

'No harm done there.' He smiled sweetly and continued. 'You remember I have a meeting at twelve. The President wants us to build two new floors on Nairobi Hospital. Another of his great ideas, but where will we get the money?'

As he made his way back to his study, Abel took out his mobile phone and made a call. It was very brief. 'Ochome? Silence him.'

Chapter Thirteen

The journey back to Cartref was slow. Sonya hoped that her boys were asleep, tired after a very long journey, but suspected that they would not be. She needed to be ready for them and she wasn't. She knew that Moses and Sammy, the two youngest, believed that when Mama returned, Papa would be with her or else they would soon be on their way home to Langata to meet him there.

Her thinking was becoming more and more confused. Perhaps an hour or two alone might help her, but seeking solitude had never been her way of dealing with serious issues in her life. Doing always worked better than brooding.

A stranger watching their progress home might have thought that one of them was ill for the frequent stops that they made. They were temporarily out of their everyday world and were travelling in a kind of spiritual and emotional bubble. A storm of seemingly disconnected thoughts rained down on them. Most of these struck but made no lasting impression but some hit hard and brought the one or the other to an abrupt halt while they tried to take them in, to make sense of them.

Maura felt a heavy guilt that she had made Sonya's situation worse. She was more convinced than ever that Abel Rubai was the man behind the kidnapping. Her Tom had survived a similar one and she had thought that she understood how

Abel would react, that a direct appeal might make him think again, even change his mind. She had been innocent, naïve, foolish. In this encounter with the powerful man she understood for the first time how ruthless, how hard-hearted he was. Please God he was not, in part, taking revenge on Simon for his failure with Tom! She shuddered and the scream of 'No!' was cutting the warm morning air before she could rein it in.

Sonya took a battering of a different kind. Scene after scene flashed in and out of her mind with the relentless ruthlessness of the worst of nightmares. She was helpless in the face of them. Her world was being turned upside down. Hopes and dreams were being shattered. Unexpectedly, she remembered her childhood days when she was the baby of the family. Mam and Dad loved to keep up some old Welsh traditions, especially the weekly reading of the Bible. She had been born in Nairobi, but she loved to hear Welsh accents reciting passages from the gospels or the psalms just before her bedtime on Sunday evenings. In that worst of times the smell of the lines of jasmine strung across the ceiling of the veranda was with her again. Most memorable of all, Dada's prayers, spontaneous, passionate and intimate were quietly spoken as if his maker were listening from His throne at the top of the veranda steps. That was what Mam had told her was happening.

Without thought or premeditation, she sank to her knees on the grassy verge, launching into a torrent of words, not so much a prayer as a release of half a dozen conflicting emotions. She was hammering on a heavy, dark door and demanding justice, mercy, forgiveness, pouring out her anger on unseen power for turning away from a good man who cared more for the wellbeing of others than he did for his own life.

At once Maura found herself caught up in the intoxicating euphoria of letting her tongue loose, joining in a wild duet of the words that presented themselves in the mouths of two defeated women.

Soon the pair of them were on their way again, arms linked, singing, laughing outrageously, seemingly past all care. The stranger who might have observed them earlier would have found it easier to understand this behaviour. The two women were, quite simply, drunk. They were being released from the chains of self. The release brought with it a relief from their fear. For a time their egos were swamped by more positive emotions. Their ordeal was not diminished, but their strength to cope was more assured. Their prayer was being answered.

Chapter Fourteen

Denis Orango enjoyed his daily cycle ride to the Karen dukas. The morning air did not have the sharp, chill edge of his village home up in the Aberdares, but he always wore his black woollen gloves anyway. This was partly for the warmth they gave but more to keep the money for the newspaper safe in his hand. Mrs Rubai sent him to pick up *The Daily Nation* because he was the fastest rider on the staff and the least likely to dawdle on his errand. She liked to have the paper by her side when she had breakfast.

The day before she had been stunned by the headline about the kidnap of Simon Mboya. Today's main news gave her a much greater shock.

'Just after midnight a tea plantation worker in Kericho found the body of a naked man on a grass verge near his home. When the police arrived on the scene it was discovered the hands of the deceased had been mutilated. Later when the body was inspected at the local police station, it was identified to be that of kidnapped Nairobi doctor, Simon Mboya, whose abduction from his medical centre in Kibera was reported in our edition of yesterday …'

Sally Rubai threw down the paper and hurried off to a downstairs bathroom. She vomited into the sink.

* * *

The Daniels family had been roused from sleep at four am by the night askari.

'The Inspector wants to speak to Doctor David. They are waiting downstairs.'

Any doubts about the news that the Inspector was bringing disappeared as soon as the two men met. A single word was enough to confirm the doctor's suspicions. 'Yes!' Inspector Kostas nodded solemnly to reinforce his bad news.

The Inspector and Sergeant Ezra sat quietly in the sitting room while the family gathered. When everyone had come, the policemen rose and moved towards the large, marble fireplace. They stood waiting for a sign from Mister David. Not one of the family had a doubt about the news they were about to hear. Their first conscious thought when they were roused from sleep was that Simon was dead. They did not need words. There was no surprise. This was an all too normal outcome when one prominent man had offended an even more prominent man who had the will and means to deal with his problem with swift, safe violence. But why did bad news so often come at this ungodly hour?

Dorothy set down large mugs of hot sweet tea on occasional tables. 'Dorothy's dawa,' she had been bringing it out for years as her simple, practical medicine to help ward off the after-effects of medical pain or, as now, to bring comfort in times of deep foreboding. There was a lot of spontaneous embracing and holding of hands taking place in that quiet room. Sonya sat between Maura and her niece, Eryl, on the large sofa directly in front of the fireplace with her eyes focused down onto the well-polished black shoes of the Inspector.

When he began to speak, the Greek intonation in his voice was more pronounced than it had been less than thirty-six hours before when he had made his first visit to the house.

Deep emotion caused dryness in his throat. Dorothy rose nimbly to her feet and brought him a mug of her special potion.

'Take a couple of sips. Good for the nerves!'

Her little intrusion set off the first smiles of the morning.

'Ladies and gentlemen, technically speaking Sergeant Ezra and I should have just one task, duty here this morning. We have never met, but I believe that you must be Mrs Sonya Mboya.' He tilted his head forward and opened his hands in what looked very like a priest's gesture of supplication.

'You are right.' Her whispered reply could have been heard clearly in the furthest corners of that large room.

'Mrs Mboya, very early this morning, our colleagues in Kericho District were alerted to the presence of the body of a man found on a grass verge close to the entrance of the Home-brew plantation. It appears that the man is ... your husband, Doctor Simon Mboya. The law demands that the next of kin must identify ... the deceased. I ask you all to forgive me if you think my manner is abrupt or even cruel, but experience tells me that there is no gentle way to bring such news. We are here to assist in every way we can.

'In a sense, our job is done but, with your permission, we would like to go a little further.' He paused and when no voice was raised, continued. 'Sergeant Kabari will explain.'

Ezra Kabari was distressed. The trembling hands holding his notes were the clearest sign.

'This is one of the worst days of my life. I am from the Luo tribe, just like the good doctor and his Uncle Thomas. My heart is breaking with yours. I am a policeman and I have failed you all. But one small thing I can do to help.

'Something amazing. I have a brother, Hosea. He has never wanted to come down to the big city here. He is a policeman, too, a sergeant in Western District. It was he who reported in to our CID here with news of this tragedy. He was given charge of bringing Doctor Simon back to Nairobi, to the city morgue. Please bear with me! However deeply what I say hurts every one of you, perhaps it is better that I speak of it now.'

Tears began to well, but the sergeant forced himself on. Breathing heavily, he got his words out with a great effort.

'These bad people who took his life ... damaged his hands, very badly. Unspeakable, but these jackals did it. Please, I want to bring him here, to this house. The inspector tells me that I am breaking police rules of conduct, but there are bigger rules and I refuse to break those, whatever the cost.'

Weeping, low and gentle sobbing disturbed the long, painful silence until David Daniels rose from his chair and moved towards the fireplace. He put his arms around the policemen and drew them close. 'Yes, friend, you have done the right thing. We want him home.'

The Inspector interrupted briefly. 'Then I can tell you that he is on his way at this very moment.'

These few words caused swift changes in several ways. Everyone sitting down rose to their feet almost as one. As people began to move about and to try and prepare themselves for whatever the next few hours would bring them, Sergeant Kabari walked over to a window with David.

'There is one more thing that has to be said, but not to everyone, not just now.' He hesitated briefly. 'Tied around the doctor's hands was a ... note written on a crudely ripped piece of cardboard: 'You won't be needing these no more, big mouth'. I am so sorry!'

David closed his eyes and groaned. Of all the people in the room only Sonya noticed how the exchange with the sergeant had upset her brother. Her tears were finished. Her reaction to those who wanted to offer her comfort and consolation surprised those who tried to give it. Far from being overwhelmed by grief, some inner source of strength galvanised her. She was full of energy, none of it negative. Her concerns were for other people. She was glad that her boys were still asleep and would hopefully remain so for a couple of hours longer. Whatever else she would have to do in that time, a big part of her mind would be given to working how best to explain to them the continued absence of their daddy. It was a time for her to groan inwardly.

Bertie planned to return to Naivasha after breakfast. The bond he had formed with Sonya and Simon in the shock of the aftermath of losing his beloved Anna was as strong as ever. He had spent two nights away from Ewan and the arrival in Karen of Rebecca and Tom in the early morning would free him to return to Rusinga Farm without leaving Maura without a lift back to Londiani when the time came. While he had the chance, he must speak to Sonya. They came face to face as she was carrying a tray of empty mugs out to the kitchen. He was afraid that his awkward social skills would not be up to the job of getting his deep sorrow and anger across to his dear friend.

'Sonya, you know how bloody useless, sorry, Sonya, but I'm not much good at the tender stuff. It still puzzles me what could have persuaded Anna to take on a crusty bloke like me.'

'Bertie, we know each other too well to be bothered with too many words. Heart talk, remember? I think we both learned how to speak it in this very room. Simon was a wonderful teacher.'

'And now he's gone. Sonya, I can't understand why you're not crying your eyes out. I feel tempted myself. It's so damned unfair!'

'Of course it is, sweetheart. If I felt it would do some good, I'd be down on the floor here screaming ... shouting, cursing, yes, cursing a god who lets these evil, evil bastards get away with this, this abomination. You understand that, Bertie. But ... Simon would definitely not approve. Can you see that shutting of the eyes and the rapid shake of the head when he wanted to say you were wrong about something?'

'What a bloody fantastic pair you were!'

'Correction, Bertie. Are! Yes, are! It's strange, but since I first received the phone call in Wales yesterday, the day before, whatever, I've been expecting it to end this way. We knew the risks he was taking. All those threats. And I've been wondering how I would react. Cold-blooded minx, aren't I?'

'Total crap, Sonya! Sorry again!'

'Bertie, he and I go on together. Now I know some people who would describe what I'm saying as rubbish. Time for shutting my eyes tight and shaking my head! Listen! I've got a lot of business to clear up here this morning. I have to speak to the boys. I'm still working on that! And I have to have my private time with Simon.'

'Look, what can this plodding Farmer Giles do to help? I'll try anything. Take me out of my comfort zone! Learnt that expression a couple of weeks ago. Not really sure what it means yet!'

Sonya pursed her lips in thought. 'The boys, you know how much they love coming up to Rusinga. Next week I'm going to have to talk to a lot of people, some unfinished business of Simon's. If I could bring them up to stay, a couple of days.'

'Long as you like. Ewan —'

He was interrupted. Sergeant Ezra had just taken calls on his mobile. 'Friends, two things. Doctor Simon will be here within an hour. And the Inspector and I have been detailed to go to Kibera. Trouble. Someone has tried to set fire to the clinic ...'

'Oh, my God!' For all of five seconds Sonya's resolve seemed to wobble. Tears were very close.

The sergeant's message was not complete. 'Doctor Sonya, no real damage to the clinic. The fools who tried the stunt, four young men, not so lucky. They came in the darkness. They did not see the local guards, volunteers. I'm hearing that for them it is too late for doctors. We will report back.'

When the policemen left, Sonya had an announcement of her own.

'There has been no clinic for two days. Later on this morning, normal service will start again. Correction! Normal service there can never be again, but,' she was biting her lip, 'we will do our best.'

The first rays of the new morning were shining dappled light onto the lawn and the driveway of the Daniels' house when a battered, old Chevrolet Estate turned in off the murram road and pulled up outside the front door. Sergeant Hosea Kabari stepped out and lifted the rear door. Before anyone from the house appeared, his wife, Maria, had time to make sure that the shroud, a white silk sheet was in perfect order.

Everyone in the household gathered in a half circle around the back end of the car, close enough to have a view of the human shape wrapped tight in its spotless covering. An ancient hospital trolley was grinding its noisy way across the gravel from the rear of the house.

After a single greeting from Sonya, 'Welcome home, my darling,' the daytime askari and a young gardener moved the trolley into position to receive the body. Hosea Kabari had placed Simon on a light wooden board which made the transfer to the trolley smooth and quick.

Not unexpectedly in a household heavy with medical people, in a copse of oleander and flame bushes, there was an outbuilding put up and equipped for times when work had to be performed at home. The granite floors and the whitewashed walls made for coolness even on very warm days. Sonya insisted that everyone who had gathered outside to greet Simon's arrival should be present inside.

The shuffling was long finished. The silence in that room went on and on and the tension built up close to snapping point. Glances returned towards Sonya, constantly, even a little impatiently. She herself stood motionless, head bowed and eyes closed. She might have been asleep. Perhaps she wanted them all, without actually asking them, to slip away and leave her alone with her man, probably for the last time.

Without warning, she moved to the top of the table where Simon's head must be. She grasped the top of the shroud in both hands. Before she could remove the sheet, Hosea Kabari gently touched her arm. 'Madam, please, I must warn you. We did not want to insult the doctor with the clothes of a stranger.'

She acknowledged his words with a barely perceptible nod and then unfolded the sheet down to the line of his shoulders.

It was a face at peace. There was a collective sigh of relief. Sonya bent to kiss her husband's cold lips. She stood back and looked around the line of solemn faces and smiled. 'Our Simon is not here. We all know that. I am already looking forward to seeing him in another place. But we have a duty to his earthly temple. I am blessed to have family who can honour him in the proper way.'

In ten minutes there were just three living humans left in that haven of peace. It was time to look at the mutilated hands. David Daniels, the surgeon with the 'stillest hands in East Africa' stood on the opposite side of the table to his sister. Her fingers grasped the silk sheet. It was she who would decide the moment when this shroud was lifted away completely to reveal the naked body of Simon Mboya. The third person present was not a family member. Less than an hour before, Maria Kabari, wife of Hosea and sister-in-law of Ezra, had been a stranger in the house. The handsome woman with the most strikingly compassionate eyes that Sonya had ever seen had not come down from Kericho just to be company for Hosea on his unpleasant mission.

'Doctor Sonya, I have brought my spices and my … equipment. I can help you. I know these things. When you have finished your task of mending his hands, call me. I will wait on the bench outside, near to the door.'

David watched Maria closely as she left the room. The tall figure glided from their presence without a backward glance. His common sense wanted to warn his sister to be circumspect before she let this woman have any part in these final goodbyes to a man, a down to earth physician who had at no time claimed to possess special gifts which had the merest hint of magic about them. It was not the time to be dishing out warnings. That could come later. But he would have admitted that this sergeant's wife had an aura of power about her, a sense of benevolent spiritual force that he had not witnessed before.

With a single, deft movement of her hand, Sonya revealed the whole body. The gasp was irresistible.

'My God! These bastards knew what they were up to.' David immediately regretted his loss of discipline. His words would do nothing to help his sister. His brief explosion of anger did not help him either. He struggled to hold back the tears, but he was amazed to look across at Sonya, the wife of this man, the mother of his children and see an expression that showed only deep pity.

In a turmoil of conflicting emotions he began his work to repair the fingers that had been broken, and hacked to the point where most of them were almost severed.

He had never before operated on a body that had been dead for upwards of twelve hours. Rigor mortis had taken a toll. The absence of normal human warmth and flexibility had made the digits brittle.

'Sonya, I'm afraid.'

'I understand, David. Perhaps it is not meant for you to do this. Maria, I'm going to call her.'

'But …' Too late. His sister had left the room and it was some minutes before she returned with Maria. He was discomfited when this stranger came straight towards him and actually touched the forearm of the hand that was holding the scalpel. She was smiling like a loving mother might when trying to comfort an uncomprehending child.

'You doctors know the word charlatan. Perhaps you suspect that I am one, that I have come to do some bad thing. Who is this woman, you are asking. You are a Christian. I know that. You will remember that Lazarus and Jesus himself passed out of this life only to return shortly after. There were many women among the teacher's followers. Believe also these two teachings. From those ancient times to this very day a small group of women have carried down some of the healing secrets.'

'Are you going to tell me that you women can raise people from the dead?'

'Of course not! Why do you seem to be afraid of me, David? If I was sick, I would be so happy if you would take care of me.'

'And the other teaching?'

Maria sighed, sensing that this man of science needed always to see things, to touch before he could accept. She would try. 'David, the barrier between us three standing upright around this table and Simon is one of our own creation. Crazy? Perhaps, but also more comfortable for us. We have long ago lost the art, the will to live with such a reality. Only at rare moments, like this perhaps, can we feel the closeness of the other side.

'Look at these hands. Less than a day ago they were beautiful creations dedicated to life. And now the clay from which they came is beginning to return to itself.

'I am not afraid. I cannot bring the warmth back to these hands. The skills they had learned are gone forever. But I can hide the wounds. I can answer the insults that they have suffered so that for a short time these fingers can be dressed in a familiar covering. When he is laid to earth, he will be ready.

'My work will take many hours. You may stay if you wish. You will see no magic potions, hear no mumbo jumbo. Sometimes I sing, sometimes I play my music. Of course, I will say many words to my friend whom I never met but only, Sonya, if you permit me!'

By the time Maria had finished her explanations, David had set aside his instruments and was sitting, a forlorn figure, on a chair close to the head of the table. While he watched his sister help Maria unpack her own bottles, cloths, small knives, spatulas and the rest, he was trying to grasp the meaning, the sense, if there was any, of what he had just heard. Sitting there in his own cool outbuilding, he realised that he was in the presence of the most remarkable woman he had ever met. Her words, true or not, were impressive for the whole new take on life that they put forward. It was the feeling of authority that she had about her which was even more impressive. She showed no sign of arrogance or vanity in her self-assurance.

He was stunned. He felt an urge to stay and watch the policeman's wife at work, but seeing his sister involved and so focused on this unmedical work, a stronger urge was to go outside, take a brisk turn around the garden and look for some breakfast.

Two unlinked notions struck him as he passed the wetlands project on his way to the back fence. The body of his brother-in-law was stretched out close by in his little home surgery, but he felt no sense of a death in the family. He wondered if Hosea Kabari was still at the house. He seemed a fairly ordinary sort of chap, so how on earth did he cope with the wonder woman he had for a wife?

By the time he returned to the main house, Sonya was upstairs with her boys. They loved using the king size bed in the big bedroom for a trampoline. Noah was concerned that Papa might not be coming to Kenton to watch him in the under nines football match for the school. For Noah it was a big competition and he was excited. Moses knew he would be let out of class to watch and Sam had hopes of missing a day of play school to travel to the big school and see the matches. He looked forward to the day when he joined the big boys in the wild running about in the coloured shirts. Papa would make sure that his younger brothers would be cheering Noah on and shouting himself from the touchline.

When are we going home, Mama? Is Papa back? I'm sure I can score a goal if he's watching!'

'Noah, we think you'll score lots of goals even if we aren't watching.'

'Oh no! Does that mean that he won't be coming again?'

Her eldest son's unconscious irony cut deep. His words and his crestfallen look almost sent her resolution crumbling. The full impact of Simon's death had not hit her yet but, for now, the dread was that she would fail her three boys. Papa was dead. This stone cold, savage truth was waiting to ambush them in the near future of their young lives. How could she lessen its impact? The angels would have found that difficult!

Before the thought could be completed in her mind, a wild idea blew in from nowhere she could understand.

'Right! Tracksuits and tackies on! Follow me!'

There was plenty of noisy chatter as they got into their kit. Moses helped his younger brother with his shoelaces. 'Hurry up, Sam, Mum's taking us on a training run around the garden!'

They clomped down the back stairs and into the garden. The boys laughed at their mother's effort to set a pace that was just above walking speed. On their way back from the wetlands, they came close to the garden surgery.

'Boys, time for a rest. Look, the bench! That's a bit of luck.'

'Oh, come on, Mum! You knew all along.'

The bench was on the far side from the door, but there was an open window just above their heads. After more talk about plans for the day ahead, a few seconds of unexpected silence allowed them to hear the sound of a woman singing. Sam slid off the bench and looked up at the window.

'There's a light on in the surgery, Mum. Come and see!'

'Yes, I know, darling.'

'Is Daddy in there working?'

'Don't be stupid, Mo! That's a woman's voice.'

'Yes, but Noah ...'

'Boys, come here.' Sonya hugged her sons close. They saw the tears in her eyes and heard the long, slow breaths. The woman's song was slow, too, and full of sadness. Child's intuition told Noah that something was wrong. He put his arms around his mother's neck and whispered into her ear. 'It's Daddy, isn't it?'

Sonya might have wished for the gift of time, minutes, perhaps hours to fashion an answer that would be just right and would do least harm to her children. But she had only seconds to prepare for the revelation that would change their lives. Even this token of control was taken away from her.

Noah moved purposefully away from the bench and his mother's grasp, leading his brothers by the hand. She hurried after them and managed to reach the open door before them. Events were running away from her. What kind of a crazy, wild idea had she given in to? Whatever it was, it abandoned her at this last moment. She had no sensible words to offer her boys.

Samuel looked around his mother's legs and caught the eye of Maria as she looked up from her work. She interrupted her singing and smiled.

'What are you doing, lady?'

'Does Uncle David know you're here?' Eight-year old Noah knew all about the idea of being careful about strangers coming into your house in Nairobi.

'Yes, he does know. Your mama will tell you.'

Sam, the smallest, the youngest, the most innocent, spoke his truth. 'That's my daddy, isn't it?'

Maria looked up at Sonya, who was standing behind the little trio, and watched for a sign. It came in the form of a brief nod of resignation.

Maria came forward, holding out her hands. The boys responded while their mother remained rooted, fascinated and alarmed in equal proportion.

'Come. There is a little step where I am working. You will see better.'

Sonya felt a sudden great heat pass along her body. It was as if she were about to melt. The scream that rose in her throat did not pass her lips. Her eyes hardly blinked as she watched the impossible scene being enacted five metres from where she stood.

Moses was the first to speak. 'Lady, has Daddy just had a bath?'

'Don't be stupid, Mo! Look, he's wearing his doctor's gloves!' Noah's superior age guaranteed superior knowledge. They might have been in a classroom with the teacher instructing them in simple biological facts.

'Is our daddy dead? His eyes are closed, but I think he's smiling.'

The calmness in Sam's voice astonished his mother. What was going on here? Why weren't these boys showing what she considered to be normal children's reactions? Was this woman some kind of witch? No! No! Sonya was ashamed of the thought.

'I tell you what. Mama will come over and we'll all sit down on Uncle David's big sofa here and have a chat. Plenty of room. No big ones. And what about a cold soda?'

Hosea Kabari was at the table when Sonya ushered her lively brood in for breakfast. He had been talking to David and Dorothy about what had happened up in Kericho after Simon's body had been brought in by a squad car.

'The sergeant and his driver made a mistake. They thought they had picked up a drunk. Too hasty. Yes, they knew their passenger was dead. Even they are not that stupid. But they did not notice the wounds. Stabbed in the upper back, twice. Very sharp knife. The blood had stopped flowing. Dried blood, not so easy to see on black skin. He had been killed somewhere else and then dumped. Once we got him into the light, well, his picture was on the front page of *The Nation.*

'So we dragged the chief out of bed. There were phone calls back and forth to Nairobi, the usual stuff.'

'But where does your wife figure in all this? She's an amazing woman. We are desperate to try … heal Simon's fingers. I couldn't see any chance and I've been in this game longer than I care to remember. She virtually said "Hakuna Matata" then she and Sonya started messing about with all those bottles and jars. My sister is just as amazing. That was her husband they had on that table. It might have been some stranger! I mean … With respect, a woman comes off the street and spins this story about healing …'

'And with respect to you, sir, when the chance comes, look at the good doctor's back. Find the place where the maniac struck. Look for the lacerations on the arm. It will not be an easy job.'

'Okay, so let's say this is all true. How in the world do you square all this with your bosses, the big lawmen?'

Hosea smiled. 'Don't forget we are not as civilised as you. Sometimes the way of mystery is the best way.'

'Look out! Here come the boys. But I'll tell you this, Hosea. I can't wait to get back out there and watch her work.'

'Doctor, Maria has many gifts, but the chiefest one is a compassionate heart.'

The next hour was a time for planning the day but also a time for coming and going. Bertie left for Naivasha after a warm but hectic goodbye to Sonya and the boys. He gave a lift to the sergeant who had to report in at CID headquarters on Nairobi Hill. He would collect his beloved old Chevrolet later. The arrival of Rebecca and Tom gave Sonya the chance to change her plans for the boys.

When she phoned Kenton, the headmaster was surprised that she could have her mind on school things at all, but she soon put him right. 'Mr Robinson, Noah has his heart set on this football match. Some friends have agreed to take the three of them into Nairobi Park for the morning. If they arrive at three …? Thank you so much.'

Dorothy had heard these exchanges. She felt reluctant but obliged to bring up what she saw as a delicate matter.

'Sonya, when are you going to tell the boys? Think about it. They are bound to see or hear something when they are in the city, and possibly from strangers.'

In reply, Sonya smiled and shook her head in bemusement. 'Dorothy, they know.'

'But how? When? I mean, I was here when they had breakfast, with all the usual arguments about Coco Pops and not wanting to eat oranges … You know?'

'Yes, I do. It all happened out there in that amazing place we thought was just a pretty ordinary home surgery.'

Dorothy sat quietly for a few moments, holding her coffee cup. The only sign of her agitation was the rapid side to side movement of her wide eyes.

'Sonya, they didn't cry. Do you think they really, truly understand?'

'They saw Simon just like we did. It was amazing, I admit. Maria says that grief will come, and soon. But …'

'My goodness, how can she be so sure? I'd better get out there and see for myself!'

Chapter Fifteen

Sonya left for Kibera before nine. She had given everyone fresh copies of her mobile number with a plea about the boys. She had a fear that they would suffer some reaction to their encounter with Maria when she was not with them. 'Please, let me know at once.'

On the way down from Naivasha, Tom and Rebecca had heard newscasts about the discovery of Simon's body in Kericho. As they drove through the gates of the Daniels' house, they expected to meet a grief-stricken family. Surprises came in quick succession. The kitchen was full of the activity of a normal morning. This did not feel like a house of death. Perhaps it was a cover-up by the adults to protect the boys. Then they learned that Simon's body was in the surgery at the back of the house and, most amazing of all, that the boys had been in, seen their father's naked body as it was being worked on by a strange woman. Where were the tears or any clear sign of deep upset?

When Maura told them about the meeting with the Rubais the day before, the young couple could only see chaos everywhere. Sonya's request to get her boys out seemed like a first step back to some kind of order. She also did not want them to be caught in the heaviest of the traffic moving across town towards the big industrial estate on the Mombasa road, so she asked them to hang on for an hour. Tom took Noah, Moses and Samuel for a kick about on the lawn.

Rebecca, taken with the luxuriance of the city garden, set out to find a quiet corner. Her walk took her past the open door of the surgery and she slowed down for a glance inside. She might get a sight of the unusual lady working on Simon's hands.

She was clear of the opening when she was startled to hear her name called. 'Rebecca, please!'

She hesitated before she turned back. She stood in the doorway and waited for this stranger to look up again from her work. Maria did not hurry and gave Rebecca time to look around the room if she chose to. She did not choose to except to take in the black coolness of the floor and the dazzling white of the walls, which seemed not so much to reflect the light as to be part of its source.

The naked shape laid out on the raised table two metres from where she stood held her transfixed and by the time that Maria looked at her again, she was conscious of a change in herself. Her initial sense of mild irritation when she was first 'summoned' to appear before this healer or whatever she called herself was transformed to curiosity, excitement, even gratitude. She had forgotten the opening words she had planned to use in this unexpected encounter. The coolness of the tone was gone.

'You are wondering how I know your name. But you are the most famous woman in this country. Our girls will be full of questions.'

Maria's smile was warm and, as David Daniels had discovered, compassionate. With a graceful nod of her head she invited Rebecca to come and be with her on her little platform. And she began to sing quietly as a housewife might do to encourage herself in her tasks around her home.

Rebecca ignored the cold shiver down her body and the heavy pounding of her heart as she prepared herself to confront the full view of the body of a murdered man.

She gasped. Rebecca had seen bodies before. The picture of the bleeding corpse of Julius would remain vivid in her memory. For her, the horror of death was its utter stillness. Looking down on Simon was different. The stillness was the same and she knew that if she reached down to touch him, the flesh would be cold and probably hard. But Simon seemed to be on the point of waking. The muscles of those arms would flex and be ready to throw a ball back to Noah. This man had not crossed over completely.

Maria carried on with her work as if she were still alone. The song continued as she worked a perfumed yellow ointment into his chest and shoulders. As she watched, Rebecca felt curiosity, but bewilderment was melting into the beginnings of fear. What she was seeing was not natural. It was interference, trying to hold back a process that was unstoppable, the dignified end of a life journey. She wanted to be back out where the birds sang in the warm air, where she could hear the boisterous shouts of this man's children playing with Tom on the lawn close to the wetlands.

'Maria, I have to get back to the boys. We' re taking them to the park …'

Maria stopped her singing, but there was no break in the slow, rhythmic movement of her hands.

'Rebecca, I heard you singing in the concert at the Bomas. My brother gave the tickets to me and Hosea. My brother's name is Paul. Before I married Hosea, I was Maria Miller. In the evening, after his work, Hosea is a pastor with the Baptist Church.'

Rebecca was puzzled. Why did Maria invite her into this cool place? Why this beginning of a family history?

'Paul Miller, he is a good friend. Your brother? He mentioned his brother once, the lawyer in Boston but never a sister.'

'Three sisters! I'm sorry that I am frightening you. I admire you so much.'

At last, she turned from her work. First, she wiped her hands on a blue linen cloth, then reached out. Rebecca looked down before she reached out herself to take the hands that were cool and smooth with a very strong grasp.

'Those boys, wonderful children. They were here. They did not cry. I think that will come when they go to their own home.'

More confident, Rebecca asked about Maria's song. 'I don't think I have heard that language before.'

'Aramaic. 'The Hymn of the Marys'. Tradition says they sang it when they were preparing the body with spices and ointments in the tomb.'

'Maria, this is too much for me. I'm lost! Why are you doing this, for a dead person?'

'I don't have the words that will satisfy you. Honouring the temple of the man that was. That's the best I can do. We have forgotten that this beautiful manifestation of flesh is not who we are. When we nurture the spirit … Rebecca, if I talked about auras, about vibrations, would it be easier? Even at this very second I can see, I can feel that you no longer have fear.'

'So you have the power to heal?'

'No! But I can help if the desire is real. And, you, too, have this gift.'

Rebecca's reply was to narrow her eyes and draw in her breath. 'But how can you say such a thing?'

'Because you have healed me. When you sang that night at the Bomas, the power of the emotion, Rebecca, electricity, it is the source of creation.'

'Please, Maria, don't misunderstand me, but you are a policeman's wife from Kericho, and you are also an angel!'

Maria clapped her hands in glee and her laughter sang around the whitewashed walls.

'Did you hear that, Simon? Rebecca, it is true that you are in the presence of an angel. I expect that he is smiling, too!'

'Well, I must look for Thomas and the boys.'

'Yes, and keep looking out for angels. One last word. You and I will have work to share, quite soon.' Maria reached across to embrace her companion. 'You will understand when the time comes. Kwaheri!'

Chapter Sixteen

From high above, the township of Kibera looked a giant, multicoloured tortoise. An intelligent eagle riding a thermal would have wondered how those humans who swarmed everywhere beneath his gaze managed to move about in these narrow places. But there were streets, narrow and dusty, houses and dukas that clung together in a cosy intimacy. Life was not easy in this city within a city and there were few who would have turned down a swap for an acre of land by the side of a healthy stream somewhere up-country. Slum was not a word that Kibera people enjoyed as a description for their home.

Sonya and Rhys made a brief visit to the ward in Nairobi Hospital where 'Welshman' Daniels was waiting for the results of X-rays to his shoulders and back. He had read the news of the discovery of Simon's body in The Nation and he was sitting on the side of his bed, downcast and close to tears. Talkative, exuberant Llewellyn was finding words hard to come by.

'Sonya, I let you down.'

'Llewellyn, I didn't have to be there to know that …'

'Since I came 'round, it's been there all the time. Why didn't they take me? I haven't got any kids.'

'It doesn't work like that, love.'

'No, I know that. But I didn't do anything, except get myself bashed on my stupid head.'

Rhys had never seen his brother so agitated. 'Look, Bro, those guys were pros.'

'Yeah, but three of them, Rhys! I've worked out half a dozen things I could have done.'

'Upset them and the guns would have been out.'

A radiologist appeared at the door with a folder and some news. 'Come and have a look. Some nasty bruises but no sign of a break. You can phone your wife. Or, perhaps …'

'No, these two have to be gone.'

News that Sonya was on her way to the clinic brought out the crowds. Rhys turned off the city road onto the narrow dirt track that was the quickest way in. Sonya was amazed to see the silent mass waiting for them outside the surgery compound. Her initial reaction was a sense of embarrassment. Feeling so many eyes all fixed intently on her was a new and humbling experience. How to deal with it presented a problem. What would Simon have wanted from her? Did she give a simple wave, hurry into the clinic and get on with the day? She visualised her husband frowning and fluttering his eyelids in disapproval.

Unknown to her, there was help close by. So many shocked township dwellers wanted to be involved, partly to work out their anger, their grief, but more to express a deep, loving gratitude to a family who had sacrificed so much for them. Twenty young men had set up a group that they named the Hospital Askaris.

Their job was straightforward. On a morning when emotions would run high, they would make sure that the intensity of the passion would be kept within the bounds of dignity and respect. After craftsmen had repaired the damage from the night attack, mothers and daughters moved in to finish the job with their scrubbing and polishing.

Simon and Sonya Mboya had set up their clinic on the edge of this neglected part of the capital where everyone was welcome to receive first-class treatment free of charge. Nairobi City Council declared the project to be a dangerous hazard, on health grounds, and only bad publicity from *The Nation* and *The Standard* forced them to grant a licence for it to open for two days a week. Now thousands of poor people were grieving. A strong man who was willing to risk his life for them had paid the price. He had offended once too often. He had died because of his love for them. This was too much, but they would get used to even this painful loss. That was too often the way for the poor people of Africa.

The wildfire spread of the amazing news that there was to be a clinic that very day had come early. There was a crazy rumour that the widow herself was coming. But there she was, unmistakable with the untidy mass of wavy hair in that very strange colour. She and Welshman's brother were already wearing their white coats. The young askaris had sorted the watchers from the patients. But she was coming and her husband was not yet even laid in the good red earth of Kenya!

The respectful silence changed quickly to an excited hubbub of chattering voices and, as emotions rose to bursting point, they found their expression in the special African way. One voice began it, calling out above all other sounds: 'Simon Mboya, waahhh!' In seconds it was the only sound, a rhythmic chant from a crowd of swaying, smiling, colourful dwellers of that deprived township, pouring out their love and thanks. On and on they sang as Sonya moved to stand close to them at the entrance to the compound. Her tears lifted the passions higher. Wailing and loud shouts, many of pain, some of anger, mingled with the chant until a single scream of unbearable pain ended it all.

In the silence, Sonya raised her arms and looked around. At that moment her wish would have been to be able to withdraw to some lonely, silent place, a garden where she could sit in peace and lose herself in the turmoil of her many confusions. But there was work to be done, and with Rhys's arm across her shoulders, she turned back towards the surgery that she and Simon had planned and paid for.

At the foot of the steps to the door of the clinic stood two old men. Both were dressed in dark suits and trilby hats and each leaned heavily on a gnarled walking stick.

'Memsahib, Bwana, our hearts are so heavy and yet there is joy that you have come to us.'

'I am Isaac and this is my brother, Gideon. We are from Western.'

'We were elders in a village on the shores of the big lake. We were fishermen.'

'We are Luo. There is much honour for us to be with you today.'

'Ah, thank you.' Sonya understood why the men had made the effort to be there to greet her and Rhys. Two Luo men wanted to give thanks for one of their own in the traditional way.

Sonya only partially understood.

'We want you to let us look after Doctor Simon.'

Sonya heard the words. Her senses had never been sharper, but she could not grasp a clear meaning. Did they want to stand guard over Simon while they waited for the funeral? Were they asking to look after the burial in the Luo tradition?

'There has been much thinking and talking. Even Sister Dorcas and her nurses want to help.'

'You mean that he should rest here? But how could ...?'

'See, just below us here, the field. The soil is good. We could plant trees and flowers. We have the people who could do this, craftsmen.'

She hid her eyes behind her hand. For the second time loving friends were upsetting the balance of the resolve that had brought her to the clinic determined to be with Simon's special people on this day of endless sadness.

'The land can be ours if you give your blessing.'

Sonya turned to Rhys for a reaction and received as a response a smile and the open palmed gesture that suggested that he could not help her beyond a single thought.

'What would Simon want?'

The two Luo elders were scrutinising her intently, sensitive to every movement and gesture. Yet they seemed unaware of the extra turmoil they were creating in her mind. They were afraid that her long silence meant that she was rejecting them but finding it difficult to tell them.

'Please, do not be offended, Doctor Sonya. Perhaps there are plans and we are too late. You know our custom of taking our loved ones back to the farms.'

'Isaac, Gideon, there are no plans but very soon ... Look, Doctor Rhys and I will see our patients and, if you are willing, we can talk again after that.'

'We will wait on this bench. Gideon likes his small sleep in the morning.'

There were many patients to see. While she was taking care of her pregnant women, Rhys was kept alert by a bigger range of medical problems than he was used to treating in his city surgery. He was well-known for his sense of fun even in the most difficult situations. His funny stories and his humorous comments were the best dawa he had to offer.

Three hilarious hours of surgery passed quickly and when the last of her ladies left, Sonya, emotionally spent, lit a cigarette.

'Sonya, what an example to your patients!' Rhys grinned impishly. 'Never seen you with a fag in your hand. Where'd you get it from?'

She puffed out the smoke, slowly through pursed lips. 'Mmn, I did enjoy that!' She stubbed the cigarette on the packet and put it back with its nineteen unused brothers.

'Know something? I bought that packet on the day Simon and I met again in London. He took me to a café near the hospital. He bought the coffee and I pulled out the pack. The look on his face! "What are you going to do with those? You're going to be a doctor. And one day you will have children." And I'm going to hell and I won't collect the two hundred pounds when I pass go!

'That was the first time I heard him laugh. Heads turned and he waved amiably. I gave up the weed that afternoon. I kept the pack, always carried it in my bag.'

She closed her eyes and a contented smile played on her lips for several seconds. She wondered if Isaac and Gideon would be waiting outside.

They rose stiffly to their feet when they saw Sonya at the door. This time they had company, two men and a woman all much younger than themselves. Isaac struggled forward on his stick and reached out to grasp Sonya's hands. His broad smile revealed an uneven set of teeth more brown than white.

'We knew that you would let him come to this place.'

Her reply was a tearful nod and a happy shrug. 'I decided

nothing. The choice was made somewhere else. I am just the messenger. But introduce me.'

The slim woman, fashionably dressed, was Gideon's granddaughter, Rachel. She had a suggestion.

'We have a small table and some chairs. You must be ready for some refreshment. We have coffee, sodas, some samosas.'

One of the two men was a lawyer, the other a stonemason. All three were originally from the north-west.

'The murder of Tom Mboya was before our time and now they have taken another of our great men. Simon's uncle is buried on Rusinga Island. You know that.'

The young lawyer's cultured voice reminded Sonya of someone. He noticed her puzzled look.

'Miller. Perhaps you have met my uncle, another denizen of the courts, Paul.'

'The politician.'

'I'm yet another Tom. Dozens of them in our part of the world.'

Isaac was becoming impatient. 'Doctor Sonya, we must make plans. Rachel, you are forgetting.'

'No, Mzee, we are forgetting nothing, not the pain, not the courage of these two special people. But Bwana Simon is going to have the best. There is little time. We will waste none of it, I promise.'

* * *

The engine of a Land Cruiser was switched off. It was parked in a dusty hollow in the middle of Nairobi Park. Its five occupants had company. There must have been upwards of thirty buffalo encircling them, the furthest just twenty metres away. They, too, were not moving.

Tom was remembering the maverick that had confronted him as he cleared the last of the vertical bog on his climb up the Great Mountain in a different age just months before. He had seen that individual off without much trouble. Then there was that time up in the Aberdares when, as a boy, he had stood in amazement watching a particularly stubborn one in a stand-off with a lion. The handsome cat had the high ground and he looked down on his opponent with a fierce glare and whipped his tail in a slow, rhythmic threat. Those jaws were ready to inflict some serious damage. Tom expected Buff to drop his head and slink off into the cover of the bush. Instead he raised his low-slung head to offer Mister Leo a good view of a broad ridge of craggy horn for his consideration. He was going nowhere. In the staring match the dour, heavy black mass of hard flesh outstayed the sleek, athletic fighting machine. Perhaps the lion did not feel lucky. Perhaps he could sniff something upwind. His tail slowed to a halt and a single sideways glance announced the end of the contest. He turned and marched stiffly away, his confidence undiminished.

Ted Manning had become an instant hero to Pembroke boys when they heard how he had saved his sister's life by shoving her across the back seat of the car seconds before a huge head had been swung and a horn thrust through the roof of their car that was trawling 'round these same plains. Kenya buffalo were never sociable to strangers. There were thirty of them just the other side of half a dozen thin panes of glass. They were full of curiosity about these strangers who had strayed into their patch. Tom was apprehensive.

Rebecca had begged him to turn back when they had unexpectedly come across the herd close to the track as they started down a steep drop in the plain. She had no fondness for any of the large beasts of her homeland. She was terrified of them and finding it hard to hide her fear from the boys. She would like to have shut her eyes tight and listened to the drone of the engine carrying her out of the park and back into the safety of the chaos of the streets of Nairobi. Tom knew he had made a big mistake by driving down the slope and that the only plan for them now was to wait until the buffalo decided to move on.

The boys' complete attention was focused on the big friends who had come to say good morning. Sammy adored the sight of the black, muscular lumps. He wanted to roll down a window, to scratch a nose or pat a flank. Noah was not ready to take any risks on the day of his big football match.

'No, Sammy. If one of those monster heads got stuck in the window here, we would have to take it home with us.'

'Crazy, man! The man on the gate wouldn't let us. That would be stealing. Daddy told us that stealing is very bad.'

'Right, Mo. And, Sammy, where would we keep it when we got home?'

'But, Noah, why do they all look so sad? When I have my friends over, we play a game or something.'

Rebecca tried to help out. 'Perhaps they are hungry. Just this brown grass for their dinner.'

'Do you think they want to eat us for their dinner?'

'Sammy, they are vegetarians. You'll learn about this stuff when you get to proper school.'

'What's a vegetan?'

'No nyama choma. So, Sammy, they won't eat you. Let's just keep quiet here.'

Noah had a more serious worry. Time was moving on. He was hoping that Tom would manage to get them out of this animal prison and back to school, and soon. In his mind he kept on seeing pictures of the playing fields of Kenton with the pitches marked out and himself running the ball at the Banda goalie.

An hour passed before there was a sign of movement outside when one or two on the edge of the crowd turned away to graze on untrodden grass. Tom switched on and raced the engine. Sammy screamed in surprise and the company moved back a step, enough for Tom to make a steady, determined charge for the open road.

Rebecca was happy that they were on their way to the park exit. Their animal sightings were few and mostly with less intimidating creatures like dik-dik and gazelle. As they wound their way along the twisting, undulating trails, Tom talked to the boys of the days, not so long before, when those plains were dominated, ruled by the creatures.

'When they built the railway from Mombasa to Nairobi the workers always had to be on watch to make sure they didn't become a lion's dinner.'

'Why did the lions go away, Tom? I wish I could see one right now.'

'Well, Sammy, I don't think they wanted to go away. We humans can be very greedy. We take things that don't belong to us.'

'Like when Moses steals my toys and I don't want him to.'

Moses, embarrassed to be accused of stealing in front of Rebecca whom he was out to impress, was officious in his reply. 'Sam, I don't steal your toys, just borrow them when you are not using them. See!'

Rebecca, sensing that emotions were beginning to show signs of tension and fearful of where even small disagreements might lead, made a suggestion that everyone approved of. 'I say that we find those picnic tables and have lunch.'

When they arrived half an hour early in the Kenton car park, most of the seven visiting schools were finishing their packed lunches in and around their coaches. Noah sat in the back of the Land Cruiser and stared out at the opposition. He felt weak in the belly area and his legs seemed to have turned to lead in two seconds flat. Some of those guys were big and they were fooling around, having a lot of laughs. Red shirts, maroon, green. Who were these people? Where did they come from? He knew where his Kenton teammates would be, but he did not fancy getting out of the car to go and join them. For sure, these strangers who were obviously proper players would start making fun as soon as they saw him in his Kenton shirt, trotting off on his skinny legs. Moses and Sam, taking their mood from their leader, shared his anxiety, wondering what he had seen out there to make him look so scared.

Tom and Rebecca interpreted what was happening with the boys in very different ways. She thought that the moment she had been dreading was about to arrive. The grief at their loss was breaking through. Noah looked bewildered and threatened, needing his mother. She began to search in her bag for Sonya's mobile number. The clinic was only ten minutes away. Tom could get them there before the tears started.

Sixteen years before Tom had travelled down from Pembroke to Kenton to play in this same tournament. It was his first game in the maroon shirt and he was the youngest boy in the youngest team. Pembroke teams always expected to win and he was in with a crowd who were, he thought, every one of them looking forward to running out onto the pitch and enjoying themselves.

'Noah, I was scared shitless.' Sam broke out into peals of laughter at this new word. 'Yes, I couldn't eat my boiled eggs. Noah, you'll be going up to the pavilion with the other teams. First thing I did was to run behind the bus and throw up into the hedge! I still remember the exact spot.' Tom paused briefly. 'I was scared. I would look a fool out there in front of our supporters. I'd do something stupid and we'd lose the match.'

The transformation was swift and solid. Rebecca put away her mobile and took out her sunglasses.

'What's with the shades, Rebecca?' Sam was laughing again, this time at his elder brother's successful take on an American accent.

'Just in case you dazzle me too much with … whatever you get up to out there!'

'You're famous, aren't you? I've seen you on the tele.' For sure, Noah was back to normal.

Close by someone blew hard on a whistle, which was a relief to Tom and Rebecca. Noah hopped smartly out of the car and followed the crowd of young footballers to their gathering point.

'Wow, boys, your brother can shift!'

'Daddy says he's fast as a cheetah!' Sam said in admiration.

Before she could allow herself another moment of panic, she was pleased to see Samuel race off. 'Wait for me, Mo! I got a Mars bar in my pocket!'

The tournament went well for the Kenton under nines. They won through to the final where they were to meet Pembroke!

'Just a minute, Ref, while I get my kit on! Someone's got to show these Kenton guys who's in charge!'

'Thomas, big men are not allowed!'

'Oh, Sam, how are Pembroke going to win without me? Don't forget Kenton have a cheetah playing for them!'

'Not a real cheetah, silly!'

The cheetah had his best game when it counted most. The big crowd for the finals cheered the serious-faced player with the skinny legs. Only the Kenton supporters knew who he was and some of those were not sure whether he should even be on the pitch. Not far from Rebecca and Tom a couple of families weren't hiding their feelings.

'What kind of a woman is she? The kid's father's probably still up in a morgue in Kericho and she's around here somewhere watching a bloody football match. I've always said that the Daniels family was weird.'

'I wasn't surprised to hear they'd got him. Death wish, a bit like his uncle. Fancied himself too much. Asking for it!'

'Keep your voice down. His brothers are just down there. Their mother's not with them, so you've got that one wrong, George. Surprised you haven't noticed since you're so fond of her!'

'Fond of …?'

'The black nightingale! Look, dark glasses. Rebecca Kamau.'

George took a couple of steps onto the pitch so that he could check. 'Damn right, Rosie! What's she got to do with them, I wonder.'

Tom was too focused on the play to pick up what Rebecca had heard clearly. She realised that the painful solution was the sensible one. She must stay quiet until the match was all over and they could move away. If the rubbish kept coming, she would reconsider.

It was Noah himself who saved the day with a dream ending to the match and the tournament. One final sprint onto a pass from his pal, Andy, and this time a low shot dribbled past the outstretched leg of the Pembroke goalie. Ecstasy and tears.

'I wish Daddy was here!'

It was not the black arms of Rebecca that embraced him in his moment of triumph but the familiar grasp of his mother who had her three sons locked together safe out of harm's way.

'Wow, boy! I saw that!'

Chapter Seventeen

That same afternoon Llewellyn Daniels was released from hospital. He was a doctor, came from a family of doctors. There would be no risks there even though his shoulders and upper back were dark blue with the biggest bruise the ward sister had ever seen. Kate drove him to Cartref and the family was still at the buttered scones and tea when the hero arrived wearing his medal.

After a short stay when she shared in the celebrations and made sure that Rebecca and Tom were being looked after, Sonya went out into the garden to the surgery where Maria was still working. Before leaving the sitting room, she had a request.

'Twenty minutes. Rebecca, Tom, I'll be back and I need your help. Please, stay!'

Maria was alone, but there had been changes since Sonya had last been in that room. She was surprised by the perfume of orange blossom that might have come from a Naivasha grove at evening time and the coolness of an underground cave was a contrast to the warmth of the late afternoon she had just left behind.

Maria had moved her working platform so that she was now much closer to Simon's head. Sonya stepped up onto the platform. She was startled by what she saw and, for a few terrifying seconds, might have believed that her husband had come back to life. The lower part of his body was draped in the white silk sheet, but the skin, where it was visible, was damp with what appeared to be beads of perspiration which made it seem that Simon was resting after a bout of exercise. The idea of a living person resting was strengthened by the blue pillow supporting his head. Over a chair down to her right was draped a surgeon's green operating gown and, on top, neatly placed, a pair of Simon's work spectacles.

'Maria, what's going on?' Sonya's voice was tremulous. 'Simon is not alive and nothing anyone can do will change that!' Irritation gave a sharp edge to her tone.

Maria took off her gloves and turned to look directly into Sonya's eyes. It was the pleading gaze of someone who thought she was being misunderstood.

'Sonya, you are right, this shell will never again carry in it the warmth of life. But I want him to look at peace in body as well as in spirit.'

'Maria, please, forgive me. You have worked so hard. It's just that …' She could hold back the tears no longer. 'He is so like the Simon I first met fifteen short years ago …' She paused to gather herself. 'I need you to help me more. You understand these things … Look! Simon has been taken from us and I want him to have a resting place where … Maria, I have made a promise to some people that, perhaps, the family will resent, dislike, hate even.'

'Sonya, your heart speaks the truth that matters. Tomorrow, when you are ready, you will take him to this place. He is ready, he is anxious to be on his journey. Let me come with you. You will not notice me! I promise. So you see, he will be with other people who loved him desperately. He gave them hope and they will take care of him for us all. And we can be with him at any time.'

* * *

When she had finished, there was a shocked silence. For a time the only reaction to Sonya's announcement came in the body language of the dozen family members and friends standing or sitting around in that comfortable room. Vibrations were doing the talking and Sonya thought that David and Dorothy were disturbed by what she wanted for Simon. They sat holding hands staring towards her but not at her. For them death and funerals were intensely personal, family affairs that should not be handed over to strangers. Dorothy was the first to break free.

'Sonya darling, forgive me. This wouldn't be my way. Grandma Daniels would have a fit if she could be here. Stuck in the past and calling it tradition. Good old Welsh ways. But my dada used to say that heaven is a place gushing with love. I think he would have approved. I'm surprising myself. What's going on around here?'

'Dot, losing Simon is like having my heart wrenched out of me. So what is this joy bubbling up inside me? It's Simon's way and it's infectious. There are enough doctors in this room for us to understand that!'

'I'll second that!' Welshman Daniels, fresh out of hospital was stiff and bent over from the heavy thumps inflicted on his back, pushed his arm into the air in triumph. 'I haven't been around here for the past couple of days. I've heard things and now I'm seeing them. It's crazy, ridiculous. This isn't normal human stuff. We aren't tiptoeing around the house with long faces. Something big is going on, like some spirit is wandering around the place. It's just right. And tomorrow …'

Rhys wanted his say. 'I was with Sonya in Kibera this morning. Isaac, Gideon, Rachel and the others, fantastic people! We're not handing him over. We're sharing him.'

* * *

Karen is beautiful and peaceful. People who are lucky enough to live out there expect to enjoy a sense of control in their lives. Things do not get out of hand. So it was in one of the old established houses in that quiet place in the early afternoon of the following day. Family and close friends sat around a large table in the garden of Cartref. Some took lunch, some were happy just to sit quietly and prepare themselves. The little surgery was in sight at the end of a path bright with a border of flame trees. Inside Simon was waiting. The dead man dominated the thoughts of the living. There was grief and a realisation of the huge gap there was in their lives now that this dynamo for good had been silenced forever. But there would be a sensible farewell where each would have a part to play, from the youngest to the oldest.

It was time. The wooden gates of Cartref were opened and the orderly departure began. The last but one car to leave was the Land Cruiser from Londiani. Tom drove with Rebecca at his side and Sonya and the boys behind. The traffic thickened as soon as they joined the Ngong Road and they became part of the crowded afternoon. To other travellers they might have been on their way to do some late shopping in one of the city malls. It was only the rare driver who looked across at traffic lights and wondered why the women and children in the next car were dressed in black.

Tom was anxious to give his passengers a smooth ride and he was relieved when the turn-off to Kibera came in sight. He was surprised to notice that the verges on both sides of the approach road were crowded with empty parked cars. Oncoming traffic was held up to allow them to turn right. The steep banks of the narrow road that would bring them to the site of the clinic were crowded, too, this time with talkative groups of men, women and children who all stooped low to get a view of the latest arrivals.

At once for Sonya the misgivings began. Had she made a terrible mistake? There was a danger that this most sacred of moments would be swamped by outside forces. Would Dorothy's cautions be justified? She had handed control over to good people, but would their loving intentions be strong enough to hold out against this hysteria of numbers? Too naïve, too lacking in foresight, she would have to cope as best she could.

Tom drove on sedately at what he judged to be a proper, seemly speed. In the short run down from the crest of an incline to a prepared parking place near the clinic, everything, everything was transformed.

Doubts, anxieties melted away quicker than she could think. They were simply not there any more. The transformation had been created for her in a flash of light and colour. After the initial thrill of seeing the complete picture in an instant, she was able to look around her and take in the details.

A huge crowd was gathered on three sides of a green oval. Tom turned off the engine and through the open window came the hushed sound of thousands of voices. It reminded Sonya of the subdued whispers of a congregation gathered in the nave of All Saints Cathedral for a great mass. A strong sense of reverence made her linger inside the vehicle. She gathered her three boys around her and whispered. 'See. All these good people are friends who have come to say goodbye to Daddy with us.'

'So many. Do you know the names of every one of them?'

'Well, Noah, I think if we checked the lists in the surgery, they would all be in there.'

'Mama, it is like the football at Kenton. But why have they made that hole in the grass?'

The open grave bordered all 'round by neatly laid mounds of red earth drew her gaze. It was a dramatic and chilling reminder of what was about to happen.

On the side of the oval close to her were more people, much less tightly packed. The smart clothes, the darker colours told the story. Friends, colleagues, local and national figures, embassy staff, Sonya took in their presence as she might a painting on the wall of a great house that she was visiting. It was there but she paid it little attention.

There were two figures who moved her with their silent, dignified stance. They were looking across at her from just inside the oval. Isaac and Gideon, the fishermen brothers from Western District, leaned on their gnarled sticks not because they needed the support but as a show of authority, like young subalterns holding their swords as a sign of order. Sonya and they exchanged private smiles.

Without a word the Luo brothers moved, one to the left and one to the right and turned inwards. Through the gap that was left two children stepped forward, side by side, the first of two long lines. They waited.

It was time. Tom slid from his seat and moved to open the door for Sonya and the boys. Every movement was slow and measured. In the great silence, every sound from that small focal point was loud enough to be heard from the distant corners – the noise of the door hinges as the door swung out, the striking of small feet as they touched the white gravel, the nervous clearing of the throat as Sonya prepared to whisper to her sons.

The boys looked about them in wide-eyed awe. They were grateful for the protection of the arms of Rebecca and their mother guiding them forward closer to the empty, grassy space. They were comforted by the gesture of the old men, two strangers who moved forward to grasp their cold hands and squeeze them and then nodded to them in a smile of welcome.

With graceful, rhythmic movements the line of children moved forward. They were each carrying a spray of white roses. They handed these over to older girls who set them down on the bank behind the grave to form the shape of a fish.

The farewell had begun. Family and close friends took their stand behind Sonya. A new sound, much louder, caught the attention. When the vehicle came into sight, it caused a surprise. Sitting bolt upright at the wheel and looking dignified, Sergeant Hosea Kabari of Western District had his wife, Maria, as his companion. She wore a black kikoi and matching headscarf. Those standing closest as the ancient Chevrolet passed by realised that they were watching the progress of the hearse carrying the body of Simon Mboya. The murmuring began and soon grew louder. Nobody in the mass of the gathering had expected the now famous doctor to be making his final earthly journey in such an ancient, humble wreck. Reaction was mixed. Casual observers who had come as indifferent spectators were already giving the show a low rating. What was this family thinking of? They were not short of money, so what point were they trying to make? Others, and they were a majority, who had been touched in some way by Simon Mboya's work, were puzzled, even upset by what seemed a lack of respect.

This was going to be no ordinary funeral, so what lay in store for them in the next hour or two?

Sonya and the family were happy to share this most poignant of moments with anyone of goodwill, but their intention was far different from a simple wish to impress spectators, to let everyone see that their Simon was receiving a good send-off. Intimacy and privacy were their natural process. Simon was the sacred heart of everything that was taking place.

As arranged, Hosea brought his car to a halt close to the family group but out of the view of Noah, Moses and Sammy.

David and his three sons, with Alex and Tom McCall, stepped forward to move the platform bearing the body from the car to the trolley that had been wheeled across from the clinic. In a matter of seconds, Simon himself was being carried on the very machine that he had used so many times in his work to heal others. He was draped to the neck in a white linen sheet, under an afternoon sky that everyone but he could see, ruffled by the whisper of a breeze that everyone but he could feel.

There was no sign of a coffin. Even the most loving and loyal of the wananchi must bear their anxiety and wait. They were well aware that white folks, even after three or four generations of living their African lives, were liable to do strange things. Surely Doctor Sonya would not abandon her man to the earth unprotected against all the weevils and worms that were on the move down there.

The voice that broke the awed silence was a familiar one. The haunting sense of loss and longing that was the very essence of Rebecca Kamau's singing shocked a thousand hearts into deep numbness as the words of Simon's favourite hymn came to them from the mouth of that beautiful woman. Two lines into 'Amazing Grace' and a crowd of diverse individuals became a chorus of full-throated African voices charged with their unique and ancient emotional power. By the time the song was ended, quiet, personal tears had been overwhelmed by the sounds of outbursts of sobbing and by loud calls for blessings and mercy from all parts of the congregation. The pain of saying goodbye was becoming unbearable.

At Sonya's request, two Luo elders had prepared themselves to say the last words. The tall, slim figure of Paul Miller embraced Sonya and Simon's three sons before going to be close to Simon himself. He bent over to touch his old friend's forehead and reached down to plant a final kiss on his cheek. When he drew himself up to speak, he had a face of stone. He was struggling to hold on to the white heat of his anger.

'Friends, we should not be in this place today. Yes, we have come to honour a good man, a man who knew how to love. But it is wicked men who have brought us here, wicked men, our own people who have taken Simon Mboya from us. Why is it such people hate the light so much that they have a crazy longing to put it out? You do not need me to tell you that the darkness around us has suddenly become a little deeper.

'You do not need me to tell you that Simon was not a sentimental, soft-headed man. He knew the risk he was taking. He knew all about the threats. He had a family, Sonya and his three wonderful sons, a family more precious to him than life itself. Simon also knew about loving strangers. When he saw brothers and sisters with a deep need, he had to answer it.

'Above all things, I believe that what we are witnessing here is not failure, not failure!' By now he was being accompanied by voices raised on every side.

'Yes, brother, yes! You are speaking true things here!'

'Sweet Lord Jesus, take our Simon into your bosom!'

'Simon Mboya, we will never forget you!'

Paul saw that a full-blown frenzy might erupt at any moment. He paused and reached out to touch the hem of the linen sheet. When he began again, his voice was firm but soothing.

'We must not keep Simon with us any longer. I say again that what has happened in these last days is not a failure. One day soon we will all begin to understand that a triumph will arise from these ashes. Soon! That is a promise!'

Years before, in his first weeks as a medical student in Saint Mary's Hospital, London, Simon had made friends with a group of young Christians. On Sundays they had done the rounds of places of worship, mainly in the Westminster area. Each Saturday night it had become a ritual for one of the group to buy a round of drinks at one of their pubs and be paid back by having the choice of church, temple, synagogue or whatever for Sunday morning. In his turn, Simon, a Methodist back home, had led his friends to Central Hall for good teaching and a warm welcome, and an unexpected meeting. Sonya Daniels, Kenya born of Welsh parents, followed the traditions of her old family and became a regular at the vibrant Sunday sessions in the crowded Methodist meeting place across the square from the great ancient abbey. So, for Simon, the ecclesiastical tour around Central London ended. And now the Christian wheel had turned back on itself.

The official farewell was delivered by Peter Andrews, a minister friend from those London days. After the reading of the triumphal proclamation of victory over death in the words of Saint Paul, those watching from far and near knew that the formalities were over. Surely Simon would be buried very soon. Then they would all return to their homes but never forget. The small green field on the southern edge of this township would be transformed into a garden of remembrance.

Two women stepped out of the gathering of mourners. They came together at the head of the platform where Simon lay, embraced and walked slowly and in step towards the opening in the ground. The Daniels men followed, heads bowed, and eased the trolley forward until its front wheels were cutting into the neat mound of red earth.

Gently and solemnly Sonya Mboya and Maria Kabari removed the linen sheet that had been Simon's shroud. It was not the naked body of a man that the bystanders saw revealed but a doctor in his green operating robe and a face that wore those familiar steel-rimmed spectacles placed lovingly by Sonya on her husband's nose. This time it was not only the mass who wondered why these women were getting in the way of the final laying to rest. The family and friends gathered close to the grave were anxious.

Dorothy Daniels, who was looking after the boys, was aware of their growing distress. They were bewildered by the strange events taking place around them. Who were all these people? Why were they here? What were Mama and the new lady doing with their daddy? They wanted to cry because of the pain that they could not understand but knew they must not. They had been told that they must be brave, even Sam who looked up in wonder at the faces of the big people and saw that no one had told them to be brave.

Of everyone waiting and wondering only Maria Kabari could see through the confusion. Maria was a Luo elder in the Kericho district. The old Luo elders from the Kibera district who had asked Sonya to allow Simon to have his resting place in their little field did not know this. They, like the thousands who had come to say their personal farewells, believed that they were looking down on a shell. The spirit which was the true life force had been snatched away before its time. What they did not understand was that the spirit, too, had been damaged by the violence of its departure. Even in these last moments there was healing to be done.

Maria turned to face Simon. She closed her eyes tight and began her final task by shutting out the world around her. She soon lost a sense of human time and place. It was a common practice with her to raise the level of her vibrations when she needed to see beyond. The many hours she had spent in the surgery in the Daniels' house were a preparation for these moments when full release would come. She was between worlds. Simon was waiting for her. The glow in his aura was bright, but in his eyes fear and pain were visible.

Her task was clear and her return was swift. She had been away for only a few seconds but time enough to have taken on a radiance from another place. Simon needed no more help.

Maria motioned for Rebecca to come and stand by her. Then she began to sing quietly. The words were in Aramaic, first sung by Mary Magdalene when she was dressing the wounded body of her master lying dead in a borrowed grave. Rebecca did not know them, but the melody was familiar and she added her harmony as a counterpoint. The three women stood holding hands in a small triangle. They were turned away from Simon. When the song was finished Maria spoke to Sonya.

'His spirit is at peace now. I know that for certain. The grieving will not stop on our side and that is natural, but the grief is for ourselves. We have forgotten how death truly is because we cannot believe. But our lives do not have to be a long cry of pain. For now it is time to say goodbye.'

The burial was over in less than five minutes. Barefooted young men stepped out of the shadows and with easy grace lifted Simon and lowered him into the coffin that was open and waiting at the bottom of the grave. When the sealing was finished, the family came with their roses and their scattering of earth. The grave would not be closed until after dark when the last of the long line of Kibera people paid their respects.

* * *

'The boys need to get away from the city, Maria. Rebecca, do you think that Bertie will be willing to have us up on the farm, just for a day or two? He did say ...'

'Travel up to Rusinga with him. He'll be going tonight. He hates being away from Ewan. You know that.'

'I'll speak to him later. He's coming back to the house, I'm sure ...'

The sound of a commotion came to them from the direction of the busy main road. There were angry men and women down there.

Chapter Eighteen

Since the early hours, Abel Rubai had been troubled by a dilemma. For an ordinary man who had played the crucial but distant part in the death of Simon Mboya, the decision would have been simple. 'Man, you do not go within miles of that funeral.' But this was no ordinary man and he suffered a powerful longing to be present when they lowered the corpse of that Luo meddler into the ground. One thought that stayed with him longer than most of those hundreds which ceaselessly whirled around in his mind pushing him first towards go and then back towards stay was a line he had read in a book many years before: 'a murderer always visits the scene of his crime'.

'But I'm no murderer and I don't even know the scene where the unfortunate accident took place. For sure they didn't do the job down there in that hellhole. Yes, I paid money and some fancy lawyer might come out with some smart idea about being an accessory blah, blah, blah! What did lawyers know about running a country, looking after the best interests of the wananchi? And those fools never did realise what was best for them. They think they have lost some kind of saint. Saint? That's a joke. This one was a true Luo, pretending to be out for the people, using them for his own purposes, just like his Uncle Thomas before him.'

For an ordinary man the decision to go was left too late.

It would not be possible to travel from his Karen home to the south side of Kibera and arrive in time for whatever they were getting up to in that god-forsaken dump, but for a Mister Big? A police car with a siren led a trio of his own reckless drivers and his little motorcade sped along the crowded roads, bullying its way through the afternoon traffic.

They were a half an hour late. Sally was just glad to hear that they had arrived so that she could open her eyes again without having to watch the risky overtaking and the near misses. What she saw surprised her. So many people were crowded onto the side of the road that they blocked the turn-off into Kibera South. The police car aggressively pushed its way into the crowd, expecting a path to open up through this human Red Sea. The driver managed fifty metres through the squashed masses. He didn't care about the bumps and bruises, the torn clothes, the bleeding limbs he left in his wake. Then his luck ran out. A seventeen year old mother with a baby on her back and a two year old boy grasping her hand, lost her balance in her struggle to stay ahead of the vehicle mercilessly advancing on its crazy journey.

The boy rolled under the wheels. The screams and the angry shouts, the thumping of fists, the frantic efforts to get to the child changed the situation instantly. Locked inside their metal box, the hunters became hunted, wild-eyed in their terror, desperate to protect themselves. Out came the guns.

Looking on from behind, Abel Rubai saw that he was trapped in a wedge of hundreds of very angry wananchi pressing hard against his cars. Lives were in serious danger here. In all four cars there were bodyguards. They were ruthless men, but he had stifled the initiative out of them. They would be waiting for his orders. As he buttoned his window down he took out his own pistol and let it be seen. The move gave him the few seconds respite he needed.

'Back! Back! Get us out! Now! Now!'

Cars moving quickly in reverse caught out those who thought that the danger for them was passed. More screams of pain followed, and frantic shouting.

A single gunshot sent hundreds dropping for cover. Abel heard the breaking of glass, but in the pandemonium it took him a second to realise that it was in his car that a window had been shattered by the stray bullet.

'Oh, no! No! No!'

Sally had taken the hit. Her eyes rolled back as she fell towards him. He fired his pistol into the roof of the car till he emptied the cartridge. He screamed at his driver.

'There are doctors up there! Get to them, now! I don't care how many of these bastards you drive over! Just get us there!'

'But, Bwana, they cannot get out of the way. There will be deaths. Better we get out. It will be quicker. The people will help us. See, it is not a big distance. I promise! I promise! Look, Bwana, look!'

The police car in front of them could force its way no further into the crush of bodies struggling to climb the steep banks on either side of the narrow road. The windows were smashed and the four men inside ducked low, trying to ward off the blows coming from stones and sticks aimed at them from outside. It would not be long before they were dragged out.

There was blood on his suit, blood on the seat. As he pulled Sally 'round, Abel saw the hole in the leather upholstery where the bullet had penetrated after it had passed through the flesh of Sally's upper arm. He kissed the wound, thinking that this might help stop the flow. She opened her eyes and was surprised to see her husband biting her arm. She frowned and then chuckled.

'Abel, what you up to? Look, you made my arm burn!'

As he pulled back, simultaneously she saw his bloodstained mouth and became fully aware of the searing pain of the wound.

'My God, Abel, what has happened here?

She saw her arm shining red down to her fingertips and remembered the loud bang that had gone off somewhere in front of her. The shouting and the screaming around them were worse than ever. She was terrified. The Mercedes was stuck fast and the trickle of blood was forming a puddle on the seat beside her.

'Please God, Abel, do not let me and the child die in this place.'

He let out a cry of frustration through clenched teeth. He turned to the open window and grasped the sill with both hands. He pushed hard into the bodies jammed outside. The narrowest of cracks opened up. Kneeling on the seat, he pushed and pulled with a frantic effort, shouting angrily as he did so. He ignored the cries and the screams of pain. At last, drenched with perspiration, Abel forced a gap wide enough to allow him to push one leg through. He managed to stand upright with one foot on the ground and one inside the car.

'Move, damn you, move. My wife is in danger. See this blood on my face? Soon it will be your blood. I swear it.'

Sonya's attention was divided. The ceremony was almost finished, but she kept glancing across to the place where the narrow track from the main road spilled out onto the open field. Why all the shouting? Why the gunshots? Her boys were upset and grabbed her hands tight.

When she saw a group of women burst through

surrounding a girl with a child who was screaming in pain, she hurried towards them. She took the child in her arms. The little boy pressed his head into her shoulder and struck out at her face with his tiny fists.

Before she could search for the source of the pain, she was shocked to see Sally Rubai moving unsteadily towards her, supported on the arm of her husband. She closed her eyes in disbelief. Her grip tightened on the child and she pressed a kiss on his cheek.

When she looked again, she saw the blood soaked sleeve of Sally's dress. She moved to put her free arm around the shoulders of her new patient and drew her away from her husband.

As she turned, Sonya's eyes caught the gaze of Abel Rubai. There was no arrogance in his look. She noticed his body shudder momentarily, unaware that the involuntary movement was caused by the power and intensity of her own contemptuous glare. Angry words and curses would have been more welcome to him.

'David, I need you.'

Her brother was happy to follow her towards the steps of the little clinic. She had never been an ordinary sister and now she was no ordinary widow. He released the boy from Sonya's arms. The child had cried himself out and David waited for his sobs to subside.

'Sally, we will soon have you fixed up.'

Abel expected to follow his wife into the wooden building. With the threat of danger gone, he was back to his confident self.

'Mister Rubai, you will not be needed.'

He felt a mixture of annoyance and embarrassment at being turned away at the door, even more so when he saw the one delivering the slight.

'So, the wash girl is now a nurse and giving out instructions. And may I ask what exactly you are needed for here?'

'It will be better for your wife. And, no, I am not a nurse. I am a friend of the family.'

'The Naivasha songbird, friend to the world. No friend of our family! Just get out of my sight!'

'I saw the blood. You will disturb the work. Please …'

'Just … go and sing a song somewhere. Look, you have an audience ready and waiting.'

'If you will come away with me from the door.'

He snarled, pointing his finger towards her face to make himself clear. 'Shut that lying mouth of yours. Know your place. I will do whatever I please.'

'I am not afraid of you.'

'What a brave little whore you are!'

'And I am not a whore. You have a bad tongue and you say foolish things.'

Before he could get out the direct threat that would get this nuisance to leave him in peace, Sally's face appeared at an open window close by.

'Abel, all this talk is upsetting things here. Please, go with the child. For my sake.'

The nostrils flared and there was a look of fury in his eyes but, without a word, he strode off, dialling on his mobile as he went. He was looking for a quiet place where he could speak, but so deep was his anger that he did not notice Tom McCall pass not two metres from him. With Maria Kabari he was hurrying towards a distressed Rebecca.

Chapter Nineteen

'Rebecca, please, I must speak to you. Perhaps you can help me. My name is Lydia. I am in danger.'

'I remember. You were at the Muthaiga that night. You wore a beautiful, yellow dress.'

Four hours had passed since a trembling Rebecca had watched Abel Rubai walk away from the steps of the Mboya clinic in the Kibera township. The two patients had been treated successfully and been taken back to their widely different homes. Now the Daniels family and Sonya were following tradition. Well over two hundred friends and colleagues of the Mboya family had come together at Cartref to be present at the formal end to the farewell to Doctor Simon. The outside lights were on and guests wandered around the garden or gathered in groups. They talked, ate and drank and talked again.

Rebecca remembered two things about Lydia from that night five months before. The striking colour of the dress had helped to make her stand out in that crowd of the smartest women in Nairobi society. But, in retrospect, more memorable was her recollection that it was Reuben who had brought her to the party. She remembered how attentive both Julius and his father had been to her when she was introduced. She herself had not been introduced, but she would not forget the wild flight of fancy that the sight of those introductions had created in her imagination. What if she and that pretty girl could have swapped places!

'Lydia, I know a quiet place.'

They sat in the large, cool room and for a time nothing was said. Lydia was anxious about the best way to explain herself. Even in the dim light, it was easy for Rebecca to see the swelling around the eyes and the bruises on the left side of her face. Lydia answered her concern with a wan smile. And she had found her way into her story.

'Yes, it was a man's work. When your living comes from selling your body, you take risks, not only with the … clients. Many women have cruel words for me. 'Whore', 'tart', I hear those two a lot. The ones who are badly hurt scream louder. Then it's 'Scum, you have stolen my husband', something like that, a bit less polite. Fortunately, for most of these poor men, their wives never find out.

'Perhaps, Rebecca, you are wondering why I say all this to you. Perhaps you think that I should not speak these things to a … I was going to say 'stranger'. But you are not a stranger to me. And I want you to know what I am.'

'Lydia, this is a place of healing. There are so many doctors in the family here.'

'I know the family. One time I lived in Kibera. I knew Doctor Simon. Doctor Sonya brought my sister's little boy into the world at their clinic.'

'We can try to help each other …'

'Before something happens …'

The two beautiful Kenyan girls looked solemnly at each other. Rebecca was disturbed. She half suspected why but was not ready to search out the full reason.

'Lydia, two days ago, I was in this … it was more than a room then, more than a place where doctors work, a kind of sanctuary. Simon was here. Maria was preparing him. I'm still confused, but I know that a special healing was happening. It gave me hope.'

'Thank you.' Lydia's smile was relaxed, almost serene as though at least part of a burden had been lifted from her. 'I am so happy that you have let me be with you. When I saw you all at Kibera this afternoon, I prayed to God that somehow ... He has answered me and protected me.'

Rebecca was surprised. 'You were there?'

'I do not live there now but have many relatives. Memsahib Sonya was holding my sister's child in her arms. I was close to you all this afternoon. I saw many things. That is why I have come.'

She looked around the room and up into the shadowy beams of the ceiling as though something in these places would help her find the right words to go on.

'I love the scent of orange blossom.' She paused briefly, gathered herself and waded in.

'I know the Rubai family, too. Reuben could have been my first customer. I was a skinny, stupid one back then. He helped me such a lot. I was at the engagement party, Rebecca. I still do not know why he invited me. I remember your green dress. You were so beautiful but so unhappy.

'I did not realise at the time, but that was when the change began in my life. Reuben found out that I knew a lot of rich men. He was angry, even when I told him about the house on Ngong Road. My small brother, his chest, he needs a dry place. Thank God he never found out about my richest customer. He sent for me not long after that night.'

Rebecca's stunned expression told her that she had understood.

'A few weeks after the time at Muthaiga the big car stopped

outside the house for the first time. Mama was in the garden. She rushed in: "Lydia, come quickly! A man is asking for you. He is not a young man. He is wearing very shiny boots. He looks important".'

'It was a big black car.'

'You are right, Rebecca, but …'

'And he told you that a very important person wanted to speak to you.'

'He took me to a farmhouse outside the city, dropped me off and drove away. The door to the house was open. I had met him at the engagement party. He said about four words to me then. Now he was very talkative. "Surprised to see me? I watched you that night. You are the only good thing that I can remember about that bad time. Anyway, my dear Lydia, I thought we might have a chat about things".'

'I was really scared. He led me into a large room. There was a fire and that was the only light. When I saw him walking towards a bed in the far corner, I wanted to run away. He slipped off his dressing-gown. Underneath he was wearing a, a safari suit, green. He poured two drinks. "Bwana, I cannot drink alcohol. It makes me dizzy". I began to cry. He laughed and he patted the bed beside and pointed to a silk nightie. "Put it on, over there, in the darkness".'

'Why was he bothering? I supposed that he would want it off again pretty quickly. He watched me closely as I took off my clothes. I have learned to be shameless about these details. I make more money that way. It was a very expensive garment. And I did not take it off. We sat in the bed and talked. He talked mostly. One hour, two maybe. He said that I was a very patient young lady and that I was helping him to return to a kind of life. He liked my hair, he liked the smell of my skin. It was good to be alone with a young woman again. Not for a single moment did I feel relaxed. Suddenly he was on the phone and the car was waiting outside to take me home.'

'Not many days later, the car came again, after dark. This happened …'

'Rebecca, how could you know this? Yes, and there was another expensive nightdress that he gave me as a present, like always. There was always an envelope with many thousands of shillings. More and more the talk was about Julius. Often his eyes were full of anger. He could see that I was frightened. "Oh, no, my dear, you must not fear me, but there are others, but they will not be so lucky. When I am ready. When I am ready. The day of reckoning will come".'

'Oh, my God!' Rebecca covered her eyes. Instantly she was back in the depths of an old terror. In the sanctuary of her bedroom, she was struggling against the savage passion of the naked Julius Rubai. Inch by inch he was forcing her thighs apart. The sweet smell of his breath was with her again as vividly as ever, the wet slipperiness of the powerful body pressing down on her. Even now, in the cool safety of a place of healing, her instinct was to run to the arms of Tom. She forced herself to stay to hear Lydia out.

Lydia was fighting a mounting tension of her own. 'Three nights ago the car came to my house for the last time. This time the meeting was very different. He did not want to talk. He wanted me. There was no tenderness. He was like a crazy man. He kept calling out his wife's name, saying how sorry he was for his sins. For sure I thought I would not leave that room alive.

'In half an hour he lost his patience with me. He was deeply troubled and, how do you say, elated in the same moment. As we dressed, a kind of miracle happened. He became calm. He told me how much I had helped him. "I am my old self again. Yes, I am ready now".'

'He placed a large envelope in my hands. "Wait outside. The car will come soon".

'But the car did not come. I sat on a bench near the gate. I began to pick at the flap of the envelope. With my nail file I made a little opening. Notes. Cash money. I was shaking as I counted. I had never seen a ten thousand shilling note before and there were a hundred of them, a million shillings. I counted again and a third time and still the car did not come.

'I knew some bad thing was going to happen. It was a trap or some kind of trick. Perhaps he had made a mistake. Perhaps he was testing me. I must take it back. He was not in the big room, but through an open door I could hear him talking on the phone. He must be calling the driver. But he was not.

'I have taken a long time. I wanted you to hear the whole story. This is my only chance, perhaps. But …'

'Lydia …'

'Rebecca, I am saying only what I know I heard. Other things … "Good work. And where is the body now? Keep it there 'til after midnight. Then dump it. There are trees in front of the Wilson plantation. Yes, even the dozy Kericho cops won't miss it there. Oh, yes, the hands. Smash them. Use a hammer. Don't worry about the white bitch and the brood … Yes, later. And the black whore? Not yet. Patience, Ochome! That one is cooking in the pot. There will be big numbers. Big payout for you, too! They made a bad, bad mistake. I will see to it that they are paid in full".

'Oh, my God, why did I hear these things? What if he put the phone down? I must get out. I took off my shoes and crept to the door. Outside, no car. The lights of the city were far away, but I must start to walk towards them. Quiet like a mouse, so the guards don't hear. Are there guards? The road is through woodland. Jesus and Mary, where is my bag? Where is the envelope?'

Lydia gathered herself before going on. Sounds were coming to them through the windowless gaps high in the walls around them. Hundreds had come to the wake. Respects had been paid, but already for most of those decent people in that beautiful garden setting, the shock and horror of the senseless killing of a selfless man were fading. The buzz of animated conversations was a clear sign that, out there, normal life was being resumed.

'Rebecca, I am sorry to have brought you this trouble.'

'Lydia.' She could get no further. The threat from Rubai. She had never fooled herself into thinking that it had gone away. But to hear it spelt out so graphically was an unexpected shock. She needed time to be alone, to talk to Tom, to be on her way home to Naivasha to be with her family. How many of her loved ones would now be in mortal danger?

'This afternoon I saw him talk to you near to the clinic. Rebecca, I want someone to know these things. He will find a way of killing me.'

Lydia did not expect to survive the week. She had gone beyond terror and was ready to live out the rest of her life recklessly.

'I was watching from a safe place, waiting for my sister to come out. I went home with her. Our people had the chance to kill him. In such a crowd who could have been arrested? We were too afraid.

'I am a nobody. He will flick me off like some unpleasant insect that has dared to climb up his sleeve.'

'That is foolish talk, Lydia. You and I are like sisters in this danger. It is our only chance. We must begin to look at him in a new way. Our way, not his way.'

'But what difference will that make? We know that he is like this giant you spoke of. But he is no good giant. How do you stand against him?'

'You do not try, Lydia.'

Rebecca looked up at the apertures set high in the walls. The dark blue of the evening sky had changed to the violet of the night. There were stars. Inside her head the weight of heavy thoughts lifted enough to let a bright gleam shine like a thin strand of gold on the margin of her mind.

'Lydia, you are not going back to your house. We will get a message to your family that you are well and in a safe place. You have friends to protect you. More than you know.'

Chapter Twenty

A test of Rebecca's confidence came more quickly than she could have feared. They had taken no more than a dozen steps on the short walk between the surgery and the main house when they were confronted by the newly minted son and heir of the Rubai family. From his manner it might have been thought that Reuben had been on the path, waiting for them. Lydia had a momentary spasm of fear that he might have just got up from the bench close to the surgery door and had been listening in.

It was a Reuben she had never seen before. The immaculately cut white suit, the elegant leftwards lean of the head, the amused condescension in the arched eyebrows and the tone of familiarity made a convincing picture of the Rubai arrogance. For Rebecca it was as if she had come face to face with a younger, smaller version of Julius.

'Ladies, how fortunate to find you in this crowd so quickly. There must have been a guiding hand.' The smile was swiftly and theatrically changed to a look of sympathy. 'Such a sad occasion. I cannot tell you how shocked and upset I am by the terrible news. I come with a message for the widow from our family that if there is anything we can do to help in some way. Perhaps you could tell me where I could find the lady.'

He did not pause as he shifted his attention to Lydia. He

was revelling in his new role of the superior being passing down his gifts of consolation and concern. Papa's confidence in him was working better than Reuben could have hoped.

'Lydia, where have you been hiding yourself? I cannot count the number of times we have sent our people to your house to check on your welfare. Your mother says that you have not been home for days. Even my father is worried about what might have happened to you. He needs to speak to you about some small matter. But you probably know that.'

He bent to look closely into her face. 'My dear, those awful wounds. Our doctor could help. No need to go to that terrible place.'

Lydia had had enough of his false chatter, his empty concern. 'What is the matter, Reuben? Why do you talk like some idiot? Have you been drinking, taking a few puffs of bhang?'

Rebecca's reaction was a badly stifled laugh. This girl had the gift and her admiration for her deepened by the minute. She herself had seen through Reuben, but she would not have had the words to derail his effort to play the role of a mini Mister Big so easily.

'Lydia, you must want to go home. Your family is anxious. There is a car and a driver waiting for us outside.'

'When I am ready to go home, I will know how to find a matatu going my way. Remember the day when we met? Tom Mboya Street?'

'You asked me for a light.'

'And you could have been my first customer. I liked you better in those days. We took a matatu from the city.'

'So, the car is over there, just outside the gates. Matatus don't come around these parts. Let's be on our way.'

Rebecca was ready to join in the fun. 'Oh, that's all taken

care of, Mister Rubai. We were on our way to a meeting. Sonya, Doctor Mboya, the widow I think you called her, has this plan, a memorial to her husband. You said that your family wanted to help in some way. We must find her. I think that a donation …'

It was Lydia's turn to feel admiration for her companion. She was enjoying the growing agitation revealing itself in Reuben's expression.

'Donation? What is this?'

'She wants to open another clinic. Money, Reuben. Your papa has some of that stuff, doesn't he?'

'This is your last chance. This is a serious matter, Lydia.'

'Is it though, Reuben? Shall I tell you something that is really important? Rebecca and I have been talking. She thinks that I would make a good nurse.'

'Nurse?' Reuben was highly amused by the idea. 'Nurse? Make sure they don't put you on a men's ward. You'd be jumping into bed with the patients. Anyway what would a wash girl know about nursing? Oh, but I forgot. Mama told me you were there this afternoon when they took her in.'

He focused his attention on Rebecca. He talked as if they were alone.

'Rebecca, we keep on bumping into each other. Not his afternoon, though. I missed the funeral, but I got to come over to that place anyway. Mama's little accident. I was called in to rescue her and Papa, take her off to a proper hospital. They told me you were there, but perhaps you were busy, or hiding somewhere.'

'And why would I want to hide from you?'

'Of course. And I had driven fast hoping, but there you are. Mama told me later that you looked stunning in black. This death business. I hate it. Don't you? And, yes, how's the farmer boy? I think I noticed him as I came in. Seemed to be talking to three little kids.'

'Shall I take your questions in order?'

Without another word of his own, Reuben turned away and trudged towards the gate on his way back to the pink palace and an inteview with his father.

Chapter Twenty-one

Only an hour before he had left the sitting room where his mama was stretched out on a sofa, still in shock. The fleshy part of her upper arm where the bullet had struck was swathed in a thick dressing. She was too upset to take in the final instructions of her husband to their son who was eager to set out for the Daniels' house, very confident that he would please his father for the second time.

'My spies tell me that she was hanging around with Mboya's lot this afternoon. There hasn't been a sniff of her at the shack on Ngong Road. She owes me a few, Papa.'

'Tell her that we need to clear up a misunderstanding. Tell her that I have something that she left behind at the farm a couple of nights ago.'

Sally was beginning to lock in to what was being said. She wanted to know more. After Reuben left the room, she sat up and asked casually, 'Anyone I know?'

Abel realised that he had made a miscalculation. He was surprised to notice how alert Sally had become. Had she been doing some faking of her own? He tried the vague, reassuring bluster that Sally was usually happy with.

'Of course, Sally. One of Reuben's friends. Poor family. One of the kids is sick and they are trying to pay for a house near the hospital. We thought we could help but … well, we think she is more likely to accept a gift from you. But after the accident and all that ...'

* * *

'So, where is she?' In the hour Reuben had been away, his father had moved to a back veranda where he was on to his third Tusker. He was looking out over the lawn towards the tall fence separating the house from a patch of unspoilt bush. One of the askaris had spotted a family of leopard out there a few nights before.

It relaxed him to sit in luxurious safety and remember the days of his youth, walking back to the shamba after a night out with his friends. Every sense was alert. One time he had been scared to hear coming to him across the fields the screams and shrieks of someone in big danger. Abel, the would-be bush boy, gave up his game of careful glances to left and right and with silent, padded steps ran for home. Just after midnight news had come that Gabe Ndoto, a good friend from Kakamega High, had been taken by a lion.

That had been a memorable night for Abel, too. His father, Nathaniel, had not allowed him to go to bed until they had visited the Ndoto home and his boy had viewed for himself the mangled remains of his friend.

They were still within hearing of the wailing and the keening of women gathered to mourn the hideous death, when his father explained: 'Did you see that, boy? Did you take notice? Gabe was a fine, fine boy and now he's just bits of flesh. No future for him. Abel, try to keep risks out of your life. Be in control. Control, do you understand me, son?'

Abel had made the dutiful, expected reply to his father's

brief advice but, as the years passed, he came to see the truth of it more and more. It pained him to acknowledge that he had failed to impress his oldest boys with this same truth.

'You tell me that you know this girl well, that she owes you something, but you cannot persuade her to travel a couple of hundred metres to speak to me. Julius was right. He said that you were weaker than mouse piss.'

This time Abel had made sure that Sally would hear nothing of the exchanges with their second son.

Reuben bit hard on his lip but held his ground. 'Papa, give me another chance.'

'So?'

'I will take a car and wait outside the house until she goes home …'

'You think she is going home? And I have boys over there watching all the ways out, just in case I'm wrong.'

'So, I will not be standing in the election.'

Mister Big frightened his son with a long burst of uninhibited laughter. The noise attracted the attention of Mama who came rushing out onto the veranda on her well- upholstered, electric wheelchair.

'Abel, Abel, what is happening? I thought there was a break-in.'

Abel's laughter shrank to a chuckle. 'Sally, calm down. You must still be in shock. Either that or this household is heading for the loony bin. I laugh and my wife thinks that the robbers have arrived. I tell our son and heir that he is about as useful as a cockroach in a plate of rice and he thinks I'm going to pull him from the election.'

'But, Papa, if you think that I am stupid …'

'What's that got to do with it?'

'But to be a good member …'

'Son, have I ever told the most important word in a successful man's vocabulary?'

'Many a time, Papa. Control. Mzee Nathaniel told you.'

'But like your big brother you never understood it. Listen. Me and your mama here have a heap of money. Control. I have two hundred men working for me. Control. If one of them makes a foolish move, he knows what will happen. You are going to win the seat of Nakuru South. Being a winner, that's my business.'

'So, you are going to be controlling me?'

Sally could hold her tongue no longer. 'Abel, can't you see that you are scaring the boy out of his wits? Reuben, you will be the MP. The people will love you and Papa will be around to help you to learn the business. Mind, you will have to ask him exactly what this business stuff is.'

'Plenty of work down there. You will have a house, perhaps a woman. When we take over our first flower farm …'

'Abel, please, no farms for a while. Look what happened last time we went hunting for a farm on the side of the lake.'

'Unfinished business, my dear. Oh, things are going to be mighty different and sooner than you think. And, by the way, that girl. Has she come to her senses yet? That's the trouble with some poor people. They want the money but don't know how to behave when you try to give it to them.'

'Mama?'

'It's all right, boy. There's been a lot of excitement around this place today. Let's all go inside. Time for some of that new season's coffee from the farm. Samson brought it back this afternoon. And when I checked earlier there was half that chocolate cake left, enough for four big slices.'

Sally was ready to turn her chair around and escape from the chill air of early night. On her way back to the warmth of the south sitting room an uncomfortable thought was nagging at her. Was he trying to hide something from her? This girl, did he owe her something? Had Reuben got her into some trouble? She could have coped with this, but why was Abel making a fuss over something that he wanted her to believe was a nothing?

Chapter Twenty-two

'This is our hospital. Doctor Simon created a miracle for our people here. You people are like angels to us. Doctor David says John is well, so he is well. He is hungry, too. We must feed him. Afterwards, he will sleep. We have the dawa from the doctor.'

Rebecca had tears in her eyes as she watched the group of a dozen women and children make their way slowly past the line of dukas and disappear 'round a corner into the beginnings of the huge warren of crisscrossing alleys and tracks and lanes that were the homes of thousands and thousands of Nairobi's poorest of the poor.

There were more tears now when she recalled the moment. This time she was sitting on a sofa in the main house of Cartref, so close to Tom that she could feel the warmth of his body. Sixteen people were scattered around that comfortable room sharing a time of memory and meditation. It was an hour and more since the last of the guests and visitors had driven through the main gates and set off into the night carrying their private memories of a long day.

Sonya was squashed with her three boys into the armchair where Simon loved to sit when he visited the house. She had asked her family and friends to recall a moment they had shared with Simon. Rebecca had been first to speak.

'I never met Simon, but I always read the articles he used to write in *The Nation*. Those stories about his days in the bush clinics were so funny and serious at the same time. One time he said he had a dream for a good hospital in every town and an even better clinic in every village.

'Thomas knows that in my heart I have longing to help the people of our town to enjoy the blessing of a new hospital. At present, it is little more than a longing, a dream. I will never forget his simple, beautiful words. If the dream comes true, that young mother will be there at the opening. Her words will be carved by a Naivasha craftsman in a cut of the finest wood we can find and the work placed where all can read them. I hope that John will still be a very small boy when he comes. "This is our hospital".'

Tom added with a smile: 'Friends, I have to tell you that, before our old Land Cruiser leaves Nairobi for home tomorrow, it will have a slab of dark wood tied securely on its roof. Yes, and I think she has marked out the best woodcarver in the town for this special work. We'll look after it till the time comes.'

Lydia was in awe of the company. 'Some of you know what I am. I am hiding in this house tonight "Grace, an undeserved gift." The Sisters of Charity were kind to our family when we lived in Kibera. They cared for us and they taught us. This word has always stayed with me and now it is helping to keep me safe.

'I was at the clinic this afternoon. John is my sister's child, but I could not watch them as they set off for home. I knew I was in danger if I showed myself. The Rubai family was there. It was their car that hurt John. It was a bullet from their people that hurt Mama Sally's arm. I watched the big man. At first, he was frightened. His boys were not close by. Perhaps these Kibera men would take this chance. Soon the danger was finished. Reuben and some policemen had come. My memory is of the words from his mouth.

'"Sally, do not worry. I am taking you to a proper hospital at once!" I hope they had angels there, too.' She paused. 'When I saw them, John and his mother, I understood how foolish I have been. Unlucky, too. One small moment and my life changed. I was playing the smart lady at the matatu stop, on Tom Mboya Street, so I took out a cigarette. I had never tried this before. Reuben snatched it away from my mouth, and now I am bringing this trouble to all of you. There will be death. I only hope that it will be mine. Doctor Simon gives me hope.'

It was to be a long time before a third person in that room was ready to share a memory. Someone coming through the front door of Cartref just then and listening for sounds of life might have thought that he was in an empty house. But if that someone had been blessed with a sensitivity to feel the tingle of fine vibrations, he might have been drawn to the room where movements in the deep silence were creating thoughts and a rising wave of hope and triumph with a purity and exactness beyond the range of normal human utterance. Try to capture these essences in words and they would crumble to dust.

One person there had the knowledge and experience to help her companions understand what new things were happening in and around them.

Maria began her song, more of a chant than a song, with words that had not been used in common speech for centuries. As she whispered her sacred lyric, her eyes searched the upper parts of the room, slowly, carefully. As each one became aware of what she was doing they let their eyes drift where she led them. It was Noah, Simon's oldest son, who saw it first. He sat upright in his mother's lap and pointed to place above the French doors that led out onto a veranda. Her reaction, when she saw the brightness, too, was to let out a sound that was part scream and part cry of wonder.

'Simon!'

The brightness had quickly formed itself into a shape, hovered for no more than a few seconds and then faded. Maria, no longer singing her ancient song, acted quickly to calm any possible upsurge of bewilderment or fear especially in the hearts and minds of the three boys.

'It was his last opportunity to be with us. It is a very rare happening.'

Dorothy Daniels held the arms of her chair tightly. She had caught the last of the brightness. The sight catapulted her back to childhood and the morning of her third birthday when she found her Nana Williams dead on the floor of her kitchen. The little girl that she was immediately lost her powers of speech. The family brought in the local minister, but the Reverend Glyn Jones made the child's situation worse with his talk of ghosts and the Holy Spirit.

'Maria, was it a ghost? You see, when I was a child …'

'Yes, Dorothy, I know.' Though her words were spoken with the utmost tenderness, they only succeeded in raising the level of panic. She was afraid that she might break down in front of the boys. Maria continued. 'No ghost, my darling. For a few moments we had a glimpse into the other side. Yes it was Simon. He has been purified and become part of the essence of love. And he came with a purpose and he left words for us. He has chosen his messenger.'

Noah slid from his mother's side and went to stand in front of the empty fireplace. His head was bowed. There was nothing solemn in his tone when he spoke. Everyone accepted that in some incomprehensible way this nine year old child was speaking beyond his conscious knowledge.

'Everything is as it was meant to be. I am well. Rise up and ride the dream. Be careful but not afraid.'

David Daniels looked on in bewildered amazement as the composed nine year old returned to his mother's side. How did these words come into this child's mind? And what was this Maria? First there was the miraculous transformation of the wounds on Simon's body and now this calm control in the face of the most momentous event he had ever witnessed. Was she some kind of modern witch? No, no, he had dismissed that idea the day before as he watched her work in the family surgery.

From where he sat, he was able to look at her front on. He narrowed his gaze. For a few moments, she became the only person in the room for him. Very unscientific ideas began to form in his mind. Could she be some reincarnated ancient priestess? Perhaps she was one of the brilliant and wise medieval mystics whose life was continuing far beyond a normal span? Focusing on her closely like this made him realise how beautiful she was in body and, more so in – he hesitated to let himself contemplate the word – soul.

She shifted her glance quickly and caught him staring at her. She smiled at him radiantly. He turned away in embarrassment.

The minor shock of being caught out in a failure of good manners brought him back into more normal, more rational considerations. 'Come on, Dai! Think it out.' That was her husband, Hosea Kabari, sitting next to her. They had three daughters back up in Kericho. She was lifting a cup to her lips. It probably contained coffee that had gone cold. This was no creature left over from the distant past.

This train of thought was interrupted. A third person ready to speak about memories of the day was an unexpected one, even to the speaker himself. Bertie Briggs moved from his chair next to his best friend and neighbour, Alex McCall. Thinking that Bertie was on his way to the bathroom, Alex stood and was ready to join him. But Bertie was picking his way across the room to the spot where Noah had been standing minutes before.

Tall and slim, he might have been taken for an officer in the brigade of guards. As usual, he was immaculately turned out, from his well-polished black shoes to the trimmed, swept-back dark hair.

So he stood in front of mainly friends, uncomfortable and struggling to compose himself for the ordeal he had willingly brought on himself. He began with a nervous laugh and a nod in the direction of his friend.

'Can't believe your eyes, can you, Alex? And, no, I have not been at the whisky.' He took a deep breath and plunged in.

'Something strange happened to me out there today. I'll try to explain. Remember three weeks ago, the accident with the runaway truck on the downside of the Escarpment road near Naivasha? I was on the road that day, just behind him and getting ready to pass. It was a long one and I would have to be quick. I found out later that the truck's brakes had failed. I realised that he was going away from me. I expected him to run off onto the verge and take his chances in the bush. You know the rest. He tried to keep a straight line and slewed into the up lane. They still don't know for sure if it was three or four matatus that he hit.

'There was a sound of metal scraping, like a giant screaming. He was sliding sideways and right across the road like a bulldozer sweeping away everything in its path. Then came the thuds, numb and deadly, as I soon found out. The screaming, the yelling and the shouting, it was like a pile of nightmares all crashing together.

'And the sight was ten times worse than the sound, so many broken bodies, pieces of flesh, red and raw scattered all over the road. And all they had to help them was blokes like me until those wonderful women and girls moved in.

'Carnage, that's the only word, a war zone, without stretcher-bearers. Soon there was as much blood on us, drying up so quickly.

'I did not see a single ambulance. The transport was anyone with a vehicle who was willing to give it a go. I carried away a family of four, mother, father, a boy holding his dead sister like she was a broken doll. I had never been in Naivasha Hospital until that afternoon. What a hellhole for sick people. Our people. Ours, mine. I dropped them off, went outside and vomited.

'I went home, cleaned up and walked my Ewan over to Sanctuary Farm. We sat under a flat-top and watched the giraffes until the sun went down.

'Anger, there was such deep anger in me. Worse was the sickening shame. My shame. Our people, my people, what a hypocrite! I had been playing games with life for too long.

'Then today. Sonya, seeing you and looking 'round and being with more of 'my' people, conscious of that shame more intensely than ever. I've been a good employer, looked after my people, but there's always been the unseen barrier. Bwana knows best. Such a mess of feelings. It would have been a good moment to die. God, the pain was unbearable.'

There was a long pause. Bertie struggled to begin again.

'A girl, perhaps twelve or thirteen who was carrying a large bunch of red roses was walking past us as part of a procession.

She turned and she smiled at me. Was it me? I'll never know for sure. Then it happened.

'A rush of warmth swept through me, from head to toe. A roaring noise in my brain shut out every other sound. My God, I'm having a stroke. I thought of those poor souls at the bottom of the Escarpment. Now it was going to be my turn. The noise became less intense, like when you turn down a blaring radio. The thunder became a single note, a blend of voices that held me with its sweetness. Gradually, even this sound faded into silence. I was back. Rebecca and Maria were singing close by. I was exhausted and at the same time light-headed. No, Alex, still not the whisky.

'That's my memory. May seem mixed up to you. I think it may have just changed my life. Who can tell? You've all been very patient.'

A round of applause and a hug from a smiling Sonya revived his embarrassment and he could not return to his seat quickly enough. He knew that, in future, he would not find it easy to hide out in little corners of anonymity when big issues came up.

No one left the room until several hours passed by. For a time quiet meditation lowered the emotional tone. Then gradually, like a large wheel gathering momentum, a single topic began to rouse, excite and unify the group. A remark from Hosea Kabari set the engine in motion.

'With your permission, this simple-minded police sergeant would like to ask a question. Why do we Kenyans allow so many of our people to die without caring enough?'

There was no shortage of answers. Corruption, graft, apathy, each of the old traditional theories that were trotted out regularly in the bars and clubs were the first to surface with the anecdotes to back them up.

'Hosea, basically we don't give a damn. And when we are blessed with someone who comes along to challenge the "system", whatever that is, wants to throttle the old ways, what do we do?' David opened his palms in a gesture of failure. 'And people like me get on with the job that's right in front of our noses and ignore the stench of the pile of manure rising up all 'round us.'

'Perhaps it's an African thing.'

'Thomas!'

"Becca, that's why you want that hospital back home. Change one little corner of Africa and the miracle will begin.'

'Money. What does Paul call it? The bottom line. This time I think my lawyer brother is right. Yesterday Abel Rubai needed help for his wife. For a moment there he was scared. For a moment he had a chance to see what the people needed. If only he remembered his days in his village.'

Maria Kabari spoke quietly, without drama.

'We get used to things. Take a walk in the city and look carefully at the people you see. Do you see the slim, handsome young men, the pretty girls with the smart shoes, the dark grey business suits? Or do you see the street kids, the barefooted women, old before their time?'

'Maria, when I saw that terrible accident up on the Escarpment … Look I don't want to go back to "getting used to things". Maybe we need to change the big men's ways. For now, I just want to change mine.'

Tom thought that it was time to spell out something.

'The dream is already more than just that. If you didn't know, we have the land. Dad, it's your turn.'

'Yeah, a piece of land on the edge of town close to where the road joins the A104. I bought it about ten years ago, the week after you began your first term in Oundle, Tom. I had this idea of growing macadamia nuts.'

'Bwana!'

'I've gone off that word, as you know, Rebecca. I've gone off macadamias, too! Must have been waiting for something better to come along.'

'Too late now, anyway, Dad. Peter's flattened the site.'

Bertie wanted to move the dream further into reality.

'You know that Rusinga is named after the island where Tom Mboya was buried. Sonya, this is ridiculous. I can hardly keep the tears back. Anna got me to build a guest cottage. We never used it. Couldn't we use it as a base, office, meeting place? Bound to be a lot of business.'

'One more thing and I'll shut up. Dorothy, what did you just whisper to me?'

'You mean I'd love to help if I had some talent.'

'Strange you should say that, Dorothy. Someone needs to keep a track on new ideas, and information that comes in. You're the smartest person I know on a laptop, you have beautiful handwriting and you hate waste.'

'And that's an offer I can't refuse?'

Chapter Twenty-three

Excitement was bubbling at the next meeting of the Big Twelve at the Pink Palace. The mood at these gatherings was always dictated by the state of mind of Mister Abel Rubai, the man from the Kenya Hills. His colleagues were not usually aware of the true reason for his bonhomie, but they were happy enough to see the smiling face and glad they would be able to voice opinions without the risk of having to endure a withering put-down if they unwittingly gave offence to their esteemed leader.

'Gentlemen, it was interesting to see so many of you at the recent funeral of the good Doctor Mboya. Unfortunately urgent state business prevented me from being there for the ceremony. As you know, an attempt was made on my life as I was arriving. The thug, an activist from an anti-government group that hides out in that vast sewer of humanity wounded my good lady.'

'I hear that CID have a number of promising leads.'

'True, Alfred, but we have to thank God that she is back on top form.'

In a brief pause, he shut down his concerned husband mode and took up his patriotic statesman role.

'I have news, but first let me confess that Mboya's passing was not a complete surprise to me. He was warned that setting up a clinic like that was going to lead to trouble. The whole operation was small scale. You help a few and you upset many more by creating resentment. "Why them and not us?" Health, education, law and order etcetera can only be handled on a big scale by governments and their agents. Too many busy-body do-gooders and in no time the position of the state is undermined.

'I have been informed by reliable sources that another anti-state, shall we say, plot, is beginning to take shape. I won't go into detail now other than to say that any danger to state is likely to show itself in the constituency of Nakuru South.

'I need your help here. After the retirement of Simon Nyache, there will, of course, be a new member up in that area of the Rift Valley. I want your approval that our candidate will be my son Reuben. He is young, vigorous, well-connected.'

The business of approval took less than a minute, another proof for Abel of how swiftly democracy can move in Africa when the need arises. Papers were duly signed. A final proposition was soon on record. Reuben Rubai was to make his first visit to the Naivasha area as prospective MP.

When the meeting had finished, Abel sat on alone at the empty table. His mood was sombre. He was tired. Perhaps he should take Sally on a holiday, make it up to her, even if he dared not tell her what he was making up for. In Paris she could go wild in the shops, only Sally never went wild about anything. She had said more than once that she would like to visit the churches of Rome, but he knew for a fact that there would be lots of steps, so perhaps not a good idea to go when she was carrying the boy in her belly.

He had slept with another woman, been unfaithful to Sally. For most of the men that had just left the room this would not have been a problem. Far from it. He would have admitted that he had enjoyed the experience. But there was this obsession about keeping control at all times. The pretty little friend of Reuben had drawn him into a mess of careless behaviour. Why had he given her that heap of money?

She had come back into the farmhouse. How much had she heard? How much? No control again. She would never have dared to speak about what she had heard. But, on balance, best to take no chances. Uchome would see to it all.

But, but, but she had chosen to hide away. It did not take him long to work out a chain of danger. McCall, the election, Serena and, at the end, Miller and Komar. Even if they did get wind of his conversation, hakuna matata. No one would believe her. Hearsay, his word against hers. But all this would be so … inconvenient. Two lawyers would smack their chops to have even this tiny morsel to chew over. No doubt there would be lies printed up in *The Nation* and *The Standard*. She must go and soon.

On that same afternoon as that meeting, Rebecca Kamau and Maria Kabari were together in Bertie Briggs' guesthouse, not far from the edge of the lake. Heavy rain was creating what Rebecca called 'the beautiful African noise' on the mbati roof, so the two women carried on with their jobs without trying to speak to each other. The unused cottage had been finished with good quality materials and ready for use as an office, headquarters.

The heavy shower stopped just as Maria was boiling a kettle for a mug of milky chai. They took their drinks and sat on the wicker chairs out on the small veranda. The air was fresh and the damp plain leading down to the lake was lush with thick, rich grass. At first, the far shore was out of sight as the grey curtain of rain moved steadily across the lake towards the heights of Eburu and beyond.

'Hosea has put in his papers for a transfer to a station

somewhere in the Rift. There are vacancies for sergeants in Gilgil and Navaisha.'

'What do the girls think about that?'

'For them, closer to Nairobi means closer to paradise. Also, if it comes quickly, it will be two more votes in the election for Thomas.'

'He will need every vote he can get.' Rebecca's tone was subdued. 'He believes he cannot win. Rubai money and favours will count for a lot. Papa thinks so, too.'

'I think Thomas is right.'

'But you will still vote for him.'

'Of course. Serena gives us hope for the future. Paul will make a good president. And you would make a good candidate for Nakuru South. You would win.'

'Win?'

'Rebecca, you are a beautiful, talented woman. Most of the red-blooded men in the country are half in love with you. The women love you even more.'

'Maria, why do you say these crazy things?'

'No, not so crazy! Let me explain. Thomas is going to be in the election, whenever Mr Big decides that there will be an election. Am I right?'

'Yes.'

'Now, maybe Thomas will win and become the Serena man for Nakuru South. Maybe he will not win. But if Rebecca McCall was the candidate, then, for sure …'

The two friends were in a state of high animation. Maria was pumped up by the logic of her argument, Rebecca by its absurdity. Maria had not yet reached the end of her reasoning.

'Darling, give me a minute and then decide if I am crazy. Mama Ngina, they name streets after her in every big town in this country. Why do the people do this? Because they love her. Mostly they love her because she was the president's wife. What was her great talent? Being herself, a big, lovely lady with a huge heart. There has never been another woman like her. Until now. Until Rebecca Kamau. You are beautiful. Everyone in this country knows your story. They could make a film about it. Even the Yankees know you are something special. You are a woman and you have topped all the men in this country. And here is the big point. You give our women ... hope. Hope.'

Rebecca looked away in the direction of her faithful friend, Old Longonot. She was embarrassed, outwardly by the praise from a woman who was the wisest woman she knew and inwardly for a sense of disloyalty towards Thomas himself. Once or twice thoughts had forced themselves into her head against her will. A woman MP for Nakuru South, highly unlikely. A young white bwana, impossible in these times.

But Maria was not finished with her words of persuasion.

'The hospital, Rebecca.'

'Maria?'

'Think about it. Mister Big and his boys give out lots of money and make promises that they never keep. Serena can show the people the field where the hospital will stand.'

'That would help Thomas also.'

'Yes, but would it be enough?'

'Perhaps not, but that is the road we must take.'

Chapter Twenty-four

Reuben Rubai was excited. He was riding in the back of one of his father's Mercedes. There was a chauffeur and a single bodyguard in front and, by his side, Frank Kisaro, the best Mister Fixit in the party. Kisaro had been given his orders. He must guide and coach the next MP for Nakuru South through the day. 'He's very green, Frank. Light touch, light touch. Got me?'

Reuben read the situation differently. At last his father had learned to trust him enough to send him out on a big job on his own. Papa wanted him to take along some office boy just in case he needed advice on 'protocol and procedure'. Reuben had picked up the expression from an article in *The Nation* and he was determined to work it into a conversation sometime soon.

The one formal meeting that had been arranged was with the town mayor and the council. That done, Papa had advised him to wander around, 'meet people, make contacts and ask questions.'

The crucial piece of information that he had been given by one of the Rubai spies in the workforce at Londiani was that the young screwball boss and his soft-headed father had flown up to the farms up in the foothills of the Big Mountain and would be out of the way until evening.

It was still midmorning, but Reuben was bored with the

business of shaking hands with strangers. He never once asked someone to vote for him when election time came 'round. That would have been too much like begging for favours. The social conscience of his youth, his desire to help 'losers', as he now described them, had given way to the Rubai trait of helping himself first and then, if there was a little something left over, well perhaps he might find a use for that later.

'Take a right here. See that sign, "Londiani Farm". We'll take the road the trucks use. That way we won't get the car covered with dust. Frank, I want to have a word with some of my voters. Smart idea, huh?'

Frank replied with a bland smile. He had known from the start that he was not going to enjoy the job of escorting this spoilt moron for the day. This one was just as bad as the boss's dead kid. But he had worked out a strategy for number one son that would work just as well with this know-all. Say little, smile a lot, keep agreeing with all the big ideas. Above all make lots of mental notes and write a few handy quotes in his little fat book. The boss would be expecting a report.

Reuben was more impressed than he would have admitted when he stepped out onto the huge concrete apron where three large Londiani trucks were parked. Three of the eight-wheelers were being washed down and everywhere he looked, he saw signs of neat practices and efficient work. He sent the bodyguard to find the manager, the boss mechanic or whatever they called the bwana in that part of the farm. Farm? Factory more like!

A small young man in blue overalls turned up and introduced himself.

'My name is Donald. I'm the junior foreman in the motor pool. How can I help you, sir?'

'Well, Mister Duck, I will soon be the MP for the district. I want to speak to the flower people.'

'You mean the field workers. If you would —'

'Don't try to be smart with me, Mister Duck, or you could soon be promoted to ex-junior foreman!'

It was curious how, after he had been accepted by Papa as son and heir, and successor to the beloved Julius, Reuben seemed to have also inherited the cool dude way of speaking of his elder brother. It made him feel impressive. South Bronx or Brooklyn, he would not have recognised either, but he had seen the films and that was good enough for him.

Eventually, he found himself with his mentor, Frank, standing outside the office of the head foreman.

'Looks like a nice chair in there. I think I'll just ...'

'No, Bwana, there are important papers in this office. The boss would not like it.'

'Oh, too bad. But if you'll just move over.'

'No, Bwana! Do not make me use the violence.'

Reuben was deeply insulted at such a threat. He thought of putting his bodyguard on the job, but the big, barefoot man in shabby clothes barring his way had a wild look about him. The half smile on his face suggested that he would relish a challenge. Frank Kisaro would have advised caution but said nothing. This kid would have reported such advice and made it sound like weakness, and weakness did not appear on the Rubai register of good behaviour.

* * *

'You don't recognise me, do you, preacher man? '

'I'm sorry, sir?

'You said the words at the party at Muthaiga. We didn't

meet. I'm the next brother down, soon to be known as Reuben Rubai, MP for this whole place.'

Stephen Kamau put his mind on red alert. He had been rushing with some late orders when the call came to return to the office. For the moment, he must shut out business worries and focus totally on this young man and whatever problem he was about to present.

'Get your people together. Some place where I can … talk to them, make a speech, yeah, make a speech.'

'But Bwana Alex and Bwana Tom are away on business.'

'What's that got to do with it?'

'I don't have the authority.'

'No problem. I can give you the authority. Right now.'

'Sir, if we stop the workers now, we will lose tonight's consignments. It will cost many thousands of shillings.'

Frank saw danger here. This big flower man was having difficulty in holding in check an anger that Reuben had not noticed. He drew his arrogant pupil to one side.

'Go through with this and you'll be answering to the boss when we get back. It won't be me that will giving your father the news.'

Self-centred Reuben was quick to assess situations in terms of profit and loss. On Frank's advice, he saw that he was not going to win this contest. But there was the matter of losing face. With great speed he switched tacks and, in the process, caught the senior foreman of Londiani off guard.

'Do you have a new woman working here, by the name of Lydia?'

'We are taking on new people all the time.'

'You'd remember this one. City girl, a cutie, not one of your local heavies.'

'I'll have somebody check it out.'

'Forget it. No good upsetting the works. Maybe, one day, I'll have one of these money making places myself. I've got other business to deal with today. Kwaheri, Mister Flower Man.'

So it was back down the driveway to South Lake Road and a left turn towards town. They had gone only a hundred metres when Reuben had new orders for his support men.

'Stop! I'm getting out. I need some air. I know this area. Charlie, I won't be needing protection. You three go back into town. Get yourselves some lunch and be back here by two. If I'm late …' He smiled imperiously, ' just wait!'

The Mercedes sped off with its three occupants relieved to have been given a freedom break. As they moved away, Frank noticed another sign for Londiani, this time pointing down a murram track. Reuben had taken the turn and as he strode along, he kept glancing to his right, through the gaps in the hedge. This was no casual stroll of a city boy seeking fresh country air. His target was specific and close at hand.

The newly built house was set on a low rise with views in all directions, across the plains to the distant hills and, much closer, to the lake where he could see the grey-blue waters riffled into tiny waves by the breeze of the late morning.

If his information was correct, she would be somewhere inside checking on the wooden floors that had been laid the day before. He pushed open the heavy oak door and stepped inside. He tried to pay no attention to the tingling sensation in his scalp and his laboured breathing. This would be the first time he had been alone with her.

'Oh, my God!' The involuntary cry was quickly followed by Rebecca clasping her hands to her face. The recall was instant and all but brought her tears. It was less than a year ago that Julius Rubai had been an unexpected and unwelcome visitor to her bedroom in the rondavel in Londiani village. She had survived his savage attack but at a great cost to her mental and spiritual wellbeing. The scars would never fade completely.

'I'm so sorry. Have I come at a bad time?' Reuben made no effort to hide his sarcasm.

'How did you know about this place?' The venom in her voice was unmistakable.

'An old friend. I just happened to be in the area. Social call. Well, that's only partly true. You see, I'm in the market for a house around and about. When I'm elected, I'll need a place for overnight stops. Pied à terre. With your education, you must know the expression. Do you know the owners? I'd like to make an offer.'

'Shut up and go away.'

He was surprised by her aggression but pleased, too. 'Oh, I do like the fire in those beautiful eyes. Anyway, do you have their number?'

'Whose number?' She spat the words impatiently. She was angry with herself that she did not have the forcefulness that would send him on his way. She tried again. 'This house belongs to Thomas McCall and myself and when we are married, we will …'

'Do you think that would be a wise thing to do? It's only months ago that your beloved Julius was snatched away from you. You and I were practically brother and sister.'

'Have you been drinking or are you just plain crazy?'

'Now that was uncalled for.'

On the surface he was toying with her, but beneath a thin veneer of calm, he was throbbing with a mixture of emotions. One of these was anger, but it was not the strongest. 'Crazy'. She had found the right word. He wanted to take her there and then. Julius had failed but only because her maniac giant of a father had been around to prevent him. He had heard the full story, eventually. Now Papa was a long way off, counting his roses and carnations. Here, far away from any possible interruption, the sweet sensation in his loins was pushing him towards the edge.

'Maria, is that you?' Rebecca was desperate to try anything, just to gain a little time, and for a few seconds she succeeded. No answering call came, but her ploy had been enough to knock Reuben off balance. A pang of doubt sparked hesitation and he saw that the moment had passed. The resultant cold fury pushed him to be more daring while struggling to present a composed front.

'I'm disappointed. It's lunchtime and you haven't offered me so much as a cup of coffee.'

'No coffee, sorry.'

'But you're not, are you, sorry I mean. Why do you hate our family like this?'

'There is no hate. I just do not want you in my life.'

'Okay, my turn to be open. Rubai, that's a big name in this country. A person should think carefully before causing problems for us. You won't sell me this house?'

Rebecca smiled. 'Never. It is to be our home.'

'McCall.' He sighed wearily. 'You still want to go through with it. Don't answer! But I want to remind you that this is not a lucky family. And Bwana Thomas has already used up any luck he ever had. You know what I'm talking about?'

'Are you threatening us?'

'Of course not.' His offended manner was not convincing.

'Good. Now I want you to leave. If you hurry they will still be serving lunch in La Belle Inn.'

Reuben was astonished. What had happened to the gentle, respectful young woman, the polite churchgoing lady, the product of the best girls' school in the country? This was the second time she had gone for him. She was beginning to remind him of some Nairobi street bitch. Perhaps she had been learning from Lydia. But this time there was no back-up and he wanted her more than ever.

Minutes before he had been ready to make a grab for her body. Now he wanted her for a wife. He stared blankly down at the polished floor. He was discovering his true feelings for the first time, sure that, at last, he had something real and wholesome to offer her. This was where Julius had made his mistake. He was just as sure that it would be difficult, if not impossible, to win her over. But it had been ingrained into the Rubais to expect to get what they had set their minds on.

It was Rebecca's turn to feel astonishment. As if by magic Reuben's cynical manner, his threatening innuendos were replaced by a humble, pleading tone of voice.

'Um, look, I know what I must have sounded like just now. Making unreasonable demands, expecting things to go our way. Things come too easily to us. But give me a minute. This is the real me. I'll lay it on the line. I think we could make it …'

Her look of bewildered revulsion did not put him off.

'Yes, I understand. But think it through. We have a lot in common.'

'You mean we're both black.'

'Yes, but …'

That was enough. His brother had been scary. Was this one simply crazy? The volatile temperament on show in front of her unbalanced her equilibrium. His eyes, the gestures with his hands, suggested a sincerity she had not seen in either of the Rubai brothers. But was she simply witnessing a display of the skills of Reuben, the actor?

The long silence between them caused no embarrassment. Both sides had retreated to consider their position. Rebecca was first to arrive at a firm conclusion. She tried hard to put on a show of pleasantness.

'I'm sure ...'

'You want a hospital? I'm your man.'

She narrowed her gaze. How in the world? And what else did he know about what she had believed was a secret shared by a very few, trusted friends?

'I must go. I have a meeting in ten minutes. Please, I must lock up.'

Reuben's attempt at complete sincerity had refined his sensitivity to a point where he did not need her words to show him her truest, deepest feelings. He understood. He had failed in his desperate bid. He wanted to scream out. This calm, stupid woman was rejecting him for the porky faced, arrogant nobody. Well, he would warn her for the last time. With an immense effort, he managed to deliver his words with the easy charm of one who was turning down the offer of a third cup of coffee.

'Well, that's my best offer. It's your choice in the end, of course. It's such a shame. Decisions have consequences, but a clever girl like you would know that. Yeah, I've got a meeting, too. Oh, yes, I almost forgot. Have you seen Lydia lately?'

She shook her head with slow deliberation. He enjoyed the solemn expression. It told him that this was a worried young woman.

'Mmn, pity. Papa wants to see her. He owes her something.'

His footsteps across the oak floorboards were unhurried. He hesitated at the threshold as if about to turn to say a final word. In a second he was out of sight and into the warm afternoon sunlight. The tension which gripped his whole body caused him to tremble. He thought it might be good to vomit, but the nausea in the pit of his stomach was dry and uncomfortable.

When he reached South Lake Road, there was no car waiting. He was too early. As he began the long walk towards Naivasha town, he looked up at the distant hills. Inexplicably, he recalled words of his mother. She had read them often to him and Julius as she settled them down for the night. There was something about getting new strength out of staring up at hillsides. As he strode along, the sense of failure, even the anger, fell away from him like an old, dead skin. The unpleasantness of the last hour and more was transformed into a new certainty, a fresh confidence. It had been a necessary rite of passage. Papa's advice was proving to be right again. 'First find out for sure what you really want. That's the hard part. Then, go and get it, whatever it costs!'

Boy, oh boy, did he feel good. And free!

* * *

As the rich, young heir of Mister Abel Rubai pondered hopefully on the future, Rebecca Kamau sat on the bench outside her future home. She let her fingers play aimlessly with her bunch of keys. Maria, Sonya and Lydia would be waiting for her in the new office room at Rusinga Farm. When she looked to her right, she could see the ring of trees that Bertie had planted to give shade to his beautiful garden. And there was the wholesome sound of young boys playing on the unseen lawns coming to her on the light breeze. She had forgotten. Sonya had brought her three sons up from the city. Ewan Briggs would be so thrilled to have boys to romp around with for a whole afternoon and perhaps longer. Their young noise helped to clear the sickly feeling of the memory of a person who meant her no good. Julius had frightened her with his veiled threats. Poor, pathetic Reuben energised her.

Chapter Twenty-five

Rebecca and Tom met under their acacia. He had flown in with his father after a successful day's business on the fertile farms up north. The rains had been on time and plentiful. They had been looking forward to splitting a bottle in celebration before dinner, but Rafaella had a message for him. The brief twilight was over, but even without the afterglow, he would have found the quickest way around the cei-apple hedge, through the shadows of the laundry garden and up the steep path to the top of the ridge.

He needed to hear no words to tell him that she was agitated. The fierce pressure of her body during their long embrace sent a clear message. She grasped him as if she was afraid that he might otherwise vanish.

The story of her day poured from her in a fluent, uninterrupted stream. As he listened, still holding her close, he looked over her shoulder out across the dark waters of the lake and focused on a single speck of brightness. He knew it was the cluster of security lights around Karura Tu. There must be guests. He took in everything she said and when the talking came to an abrupt end, moved his head and shoulders far enough backwards to be able to look straight into her face. His expression was blank and empty of emotion.

'Thomas, you were not listening! Since afternoon, I have

been hiding these things in my heart. And now you are going to tell me that I am foolish …'

'Darling, you have the gift. You would make a wonderful actress …'

'But you are so stupid sometimes. I am not telling you a fairytale.'

'I heard every word and I am very angry. I should have been here. Dad could have taken care of all that farmer's talk.'

'He came today because he knew …'

'He's an airhead, Rebecca, but a dangerous one.'

'The Rubais, they will never wash out those spots. Papa says we must not hate … Yes, I forgot. Papa said that this one came to his office. He was asking about Lydia.'

It was pleasant to stand on that ridge. The breeze carried the freshness from the cool heart of the lake. Looking up to their left, they watched the headlights of the evening traffic marking out the diagonal of the A104 as it made its steep descent down the Escarpment to the valley floor.

'They know that Lydia is here, 'Becca?'

'Yes. Thomas, how can they know these things? It is a kind of magic.'

No, just plain, simple, old-fashioned money. Does anyone over at Rusinga know about this visit today?'

She shook her head sadly and for much longer than was necessary to make her answer clear.

'Just as well we're going over later.'

'I'm afraid, Thomas.'

It was past eleven, but no one was ready to move away from the comfort of the cosy sitting room of the guesthouse at Rusinga Farm. It was the first gathering to talk about the hospital since the meeting at the Daniels' home after Simon

Mboya's funeral. Sonya had brought her three boys up to spend time with Ewan. She was glad she had stayed on.

For an hour and more the enthusiasm that had excited them down in Karen was recaptured. There was no shortage of ideas and, now that they had all seen the land donated by Alex, practical plans were being thrown around. How big, how many beds for general care, how many for maternity, one or two storeys? These and a dozen more were all given air time. Sonya, the medical fundi, was making notes, sharing opinions, often smiling and weeping both at once. She was being part of the fulfillment of the dream of her darling Simon.

Rebecca could carry her pain no longer. Her serious expression and her downcast eyes were warning enough that bad news was coming.

'Reuben Rubai came calling today. I was over at the house on my way here. He was suddenly inside.'

'So that is why you were late.' Puzzle solved for Maria but no sense of pleasure.

'I am so sorry for my deception. I wanted to tell Tom first.'

'How was it?'

'Sonya, he's a Rubai. That should tell you a lot. Tom calls him an airhead. I did not understand before how much the Rubais are crazy for marriage. Yes he did, Maria! I wonder if this one is just plain crazy.

'And he knows we want to build a hospital.' There was a collective gasp. 'And they want Lydia.' This news stunned them much harder. 'I would have said nothing if she had been here with us.'

'She and the boys are stretched out in Ewan's room. What a noise! She was trying to tell them a story. I heard something about snakes and a talking cat. She was loving it. She's beginning to feel safe here.'

'Bertie, has she been out at all?'

'Out in the garden, with Ewan, Sonya. With Noah, Moses and Sammy. No one else was here.'

'I heard the boys from our new place. Our friend had left just before. I could see him through the window, hurrying off towards South Lake Road. I don't think …'

Bertie's Westminster clock began its long midnight chime. No one tried to talk over the comforting sound. Maria spoke the first words of the new day.

'In the morning, we will talk with her about a new place. Not easy to hide away from these vultures.'

Rebecca offered a possibility. 'You know that Mary Wajiru is coming tomorrow. We are going to New York on the weekend. She could come with us.'

* * *

At ten-thirty pm, two large cars pulled away from their parking spot in front of the Acacia Club in a side street off Kenyatta Avenue. Their journey from Nairobi city centre would be a leisurely one. There was no need to rush. Travelling up and back would take much longer than the job itself. Drongo Gusil was puzzled.

'Boss, why is we always doing night jobs? I was enjoying myself back there.'

'Now you tell me! Half a dozen good people came up to me in the club just now begging me to give them a spot. Perhaps you don't need the money like the rest of us. Four times the going rate sounds pretty good to me.'

'It was only a question. Sorry, Boss. I like being out after dark. The roads are quiet. Yeah, lots of things. Any chance of a bit of music?'

'Drongo!'

'It stops me hearing the engine here. The noise reminds me of my woman. She snores terrible, all night sometimes.'

'Well, bet you don't get four times the going rate when she's around.'

'That's very true. Thank you, Boss. Never looked at it that way. Yeah, yeah. Okay if I put my head down, drop off for a few minutes? Wake me when we get there?'

They took the long way 'round to Naivasha. The bars in town were open and the street girls were enjoying the cool night air with their customers.

'Boss …'

'Yeah, I'll buy you one on the way back.'

They pulled into a lay-by on South Lake Road, left a guard and set off on foot.

'Before any of you ask, it's called the element of surprise. Read that in a book one time. From now on, cut the talking and be careful where you put your feet! This is no city street.'

But there were lights. In the distance Oserian Farm was lit up with their blocks of man-made sunshine, trying to fool the plants into thinking it was daytime. Dotted at intervals around the lake, pools of brightness shone where the security lamps picked out the locations of the farms. The silent group was making its way down a track towards one of these pools.

A very bewildered Drongo put his hand on his boss's arm and whispered, 'Boss, you sure we're in the right area? Do you think there's any snakes around this place?'

'Drongo, see this tape in my hand here? Open your mouth once more and you'll have a thick piece of it plastered across it! Just follow the hand signals like always on a job like this.'

They were close enough to see that their destination, the farmhouse over to the right, had two separate buildings, just like the plan showed. The larger one was in darkness. In the smaller, one room had lights on. The front door was unlocked. They could hear every word spoken inside. The boss gave the signal. Drongo grasped the doorhandle and turned it silently. He loved these moments. They gave him a rush of excitement. He was glad he came.

* * *

'New York for the weekend? For our friend Lydia? I do not think so.'

Of the eight friends sitting around that room, only one did not become rigid with shock. The quiet end to a long evening was transformed into a nightmare scene of surreal horror. Three men were standing just inside the door. They were grinning smugly, pleased that they had been able to get so far undetected. She must be in here.

Tom McCall, sitting in a shadowy corner, was as surprised as his companions, but something else held his attention. He instantly recognised the cultured voice of the spokesman. He had heard it often enough during the most critical two days of his life. The intruders had made no attempt to disguise their appearance and to Tom, the arrogantly relaxed posture of this portly man was unmistakable. Seven months before he had stood facing him in a rocky canyon on North Lake Road. Between them lay Bertie's Harley, tipped over in the skid Tom had made when confronted by half a dozen hefty, dark-suited men very like the ones who had just forced their company on this midnight gathering. Kidnapping had been their business then, an attack that had, amazingly, not ended in the death of the victim.

Lydia, thank God, she was in the other building and

perhaps asleep. The still anonymous leader was direct and forceful.

'We know she is here. Show us where she is. We will vanish into the night like brothers of mercy.'

Tom's spat out his words, calmly. 'You disgusting bastard! So you threaten us, insult us and cover your filth with your sophisticated lies, your sweet talk. Brothers of Mercy! Brothers of Hell!'

Patrick Uchome, still anonymous to Tom, recognised a voice from his own past. He moved two steps towards the shadowy corner to make sure that his memory had not deceived him.

'Thomas McCall, my intuition told me that we might find you here. Meddling McCall, is that sweet enough for you?' The mocking, light-hearted tone suggested a man enjoying the superiority of his position. 'Do you know, I have been hoping we would meet again. Something we need to clear up. Those stories in the newspapers after your little adventure up north. All those lies you told them. Naughty boy! No mention of our part in your rescue.'

'Get lost and take your bully boys with you.'

Uchome turned aside. He was losing patience. 'She is here. We know that. Don't force us to search. The boys tend to be, shall we say, destructive.'

When no positive reaction came, he raised his voice. 'That's it. You have thirty seconds. Drongo!'

There were now six dark-suited men standing in a line behind their leader. The smallest of them reached inside his coat and pulled out a pistol. Mister Uchome was surprised when this obvious raising of the stakes made no impression. There was no fear in the faces of these people. They sat around watching him as if he were playing out a role on some stage.

Maura McCall shifted to the edge of her armchair. Wide-eyed, with her forehead wrinkled, she stared at the fat man in the expensive suit. Less than a year ago, this foppish creature who gloried in his cold, ruthless nature had her eldest son in his power. How much blood did he have on those soft, sensitive hands? Tom had escaped death. She had accepted the miracle without trying to look for explanations.

'You have come to the wrong house. We have nothing for you here.'

'Except for the girl.'

'She's in a convent working with the sisters.'

The laughter was uproarious with plenty of doubling up and hand slapping.

'Mama, we get paid for our work. We don't expect a cabaret.'

Sonya watched these strangers with a horrified expression. Could these have been the same men who had taken Simon? Now they had come for Lydia, shamelessly, as though they were collecting her to take her to a smart party somewhere. Her next thought stunned her. These men were paid murderers. They killed without mercy, for money. Without a backward glance, they walked away from the corpses they had fashioned from the warm flesh of human beings. They have no conscience and they have no fear. And we, we have fallen so low that we pay attention to these thugs. We have helped to create a situation where we tolerate them as part of the fabric of the life of the country. She wanted to scream out her anger, but the energy had been sucked away from her by a sudden onrush of despair.

Maria sensed her distress and moved from her chair to comfort her.

'Tie them up. The girl must be in the other house. Charlie,

Zac, start with the one in the corner. Alfred, Buba, the other men.'

Tom, the one in the corner, rose preparing to fight the two heavily muscled men stepping towards him.

'Do not fail me on this one, Charlie!'

Patrick Uchome, trembling with anger, barked out his order through clenched teeth. Slim, wiry, Maura flung herself at the one closest to Tom, catching him off balance. He went down, pushing over a table with half filled mugs of coffee.

'Mother of hell, I'll kill you for that!' The one called Charlie reached for her ankle. Alex, fired up, stepped hard down on the grasping arm. But he could not avoid the fist of the one called Zac. He slumped to the floor striking his head on the arm of a chair as he fell. Wailing and shrieking, Sonya waded in, flailing her arms at whatever she found in her way.

Above the chaos of noise, Uchome screamed a new instruction.

'Drongo, now!'

Obedience was instant and two shots were fired into the ceiling. Calm returned. Drongo grinned smugly, pleased that, with two swift movements of his finger, he had given a demonstration of his power. He looked across to his boss, expecting to see a look of gratitude. Instead, the portly man was perspiring freely, surveying the scene with bulging eyes and breathing hard through flared nostrils. Drongo quickly looked to his front again. He had never seen Uchome like this even on really tough jobs.

A few moments of peace followed during which the women gathered 'round the limp form of Alex stretched out on the carpet in front of the empty fireplace.

* * *

A man was riding a bicycle on the way from one of the town bars. He had touched no alcohol while he talked to two old school friends. He had been seeking their advice about an interview that had been arranged for him the next day.

'Inspector Caroline is a very unusual woman, Hosea. I think she'll like you. She is slowly getting rid of some of the bad cops who see their job as screwing money out of the people they are supposed to be helping.'

'Yeah, the job is yours. It will be good to have you. Perhaps we will be able to persuade you to have a couple of beers. Off duty, of course.'

Hosea Kabari had never felt happier. Alone under the night sky, he began to sing to himself. It had not taken him a long time to learn the melody from the girls, but patient Maria had spent many hours getting the words into his head. One of her 'songs of Mary' was his favourite and always cheered him up.

Yes, he would like living in this place. He loved the dark green hills of Kericho with its endless sweep of tea plantations. There the rain came every afternoon like a welcome friend. Here on the dry plains where the valley spread wide, he would be close to the waters of the lake. He could go fishing. The girls were excited about living so much closer to Nairobi and Maria would be able to give herself to her new work.

It was an easy ride along a flat, smooth road. Only one thing troubled him and that came shortly after he had turned off onto South Lake Road. There were no shambas to be seen on this part of his journey, not a single soul out at this time of night. So why were those two expensive Mercedes saloons parked on the verge close to the spot where he would leave the road to join the track that led to the house where he was to spend the night? Something told him to overrule his policeman's instinct to stop and investigate. He made a note of the numberplates and, once on the track, dismounted to walk the rest of the way. On foot, he could be more watchful and wary. He was surprised to see lights on in the house that was his destination.

He was even more surprised to hear a commotion in the house that was now less than fifty metres away. He set his cycle down quietly and crept closer.

* * *

Patrick Uchome had never met a situation like this before. He was barely in control. He knew it and, worse still, everyone else in the room knew it. His advantage lay with the gun and the threat it posed. If he was bold enough, he might save his credibility as the most successful Mister Fixit for the rich men of the country, the solid performer they could come to when a problem needed sorting out.

It was possible that there was already one person dead in the room and he resolved that he would risk a killing if any of these idiots he was dealing with tried to thwart him. Yes, that was it. Caleb would phone for the cars to be brought right up to the front door. But the first task was to immobilise the opposition. He did not want another death. That would make for a very messy job, something his professional pride would loathe. He must intimidate them.

'No more fucking about! Got it? Cross me again and you'll be dead. I'm ready to take you all out. Boys, get the ropes. Don't waste time with gags. Come on! I want out of here, with the girl.'

For a whole lot of reasons, Mister Bertie Briggs did not see things the Uchome way. He turned, stretched a long arm out and pointed his index finger towards Uchome.

'No! No! No! Got that? Yes, the girl is here! Perhaps it's imp —'

Uchome, grim faced, was ready. 'Drongo, the heart or the head! Double bonus if you do it in one.'

There was a single shot, but it did not graze any part of Bertie Briggs. The gun dropped to the floor from the bleeding hand of Drongo Gusil and he screamed with pain.

Five heavily built men rushed for the door and out into the night air, ready to fight for their lives against whatever unseen threat awaited them outside. Hosea Kabari stood aside and watched them go.

Back inside the room Patrick Uchome picked up the gun and turned it on his faithful but weak accomplice.

'Patrick, I've never …' The third bullet fired in that small room that night took a second life.

It was a coincidence that the person Uchome seized to act as his shield to take him to freedom was Maria Kabari. The stench of cordite was an alien smell in that peaceful home. The new drama, the new struggle for life and death was too much for some of the friends who saw clearly what was happening and could do no more than watch powerlessly. Rebecca vomited uncontrollably into the fireplace, comforted by Tom. Maura and Sonya were bent over the unconscious body of Alex. Bertie stood staring rigidly down at the dying form of his would-be killer. His whole body was locked into a muscle spasm.

Hosea smiled. The dearest thing in the world to him was being held 'round the throat by a man who was temporarily close to insanity. His weakness gave him strength. He placed his police weapon carefully on the floor, stood up and looked directly into Uchome's eyes, a fearless gaze. When he was ready, he stood back from the entrance and motioned Uchome out. With the gun pointing at Maria's head, Uchome shuffled through the door, threw her down and ran off.

Hosea lifted her gently, grasped her to him and whispered, 'You see, darling, sometimes it is no bad thing if a husband returns late from a night out.'

During his career with the police, Hosea had been witness to many very ugly scenes. He had been an officer on duty in Western District in a time of political rioting. Two hundred Kikuyu had fled from their village to take refuge in a Baptist church. Hotheads from a rival tribe had locked them in and set fire to the building. There were no survivors. For a week, he and two constables spent their working day fetching and carrying for medical people, sifting and sorting through the burnt remains of friends and their families. It had been a great struggle to find the will and energy to return to any kind of work where human beings were involved. Maria brought him through.

Now in a room in a house in the town that would soon be his home, he had seen the life of his wife threatened, come upon a cottage where new friends had been catapulted into a state of shock by an invasion of ruthless city thugs. Yet no hard words were being spoken, no tears shed. Sonya Mboya was kneeling over the prostrate shape of Alex McCall who was possibly fighting for his life.

His own wife, the strongest person he knew, was kneeling too, with an arm around the shoulders of Maura McCall, supporting her with the most powerful medicine she knew. There was no spoken word, but Hosea could almost feel the vibrations beaming into her friend's consciousness from Maria's totally focused arrows of prayer.

Ever the practical husband, Hosea began to move around the room, restoring order. He picked up the fallen table and reset the coffee cups on the tray. With great tenderness he lifted the body of the man in the dark suit, whose blood had dried to hardness, and set it down on a bench under the veranda.

'Rest easy, brother.'

He moved on into the kitchen and soon the reassuring sound of a kettle boiling helped to rebuild in a small way a sense of normal life starting up again. The cups were rinsed and refilled. Hosea sat at the table and waited. Tom and Rebecca were the first to join him. Bertie, pale and abstracted, sat himself down heavily, his mind unable to move on from the vision of a gun pointed at his heart, still in a limbo between life and death. He did not attempt to grasp a drink in his trembling hands.

'I've made three calls.' Hosea was aware that practical steps had to be taken to make the outside world aware of the madness that had shattered the peaceful night of the lakeside farm.

Maura was finding it difficult to sit still. Her hands were in constant motion and her nervous gaze was fixed on the motionless shape close by on the floor. Sonya tried to give her some hope.

'Alex is going to be well. But we must move him to a hospital.'

'Sonya, you're a sweetheart but ...'

'I could not lie to you. My own pain is too fresh to insult you like that.'

'Maura, there is no ambulance at Naivasha Hospital. Just two nurses on duty. I phoned ten minutes ago.'

'Thomas, the plane?'

'Rebecca, no. Too dangerous.'

'Inspector Caroline will be here any minute. She lives close by. And Maria, Paul knows and he should be here within the hour. Friends, it must be done this way. There is a dead man out on the veranda. And Alex … we must be very careful.'

Hosea left the room when he heard the sound of a car arriving. 'It must be the inspector.'

The stereotype of a Kenyan policewoman presents an unflattering picture. Travellers passing through Jomo Kenyatta Airport will usually catch sight of a pair of them patrolling the corridors or the baggage hall, squat ladies with the ubiquitous pear-shaped bottoms and unflattering, dark-blue ankle socks. God forbid that they would have to respond to a desperate call of 'stop thief'.

Inspector Caroline Miggot had become a little bored with the look of surprise on the faces of strangers, especially Europeans, when they first met her. In or out of uniform, she displayed many impressive qualities. Her use of make-up and her taste in her off-duty clothes revealed a sure touch. She knew exactly what worked well for her good figure and handsome face. In her work, she was energetic and scrupulously honest. She saw crime as a disease. With those in the know she was considered the best cop in the Rift Valley.

Hosea had given her a general picture of what he knew had happened on Rusinga Farm that night.

'Mrs McCall, our second meeting and another bad business. I'm so sorry. Last time we had a good outcome and this time, too, we have strong hopes in our heart.'

For a few moments, the warmth in this young woman's smile blotted out Maura's anxiety about her husband. She motioned Tom to come and join them.

'You never met Tom.'

'No, but I saw many pictures. I still call you the 'miracle

boy'. The day you came home was the best day of my time in the force. But we have new work here.'

The very presence of this unusual officer of the law lifted the spirits of everyone in the room. She grasped the details of what had happened with a series of probing, clear questions. She quickly mapped out a list of priorities.

'We must get Mister Alex to a Nairobi hospital. I know that the hospital here cannot help us. I have a suggestion. Perhaps you will find it too … distasteful. My car is a very old Volvo, but it has never let me down. And it is an Estate. A person can lie flat down. I must be straight with you. Outside on a veranda there is a dead man.'

Maura bit her lip and screwed her eyes tight. 'Of course, Inspector.' Through a tearful smile she added, 'I don't think they will be much bother to each other.'

'Of course, there will have to be statements and more questions, but they will come later. Hosea, will you drive?'

'Can you trust me?'

'Our new district sergeant? On his first job? I will telephone CID on Nairobi Hill. They will meet you at the hospital. Mrs McCall, do you want Tom to be with you?'

Maura hesitated. 'Tom, you know your father. When, if, no, when he gets over all this,' the tears were flowing again, 'he'll be …'

'Right, Mum, trust me. Stephen and I won't let him down.'

'So, will you come with me, Maria?'

Temporarily Tom and the inspector were alone together in the sitting room. Bertie, more animated now, had crossed over to the main house with Sonya and Rebecca to check on the four boys and Lydia.

'Tom, the next hour will be a 'specially painful time for all of us. There'll be some remembering to do. The danger is over for now, but the gang and, more important, the person who is paying them, are not finished.'

'Inspector …'

'Caroline, please.'

'I recognised two of them from before. The little one who was shot … Drongo. He seemed a, well, until he pointed a gun at Bertie …'

'Mister Briggs?'

'Yeah. But, right at the very end … I'm sorry that it's coming out a bit all over the shop. The boss, the fat one, I saw him in the canyon on North Lake Road. Wasn't trying to hide himself. No need. I'd be a goner in a couple of hours. But the name, Patrick, it was Drongo's last word, almost. It was the first time I heard it. Not much help, I suppose.'

'Wrong, Tom. I know what most people think about the police in this country, but down on Nairobi Hill, the CID have some very impressive equipment.'

'Do they have the name Rubai on a list?'

Caroline sat back in her chair. Her unspoken reply was a look that mixed irony and amusement in about equal parts. Her actual words were less clear.

'Not to my knowledge.'

'Just a thought.'

For a time Bertie stayed behind in the main house. He and Sonya had been relieved to find their children fast asleep, stretched in a line across the largest bed in the house. Lydia was curled up in a blanket in an armchair close by.

'They had come for me. I know it. I was waiting for them, listening to the boys breathing. Without these beautiful children … I am very ashamed. When the shouting began and the noise of the guns, I wanted to run away and hide out in the darkness, anywhere. But what if I was not here and they came? These kinds of people are crazy. Where is a safe place? So this time, they went away. They are getting closer. Perhaps I will be dead soon.'

Her three new companions had no reply that was both honest and comforting.

Rebecca, Sonya and Tom contemplated the blank sheets of paper set in front of them on the table.

'Write what you saw and heard. Sometimes it is better when the memories are fresh, sometimes not. A word, a phrase, perhaps a paragraph will do. Later on they will be like triggers for the mind. Doctor Sonya … I was so sorry, so angry to hear …'

'Inspector Caroline, when I was up in the bedroom looking down on the boys, I thought of a line from Simon's favourite piece of scripture. "Though I walk through the valley of death", and how does it continue?'

'"I will fear no evil".' Papa loves it, too.' Rebecca wondered how her father would react when he heard the news.

'When I look back, there was that first call from my brother about Simon. On that moment on a rainy morning in Wales, I can see now that I entered some dark place, but all along I have been sure that, whatever I had to face, I would be able to cope. So where's the problem in writing things down?'

Tom was the last to finish writing, and as he leaned back in his chair, Bertie joined the group.

'She wanted to stay with the boys. I got her to drink a half tumbler of warm whisky and honey. Out like a light. Do her good, don't you think?'

Before he could ask what the paperwork was about, another visitor arrived. Paul Miller was as immaculately turned out and unflustered as a man on his way to a high-class garden party at some famous country house. Paul's entry added to the sense of confidence that Caroline's compassionate professionalism had brought to the emotional chaos she had found on her arrival. He had spent a year at the Harvard Law School and had a gift for seeing quickly through to the core of any brief he was given. He and Caroline had met several times when she had been a station sergeant in the Langata district of Nairobi. He had been familiar with the main issues of the troubles that night in Rusinga Farm long before he had turned on the engine of his Pajero to set off for Naivasha.

He and Caroline spent no more than ten minutes in intense discussion while everyone else in the room listened and watched in admiration at the speed of their exchanges, their grasp of detail and the ideas that sprung from their energised, excited intellects. When they were done, Caroline spoke first.

'This is not a complex problem, but it is a problem. Tom, those names you gave me. Drongo is on the records as David Gusil.'

Paul took over. 'Your Patrick, surname Uchome, fancies himself as a couple of cuts above the people he employs, mostly out of work thugs from the rougher parts of the city. There's a list of charges against them a foot long, just from tonight.'

Caroline took up the explanation.

'Before we charge them, we have to catch them. And these are a ruthless bunch with a nasty habit of getting to witnesses before we do.'

'Unpleasant as they are, they are little fish. The big fish, our Mister Killer Shark who never gets his own teeth messed up with blood, we all know his name.'

'We do.' There was a cynical edge to Tom's tone. 'But Mister Abel Rubai is not on the list.'

'You are right.'

'And there's a girl asleep over the way who is going to cop it from him sooner rather than later. We are her only hope, her only hope.'

The silence that followed was long and intense.

Lydia Smith, what was she worth? The unspoken question was in everyone's mind, one way or another.

Paul quietly left the room to sit on the bench under the veranda. Less than two hours before a dead body had lain where he sat. He knew it. Do the dead leave behind tiny traces of themselves? Maria would be at home with a question like that. He had never seen this girl, but his heart was warm towards her. Supposing they tried to protect her, where would it lead? Where would they bottom out? Every path Paul followed to find an answer to the question brought him to the same destination. A minor confrontation with the Kenyan colossus would be risky. Oppose him when the stakes were high and you would provoke him to bring out the iron fist.

Caroline sat at the table with pen and paper, alternately doodling and writing down random thoughts. She eventually arrived at two possible conclusions, the noble one and the sensible one.

Tom, who had inherited his father's gift with numbers, leaned forward with his head bowed. A stranger might have speculated that he was dozing after a hard day or maybe praying. In fact, he was composing a simple equation, a kind of mental balance sheet. He found nothing to put in the negative column of his accounts sheet.

It was Tom who broke the silence. 'Yes, we are Lydia's only hope. I'm in, whatever it takes.'

Caroline smiled. 'I have two possible ways to go. Tom, yours is not my sensible one, but it's the better one anyway. You might hate me for saying this, but my brain tells me that we should try not to be sentimental on this. Abel Rubai is in desperation mode. We could all go down – but I'm in, too.'

'I nearly died here tonight. If Hosea had been one, two seconds later … A few days ago Simon was taken from us. In this last year, Thomas, you could have gone twice. Anyway, what do you make of this? When we were all sitting around just now, I think I dozed off. Either that or I had a sort of daydream. Haven't had one since my Pembroke days. I, well, I, er, went off on a strange journey. Bertie Briggs was dead. He, I was on the other side, looking down at this farm. I love it here. I could see into two rooms. In this one, half a dozen of us were sitting around. Yes, I was still here, damned if I know how. Anyway, I was then looking in on the big bedroom next door. Four little ones with their lives in front of them and close by, another little beauty with her life waiting to unfold.

'Suddenly darkness dropped on us like a heavy curtain. Someone started singing down there, a female voice, a single note. To start with it was a sweet sound, but soon it became louder and shrill like a siren. Next it was a scream, even louder and filling the sky, up and up until, with a final burst that would split the earth in two, silence and the darkness clearing and a shape clothed in shimmering white silk, floating out across the lake. Then it was me again, watching myself on the other side, alone until the silky shape appeared coming towards me slowly, gently like a feather on the breeze. As it passed by, hardly moving now, a face turned to look at me, a woman's face so beautiful that my only reaction was to gasp in wonder. She smiled and breathed a single word: "Forgive".'

The silence in the room was as deep as the sleep of death. The concentration of his companions on Bertie's words had been so intense that every other sound had been shut out. So they had not heard the car pull up outside and the silent return of Maria and Hosea. They moved inside the door only when Bertie added his short epilogue, his resolve: 'Count me in, whatever it takes.'

Tom, who knew Bertie better than anyone in the room, was staring at his old friend in amazement. Bertie, who would normally keep his emotions strictly under control, who would be embarrassed to listen to, let alone utter what he described as airy-fairy twaddle, merely smiled and nodded as if he had just made a very practical pronouncement on what prices he expected to receive for his next consignment of roses in the Amsterdam flower market.

Maria's reaction was very different, but first she had a message for Tom. She was shaking her head and smiling. 'Thomas, your father is a man with a sense of humour. We were almost at the hospital, just about to turn off Ngong Road, when Hosea had to brake sharply. Hardly a word had been spoken since we left this house when Alex suddenly sat bolt upright and looked around. He caught sight of David Gusil lying beside him stiff and obviously no longer in this world. "My God, are they so short of graves these days that they're burying us two at a time? Do I know this man?" I know I should not be smiling and I mean no disrespect to Mister Drongo —'

'But you can take it,' interrupted Hosea, 'that Alex McCall is well. He wanted to travel back with us, but your mama stepped in. But it will be no long time before he is back home and giving orders.'

'But how? What happened?' One strong emotional

experience after another sent Tom's mind reeling with a mixture of wonder and delight.

'Tom, it's the usual story. We've forgotten the simple way where you expect without needing to understand every detail. Best to accept the reality – and rejoice!'

Hosea sat down and nodded his agreement. Glancing around the room at each person in turn, he wanted to let them know that his wife had been lifted into a dynamic level of perception. She was not finished yet.

'You have a very fine car, Caroline, such a smooth and peaceful engine! Hosea and I were so excited by what had happened to Alex, that, on our way back, we talked like a couple of mother hens sitting out on our patch on a warm afternoon. Lydia Smith, she was at the heart of it.'

Sonya smiled and let her head rock back in surprise. 'Coincidence, no, synchronicity. I hope that girl's ears are not on fire with all these words about her spilling out.'

'Come on, Maria. Out with it.' Paul chuckled. 'I haven't been your brother all these years without being able to recognise when the mood is with you.'

Brother and sister slapped hands in delight before she went on.

'Bertie, you have blessed us all. I don't believe that this daydream, or whatever, is an accident. You have struck a seam of pure gold here and we must not waste an ounce of it. We have the privilege of seeing the road ahead. If we look hard enough we will see this girl along the way waiting for us.'

'Maria, I have listened, but do I understand? You just heard it second-hand and understand straightaway. You people are much wiser than me.'

'Rubbish, 'Becca.' Tom reached across and squeezed her

shoulders. 'You are the wisest person I know. And I am not being biased.'

'But, Thomas, do I really understand? This is such a new thing for me.'

'I'm not too sure myself. Abel Rubai wants to silence Lydia. We want to stop him. For a quiet life we hand her over. Protect her and we could all be knocked off. He's afraid. Serious stuff.'

Chapter Twenty-six

'Uchome, please explain.'

Outwardly Abel Rubai looked very calm. Casually dressed and at ease in an armchair in the sitting room of his farmhouse on the outskirts of the city, he poured himself a fresh cup of coffee. Patrick Uchome had not been invited to join his very generous paymaster but stood watching him stir his drink for what seemed a ridiculously long time. Uchome had seen the boss play little mind games before with others he wanted to unsettle. Now he was the victim.

'Boss, as I explained on the phone ...'

'Uchome, let me remind you. Passing on information is not the same as giving satisfactory explanations. As I understand it, your men, your best so you assured me as recently as last evening, ran away from the job. And let me remind you that I emphasised the importance of this one. "No problem, Boss, we'll have her back in next to no time". Your words?'

'See, as I explained, the layout of the place was confusing in the darkness. We went to the little house. The lights were on. Not there. We were just about to go to the main place, on the very point of finishing the job and suddenly guns were going off. Drongo went down. Boss, the boys thought it was the police, so they took off. I stayed behind. It turned out that it was a cop, some kind of crazy who was just coming back from a night out in one of the town bars.'

'Bullshit, Uchome.'

'But, Boss …'

'Shut up and just listen. You messed up and you know it. But, but, perhaps you can give me the truth on something else you said on the phone. McCall, the older one, tell me again.'

'Things happened pretty fast, but this is kosher. McCall went for one of the boys. Zac, one of my best, moved in. One smash on the jaw and McCall went down. Hit his head on a chair as he fell. Out, maybe worse.'

'Hospital job?'

Uchome, his expression hopeful, nodded his head. 'Yeah, but not the local dump. I was there once …'

Abel had switched off. Uchome had also seen this side of the boss's behaviour where he sat forward in his chair and gazed sideways at the floor. His only bodily movement was in the eyes. They flickered this way and that or alternately were hidden under eyelids that closed with langorous ease. Uchome stood rigid and made sure that even his breath would not break the stillness of this effort in concentration. He was sure that his boss was working towards some decision about his own immediate future. He was partially correct.

'Leave us. Just go outside somewhere, out of earshot. I'll call you when I'm ready.'

'Leave us.' Uchome looked around expecting to see someone whom in his state of nervous tension he had not noticed, perhaps in one of the dark corners. No one.

As the servant nervously awaited his master's summons, striding up and down the gravel driveway, he longed for one of the long Havana cigars he bought for himself on his birthday. Inside, Abel was making phone calls. In the first four, he was seeking information. He was encouraged by what he was told and the news persuaded him that the plan could work. He set a target of five am for completion, just three and a half hours away. It would not be cheap and there were big risks involved.

Another half a dozen calls and it was all set up. Uchome would be the man to guide it home. Abel smiled at his own smartness in choosing the very person who had just failed him, to rescue the situation. Uchome worked more happily on city jobs. He was familiar with the details and, best of all, this time, his man would be keen not to stuff up on a second and probably last chance.

The person who had failed his generous employer had issues of his own to deal with before he felt fully prepared to ride into battle and redeem himself. He had turned the gun on Drongo. He had temporarily lost control of a situation and panicked. But Drongo! Of all the men he had taken on jobs, Drongo was the only one he would have called a friend. And Drongo had never let him down. For a person in their business Patrick Uchome had an amazing distaste for violence of any kind. Why had the big man insisted on sending in such a heavy brigade to bring out one slip of a Nairobi tart? The kid must have something mighty serious on him. Yes, Uchome was well aware how much the Knight of the Pink Palace loathed even the minutest possibility of having the tiniest spot of dirt besmirching his shiny armour. And he could not forget the large piles of shillings he had accumulated for finishing off little jobs for big paydays. And when this business was finished, he would have to be the one to tell Drongo's wife the bad news. Hell, he was tying himself in knots here. Work was the best cure he knew for dealing with this kind of garbage.

At four am an ambulance stopped at the barrier of the main gate of Nairobi Hospital.

The gateman was not happy about what he saw. These

paramedics were strangers to him. In his many years at the hospital he had become familiar with practically every member of staff. He put a call through to the central office and was surprised that it was transferred to Doctor Peter Umbaka, a very senior consultant in cardiothoracic.

'Yes, fine. No, you wouldn't know them. They are from a private place up at Nakuru. They have a patient to pick up. They know where to go.'

At this early hour, Peter Umbaka was normally fast asleep in his Langata home. But the call had come and, as usual, he obeyed the 'request' immediately and left for the hospital. This was the fifth occasion when he had been asked to help the people of Kenya in this special way. Five times he had covered his tracks with an elaborately spun web of lies. He had more than repaid the debt in full. Never again would he protect himself with another man's blood, yet knowing full well that when, in the dead of night, that amiable voice chilled his heart with inquiries about the progress of his children, the wellbeing of his beautiful wife, he would, trembling with panic, be waiting for the casual afterthought, 'By the way, I was wondering if you could see your way …' He would surrender meekly and ease the conscience with another bottle of his favourite Scottish medicine.

Patrick Uchome's medical team was swift and efficient. The drill was simple. Maura McCall was lured from her husband's bedside by the request of a bogus but polite clerk to accompany him from the private ward to central office to fill in some forms. 'Admin stuff. Five minutes and you'll be back here. Promise.'

He did not lie about the timing. Next, three impressively kitted out doctors, with stethoscopes swinging from their necks, moved in to check over a drowsy patient. In seconds he was feeling much drowsier after a single injection of strong sedative. A quick transfer to the waiting trolley and within two minutes Alex McCall was speeding from the fifth floor in a lift operated by a one-time hospital clerk.

Tom and Rebecca decided to walk the few hundred metres back to Londiani. Just before leaving Rusinga, there had been a call to the hospital to check on Alex. Maura's relief and excitement came down the line in a rush of words. She could not give any explanation for the sudden resurrection of her husband.

'Hosea braked hard and we all pitched forward and … Perhaps he had only been in a very deep sleep. He's having a scan first thing tomorrow, today. I'm in a kind of dream world. Try to get down by about lunchtime. We'll know more by then.'

In the days when they thought that their love was secret, all their meetings were after dark. From time to time, Rebecca still visited the acacia, a flat-top set on the grassy bank between the laundry garden and the lake, her special place. In the conversations which she enjoyed with her tree while she waited for Thomas to join her, it had been agreed that the view up there must have been as good as Mother Eve's in her special garden. The blend of beauty made her gasp with the wonder of things. Below them, and stretching into the distance, the grey, metallic gleam of the surface of the lake lapped onto the black sands drawn by the pull of the full moon. The dark silhouette of the hills all around was the wall and the arching canopy of the starlit sky the ceiling of their private world.

Tom and Rebecca did not return home directly but rounded the silent bulk of Big House, passed through the laundry garden and followed the winding path to their old meeting place.

'Thomas, are we the only hope for Lydia?'

'How many times have we stood here together?'

'Many, many.'

'What's wrong out there tonight, Rebecca? Where has the innocence gone, the feeling of protection in these hills? They have been here forever. I have never felt danger up here before.'

'You sound just like Papa when he listens to the news broadcasts on Mama's blue radio. It was a present from —'

'Grandfather Don. Do you know it's nearly three years? How many times did he bring our little white Cessna in off the lake to a safe landing on that bumpy strip he had helped to cut out of the woodland across there on the island? He taught me to fly. In the end it was those two wilderbeest fooling about on the muddy ground that took him. Such a small, almost silly thing.'

'Perhaps we are fooling ourselves. These beautiful hills, these stars are not interested in us. You say that innocence has gone. Perhaps it was never there. Has hope gone, Thomas? We are her only hope?'

'Lydia? She knows a dangerous secret. If only she had not gone back into that house.

But Rubai, how could a girl like Lydia be a threat to him? Even if she went to the cops with the story …'

'Caroline and Hosea know of it.'

'I bet he's more scared of Sally finding out that he's been spending time with Reuben's friend. God forgive me for saying it, but these are evil people. If only Mary and I had not sung in that concert in the Bomas five years ago, if only Julius had not been there to see me and … Thomas, these "if onlys", is this how it is meant to be?'

'But they happen, and we can only do our best with them.'

'Thomas, listen. I have not spoken of it before. Please, this is very hard for me. As I was leaving the village when I was frightened for you, I met Rafaella. She said that, after Grandfather Don was killed, she learned that there is not always the happy ending. You cannot go out with your big stick and fight those who want to crush you. You wait and you hope you come through.'

'So, we abandon this girl so that danger does not come to us?'

'I don't know. I almost lost you once. Tonight your father ... Thomas, I don't know. He will strike down everyone in his way. I am very frightened. I want a happy ending, for us all. Lydia, we must be with her. Tell me that there is a way through.'

Tom had one arm around Rebecca and the other around the trunk of the flat-top.' Don't let anyone tell you that this beauty is not alive, doesn't feel things. He's been through a lot with us.'

A familiar voice called out of the darkness. Luka, the night askari with his twin brother Erik, knew that Tom and Rebecca were up by their tree. It was part of their job. He was in a big panic.

'Bwana Thomas, Bwana Thomas, you must come quickly! Memsahib Rafaella needs you!'

'Thomas, there have been three calls.' He had never seen his grandmother so agitated. She was struggling to keep her composure and get her news out clearly. 'First, your mother. She was so excited. Alex was back with us. That is how she said it. An hour later she spoke again. He has gone, Thomas.'

'What do you mean "gone"?' He knew the answer. The warm wrench that grabbed his stomach as soon as he heard that chilling, simple word told him every thing. The third call drove home the truth of his fears.

'A stranger's voice. "In twenty minutes I will speak again. Make sure that the little farmer boy will be there next time".'

The agony of the wait did not last long.

'Ah, farmer boy.' Tom did not recognise the voice, but the note of triumph it carried was unmistakable. 'I have this person here with me. You know him well. He is in good spirits and will speak in a moment. We will be happy to bring him home or drop him off in some place of your choice. Just one small condition. You have an ungrateful little whore hidden away with you up there. Someone needs to speak to her, check out a few things. You know, the usual stuff.'

'That's just it. I don't know.'

'Perhaps this arsehole will help you understand. Speak and don't try anything.'

Down the line Tom could hear his father's laboured breathing. 'Hello, Tom. Another fine mess I've got us into.'

Another voice in the background shouted, 'I'm warning you! Get to the business.'

'Dad, stupid question, but are you all right? They haven't hurt you or anything?'

'No, son. Perfect gentlemen.' The irony was light, but what was that tremble in the voice? 'Don't worry, but you must not bring the girl. I'm not worth a young life. She's had enough trouble …' The phone was snatched away and the sound of a hand slapping flesh was clear.

The original voice returned. 'Mister McCall, your daddy is … confused just now. Understandable. He's had an exciting night.'

'You're right. My father is confused. The girl was here. Was, I said. Two days ago she got on an *Eldoret Express*. I took her to the coach myself. She said she was going to Gilgil. We tried to tell your other lot when they called.'

'Rubbish. Get her! Bring her in. You are very fond of your daddy. If I mention the word Kakamega?'

Half an hour before, Tom had been looking forward to getting horizontal on his bed. Now the thoughts were coursing 'round in his brain at lightning speed. How could he buy themselves time? How could he persuade such a suspicious, impatient set of crooks to accept a lie? He must stall.

'You have to give me time.'

'No! I've got deadlines.'

'Okay, forget it. I want my father back here, but I have to find the girl first. Can't you get that through your skull? I've had enough of this. When I put this phone down, I have other calls to make.'

'Like to the cops?' There was a gloating roll of throaty laughter, followed by a long pause. There was the sound of voices, but they seemed far away. Someone had a hand over the mouthpiece. At last the voice returned clear but threatening.

'Noon. You wait for a call from this side. We'll tell you where to bring her. I don't need to tell you what will happen if you break your word.'

'Our word. That's rich!' Tom was ready to launch into a burst of angry moralising but managed to put the phone down without saying anything else.

* * *

'Bertie, I'm coming over. Bad news. I'll explain when I see you.'

"Becca, I need your help. Urgent. Phone my mother and explain about Dad.'

'Thomas, she will want to hear this from you. But …'

'Maybe, but Dad needs my help even more. Tell her to stay where she is. Tell her I'm on my way down if that will hold her.'

'I will, Thomas.'

'When I've got my head 'round this, I'm going to call the Daniels' house in Karen. They'll pick her up from the hospital. When you've finished here, come over to Rusinga. God, what's going on?'

Tom found them drinking yet another mug of coffee. Sonya had gone to be with her boys and Ewan. Tom was surprised and apprehensive to see Lydia on an armchair and wrapped in two warm sweaters. She looked up briefly and greeted him with a weak smile before turning back to the task of disentangling the knots in a silver chain. Maria, Bertie and Hosea were grim faced and concentrated. The words 'bad news' were crowding their minds with possibilities, none of them hopeful.

Tom was anxious to share his news, but the presence of Lydia troubled him. He had been ready to speak openly and full on, but now he had to make sure that he would say nothing to make Lydia's fears much worse.

But he had underestimated the strength and courage Miss Lydia Smith, daughter of a captain in the Royal Engineers, the father she had never set eyes on. Tom uttered three words: 'They've got Dad'

And she shocked them with her comment, 'And they want me to take his place.'

She might have been asking for another sugar for her coffee. 'I am ready. I cannot win. Better this way. I can save the life of a good man.'

In the theatrical silence that followed, Bertie, Maria and Hosea were the audience waiting for the plot to move forward. Tom, struggling to find his next words, was conscious of his weakness. He had no heroic solution to offer, did not possess the wisdom to give hope and was frightened that he might cop out and lapse into the drivel of totally useless cliché. He was not at the heart of the drama. He had a kind of choice. The villains did not have him directly in their sights. For Lydia and his own much-loved father, it was the raw business of life and death.

'Dad says that you must not go down there.' His voice was croaking out of a dry throat. 'He insists, says you've got a life ahead of you.'

Lydia set down her silver chain, looked him directly in the face and smiled warmly. 'Bwana Thomas, you know the word naïve?'

'Of course, but …'

'Suppose I stay here or hide in some cave in the mountains, perhaps they will take life away from your father. I think these devils would do it. Do you think that they would then wash their hands and go home? No, Thomas. No, they come in search. They will pay money for news of me. I am a nobody. Yes, for the first time in my life I will be a famous person.'

Maria calmly interrupted. 'Lydia, you are speaking a truth. But there are other truths even in this hard place. You know that I have a husband.'

For the first time since Tom's arrival, some of the resigned poise went out of Lydia's expression. *What is going on with this woman? Perhaps she smokes the bhang. Perhaps …*

'Hosea is a very special man. He understands me. He does not laugh when I tell him about a gift I have. Gifts like this are not … fashionable in these days. If I tell you, Lydia, that you are going to be an important person, perhaps you will laugh at me.'

'No, I will not laugh. I will thank you for your kindness to me …'

'But you will not believe me.'

Lydia's reply was a shy shake of the head. 'Because you

think I am trying to be "nice" to you. How can it be nice to tell you lies? You test the truth of electricity by turning on a switch. I want you to test my gift in the same way. Experience it.'

Bertie was in new territory. 'Maria, I've never met anyone like you. I respect you such a lot. But, how shall I put it? We have a kind of triangle here – Lydia, Alex, my dearest friend and a first class bastard – pardon my French called, shall we say, Rubai. Who's got – some big wig Nazi said this, I think – yes, who's got the big battalions? How can we work this without taking on casualties? Do you follow my drift?'

'Perhaps you are right. But there are other ways. All bullies fall in the end, even rich ones. And we have nothing to lose.'

'Except your own lives.' Lydia the realist was back in command of her thoughts.

Rebecca returned with news about the calls she had made.

'She was amazing, Thomas. She was actually pleased about the news of the kidnap.'

'Thank God. There is still hope. She promised to stay put. She does not know yet, but the Daniels will be with her soon. Mary Coulson, too. She is down, staying with Philip and his family.'

'They'll look after her.'

Lydia slipped nimbly from her chair to kneel by Tom's side. She spoke quietly, looking up into his face as she did so.

'Phone them now. Please, before all my courage goes.'

'They wouldn't give me their number.'

A heavy lethargy held him firmly. The shock of the series of threats to him and his loved ones had created a numbness which prevented him from getting a proper grip on the reality of what was going on. Yes, he knew that his father was in mortal danger. Yes, this girl looking into his eyes was ready to give her life for a comparative stranger. But his awareness was remote. Events were happening at a distance. He was a spectator, not a participant. He knew that so much depended on him, but he had nothing to offer. And time was passing.

He closed his eyes tight and looked in on himself. *Get a bloody grip, boy. Do something, you cretin!* Not a single idea sparked into life for him. He was teetering on the edge of a bout of deep self-pity. He felt a hand touch his neck and a soft cheek pressing close to his face.

'Thomas, do not torture yourself. Pray with me'

'Sweetheart, my whole guts, my whole heart is reaching out and there is no reply. Nothing.'

He heard a voice coming to him from a distance. He recognised it as Maria's. It was calm and soothing.

'Thomas, focus now, now, on one single idea, hope, thought. Just one. Shut everything else out. See it clearly. Hold it up in front of you.' There was a long pause before she continued. 'Keep it there until it becomes a part of you. Then decide!'

He was breathing hard as if he had just finished a bout of heavy exercise. For the others watching him was like looking in on a soul in torment. They longed for him to return to himself. He was driving himself to a state of collapse.

Suddenly it was all over. He had come through. He stood up and let out a final deep sigh.

'I know what to do,' he said wearily. 'It's so obvious, but I was never one for getting the point quickly.'

Rebecca was more anxious than ever. 'Thomas, let me help you, whatever it is. This is a nightmare, but even such things come to an end.'

Maria, still calm but more forceful now, began in a voice a little above a whisper, 'So, you will get into your car and drive carefully home. You will step down but leave the engine running. You will go up to your bedroom and return to the vehicle and drive out onto South Lake Road, turn right at the junction and make your way towards Nairobi.' She stopped abruptly and opened out the palms of her hands as if to invite him to complete the narrative. He took up the offer.

'Hosea, where did you find her? Maria, what can I say?' He reached out for Rebecca's hand. 'I'm going to kill him.'

'No, Thomas!' Rebecca's scream did not weaken his determination. He moved towards the door. 'Someone should have done it years ago. Don't anyone tell me it can't be done. I'm up for this.'

'It can be done, but there is a better way.'

'No, Maria. I cannot save my father. I don't even know where they're keeping him.'

'I think I know where that place is.'

Tom, they all waited for Lydia to continue. She picked up the silver chain and twirled it around her finger, staring at it intently as she did so. 'I will have to guide you there. I have been there. It is a farmhouse. It is near a road and it has no fence. These things I remember from the night I ran away. I had to hide outside for many minutes.'

'Can't come. Too dangerous.' Tom tried to sound firm but realised that what she offered was the only hope he had of getting to his father before the noon deadline.

'Show me and then you can come back.' So much for his firmness.

In five minutes arrangements had been made. Rebecca was to be dropped off at Londiani. She would tell Rafaella what was happening. Her father, too. Bertie was to stay at Rusinga.

'I'm going to sit downstairs over there. Switch the radio to World Service to keep me awake. I'll have two guns loaded.

The night askaris ran off when they saw that first mob coming. Can't blame them, only youngsters.'

* * *

Dawn was still a long way off when the Land Cruiser with its four passengers reached the dual carriageway that would have taken them down into the city centre.

'No, not this way. We must go to the left, towards Dagoretti Corner. It is not far now, when you are travelling in a car.'

Tom was driving on sidelights. When she added, 'We must slow down now. It is there up on the left,' he slowed the Cruiser down to a crawl.

The long, shadowy farmhouse was in silhouette on the crest of a low hill, picked out by the lines of security lights surrounding the building. Tom pulled off the road and cut the engine. Through the open windows the only sounds that reached them were the gentle breezes moving through the branches of a craggy pepper tree just off the roadside. They waited and watched. There were no obvious signs of any guards.

'This is the place. Mister Rubai likes to think that it is a secret house. Perhaps I am mistaken, Thomas. I am very sorry.'

'Don't worry. You've given me hope.'

There was no plan. There had been talk on the way down but, with no proper idea of location, the only fixed thought they had was that they would have surprise on their side. Maria disapproved of the guns that Tom and Hosea insisted on bringing, 'just in case'.

'Maria, this is my kind of work. You have been very quiet on the way down.'

'Not much talk. I love looking out at the darkness. It makes me feel calm.'

'Mmm. Talking to the stars. So, what have they come up with?' The hardened police sergeant teased his wife.

She was up to his mild sarcasm. 'I have a question. Imagine that you are one of Rubai's men inside this place. What would tell you that unwelcome strangers were prowling about outside? Too difficult?'

'Er, perhaps footsteps.'

'Especially the heavy boots of a sergeant or a farmer. One of your steps and they'd be out here chasing us away.'

'So?'

'So take those boots off and skip around this place like a pair of ghosts.'

'But ...'

'Too painful for those tender little feet. We will show you. Lydia, shoes off and follow me.'

'But ...'

They slipped out of the back of the car and, bending low, disappeared along the side of the house.

Hosea was annoyed. Tom was anxious and bemused. These surreal events kept on happening. Now he was left wondering if he would see these two wild women again. If his father was actually inside, he would surely be tied up. One careless move by these amateur detectives and a lot of blood would be flowing. A gang of humiliated thugs would enjoy taking their anger out on anyone who got in their way. And what a bonus when they discovered that they had taken care of the pest Lydia without even realising it.

Ten minutes passed with no sound coming out of that dark shape. Was that good or bad news? Tom and Hosea spent the time looking about them and exchanging worried expressions but saying nothing. Hosea knew that sooner or later they would have to leave the relative sanctuary of the car and make a two man assault on a Rubai stronghold. This time he would take his gun.

There was the sound of footsteps from behind. Gun in hand, Hosea crouched behind his seat for protection. A tap on the roof sent their pulses soaring. Three figures climbed in behind them.

'The mice have returned with the cheese!' was Maria's whispered call of triumph.

'Now, take it away Mister McCall, Junior!'

'Bloody hell!' and a huge sigh of mingled shock and ecstasy sent the driver's hands into an uncontrollable tremble. The last thing he felt capable of was starting the engine and moving off. The realisation that they were still in danger of losing all their gains was enough to steady him.

A carload of tears. The sluice gates opened. Hosea was shaking his head in relief and amazement. Alex McCall sat between his two rescuers, head down and stunned. Tom, gradually taking in the impossibility of his father's rescue, was exhilarated by his free passage through the open countryside as the first rays of the sun opened up a new day. Blue smoke rose from a cluster of shambas. The longest night of his life had come to an end.

Lydia grasped Alex's hand and squeezed it. 'Bwana, you were willing to die for me.'

'Yes, Dad, I know you told me not to mouth off about what you told me.'

'Mouth off! Tom, thank goodness your grandmother can't hear you.'

'She wouldn't mind this time. Yep, and since we are on the subject, Lydia wanted to take your place.'

'But how could this happen?'

'Hosea, don't look so startled.' Maria wanted to move on. 'Okay, let's enjoy the moment.

'There is still a lot to do.'

'How?'

'Lydia, that's how.'

'No, Maria, you know ...'

'She led, I followed. You'd make a great dancer, Lydia. I was just company.'

The front door was open, not a guard anywhere. Empty bottles on the floor.

'We were dealing with idiots, arrogant ones, as usual, four of them.'

'Snoring in armchairs.'

Alex took up the story. 'They had tied me to a chair in a bedroom. Bars on the windows, door locked ...'

'With a key in the lock, outside.'

Lydia and Maria wanted to move on, to shake off the memory of the farm. Had they simply been lucky or had there been some other factors at work, unknown, even mysterious? They did not want to find out. Tom glanced in the rear-view mirror and was disturbed to see his father upset, perhaps on the verge of tears and not from joy this time.

'Tom, is there something you are hiding from me?'

'Dad?'

'Your mother, has something happened? You know, in the hospital. Look, don't try to hide anything. I —'

Tom held up his hand and delivered his message low key. 'She's fine. She's with Dot and David. We're on our way. Mary's there, too.'

'Thank God, thank God!' A huge sigh of relief was followed by a huge smile. The image in Tom's mirror was transformed.

* * *

The last time the Daniels' sitting room had held so many people had been the evening of the day when Simon was buried. Now, just days later, a heavy breakfast was laid on as a dozen friends enjoyed the chaos of trying to make sense of the events of the previous twelve hours.

Maura discovered that her husband was safe only when she actually set eyes on him as he came into the room where she was sharing a quiet time with Dorothy and Mary. David had announced noisily, 'Maura, someone to see you.'

She gasped and closed her eyes as the rush of euphoria took hold. She felt herself being pulled up out of her chair and held in a familiar embrace.

'Alex, Alex, thank God. I thought …'

'It's all over.'

'That doctor and those others in the ward, how could I have been so stupid?'

Eryl eased the mounting tension when she insisted that the unexpected guests sign the cast on her broken arm.

'When this comes off, I'm going to look after it like a family treasure.'

'Look through the window.' Maria spoke quietly, but there was authority in her voice.

'The sun has brought us a new day, a blessing that we take for granted. Last night a man died and there is no joy in that. He meant to harm us but he failed. Lydia is here. Alex is here. We must not be too comfortable with these blessings, this miracle. And beyond even that there is some change yet to come. I feel it. Only our own fear and laziness can stop it.'

'Maria, when do we stop? The change, I believe you, but will it come today? To be alert, we need rest, sleep.'

'Hosea, I'm supposed to be the practical one, the wife, the mother and all that. But you have the greater gift and you are right. One more thought. We must have the discipline never to forget the very angry man who lives around the corner in his big mansion.'

Chapter Twenty-seven

At eight o'clock, Abel was enjoying breakfast with Sally and Reuben. He was relaxed and pleased with himself. By his smart thinking he had come out of a potentially disastrous night with a handsome profit. The deadline was four hours away. His hostage was safely hidden, ready to be brought out for the exchange. Exchange. He would delay a final decision about that.

He was convinced that the McCalls and their crowd would not hang on to the Kibera tart. They would be awfully nice to her, but common sense would win out. They would rationalise their decision in the logical European way. And had the stupid girl heard anything of his unguarded conversation a few nights before? He would make a show of asking a few questions, but by nightfall, she would be gone. And, probably, dear old Alex, too.

Ten minutes later he was shut in his screen room, holding in check a massive rage. Oh, yes, Abel knew how anger was a blight on clear processes of thought.

'Uchome, what went wrong this time? And what do you mean, "they lost him"?'

'Boss, I checked every half hour. Six o'clock he was there. Half an hour later, gone. They heard nothing, saw nothing.'

'They were drunk!'

'No, no. They are country boys, superstitious. They swear

it was magic, the spirits at work. They had been edgy up at the Naivasha place. They had seen a big black dog. He could have been noisy. They shut that one up with a Masai spear straight through the belly.'

'Black dog?'

'It had turned into an evil genie. It was after them. They ran off into the bush.'

Abel groaned. The next thing Patrick Uchome heard in his coming down the line was a low cackle of laughter. Abel was in danger of a rare defeat. Incompetent fools had let him down. The irony was not lost on him that it was another McCall who had slipped out of his grasp. The McCalls, the curse of his life.

Wearily he asked the question whose answer he already knew.

'And where's McCall right now?'

Uchome pulled the phone from his ear and squinted at it with a very puzzled look on his face. He'd better be right on this answer.

'I'm making inquiries, Boss,' he lied.

'Good. I'm glad to hear that you haven't made plans to take off for the bush yourself. You know that I am going to be the winner here.'

'Of course, Boss.'

'Then wait for me at the farmhouse. I've got a few arrangements to make in town first.'

'I'm already there.'

'Any sign of black dogs?'

Just after his driver had pulled out onto the road and turned left for the city, an askari leaned his bicycle against the wall of the Pink Palace. He was delivering a letter to Mrs Sally Rubai, marked 'Personal'. It had been sent from a house just around the corner.

Chapter Twenty-eight

And then there were six. The Land Cruiser made one stop on its journey north. 'Kisumu Cottage' was the city home of Paul and Miriam Miller. It was set in its own grounds on a leafy street in the suburb of Langata. Miriam was out on the driveway packing the Pajero with bags and musical instruments and about to bus her two boys to Kenton School. Joshua and Jonathan loved seeing their aunt and uncle from Kericho district, so there was noise and enthusiastic high-fives of greeting.

Attracted by the hubbub outside, Paul came to the door. At the sight of his unexpected guests, his eyes opened wide and his face lit up in an incredulous smile.

'How?' He held his arms out wide, inviting an explanation.

'Later.' His sister, in bossy mood, turned him around and ushered him back inside with a firm push. 'We need to talk!'

The story came out in broken pieces from six sides. He locked away every word of every speaker in his lawyer's memory bank. When it was finished, Paul turned to his sister.

'Right again. We do need to talk. Right now Mister Big Ego will be working on his backlash. Do you think it's possible for a black man to become incandescent? Who was it who said something about big battalions back up in Rusinga, about two years ago?'

Hosea recognised a danger. 'He'll know that we're all very

excited just now. This could be a weak point for us. Relax too long and he'll nail us.'

Alex agreed. 'Bertie's got a saying, "Get your retaliation in first".'

Lydia, sensibly realistic in her eyes, took up the point.

'I don't know what that big word means, but the best way out is still the same as yesterday.'

Maura, a patient listener so far would not let this idea pass. She replied with a compassionate but firm reprimand. 'Lydia, no, no and no. You're ours. You saved my husband's life.'

'This man is crazy and I do not want more danger for you.'

'My turn for a saying.' Maria, still full of energy but with an edge of impatience in her voice, went on. '"Be as innocent as doves but as wise as serpents". Time to let the old serpent out of the box and do a bit of spitting of our own.'

'Oh, oh. I've seen this before. Out with it, Maria. I'm only your dim-witted little brother, but I know when you've got some scheme on.'

'Well, do you think this could work? We round up Uchome and his boys and put them before the courts. Murder, kidnapping, there must be a long list.'

'First, we don't do the rounding up. That's a police job.'

'Hosea is a policeman. Inspector Caroline, she was there, don't forget.'

'Okay.' Paul leaned back in his chair and gazed at the ceiling. After a few moments' thought he had an answer. 'Yes, could be done. We'd be up against some smart lawyers.

'We could get lucky, but it would take time. What about this for a starter? I've got friends working on *The Nation*, all good Serena people. We feed them a story, for their front page. Give them an angle. What about "Another miracle escape"?

'Would they include names, one name in particular?'

'Not yet, Tom. Innuendo, hints, mystery with scope for pointing the invisible finger. Most readers would work it out. Mister Big would certainly know. "Crazy". I think you've hit on the right word, Lydia. He's crazy for control. Julius was spoilt but not more than his father. He loves hurting people, sometimes just for the hell of it. And, my friends, we are his number one target of the moment. Don't go anywhere without a phone.'

* * *

On the long leg of the journey up and over the Escarpment, Lydia was glad that hardly any words were spoken. Only she and Tom remained fully awake. He was tired himself and concentrated hard on taking his passengers home safely. She was in new territory and fascinated by so much that she saw. She fell in love with the blood-red colour of the earth in the high verges where the engineers had cut their road through low hills. When she looked out from the highest point she gasped at the vast patchwork of fields and woodlands spread out into the hazy distance. Black ribbed Longonot and the flat, blue plate of the lake came on her in quick succession. For the first time in her life she had an inkling of the vastness of her country. Surely it would be no easy job, even for a rich and powerful man to find one small woman in all these hidden places.

'Lydia, how would you like to spend two weeks in New York?'

Lost in her own landscape, she misunderstood Tom's words.

'You mean go to the cinema or something?'

'Rebecca and I are going over. She has a lovely voice ...'

She laughed. 'Everyone in the country knows that.'

'She's going to sing with Toni Wajiru again, to raise money for the hospital.'

'Do you think they would let me work in a hospital? I could earn money to pay for my journey.'

'Yes, well …'

'But I know for sure that you must have a passport.'

'Lydia, half an hour and we'll be home. Have a think about it.'

And she did think about it for at least thirty seconds. Such a journey would be impossible for her. She would explain to Tom when he was with Rebecca again. She had more pressing matters to come to terms with.

So far that morning the new things in her life had been objects, mountains, plains, the gardens of fertile shambas lining the sides of the A104 and heavy with crops. From now on, these objects would be peopled mostly with strangers. What would they think of her? Everyone in Londiani was familiar with her, but she had heard the plans for the day ahead. Two gatherings were to take place and it was clear to her that these were places to be, times to enjoy, in the eyes of everyone else, at least. How could she explain to the family that was being so kind to her that she saw them as ordeals where she would struggle to maintain her composure.

'And, Lydia, what work do you do down in the city?'

'It must be really exciting to be down in Nairobi. So many things going on.'

Perhaps they knew about her life. Perhaps it might be best to be completely open, even to the point of brazenness. 'You might call me a lady of the night, but I can assure you that my clients are men of the highest class.'

She was sitting alone out on the veranda when Maura and Rebecca came to take her down to the flower fields.

'I think you'll enjoy the walk. Shade all the way and the air off the lake is so fresh.' Maura enjoyed showing off her home to newcomers. 'Yes, and a bit of news. If you decide to go with Rebecca and Tom on Sunday, Mary Coulson would like you to stay in her lovely home in Gilgil until you leave. I'll be with you. Think about it.'

'But why are you doing all this for me? I am not a good person.'

'Yes, that's why you risked everything when you didn't have to and saved Alex's life.'

'Madam, I must tell you a terrible thing about myself. When Maria and I went to that farmhouse, I was carrying a very sharp knife in the pocket of my coat. I was ready to use it. I know the way. My uncle, Mama's brother … I saw it happen.'

After a stunned silence while her companions took in the implications of what they had just heard, Rebecca was the first to recover her composure. Neither Lydia nor Maura understood that Rebecca's tears were set off by a memory of the lowest point in her life when she sat on the balcony of her room in the Flamingo Hotel in mid-town New York contemplating the possibility of taking her own life. Her actual words of reply distracted Maura and Lydia with its bizarre quaintness.

'A sharp knife. That could be useful tomorrow. You know, if we do manage to catch any fish up in the mountains.'

More silence until the call of duty prompted Maura. 'Come on, ladies. Don't want to be late. Special occasion, you know.'

Chapter Twenty-nine

'Abel, a strange thing has happened.'

'Now what could that be?'

Abel had called back in the house to pick up some papers. He was between meetings and was anxious to be on his way to the farm where Uchome was waiting for him. He was finding it hard to hide his indifference to this latest of Sally's little difficulties.

'I have received a letter.'

'We receive many letters.'

'But not like this one.'

Abel had learned that, when his wife had one of her problems, it was quickest for him to hear her out, offer a solution and move on.

'So?'

'Only a few minutes after you left this morning, Isaiah, one of the day askaris down at the lodge ...'

'I know Isaiah. I see him every day.' He regretted his interruption. It would only delay his departure.

Sally was well aware that her husband often found her problems a nuisance. He would soon change his mind.

'Isaiah said he had found this letter on the floor just outside his office, "like it had dropped from the sky".'

'Written by some angel and sent to me, air mail!'

'It was addressed to me. Let me read it. It is not long.'

Abel nodded irritably.

'Madam, the skies above Africa are heavy with the stench of death. We are afraid and desperate. Even our own beloved country is infected with this poison. We send our blessings to your family. We need a strong man to lead us out of this dark valley. Your husband is such a man. It is not easy to speak to this busy leader who already carries many burdens. We beg you to seek his help for our people.'

'And that's it?'

'Yes, but …'

'No address? No name? Sally, this is plain rubbish sent by a crackpot or a coward, probably both.'

'So you cannot help?'

'I shall be out for most of the day. I promise I will think about. We'll talk later. Sally, I have someone in the car waiting for me.'

* * *

Abel had been assured that no one was better at the business. But, when Angelo Rossi was dropped off at his office in town an hour before, he wondered if his American associate had misunderstood his request. He was soon convinced that his money was not being wasted. Rossi was younger than Abel had expected and he said so. The reply was sharp.

'Mister Rubai, this is a young man's work. You learn early, make your pile and then retreat to some pretty part of the world.'

'I see.' Hearing Rossi speak brought him his second surprise. Rossi was a small man, neat and muscular with stereotype Italian looks, olive skin, dark eyes and shiny, black hair swept back from his forehead. But the accent was good quality, cut-glass English. This man had style and presence. Abel had seen such men in the gentlemen's clubs in England, the product of the best of the country's public schools.

'So now it's the accent. Simple. My father was a self-made man. For his firstborn he wanted what he saw as something better than the Bronx school where he and his brothers learned a lot of lessons about survival on the streets of a hard city. He asked a big man in Chase Manhattan for advice. He sent me to Eton. You've heard of this place, I know. You had a boy there. Well, I met a lot of clever people in that place, learned a lot about a lot. The downside was that, when I went back home, I was late coming to those street lessons. But I'm a quick learner, as you will soon discover. Also, my family said that I talked funny. My mother liked that. Made me sound special, she said. So, I thought that I would run with that. I think it works. Of course, I can toyn on da Brooklyn, if I need that stuff.'

Abel was impressed, and excited. This one was different, definitely a professional.

Not much was said on the ride out to the farm. Rossi spent his time taking in the one amazing sight after another he saw by just looking out at the people and the places they passed on the way. It was his first time in Africa. He understood that his line of work was not often called on out there. The locals had the market covered.

Abel was happy to let his fellow traveller enjoy his exotic adventure. He was troubled and annoyed with himself for being so. He could not shut out of his mind the absurd letter that Sally had read to him. Who was behind this nonsense and why had they sent it, and sent it to Sally? He recalled a similar message, plea, that he received, delivered to him at home by Sonya Mboya and Maura McCall. Did they think that they could use Sally in some way to undermine him?

The unpalatable truth was that they were succeeding. He loved Sally and he was desperate to retain her good opinion of him. It was a silly weakness but a real one.

He was afraid that these little invasions would begin to sow a seed of doubt in her mind. But he was too far in now and the only way through was to keep wading on. This was one reason, the main one, why this ruthless, efficient fixer was sitting next to him on their way to his private lair outside the city. He had brought him to solve his problem with the McCalls, but he could throw in the tart. He was paying enough. One extra should cause no dramas.

It was a meeting for three. This time the guards, six of them, were posted outside. Abel was curious to see how Patrick Uchome reacted to the new man on the Rubai enforcement team. Uchome had overseen two failures in the last twenty-four hours. He had suspected for a few weeks that the boss was up to something and it was his bad luck that this muscular midget had arrived at this worst of times. So there was a handshake but no smiles. Uchome was wary and it showed in the attempt at relaxed swagger in his body movements.

Rossi was genuinely at ease and keen to get down to work. When he turned down the offer of a drink, 'No, Mister Rubai, we celebrate after the job is done,' Uchome turned towards his boss with his eyebrows raised on a scowling face. What was going on here? This guy is English with looks like that? But he had no time to work out the puzzle.

'Mister Rubai, now that we are face to face, I want to know precisely what you want of me. Who, where, when and what. Forget about the why.'

This time Rubai was as puzzled as Uchome, but, while his Kenya man suspected that this newcomer was too fast with his tongue, Abel was, once more, delighted. New York had come to Nairobi.

'Mister Rossi …'

'Alfredo.'

'Yes, well.' For a few moments Abel was stumbling about setting out his wishes. He remembered how uncertainty had undermined him once before. He had failed to allow Uchome to finish the McCall kid months before. The picture on his desk of Sally smiling at Julius taken on his last day at his English school served its purpose again. It cleared his mind and focused his thoughts. At once he became more fluent.

'Alfredo, I'm not quite sure how far you …'

'Mister Rubai,'

'Abel, please.'

'Mister Rubai, anything, anything you want me to do will be my pleasure.'

Abel hesitated, took a deep breath and opened up.

'Alfredo, for many years I have been a man who has kept his important business close to my … heart. Uchome here knows this. That is why he is going to leave the room now to check on things outside. I'll call you in later.'

Patrick Uchome was on his feet and out of the room quickly, and glad to be going. Being privy to the boss's deepest secrets could be interpreted as a kind of delayed death warrant.

'Hate is a big word,' Abel continued.

'Excuse me, Mister Rubai, but are you sure you want to go through with this? No more philosophy, please. We're wasting time here.'

'McCall, they are a family who have been a curse on my life.'

'How many people and do you want to get rid of them all? You will appreciate that numbers will dictate methods.'

'Of course,' Abel lied. He did a rapid calculation. 'Six, plus or minus.'

'Mmn, okay, we'll pick up final details on that later. Now, where do they live?'

So began a long and detailed interrogation, mainly concerned with people. He wanted to know about ages, physical and personality details and he insisted on spreading his inquiries beyond the immediate family.

'This Bertie Briggs sounds important.'

'Another of the old-time bwanas who cannot get it into his head that this country is not ruled from London any more. Arrogant white Europeans who think that they are real Kenyans.'

Abel was working himself into a rage. But this was not the red-hot boil-up that he experienced on the night of Julius's death and which was repeated many times in the months that followed when thoughts of that devilish family came into his mind. The emotions now were cold, the anger, the hatred, the longing for revenge. To him the reason was obvious. And at last he had found the man who could bring him peace. Those days of frustration that were all too common when the local boys were on the job were about to end.

'Mister Rubai, you have given me everything I need for now, except for locations, but I understand that Mister Uchome will supply all that information.'

'Yes, indeed.' How like an ordinary business transaction this was. Put your signature on a contract, write a cheque and problems disappeared, as easy as switching a light on to bring brightness to a dark room.

'Patrick, get in here and bring your stationery.' He stood and offered his hand to his saviour. 'I have to leave you now.

My boys will see you back into the city. Anything you need, anything, they will organise it.'

'The rest of today I'll be making preparations. I will be in Naivasha in the morning. I'll be in touch.'

'Mr Rossi, I want these people to hurt. Don't worry about the girl, Lydia. We'll see to her later if it's a distraction. I think, maybe, that she is less … No matter. We will meet again very soon. Uchome, take care now!'

Chapter Thirty

News has always travelled fast across the plains of East Africa. Now that a little more of the light of civilisation has come to silence the mysterious messages that were sent on the wind by the romantic beat of the drums, the family mobile does a more efficient job. Or so some people believe. No more need for the sensitive ear to interpret the latest bulletin from the bush.

By the time Tom had turned off South Lake Road onto the bumpy murram of the track that led to Londiani, a dozen stories were flying up and down the villages of south Naivasha. A single phone call from Paul Miller's house to Rafaella and Angela who were together in the McCall kitchen had created a score of rumours. Variations on the basic themes of murder, kidnap and rescue brought great excitement to the beginning of the working day. But could so many twists and turns have been possible in so short a time, between bedtime and sunrise?

Stephen Kamau, the trusted chief foreman, heard some of the different stories and understood that no work would be done in the fields that were noisy with continuous chatter. He gathered his people together into a large tent that had just been cleared of its last row of roses. By the time he stood in front of them, Rebecca was at his side. She was smiling.

'It must be good news. Rebecca knows all the secrets of this place.'

Stephen was brief. He focused on the kidnap of their beloved Bwana Alex and his rescue, his 'miraculous rescue'. 'Bwana will soon be safely home. I think he will come down to talk to us later. For now, let us thank and praise our loving Father for his goodness and mercy, and return to the tasks of the day.'

There were two meetings later that day. As Bwana Alex slipped into the large tent, the excited hubbub of expectation soared into a loud, prolonged cheer that itself turned into a more traditional harmony of blended voices. The improvised choir of a thousand accompanied itself with rhythmic clapping and swaying movement. As he walked among them, his workers, his friends saw some proof of his ordeal in his pale face and sunken eyes. They were distressed and angry that violence had come again to bring danger to the McCall family, their family.

He returned to the jua kali platform and raised his arms in triumph, wearily some thought. As he spoke his words of thanks, very few even in the front row paid attention to the slim, pretty figure behind him standing between Rebecca and Signora Rafaella.

Lydia was entering a new phase in her education. The years spent in a way of life that most of those in the crowd in front of her would have described as sordid, if not downright disgusting, had taught her many lessons. She had learned to read characters quickly. Her life might depend on her ability to pick out the customer who came to her wanting more than to use her body for a brief, intimate encounter in the privacy of a bedroom. Some men thought that their money bought them the right to indulge their wildest sexual fantasies. There were friends who had been murdered by such sadistic perverts.

For now, she enjoyed looking up and down the rows of these flower people with families to return to when their work was over. Why could she not have been one of these girls, with their glowing faces, their colourful kikois? But she had chosen to sell her body, not her labour.

Alex and Stephen chatted for a few moments. A loud cheer went up when the big foreman announced that work was over for the day. The large crowd of workers dispersed quickly through the open sides of the tent.

Half a dozen girls made straight for Rebecca. They had been friends from their schooldays before Don and Rafaella McCall had sponsored their foreman's bright eldest daughter at Santa Maria in Nairobi. Rebecca was no longer the famous singer but one of the Naivasha gang, noisy with their shrieks of uninhibited laughter and high spirits.

Lydia was welcomed into the group. It was a new experience to be in such company. Her city friends seemed older and wiser with their pretentious air of cool, street smart ways. They would not have been so ready to embrace a stranger so wholeheartedly. These flower workers had kept some of their girlish enthusiasm, their love of getting up to things.

As they made their way up to South Lake Road, the bubble of excitement moved along slowly, a colourful piece of Africa, enjoying life to the full.

'I want to show you my favourite place.' Rebecca and Lydia were strolling back to Londiani after the last of the girls had boarded their matatu to their homes on the other side of town.

'The washing garden. It is beautiful, Rebecca, but a surprise, too. Where is the machine for the clothes?'

'There isn't one. Plenty of hot water from the boiler. See,

over there. We carry it to the two troughs, put in the powder and work away, like baking bread, only better. No flour on the hands and the hot water is like dawa. It makes you feel good. I love being on the stage, but this is better. I think there is water. I will show you.'

In ten minutes the girls were caught up in the rhythm of the kneading and the slapping and the rinsing.

'This is a good place to think. To talk, also. Lydia, New York, will you come with us?'

'On Sunday? I think I must go back to Nairobi. My family will be worrying.'

'But someone will be watching the house. We could send a message. Paul will take it. And he is working to help you travel. So it will be easy for you. Just two weeks.'

'New York, is it like Nairobi?'

'Come and find out.'

'Do you think they will give me a job down in the fields? Those girls, your friends, are they happy?'

'Yes.'

'Rebecca, suddenly, why so sad when you say this?'

'Listen.' Rebecca let the sheet she was washing fall back into the hot, soapy water. 'Look around. Beautiful Kenyan garden. These flame trees, the bougainvillea, the bananas over there in the corner. My favourite is this big hedge between us and the house, cei-apple. You can eat those yellow fruits. But it is a hidden place.'

'But how can this make you sad?'

'Those girls, my friends, many of them long for one special thing. They want their own toto, to carry on their backs in a shawl. This will make them feel like proper women.'

'So they will get married soon?'

'Some, but not many. A man will give them the child, but

there will be no marriage. A child is good but the men, well, not often. They will drink. They will take their money and beat them. But there is something else.'

'They are afraid that their family will be angry?'

'No, they are excited and they feel no fear. But I do, for them. I have been in the hospital here and spoken to a lady nurse from another country. Many of the babies die, some of the mothers. There is no love in that place, no compassion, not many things to help when the baby is coming. In Nairobi yes, if you have money. I am sorry, Lydia, but this sadness is close to my heart. I am blessed many times over. I will use these blessings. Soon the workmen will get our land ready for the new place. So many people will help us. Some will be coming to Londiani tonight. You will see them. And it is going to happen.'

* * *

Peter Bellengeri owned a cattle farm on the other side of the lake where he kept two large earthmoving machines. Fred Sawyer was the leading building contractor in the Nakuru district. Sonya Mboya had spent her working life in hospitals, mostly in maternity wings.

Rebecca was thrilled to see all three of them together for the first time on the veranda of Londiani. The sundowner was still going on long after the darkness settled on the valley and the lake had been transformed into its nocturnal steely grey.

The story of the day had been repeated for the newcomers. The mood was convivial and optimistic when the conversation moved on to the idea of building a new hospital for the town.

Rebecca was sitting against the backdrop of the night sky as she set out her dream. Her natural beauty was enhanced by the passion of her belief that powered a glow in her face that held her listeners spellbound. For the hundredth time Tom fell in love with her. Once again the strength of her feeling and her fluency convinced him that she was the one who should be standing for Safina in the election and not him.

'I love this place. We all know that our people, we, need many things to give us what is important in our lives. Families want clean water that is brought into their home. Our children need schools with books and teachers who really care. The list is long. Why do I believe that a hospital comes first? Because that is where the lives of so many of our people begin, those dangerous hours when we make our journey from the womb into the world. Thomas and I hope to be married soon. We want our babies born close to home and we want the best for all our mothers-to-be. Bwana McCall has given us the land. I know he does not like that name and I promise that I will not use it again. But we must honour his gift and we must begin to honour it tonight. Am I foolish to speak out this dream?'

Enthusiasm tempered by realism was the hallmark of the discussion that followed this longest single public utterance of Rebecca's life. By the end of the evening her dream had become a project. Temporary appointments were made to give some focus to different aspects of this newly born plan. It was reasoned that, without these, the blurring of areas of responsibility could undermine the practicalities that dreams must have to become realities. Tomorrow might become next week, next year and, eventually, never.

Rebecca sat silent but wide-eyed with delight to watch the way that the three people in the room who could be described as experts set off ideas in each other. As Fred Sawyer, Peter Bellengeri and Sonya discussed possibilities, she could visualise the new place not as an empty, lifeless shell but a thing of beauty alive with human activity.

'Contracts, costings, materials, all dull paperwork will be the practical strengths here.'

'Totally agreed, Peter. We will need a clerk of the works almost straight away.'

'Fred, you and Peter could organise that.'

'Oh, yes, Alex, if you trust us.'

'Course we do. Otherwise you wouldn't be here tonight.'

'No, Alex. I've seen too many scams and rip-offs, sometimes by so-called honest businessmen you thought you had on your side. Make haste slowly.'

'But this is going to work, for sure. A lot of lives are going to be changed, Rebecca. I want to be part of this. I want to make a proposal to get us going. I had a walk around the land on my way here. I hear you and Tom are off to America on Sunday. Two weeks?'

'Yes, Peter.'

'There are no plans yet, but by the time you get back, I could have my machines over again to finish clearing the site. Alex and Bertie, you could come over. We'll have a rough area ready. We need plans. The council will have to approve, etcetera. Come on. Let's get going.'

* * *

Maura and Lydia were back by seven from their overnight stay with Mary Coulson in Gilgil. Two four-wheel drives were packed and loaded for the safari up into the south-western side of the Aberdares, a treat for the boys, a time away from houses and crowds. Lydia rode with Sonya and her boys. Bertie drove, excited by the prospect of taking Ewan on his first adventure into wild country. Tom led the way off the A104 onto the lower slopes of the Kinangop. His only passenger was Rebecca, but they were loaded with the tents, the sleeping-bags and the rest of the ridiculous amount of equipment and supplies needed to spend a single night out in the open on a cold mountain.

The boys were into a magical new land. They loved the bumps and lurches as the Pajero clambered relentlessly up the stony track that, in places, was more like a dry river bed. Sonya thought that too much of such a rough ride would bring on the nausea she invariably felt on long journeys by air, but this was a triviality compared to hearing the delight of her boys as they shrieked and laughed at every new bounce and roll.

Ewan, belted in at his father's side, was less assured. He was strapped in tight and his view was limited to what he could see above the level of the windows and that meant the endless green of lush foliage broken occasionally by squares and triangles of blue sky and heavy sacks of grey cloud. For a time Bertie wondered if it had been a mistake to bring a boy, not yet three, up into this mass of forest and thicket. Had he brought him for selfish reasons, too eager for him to start experiencing the great life outdoors? But, at last, infected by the happy noise coming to him from behind, Ewan reached over to touch his father's arm.

'Dad, can we come up here to live?'

A relieved Bertie turned to smile at Sonya. 'What about a couple of songs to let the forest people know that we love being up here with them?'

'I don't know any songs all the way through.'

"Course you do. Here's one. Used to sing it at Pembroke. You heard it last bonfire night. "Old MacDonald had a farm!" Yes?'

After singing themselves out, the travellers settled into a happy, dozy state, lulled into silence by the heavy sound of an engine working hard in a low gear. Nearer the top, the road became less bumpy, but the boys and Lydia were surprised by the chill on the breeze blowing in through the open window. So the windows were wound up and there was a struggle to put on anoraks. A heavy shower rattled on the roofs and for a time blotted out the now more distant horizons. When the rain stopped, it was time to get out. They had reached the flat, open glade that was to be their base for the next twenty-four hours.

Noah and his brothers stepped down onto the sodden clumps of grass and looked around. No sign of blue sky up here. The silence was broken only by the drip of thousands of droplets of water sliding from the leaves of the trees close by. Tom unloaded the boxes of rubber boots and thick, woollen socks. The boys did not like the chill, damp air, did not see it as a refreshing change from the heat they had left behind on the plains. Even the slightest movement of their bodies up in this alien land helped the cold to tighten its grip on every inch of their skin. But there was a remedy close at hand.

A mug of hot sweet chocolate warmed their hands and cheered them up. As they drank, the boys looked 'round again to find that the landscape had changed miraculously. The damp trees suddenly showed off their solid branches at comfortable heights, inviting young legs and arms to heave themselves up and explore the mysteries of the overhanging foliage. For Ewan, all the attraction was at ground level. Those muddy puddles in the tracks were wider and browner than those he splashed through in Rusiga, even when the long rains had lashed down on the night before.

While the boys played, the adults worked. The little patch of green became a proper camp. The gas stoves were soon full on and heavenly smells were helping to change the playground into a paradise.

'Daddy, can we come here to live? Please!'

'We'll have to ask the bwana of the mountain.'

'Where does he live? Can we go and see him, now?'

'Ah, well, I think it's his day for being over by the big mountain.'

'Bigger than this?'

'Yes. And, Ewan, I don't think he likes houses in his kingdom. Nests he likes and dens, but our houses with their fires and their chairs. I don't think the dragon …'

'Dragon?' Sammy grabbed Moses around the shoulders and peered up into the trees with a mischievous grin lighting up his face. 'I hope he lives up on that big mountain!'

'Is it a pretend dragon, Daddy?'

'Well, boys, I'm not sure. I've never seen him, but I know for sure he likes good Kenya boys who look after the forest.'

The quiet time after lunch was brief. Tom made an announcement.

'Who wants to go fishing?'

Four young bodies flashed into full-on energy.

'Any of you ever heard of the Karuru River?'

Four foreheads beetled in puzzlement. Tom and Bertie smiled. 'Bertie and I have been up here lots of times, with my father, Eddie and Rollo. Always managed to catch something.'

'Any sharks up here, Tom?'

'I'm not sure, Ewan. I remember one time your mother …' Tom stopped abruptly, angry with himself for his carelessness. He looked across at Bertie and shook his head, regret written all over his face. Bertie had recovered his poise and almost had it wrenched away in the next second. Ewan explained to his three young friends unemotionally.

'I never saw my mummy. But your mummy did. Daddy told me she was there.'

Bertie steeled himself. 'It's all right, Tom. Yes, Mummy was up here, too. Tom's right. She caught a fish so big it made enough supper for seven people.'

'That must have been a shark!'

'You know, I can't really remember for sure.'

'I say we go and see what fish are there today, just waiting for us.'

'Oooh, Daddy, like you say, let's put our best foot forward. Sam, that means hurry.'

* * *

Rebecca, Sonya and Lydia were in sombre mood as they finished their domestic chores. When they sat down together for yet another coffee, Sonya explained to Lydia.

'Yes, I was there. I had been watching Anna closely since we first heard about the pregnancy. "My miracle baby" she called him. She and Bertie knew the risks. When she came in for the birth, she told me straight away. "Sonya, promise, if things don't work out, let me go and save the child". When Ewan was just about to come Bertie drew me to one side. "I hate to ask this but, Sonya, whatever happens, don't let my Anna go. Please."'

'Oh, Sonya!' Lydia reached out to touch Sonya's arm.

'You know, I've been working with mothers and babies for so many years, but the mystery of those precious moments is there every single time. Gynaecologist is a fancy name but, really, I'm no more than a bystander trying to help. The big decisions are made elsewhere. But that was my worst time. I wanted them both, but I didn't have to fool myself for a single second that I was playing God. The little one was a fighter from the very first moment. Anna saw him, heard him cry but …' She covered her face and wept quietly. 'The pity of it. When I brought his boy to Bertie, we just cried our eyes out.'

The three women sat quietly in the privacy of their thoughts and listened to the sounds of the fitful breeze and the screaming calls of a pair of black kite skimming their way to the open plains further up the mountain range.

* * *

The fishing party returned earlier than expected. Sonya was talking to Lydia when they arrived.

'Simon and I loved it in America. The boys hadn't come along then. We were both offered jobs in Doctors Hospital. We thought about it but, well, NewYork for a holiday, yes, but where could you find a place like this… My God, what's this?'

The three of them ran to the edge of the glade. Every one of the fishermen looked as if they had not been by the river but in it. Bertie led the way with Ewan crying in his arms. Tom followed and he was carrying one of the brothers – it must be Sammy – in his arms. The boy was silent. Sonya ran to him. She saw the blood on his blue anorak and then a wound to one side of his forehead.

Moses and Noah ran to their mother and buried their heads in the folds of her coat. The tears held back for so long were released mingled with sobbing, desperate pleas from Noah.

'Mamma, is he going to be all right? I didn't push him. He just sort of slipped …'

Tom took over quickly. 'We were coming close to the falls. The boys wanted to look down to try to see the bottom. Ewan slipped and fell into the mud. Sammy went to help him up. He skidded and slid over.'

'And fell to the bottom?' By now, Sonya had taken Sammy in her arms. He was warm and breathing gently.

'No, Sonya. Barely five or six feet.There was a slab of rock down there. Bertie had him back up in seconds. As you see, we all got a bit wet. Spray mostly.'

She held her little wounded soldier tight, closed her eyes and prayed hard.

Frantic activity. While the women undressed the boys and dried them, Tom and Bertie broke camp and packed the vehicles. In ten minutes the engines were revved and the journey back down to the plain began. The boys, wrapped in heavy blankets, sat tight together in the back, except for Sammy who lay upright in his mother's arms. She had done the first aid. There was no more bleeding, no broken bones.

That same morning Alfred Ross had been doing a lot of reading. By eleven he was driving quietly from his hotel on the edge of the Nairobi city centre to the Highlands. He travelled alone in a second-hand, battered Range Rover, supplied at his request by his client. He was enjoying himself. Alfredo was always happy when a job involved a slow build-up. The bonus here was that he would be taking on a new identity, getting to practise a little acting, always a pleasure. He had not yet made up his mind whether it would be a professor of anthropology or a freelance newsman out on a special assignment. At times like this he always blessed his father for sending him to school in England. The accent alone was worth the investment. Up-market London seemed to inspire trust in a way that Brooklyn did not.

He enjoyed the brightness of the African light and was fascinated to observe his fellow travellers. At home he mostly used taxis or was driven by a chauffeur. Here the driving was erratic but relaxed. There were so many people on the red earth verges, most of them on the move. There were kids everywhere, on their way to school dressed in different coloured sweaters. Uchome had been right about the views, especially from the highest point of the climb.

'Look out for the volcano to your left. Just beyond, you'll see the big lake.'

This Africa was full of life. No dozing at the wheel out here. Get the job done and stay away for a while. He knew that when he was finished, it would the first plane out. One day it might be different.

Once onto South Lake Road, he pulled over for a final check. Londiani. The finger post pointed down a track to his right. He considered walking to the farmhouse two hundred metres away. Its pitched roof peeped out from a tight circle of dark green trees. Beyond, the blue waters of the lake sparkled on that bright, warm morning.

A beat-up old car pulled in behind him. Alfredo had been too relaxed on his journey from the town centre. Yes, he had noticed a car behind him, but it was way back and, after all, they were both travelling on a public road. The three occupants had spotted him as he pulled out of the Amin filling station. Smart car, to them, single white driver. This could be interesting and profitable.

In his side mirror he watched them stepping out, three scruffily dressed skinny youths with the oversized basketball boots and the loose jeans. He had seen such characters everywhere he went in the world. He was fully alert now. He took something out of his pocket and held it under the flap of his coat. As they drew alongside, he rolled down the window and smiled affably.

'Good morning, gentlemen. A nice, fine day for it.' As a schoolboy in England he had heard the locals use this expression many times, without ever knowing what the 'it' meant.

The laid-back, lazy manner of the young men was no surprise, nor the passable attempt at the down-market Bronx accent.

'So what have we here? Nice wheels, Mister Englishman. How much they cost you?'

'I beg your pardon?'

The spokesman, and presumably the leader, leaned on the windowsill and checked out the interior of the Range Rover as he spoke. 'Maybe you could give us a ride to Nairobi. Meeting with our business partners.' He grinned towards his companions. 'Better yet, you step out and let me drive.'

Alfredo pleased them with his quick cooperation. He closed the door behind him and took a step backwards on the verge, not such a pleasing move. When they saw him standing in front of them, they could not resist a comment. Their surprise caused their man to forget the pseudo accent.

'My, you're small for your age,' he chuckled. 'You haven't escaped from some place?' The loony house up in Gilgil?'

'I was just going to ask you the same question.'

The tension was mounting. There was something annoyingly arrogant in this little man. The tall companions behind the man of the mouth stepped forward and reached for their pockets. Too late. Three bangs later and they were screaming with the pain of their wounds. Their lives were in no danger. Alfredo, as usual, had selected his target areas carefully. Fearing another onslaught, they hobbled back to their vehicle, switched on and began a turn.

'The hospital is that way!' Alfredo mocked, pointing towards Naivasha town.

He heard the shot almost simultaneously with feeling the

burning sensation in his left upper arm. Flesh wound, just one level up from a graze, but there was blood. He was very, very annoyed with himself.

Alfredo removed his coat to check on his wound. As he did so, he heard the sound of footsteps of someone running up the driveway towards him. In seconds two men appeared calling out something in what he took to be Swahili. On seeing him, they switched to English.

'Bwana, we are coming. We heard shots. You have had some trouble, yes?'

The brothers, Luka and Erik, night askaris at Londiani, had been on their way into town to visit family and to look around the matumba on the hunt for bargains. Thrown temporarily off balance, Alfredo suspected for a moment that these two were part of the attack squad. He soon realised that these tall, smartly dressed men were on his side. When they noticed blood that had saturated the arm of his white shirt, they scrunched their faces into a look of shared agony.

'Bwana, so sorry, so sorry. Please, come to the house. The memsahibs are at home. They are very clever ladies. They will help.'

Erik, the brother who had not spoken, took a large blue handkerchief and held it out to this mzungo in distress.

'I'm fine. Just a scratch. Come on, let me drive you down.'

It was a strange and unnerving situation for Alfredo. He was sitting in the kitchen of two of the women he had come to assess with a view to killing. He had seen their photographs and knew their names. Rafaella, the older McCall woman, was a surprise. The Italian accent had not been completely lost after her many years in Africa and she was a real beauty, a Veronese princess in exile.

'I was not much more than a girl. My father and his friend

had been out hunting for birds. It was the last time for Papa. Mama and I were in our kitchen, just like we are here, pulling little balls of lead out of the bottom of Tullio Capello with a tweezers. Papa was jumping up and down on his gun. Mama said, "Blame your eyes, Tonio, not the poor gun!"'

Alfredo was happy to be the quiet patient, listening to the kitchen talk. One awkward glance from the younger McCall woman put him on his guard. The question was about to be asked. She looked at him sideways, like a naughty schoolgirl about to be impertinent.

'What exactly happened, Mister Ross? Shootings in broad daylight, that's a first around here.'

Alfredo smiled dismissively. 'Please, Fred. It was my fault. It's my first time in Naivasha. As I came down the steps of the bank, a young man was leaning against my car, waiting for me. He was smartly dressed and polite.'

'"Sir, I am applying for a position on one of the flower farms by the lake. If you are driving out of town, I could get down on the turn onto South Lake Road". I didn't know the way so he guided me. Trying to be helpful, I took him further. As we came to your entrance he pulled a gun and told me to hand over my wallet.'

'Oh, no!'

'Oh, yes. But there's always karate. Comes in handy sometimes. Too easy, really. Next thing we were out on the road with his gun on the tarmac. I picked it up and he ran back towards town. I fired a couple of shots into the road to encourage him.'

'But your wound?'

'Carelessness from me. As I grabbed it, well, I think I actually shot myself.'

A thoughtful silence on the women's side ended with Maura throwing up a bright idea.

'Inspector Caroline or Hosea, Naivasha police, but honest ones, efficient ones.'

'No, no. I'm an American citizen. Oh, yes, I know, the English accent. If we call in the police, there'll be a big fuss. And I think the kid has had rough justice served on him.'

From the bedroom window, there was another majestic view for Alfredo to enjoy. He had gladly accepted the order that he must lie down for a time, just in case of delayed shock. He watched the afternoon shadows as they gradually shifted across the plain. The only shock he experienced was that the turn of events had dulled the sharp edge of his plans. Two of his intended prey had been kind to him. This was useful. He wanted to observe, but he did not welcome the warm intimacy. For a time he questioned if his resolve might be undermined. Common sense and some simple reasoning soon helped him over this hurdle. These people meant nothing to him. In his time he had put away some attractive, undeserving victims. Conscience was not a part of his baggage. And his temporary employer was offering him a very big payout. There would be no problem when the time came.

The noise of activity outside roused him. He checked his watch. He must have been dozing in that armchair for at least an hour. From the window he saw two men and five women in conversation by the open doors of a newly arrived Japanese four-wheel drive. He knew the two McCall women and their maid Angela. One of the other two must have been the famous Rebecca. No exaggeration about her good looks even from up there. He felt sure that the second young woman was the one who must have troubled Rubai such a lot. He would check later. As for the men, easy, boss man McCall and the dreaded son, Tom. They were not a joyful group. That was obvious.

When he was introduced downstairs, he attracted little interest beyond the fact that he had been wounded on the road just outside the property. He soon worked out that the three young people had returned early from some trip into the hills. Some young kid had fallen into a river and knocked himself out. The animated conversation around the healing ceremony of the tea taken on the large open veranda presented him with the opportunity to observe without being noticed, except that, from time to time, the other young woman, ah, yes Lydia, gave him what his grandmother called 'an old-fashioned look'. Another African beauty, the mud stains on her clothes gave her an extra attraction.

Stupid of him, but there in that comfortable atmosphere, he understood, for the first time, that he had tumbled into a family that was close-knit and caring. Pressed to stay for dinner, he was introduced to four new people. For a time he believed that they were two married couples until he picked up that the man, Briggs, was a widower and the woman next to him had recently lost her husband in a brutal murder he had read about in *The New York Times*. Sonya Mboya was a doctor and it was one of her kids who had fallen into the river.

When Hosea Kabari, the sergeant in the local police, arrived he brought his wife. That was a surprise. There was something striking about this Maria, yet another good-looker. But this one radiated an inner strength and possessed a poise he had rarely seen in any human being. Before they sat down, he had been persuaded to take off his shirt for this woman with the firm yet silky hands to examine his wounded arm. Her cool touch soothed the irritation. Perhaps they were right with their suggestion of a gift of healing powers. Even the doctor seemed to believe in the idea.

He gathered a lot of information that evening, perhaps too

much. His memory was his notebook. It had logged in news about plans for a new hospital. He had discovered that this Tom and the singer would be back in New York before he was and raising funds for the project that would fade away with the passing of the dreamers who had thought it up. The plan was for them to be away for two weeks. He would make sure that they were back in less than one. They were taking the Nairobi whore with them, presumably to try to hide her from the boss. Should he tell Mister R that he had run the troublesome female who had bothered him so much? He registered a no on that tiny dilemma, without being able to give himself a satisfactory reason.

One intriguing but seemingly irrelevant piece of news that came out that evening concerned the injured kid, little Sammy. He was still unconscious when they returned to the Briggs place where this Sonya and her boys were staying. Mama was puzzling on her own dilemma. Should she risk taking him down to the city straight away or wait until morning?

Without warning and without explanation, Maria Kabari had turned up at Rusinga Farm.

'I think I can help Sammy.'

Sonya showed no surprise. How could she have forgotten the hours that Maria had spent with Simon in the coolness of the private surgery in her brother's house? Maria had a gift and Sonya trusted her. Soon Sammy was with his brothers and Ewan out on the big field bordering the house where they were daring each other to see who would get closest to one of the waterbuck grazing quietly in the late afternoon. Sonya did not try to look for sensible reasons for yet another transformation.

Chapter Thirty-one

Fred Ross left early. He had arranged with Alex that, next morning, Stephen Kamau would escort him around the flower farm.

'One of my courses in New York State was on the flowers of Africa. The roses around the room here, I've never seen better specimens. Got to take my chance. You don't mind me taking pictures?'

Those left behind at the dinner table did not expect to see him again. Another ship had passed in the night. Life went on and plans became reality. Next morning, Sonya returned to Nairobi. She and the boys became temporary residents at her brother's home in Karen.

Later in the same day, Peter Bellengeri brought his heavy machinery to the Naivasha site. As a symbolic gesture, he climbed into the cab of his earthmover and sliced away a few more swathes of topsoil. The new building was on its way. As he was checking his work, Bertie turned up. He was on his way back to Rusinga with Ewan after a drive 'round Nakuru game park, a treat for a small boy who was missing his friends.

'What do you think, Bertie? I'm guessing that the main entrance should be about here.'

His old friend was in reflective mood. ' Bloody marvellous, Peter. As I drove in, it struck me that this bit of land has been lying untouched, at peace for thousands of years, until we come along and the long wait ended. I hope we can put up something beautiful. Our people have had to put up with tenth rate for too long. I wonder if we can do it.'

Rebecca and Tom, with an excited Lydia, set off from Jomo Kenyatta on their long journey to the north-west. Just as on their first arrival at Kennedy Airport earlier in the year, Toni Wajiru and Mary were there to meet them. When the chauffeur driven car returned to the daylight on the Manhattan side of the Queen's Tunnel, there again, on either side of them, was the display of streets and buildings, the world famous cityscape that, to most visitors was the essence of the place. For Lydia, it was just like being in a glamorous film – the canyons of concrete and glass, the broad sidewalks crowded with people on the move and the noise. When a police car passed them with its siren blaring, she watched it go by in amazement and, when the officer on her side looked across at her, waved and smiled, she put her hand to her mouth and was too late to wave back.

But there was something else. Lydia had not been in Bertie's guesthouse on that night of mayhem on Rusinga Farm. Those who had been there were now scattered and out of reach of each other. They could not know that their common experience still bound them in a way that only Maria understood fully. Tom would have seen something of it in an attack of the Celtic melancholy that his mother sometimes teased him with. Maura and Alex would have put it down to delayed reaction to the close call that hit them twice within a few hours. For Bertie and Sonya, it was a recurrence of the sadness of loss. Sonya had fought a losing battle in the delivery room when Anna had managed to present Bertie with a son at the cost of her own life. The happy hours with the four playmates at Rusinga were over and she was back to long nights in a room alone.

But Maria saw that a euphoria which sprung from excitement and hope when they had all been together planning a great venture in Bertie's home and raised to even greater heights when danger threatened them could not stay up in the heavens forever but must fade. In their aloneness, doubt would snake its way in and undermine their confidence, a variation on an old theme. United there is a glimmer of a chance, separated we see the raw truth of reality.

* * *

Sally Rubai was enjoying life. The arrival of the new Julius was not far away. The latest scan showed the little fellow perfectly formed and moving about. The attack on his mother seemed to have had no bad effect.

'Now don't be impatient down there. Your mama is taking good care of you and she wants you to herself just a while longer. This will surely be the last time, so let's both enjoy ourselves.'

Her portly curves were not shrinking. The idea that she was eating for two suited her just fine. She did not have any guilty thoughts when she took on board that extra scoop of ice-cream or another slice of cheesecake. Her sweet tooth had never been so indulged.

Abel was more attentive to her than he had been for a long time. She thought that it was the excitement of having a new Julius in the family. After all, she was the vessel that was carrying the sacred cargo and it was only right that he should make a fuss of her. He was smiling, buying her presents, bringing her coffee from the table to her chair, just as he had done in their early days in Nairobi, before Julius had come along.

And he was a man relieved beyond his expectations. Friday, May 25th, Abel recalled it several times a day, always in vivid detail. The passing of the weeks made the memory more painful. The litany of 'if onlys' grew longer, each time he revisited that fateful evening. He had experienced the two extremes of emotion in the space of a single half hour. The joy of sitting in the dining room of Muthaiga and watching his handsome son showing off his bride-to-be had been shattered by the shock of despair of seeing that same boy, stretched out, lifeless on the cold, damp grass.

The coming of Alfredo Rossi lifted his spirits. This young American, himself just a little older than Julius, was about to exact punishment, to bring him the sweetness of revenge. The McCalls would have to pay in full. Several times a day Abel indulged himself in the pleasure of anticipating a new, cleansed world. At last he would have fulfilled his duty as a father and brought himself peace of mind.

Chapter Thirty-two

Alfredo Rossi made an adjustment to the strategy he had worked out for the most lucrative job of his career so far. The day after the supper in Londiani, he had turned up early for his tour of the flower fields. Stephen Kamau had chosen Gideon Moyale to be his guide. Stephen was surprised that he did not see his young next-door neighbour for more than two hours.

'Bwana Kamau, that man wanted to see everything. He made notes in a small green book. He asked so many questions, even about where the power points were placed. I think, perhaps, he is planning to grow flowers in his home in America. He is fond of roses, especially yellow ones.'

'Is he gone, Gideon?'

'I told him that he should speak to you. "Bwana Kamau knows more about flowers than anyone else in the country". He said to thank you for your kindness, but he was returning to Nairobi. I think he said to the airport.'

'He is a clever man, I think. You got on well with him?'

'He said that he thought I could make much money in his country. "You grow the flowers and I will open a shop to sell them. Big prices".'

'Did he ask if you would go over to help him with this new farm?'

'Bwana, if I had the money to go to this America, I would

be going to see Rebecca singing. I told him that you are the man he needs over there.'

'Better to wait till she comes home to sing, just like me and her mother. But if you are going you must hurry. In two days she will begin. Sure you got enough shillings for the trip?'

* * *

Alfredo was a smart thinker. 'Killing two birds with one stone.' His housemaster in Eton told him more than once that Americans had a gift for this remarkable feat.

'But, sir, how come …'

'It's a metaphor, boy. And, in this case, it is a compliment. You're just about the smartest operator I've ever come across. Have I got the lingo right, Rossi?'

'Alfredo, we thought you were in Africa.'

'Mama, in a strange way I am.'

'I told your father that sending you to that school was a mistake. So you come back with this crazy voice which I like very much, but you talk like you have had an accident to your brain.'

'Alibi, Mama. That is a very important word to the men of the Rossi family.'

'Now, there is a word that I do understand. Do you need Papa to help you?'

'Mmn, not this time. I will be here for two or three days.'

'But you will come for supper.'

'Tonight, no. I am going to a concert.'

'With a girl? Constanza, the banker's daughter, perhaps. She's not yet got a husband. I know she is no beauty, but she is not very tall either.'

'Thank you, Mama. No, not with a girl but to see a girl, to listen to a girl. All part of the alibi. I am being very careful.'

He had a ticket for the second night of the new program of the Wajiru band at the Flamingo Hotel in Mid Town.

* * *

Paul Miller had an older brother who was also a lawyer, Barnie (only his wife Phoebe used his full name and that when Barnabas had committed some grave offence like being late in picking her up from a hair appointment). The family had lived in Boston for over fifteen years. Many times Barnie tried to persuade his brother to join him.

'"Miller and Miller" on a polished brass plate. How does the idea grab you? When Tommy and Chris graduate from law school, we could be a big-time outfit.'

The brothers were in weekly contact. Barnie had great admiration for Paul and there were occasional pangs of guilt when he saw how hard Paul was working to change some of the worst ills in the old country. But then it was easy to find good reasons not to break away from a pleasant and productive life and a seductive lifestyle. In the time since Paul and Daniel Komar had set up the Serena party, the situation had shifted.

'Paul, the big men will be keeping an even closer watch on you.'

'I know, man, but there's no choice.'

'Oh, but there is. And you've made the right one. Be patient with me, brother of mine. Give me time, give me time.'

Barnie was excited to hear about the idea of building a hospital in Naivasha. As boys in Kenton, he and Paul had enjoyed many Sundays on school outings to the yacht club on the lake, learning how to sail, with the added thrill of watching out for the hippos who loved to wallow close to shore on sunny afternoons. When he heard that Rebecca Kamau was coming to sing with Toni Wajiru in New York to raise funds for the work, he was on the phone at once to the Flamingo Hotel. Toni and Paul had been scholarship boys together and the families had been friends ever since.

'Barnie, come on the second night. Yeah, sometimes we can be a little nervous on opening night.'

Two days later, three of the American branch of the Miller family took an early train out of Boston on their way to Grand Central Station. Debbie had passed up the chance to meet the famous Arnold Brookman to join her parents on this special outing.

'Mom, I can always read his books, but Dad says we'll get to speak to Rebecca after the show. No contest. And what's this about some shopping?'

After checking into the Flamingo, Barnie arranged to meet his two women in the late afternoon back in the hotel for an early dinner. At four, they were sitting together in the Kisumu Room. Harry Thuku had given his ground floor public rooms the names of Kenyan towns. 'Makes me feel close to home and I think the customers like it'. The family swapped stories of their day over several cups of coffee.

'Dad, was it the zoo or the lady with the lamp this time?'

'Neither. I did a lot of walking, took in a couple of galleries, but, my dear child, my great achievement for the day was this. You missed the "great man" to come here, so, well, I hope you haven't read it. Mister Brookman's masterpiece, that's what the lady in the shop told me.'

'"Public Buildings Right and Wrong". Dad, this must have cost a fortune!'

'And such a boring title. When I said this as I was paying, I was put in my place. "Only a philistine would make a remark like that!" and no hint of a smile on her face.'

'And, of course a cookbook for your beloved wife.'

'No cash left in the wallet.'

Debbie had been flicking through a few of the pages of the heavy volume. 'Dad, I really am grateful. In college, I looked at this book so many times, but to actually own a copy, it's a wow! moment.'

Later Barnie and family had their first experience of Harry Thuku's 'Spiritual Space'.

At great expense, and at some risk to the whole structure, he brought in contractors who had gutted the third and fourth floors and converted them into a single theatre, concert hall. The investment paid off. The combination of a restaurant serving the best African food in Manhattan and a showcase for top-class music of many kinds was a winner.

Rebecca Kamau was back for a short season and this was the best of the best. Earlier in the year, the unknown amateur from the African bush had won over audiences. She had a voice, she was a beauty, but most of all she had a remarkable presence. Her movement was sinuously rhythmic and there was what one critic described as 'a spiritual force in her delivery'. Another saw her singing voice as a combination of Ella Fitzgerald and Jesse Norman. Rebecca ignored all the attempts to portray her as a singing sensation.

'Crazy talk.' She enjoyed the applause but, most of all, she was intoxicated by a feeling of ecstasy when her voice rose up inside her. For those minutes of performance she was possessed. God was willing her to take new risks with His gift and she was ready to push herself to her limit. And, when it was over and she returned to her dressing room, she was happy to be the wash girl of Londiani again, the future wife of Thomas McCall. She understood her truth and there was no danger of addiction to the powerful drug of fame.

Her joy was to be back on stage with Mary and the band.

Tom had seen Rebecca on stage many times, but for Lydia, being in the heart of a great city, in the company of so many smart, sophisticated and rich concert-goers was overwhelming. It could not be happening. What would it be like when her new friend actually appeared on the stage?

For Lydia and for many others who sat entranced as they looked up at the 'black angel', as the woman in the next seat described Rebecca, the sounds they heard from the mouths and instruments of those supercharged Africans were almost otherworldly. Audience and performers inspired each other to undreamed of heights. After all, this was just another concert in a city where there were a hundred concerts happening on any given night.

A standing audience drowned out the sound of much of the final encore. Toni and his boys were considered to be the best of the African bands seen in New York for years. Toni himself was a gifted composer and in his lyrics he captured the heart and soul of his beloved homeland, a spiritual experience for a spiritual space. But when Rebecca Kamau stood up in front of a packed house, those ten men and Mary, Rebecca's best friend, who shared their duets, reached levels of brilliance that had them in awe of themselves. They had broken through to the place where, for a few moments, they tasted the pure essence of what music can mean.

Not far away from Tom and an emotional Lydia, Debbie Miller was sitting, head down and weeping. What she had seen and heard had disturbed her. She was a proud American and loved her New England life, but the foundations of her confidence in the rightness of these privileges were rocked. Africa, Kenya, Nairobi. What had she lost?

At last, the audience began to move away. Barnie and Phoebe smiled at each other. Mama held her daughter's hand while Papa leaned back and looked around. He and Tom recognised each other. Barnie cupped his hands to his lips and said quietly, with a smile, 'Look what your girl has done to our girl. Musical dynamite! But hey, it's still on to meet Rebecca?'

'Yep. Give me five minutes and I'll come and fetch you.'

Two long sobs and Debbie was sitting upright. She shook her head and laughed gently.

'Okay, I'm coming back. Sorry about that, folks.'

'Sweetheart, I envy you.'

'Strange thing, I've heard most of those songs a dozen times and more, but being here, well, I wish life could stay like this. No, I don't! My heart couldn't cope. Tell you something. I'm not sure if I want to meet her.'

'And break the spell?'

'No, Mom. I wonder what I could say.'

Barnie soon sorted his daughter's dilemma. 'Okay, it's getting late. Let's go straight to bed.'

'No, no!'

'So when you meet the Queen of the Night, just tell her that you think she has a very pretty voice and curtsy. Debbie, I think you may be in for a surprise.'

When Tom returned, a voice called out from the back of the hall. 'Thomas McCall, remember me?!'

Fred Ross, in evening dress, with his black hair swept back, skipped down the steps towards the little group who had, by now, all turned in the direction of not the expected tall, fair Englishman with the cultured voice but the swarthy, bustling figure, small but with the build of a middle-weight boxing champion. As he moved towards them, he was smiling and whispering repeatedly under his breath the single word, 'Alibi'.

There was a party. Harry Thuku had specially dressed up his Nakuru Room, his favourite venue for celebrating with invited guests. Alfredo was surprised to be invited. He had made his point. He had been seen and noticed. He was back in his hometown. Toni and the band were still in their working clothes and the other twenty or more guests were hoping that sometime in the next few hours, there would be more night music.

While Rebecca and Mary were showering and sprucing, everyone else busied themselves in pleasant circulating and chatting and checking on where they were sitting on the very large round dining table. An extra place had been set for latecomer, Fred, between Lydia and Monica, the bubbly, handsome wife of Charlie, the drummer. Tom was holding a place next to Debbie for Rebecca.

'You know Paul Miller, my father's brother.'

'Yep, changed my life. Made a big mistake. Got me to be a candidate for Serena. Wrong choice, of course. Rebecca, she would have been a winner.'

'But Rebecca's got such a talent for music. Why would she want to spend her time …?

'Because it might just help turn a dream into a reality. Talk to her about the hospital.'

'Hospital?'

'That's why she's over here, to raise money. Hospitals don't come cheap. We've got the land …'

'What about an architect?'

'Another expensive item? No, not yet.'

'Not if I did it. Wouldn't cost a shilling. Don't look so amazed. I'm qualified and I'm good.'

'Hang on. I'll make a slight adjustment to the seating on this table.'

Monica Mgoya loved meeting new people. This one intrigued her. She fixed her dark eyes on her table companion. Fred Ross was also intrigued, discomfited to have this chunky African lady, with the sexy laugh, the heavily lipsticked mouth scrutinising him closely. He was on his guard.

'Toni used to have a fellow called Henry working for the band. Spoke just like you. English, and, I'm sorry to say, a very bad person. In the penitentiary just now. I never trusted him.'

Alfredo cleared his throat. 'It can be a problem sometimes. I'm Italian. New York. When the family is having a big party, it's the same old jokes.'

'Could be they envy you, having a voice that makes you sound like what some folks think has to be a gentleman. No doubt your young lady doesn't make jokes.'

'Young lady? Ah, yes, no, not my … young lady. This is Lydia. We met in Kenya, at the McCalls', just a few days ago.'

It became a three-way conversation. 'Do you sing, dear?'

'Sometimes, when I feel happy.'

'Hmm. When you're working …'

'No, never when I'm working. I don't think the customers would like that.'

'Customers? No, I don't suppose. Do you work in a bank? I was working in a bank when I met Charlie.'

Alfredo was enjoying the contest going on between his dining companions. This Lydia was in control. The band lady obviously liked checking newcomers out in her friendly way. She was always on the lookout for a good story that she could share later with the rest of the girls. Abel Rubai had told him enough about Lydia Smith to understand that she could have given Monica her most sensational story ever. Monica had not finished.

'So, what line of business are you in?'

'You could call me a social worker. I work with people.'

Alfredo broke in. 'Interesting. I work with people, too. Helping them on their way.'

Just at that moment, he was conscious that one of those he would be 'helping' along was sitting on his right. He was impressed with Lydia, a girl with good looks and a sassy temperament. But the boss considered her to be some kind of threat and he always went with the money. When the time came, and that would be soon, the ice would return to his veins, the job would be finished and he would move on. He took a perverse pleasure out of the invisible hold he had over his future victims. *I know something about you that you will only discover at the very last moment, if ever.* After dinner, he sat with her in a quiet corner and gave her a rundown on his hometown. She was full of questions and laughed a lot.

Rebecca had developed a pattern for concert nights. A regular rhythm had imposed itself on what she did, what she felt. She looked forward to every shift of mood, the tension of the minutes before she set foot on the stage, the elation of the magical moments of the performance, the languid sense of wellbeing as she wound down and returned to earth.

Tonight was different. Tonight she met Debbie Miller, a new, young architect. As part of her course she had completed a research project on designing public hospitals. For two of the partygoers, the celebrations lost their attraction. In imagination, Rebecca led Debbie to a patch of ground on the edge of Naivasha. 'We are desperate for a new place. Just ask Paul and Miriam. You should see ...'

Tom, sitting next to her, sensed danger for her in this mad rush of enthusiasm. "Becca, tomorrow! If Debbie can stay over for the morning ...'

'Try and stop me!'

'There. After breakfast, get around a table. I'll provide the big sheets of paper and the etceteras. You'll remember more after a, well, a sort of rest if not much sleep.'

* * *

Alfredo and his younger brother, Lucio, spent much of the next day working on their father's books, 'the family books' as Lucio Senior insisted on calling them. There were no financial secrets in the immediate family, so that there was no surprise for the sons when they saw how much money Papa had amassed and deposited in banks all over the world. The job was easy because of the meticulous entries, all handwritten by their father in black ink. From time to time, Alfredo allowed his mind to drift away from the pages of numbers. When he had a contract on, he carried all the details in his head and was constantly making tiny adjustments to his program. He had a ticket to fly back to Nairobi next morning and was looking forward to the end game. He was confident that he had an alibi ready, if it should come to a situation where he would need one.

But the party in the Flamingo held his thoughts, too, and Lydia was right there in the middle of them. Rubai called her the whore from the slums and yet he admitted that they had enjoyed a few hours together. Perhaps it was the girl's openness in combination with a shy innocence that was the attraction. He himself had been flattered by her eager enthusiasm for his stories about New York. He did not find it difficult to rationalise this reaction. It was natural to have an interest in a future victim and coming to terms with all these figures in front of him was becoming something of a bore. Little black squiggles in a book were not as engaging as the memory of a beautiful black woman.

And, as the afternoon wore on, he considered a return to the Flamingo. He knew that the evening performance was sold out, but that was a minor problem. Anyway he was more interested in watching than listening, watching without being seen.

When the audit was finished, Lucio, on his way to Little Italy, gave him a lift as far as Mid Town. Alfredo booked in for dinner at the Flamingo and took a wander northwards towards the Rockefeller Center. It was his favourite building in the city, though he had been inside only once. Sitting on a café terrace with a beer, he indulged himself in more watching. For Alfredo this was like going to the gym for a sportsman. He was honing his skills. He would pick out one of the hundreds of those strolling by and 'do a job' on him or her. After giving a name, he built up an imaginary dossier of personal traits, occupation, family, ending with an assessment of how he or she would react if they found a bag stuffed full of hundred dollar bills or were confronted by some punk threatening them with a gun.

For once he did not enjoy the game. He was not sharp enough. He had created a bunch of clichés. Instead of honing his skills, he cast a slight shadow of doubt on his self-belief.

He finished his third beer and phoned the Flamingo to cancel dinner. Then it was down to the subway at Rockefeller Plaza and home to join his mother and father for supper.

After an early night he was out on the streets by four and on his way to the airport, back on the job and looking forward to returning to Africa.

The bars on the ground floor of the Flamingo only closed when the last customer decided that it was time to go home. After three, the loudest sound was the comfortable low hum of the machines of the cleaning ladies. Not long after they had begun work, the relative peace of the early morning was broken. Of the five women making their hurried way to the exit door, four were in a state of mild but excited panic and the fifth was biting her lip and struggling to hold herself together in spite of the pain in her lower abdomen. Harry Thuku was holding the front door open with the driver of the limousine whose engine was running and ready to go.

Terri Burgon, the wife of Tommy, the band's trumpeter, was in labour. Monica Mgoya , the mother figure of the Wajiru group, was struggling with her three companions to glide the first time mother to be out of the hotel and on her way to the hospital. Rebecca and Mary were still buoyed up by the excitement of the concert. Lydia had heard the commotion outside her room and came out in time to help Tommy in his struggle to balance three bulky bags as he trailed his wife in the direction of the lift.

General Monica insisted that Tommy sit with the driver and count slowly up to a thousand.

'Keep you out of trouble. And don't be nervous. This is going to be a great night, day, whatever. Colin, not too fast and, please, watch out for the potholes.'

Monica realised that total silence would be their enemy on their way to Saint Luke's. It would give Terri time to worry and, maybe, bring on the arrival of the little one. She talked as if they were all sitting 'round a table, drinking coffee and having an old-fashioned gossip.

'Did you see those people sitting in the front row last night?

Ali Baba and his people, three men, six wives and the forty thieves, waiting in the cars outside.'

'Mon, all I could see from the stage was a row of dark glasses and the occasional flash of gleaming white teeth.'

'Mary, you missed a treat. The dresses, every one white and weighed down with, well, if those stones were real, where were the security boys?'

'Is it always so busy in the middle of the night?'

'They don't have nights in this part of the city, Lydia.'

They turned left off Broadway. Conversation died. Terri's pains were coming more frequently.

'How far now, Colin?'

'Get you there in five, if the lights stay friendly.'

'Terri is some lucky girl. Twenty minutes. I was four hours with Charlie junior. Girls, you go back with Colin. I'll stay on a while, to hold Tommy's hand. The way he's going on, if a cop came along he'd arrest him for being on something!'

The conversation on the return journey was animated. Rebecca had seen something that lifted her spirits.

'That's what we need. Imagine a place even half as good. But ours is not going to be just half as good.'

'We didn't see much, 'Becca. Lots of corridors, the labour ward office, three nurses, two doctors.'

'Mary, the feel of the place. They care for the mothers in there. Didn't you think so?'

'Sweetheart, it was the luckiest day of my life when the sisters put us next to each other in the same dormitory in Santa Maria. You have such wonderful dreams for people.'

'Yes, a dream, but soon it will be a new truth, a real building, and beautiful, too.'

'Poor Tom!'

'Why you say that?'

'He is going to have a lot of listening to put up with for the next few days.'

'Wrong, Mary. Debbie, she and I have a lot of work in the morning. Thomas has to go out shopping to buy a present for his mother's birthday. By the time he comes back, we will be finished. No more talk till we go back to Kenya. Not much anyway.'

'But he hates shopping. Even I know that, 'Becca.'

'One of the boys in the band will go with him. Unless ...'

Mary and Lydia exchanged glances. Mary spoke for the two of them. 'Of course we will. I think I know the best place for little boys to buy important presents for mamas.'

When Tom returned to the Flamingo in the early afternoon, Debbie had just left for the. station. 'She is coming over. The whole family, sometime in the week after we return. We have a proper architect, Thomas. Perhaps in six months ...'

'Don't forget that we will have to ask the Naivasha council ...'

'Don't be ridiculous, Thomas!'

'You can always try an envelope with a few shillings inside.'

'Thomas, you will soon be an MP. You can give permission. When the people know about the new hospital, they will all vote for you. Hakuna matata! There, that is all organised.'

The days passed quickly. Terri and Tommy brought their handsome new son back from the hospital. Debbie and Rebecca were in regular contact bouncing new ideas off each other. There were two phone calls from Londiani.'

'Peter has finished the base. If it's not quite right, it can be adjusted to suit, easily. He's started landscaping.'

* * *

This first message was from Alex McCall. The second, from Rafaella was quite different. His grandmother was clearly distressed. There was a tremble in her voice and she seemed to be fighting back tears. 'Tom, please come home at once. A terrible thing has happened. Please forgive me. Caroline is here. She will tell you.'

'Thomas, Caroline Miggot, Inspector Caroline.'

'Caroline, what's going on?'

'There has been a fire on the farm.'

'You mean the house?'

'No, just the farm. It started one hour after the workers began their shift.'

'How bad? Anybody hurt? Of course there are. I …'

'Thomas, give me a few minutes. I will tell you everything I know. Eight o'clock, there were explosions. Two flower trucks were blown up in the yard. Four more explosions in the sheds and the fields. The flames raced along the canvas walls and the netting like a crazy thing. No fire brigade, of course, and the farm hoses could not cope. The smoke could not get away until the ceilings were destroyed. Thomas, there have been deaths. Many were choked and many burned. Big House is like a hospital. Your mother is in charge. So many have come to help.'

'My father?'

'He had just left the yard and was on his way to his foreman's office. He was blown over by the blast. He is unconscious, but he is going to be all right. Bertie is sitting by his bed. Stephen Kamau …'

'God, he's not dead!'

The hesitation before the reply terrified Tom. 'He was carrying his people out into the fresh air. He was crying and praying all the time. His young assistant said he was doing the work of ten men. He saved dozens of lives.'

'And lost his own?'

'I cannot tell you. That is God's truth.'

There was a long silence. Tom thought he had lost the line, but at last, Caroline began again. 'It was not an accident, Thomas. Of course, it could not have been. And Hosea, my new sergeant, Maria's husband, found, well, shall we say for now, devices. It was a very clever piece of work. It's my job to find him, more likely them. I am starting this minute. I am so sorry about this. We will speak again soon.'

'Thomas, you have not gone?'

'How are you coping, sweetheart?'

Her girlish laughter was the sweetest sound that had come down the line to him since he picked up the phone in his hotel room.

'At least you did not use that awful word. And I am better now. This minute a message from Bertie. Your father has just woken up. Angela is making a hot, sugary drink, and a double whisky for his best friend.'

'Stephen?'

'No news yet.'

'What do I tell Rebecca?'

'No one has been able to find him. Thomas, some were so badly burned. Say nothing to her or at least be vague. It is unbelievable. Those poor young people. You know they love to sing down in the tents. The whole house shook. Your mother ran out. She saw the flames over on the farm, and the smoke ...'

'All right, all right. I'm going to put the phone down right now. We want to be on our way ... very soon. We'll phone from the airport on this side.'

Chapter Thirty-three

Two evenings after the day of the fire, the news program on television was once again given over to the 'horrors of the Naivaisha tragedy'. Two screens in rooms separated by ten kilometres in the city of Nairobi were being watched with the closest attention.

In the pink mansion in the heart of Karen, three members of a single family watched the unfolding story with different private reactions. The pictures of the lines of bodies under their protection of white linen sheets, the smouldering tents, the neat rows of blackened rose bushes told their graphic story once again. Messages of condolence from heads of state in Africa and beyond were replayed. Henry Akamba, the maverick *Nation* journalist and television interviewer, gave a hard time to two more top cops.

'Do you people think that there is any chance that, for once, you boys in blue could actually come up with some successful policing here? I mean, do any of your men even know yet what caused all this mayhem? Where are you at, exactly in your … investigations?'

Mister Akamba was talking to the wrong policemen. Rather, he could not know that a female Naivasha inspector was making real progress. No report on that.

The human touch, that's what audiences wanted. What more intriguing aspect of this massive event than to watch the arrival back in Kenya of the most famous woman in the country, called home from the glamour of a concert tour in New York itself? And that was the next segment of the program.

There were pictures of a plane landing in JKIA, Kenya Airways when she, Tom and Lydia were flying British Airways. Carrie Eagleton of CNN was providing the voice-over.

'Rebecca Kamau and fiancé, Tom McCall, flew in this morning. Bravely Ms Kamau agreed to meet the media, for ten minutes, as long as no one followed their car over to Wilson Airport where a friend was waiting to ferry them home.'

There was a series of bland questions and defensive answers before they set off. Rafaella had flown down with Laurie Buckle. On seeing her, Rebecca shed tears for the first time since hearing the news.

'Papa?'

The single word carried the full emotional charge that had built up in thirty sleepless hours when an anxious mind fought its battle between hope and despair. Rafaella was ready. She had only her own truth to offer.

'Darling, he has not been found, yet.'

'"Yet". Such a tiny word to carry such a heavy weight. Many were burned …' Rebecca broke down. The mixture of pity and fear and guilt in her heart was unbearable. Through the sobbing, she forced herself on. 'How many?'

'Forty-five. Everyone is accounted for …'

'Except one.'

The engine of the light aircraft droned on, the only sound in the warm cabin five thousand feet above the vast open plain divided into thousands of small shambas. To their right, the thin, snaking A104 was clearly visible as it crested the high point of the Escarpment. But Rebecca was looking left. Old

Longonot. It was Papa who had introduced her to this dark peak which been a constant friend ever since. With an effort, she forced her eyes to look ahead and caught her first sight of the blue waters of home.

* * *

The only sound in the large sitting room of the pink mansion was the patter of talk coming out of the speakers of the large plasma screen. Darkness had fallen outside, but no lights in the room had been switched on. Three faces were illuminated by the flickering coloured images. Anyone who looked closely into those faces would have found only one that revealed the true feelings of the heart.

Sally was over the tears and the initial shock of seeing the scenes of horror in a place she knew and loved. The ache was as painful as ever. She found no relief in prayer. The foundations of her faith were rocked. She felt inadequate and unable to cope. If only she could have talked to Maura, been with her. But would she have been just a well-meaning nuisance in a situation that needed much more than kind, sympathetic words?

For her, seeing Rebecca surrounded by a crowd of men and women who were interested not in her but her story reopened the wound.

'Why can't these leeches allow grief to be private? Thank God they have not asked questions about her father.' That powerful, good man. What had happened? Why have they not found his body? She thought again of the lines of the dead laid out on the lawn close to Londiani. Surely, surely he must have been with them.

Her son and her husband suffered no such tender thoughts

as they watched those same images. For the third night Reuben had sat with his parents while the news was on. He found what he saw interesting, much better than the usual stuff that KBS had on. It engaged his mind like a half decent film. The people involved were distant, out there until that latest broadcast.

This time he was riveted. The sight of the piggy-faced farmer only irritated him, but he was shocked to see Lydia as the third member of the group that was being interviewed. What was she doing there? Nobody was bothering with her. Nobody mentioned her name, but she sat next to Rebecca as if she were her sister or something. He screwed his eyes tight in his concentration. Rebecca was polite and patient. If she resented giving precious time, she did not show it. Reuben wondered if anyone would dare to ask something about her father. Nobody did. Reuben finally realised that the reporters were content to have her to themselves for a few minutes, to hear her voice replying to their friendly inquiries.

Mother and son would have been shocked if they could have known the reaction of the master of the house to the startling events taking place eighty miles away in dreary Naivasha. Outwardly, his serious expression and his neutral comments suggested that he, like everyone else, was struggling to give this national tragedy some perspective.

Inwardly, the man was rejoicing, secretly and carefully. It thrilled him to know that he was the driving force, the puppet master, the sponsor. The world was tuned in to Kenya, eager for news of what he could claim was his work. And the best part was yet to come.

He had seen the pictures of the lines of bodies and felt no pity and certainly no shame or remorse. These were the casualties of the greater good, his vengeance. Hundreds of his own people had helped the McCall family to create the lakeside farm that was dedicated to producing flowers, colourful, delicate and meant to give pleasure. He revelled in the blackened destruction.

'Abel, what can we do to help these people? They were always so kind to us when we visited. You could send some of the big machines to clear the mess.'

'Get John to make some of that Colombian coffee. While he's at it, tell him to bring some pieces of the fruitcake your sister sent you.'

Having given his order, he turned towards his wife. His solemn expression suggested to Sally that he was as moved and shocked as she was.

'Karma, Sally.'

He held her gaze and waited. When he saw that his words had struck home and the big eyes and the slack jaw warned him that the reprimand was about to come, he went on.

'Sally, all this, er, stuff is most unfortunate. But your kind heart blinds you to deeper realities. These people have been kind to us? My dear, they have always looked down their noses at us. Because we have money they have tolerated us. Like so many of our European citizens, their forebears stole the very best land and used the cheap labour of our wananchi to set up their privileged lifestyle. The White Highlands. White, Sally. And now? Karma is a very good description. We have watched the television. We have read the newspapers. Where did you read that a single white person was burned to death?'

'Abel, the pain of Julius's death is still strong. But your hard heart is blinding you, too. Compassion, forgiveness, these are not weaknesses. And hope. Don't forget that God has helped us create a new life in my belly. We can be healed.'

Reuben wished he was in some other place. He was

embarrassed to hear his parents talk in this way. He was relieved when the coffee and cake were set down on the table and took the chance to excuse himself.

'No more coffee for me. I find it keeps me awake if I drink it so late.'

'So late? But it's only half past seven, boy. Yeah, you just go. I'm about finished here, too. By the way, Sally, my people checked with Londiani about sending some of our big stuff up. Bellengeri was already on the job.'

'Abel, why couldn't you say before?'

'Well, you know. Look, just pass me a thick slice of that cake. I've got work to do.'

Alfredo Rossi had just switched off the same news program and was about to return to some more study of his file on the next and final stage of this lucrative job. So far he had used his intelligence gathering with spectacular success. The television pictures proved that. Not one of his clever little bombs had failed him. Knowing the positions of all the power points had been crucial. As for the deaths, he did not see that the blame was his. The electronic devices were not killing machines. Those stupid Africans had panicked and let themselves be caught out.

His mobile rang. He was angry but tried to hide this. Against all his advice, this very pushy man had contacted him. But then, who was paying the bills?

'Mister Rubai ...'

'How did you know?'

'Because you are the only person in this country who has this number. This call is not a good idea.'

'I understand that, but I had to congratulate you on such a great piece of work.'

'But the job is not finished. The tricky part is still to come.'

'And I want to ask you a special favour.'

Alfredo made no response, hoping that his employer might just get the message at last, think again and ring off. No such luck. The man was off again.

'I want us to meet. Yes, I know, but this is something very important to me. I'm ready to double the money.'

'But I don't want to leave my room here until I'm ready to go back up to complete the assignment. Remember, the one that is costing you a lot of money.'

'At the farm tonight. Two o'clock. No one will see you.'

'No one will see me!' Alfredo's tone was meant to spell out his frustration. He was wasting his time.

'You sure you're not English? That voice sounds like it belongs to Lord Something.'

'Right. I didn't tell you, it's Lord Brooklyn.'

'I'll phone again when we're ready to move. And, relax. No one will see you.'

'Better be a big laundry basket!'

Chapter Thirty-four

As Laurie Buckle taxied his plane along the airstrip on Crescent Island, a small group stood waiting impatiently at the far end for the engines to stop. Rebecca was not surprised to see the McCall family there, including Eddie and Rollo, called home from their English school. But her mother and sisters, this was a first for them. The smiling face of her father was not there. Rebecca let go. She was soon holding her mother, Jane and Martha in a close embrace.

'So, he is not found.'

Her mother smiled tearfully and shook her head. 'No, he is not. They did not find him with the others who did not escape. How could he just vanish like this? Child, what do you think? Am I foolish to hope?'

'No, Mama. Hope is never foolish. Martha, do you remember Papa saying that?'

'No, 'Becca. Mama sent us to school today. Everyone was saying sorry to us. Jane ran home. Mister Bweiga let me do my work in his room.'

Rafaella put her arms across the girls' shoulders. Come on. You are forgetting the cake we made for the homecoming.'

Jane had lost her enthusiasm for the project that had distracted her earlier. 'I do not feel hungry now. Rebecca is home now, but she never eats cakes. Perhaps we could save some for Papa.'

Maura could see where all this negative emotion could lead and pressed for a return to Londiani. 'Don't worry, Jane. Eddie and Rollo are always hungry. You make sure that they don't scoff the lot.'

Tom helped out. 'Scoff is what boys in English schools are always doing. They will eat every crumb, if you let them.'

The acrid smell of burnt vegetation and timber was strong in the air as they all made their quiet way back to Big House. Tom was glad that from where they walked they could not see any of the devastation not fifty metres away.

Inspector Caroline and Sergeant Hosea were standing on the steps of the veranda and looking down towards the lake when Maura led the families around the corner from the laundry garden to the front of the house.

'Maura, we are very sorry for dropping in like this without letting you know.'

When Caroline gave no reason for their unexpected visit, Alex was not the only one who believed that there must bad news about Stephen, the worst. Caroline knew that any attempt at polite pleasantries would neither be useful nor welcome. Rebecca went forward and grasped her friend's hands.

'It's Papa, isn't it? You've found him. Is he …'

Hosea stepped in. 'Rebecca, everyone, I suggest we all sit down for a few moments. There is a lot to be said and we must be calm if we want to avoid any confusion.'

Caroline made a request. 'Maura, with your permission, I want you, Angela and the girls to sit at this table, close to Hosea and me.'

The tension mounted. Angela found the situation doubly difficult. She was being asked to go against her instincts and custom by sitting down in a place where she was much happier serving the needs of Bwana McCall's family. Worse still, she was afraid that she would let herself and the girls down in the way she reacted to the worst news of her life. She grasped her daughters close.

Caroline was quickly into her news. 'Yes, we have found Bwana Kamau.'

'Papa is alive! When is he coming home?'

'Martha, sweetheart, help me. I will be as quick as I can. For all of us.' Caroline took a deep breath and began again.

'It was the morning of the fire. The flames were finished. It was quiet out on the fields. Hosea and I walked down towards the lake. Maria was with us. We needed a time to gather our thoughts. A terrible thing had happened and it was our job to find out why it had happened. And we found him.'

Caroline did her best to ignore the gasp of surprise and quiet sobbing.

'He was lying on a bed of reeds with a pair of waterbuck cropping close by.'

'But was he …'

'Rebecca, Rebecca.' Another deep sigh before she went on. 'He looked as if he was in a deep sleep. His face was serene, but his clothes were burnt rags.'

'Caroline, why didn't you bring him home? All this time …'

'Angela, I told you that Maria was with us. No one here has seen her since Monday.'

Caroline hesitated, half expecting Rebecca to say something, but Stephen's firstborn merely narrowed her gaze. The beginning of a new thought was troubling her.

'Angela, his chest, his arms were burned. Now the hard part. Our bodies are fragile and when they are burned very badly, we cannot save the life.'

The members of the McCall family, except for one,

anticipated Caroline's next words quite wrongly. Rafaella felt a flutter of hope.

'Maria said medical teaching would say that his wounds were too bad. But Maria, well, she told me to bring my car … Stephen is in Nairobi.'

'Nairobi?'

'Rebecca, you know the place.'

'The little surgery, Hosea?'

'But nobody spoke about this.' Angela was halfway between puzzlement and anger. Caroline reached out to grasp her hands.

'We were afraid to give you false hope. Rebecca knows what Maria can do, but sometimes …'

Hosea took it up. 'Caroline stayed with him. Maria and I rushed home. Soon we returned and prepared him for the journey. Caroline phoned ahead and we arrived in time to see the Daniels family set off for Londiani. Thank God, Sonya stayed behind. Like for all of us, I had been thrown into an unreal world. One hour I stayed with them, to help them lift him onto the table in the surgery.'

Angela's body was shuddering with grief as she dropped her head towards the table, drawing Martha and Jane with her. Rebecca struggled to speak for her mother.

'Mama would bless you for loving us so much.' Many seconds passed before she was able to go on. 'So, you have come to tell us that you are bringing him home soon …'

'No.'

Rebecca did not expect such abruptness from Caroline, but the inspector had not finished.

'Angela, you can see that Maria is not with us.'

She gave the families time to take in what she said before going on.

'Maria and Sonya have not left his side for three days. Rebecca, remember those hours when you were together with Simon …'

Rebecca's face burst into a shocked, wonderful smile. 'But …!'

'This morning he spoke. It is not finished. The danger has not passed. Please, remember this. But it is time for you to see him.'

* * *

The door was open, but the light spilling out did not reach far into the darkness. Inside a woman was singing. Her voice was soft, but her words were clear though they were in a strange language.

'This is a spooky place.'

Jane longed to be back in the rondavel village. Her friends were there and she missed their noise. She did not feel safe here with the shadows all around.

"Becca, is Papa really in there? Will there be lots of strangers inside?'

Rebecca wanted to be quiet. Her sister would have her answers soon enough. They were not quite at the door, but a call came from inside.

'Angela, bring the girls in. Stephen is waiting.'

The air inside was heavy with a sweet perfume, chilly, too, like in the early morning out on the lakeside. The high windows in the walls all around were inlaid with coloured glass. A large table raised off the ground was the only furniture in the room. On it was laid a figure draped in a white robe. The head was at the other end where two women in yellow robes and multicoloured headscarves stood close together on a platform. Martha, more bold now that she was inside asked, 'Is that Bwana Kamau on this table? He is our father.'

Angela had a greater worry. 'Maria, Memsahib Sonya, is there witchcraft happening here? Stephen does not approve of those things.'

'No, Angela. Rebecca will tell you that we are using ancient teachings. All our medicines are mentioned in the Bible – oils, herbs, the bark of trees. Think how many times the writers tell us about oil for healing. For sure, his skin approves of our healing ointments.'

'Can we see him?'

'Martha, I cannot understand why you are all holding back.'

Rebecca was pushed to the front to lead the way. The line of Kamaus moved slowly, each of them struggling to keep a hold on the mix of conflicting emotions. When they stepped up onto the platform, they discovered that their bwana was asleep. Anticlimax, but at least it spared them the task of coming up with the perfect opening words. The covering of the white sheet was folded back to the waist.

Stephen's four womenfolk showed their astonishment in their own way, but the gasp, the clapping of the hands to the mouth was a shared reaction.

'Maria, but how …?'

That was as far as Angela could speak out her feelings. Her eyes moved quickly to take in every square inch of that familiar muscular body. She had helped to lay out the corpses of the mostly young people who had perished in the fire just days before. Where there were burns, the flesh was crusty and peppered with ugly red sores. But here in front of her, Stephen's flesh was undamaged but covered in a skin that had the texture of soft leather. There was not a single blemish of a sore. Sonya explained why this was so to a bewildered Angela.

'Maria is a healer. I'm a doctor. I studied in a famous London hospital that did wonderful, amazing work. My main task now is to help mothers bring healthy babies into the world. Maria's teacher? She will tell you.'

'I only wish I could. I know that the knowledge has come down to us from long, long ago. You remember that Jesus himself had many followers who were women. Some say that he spent many hours instructing them. Some say that a woman, Dorcas or Sophie perhaps, wrote down this teaching. It is a mystery. There are prayers and songs, all in the languages of ancient times.'

'Mama, I have watched Maria at her work.'

'Angela, the danger is not finished. We have taken away the pain of his body. Now there is the pain of the heart and the mind. Sonya's word is "trauma". Bwana must want to come back to us. Wait! He is restless. Angela, place your hand on his forehead. I will sing. My words will be Aramaic, Jesus' own language.'

She began. The voice was soft, but it filled every space in the room with a sweetness and power that cast a spell. Jane and Martha buried their faces into their mother's side and clung tight. For their young minds it was as if they were being carried off into some mysterious land where the safe familiar ways had deserted them. They did not utter a single syllable, afraid that they would be noticed.

This music went on and on until another sound pierced their ears. It was laughter, coming from close by. It was the melodious chuckle that they heard a thousand times. The healing was complete and their father had returned to them.

* * *

'Not many people around at this time of night. But, even at this hour, I could not risk a meeting at your hotel. I would be recognised and, well, it would cause problems. You understand these things.'

'Understand, yes, but I don't like it. My work is delicate in certain ways. My timing has to be perfect and I do not like showing myself around. You want value for money? Trust me. So, Mister Rubai, what gives? You have some special request. Tell me.'

'Yes. This family, these McCalls, these opportunists, these robbers …'

'These killers of your son, I understand. Revenge, a lot of my clients are into this.'

'I want their punishment to hit hard, to hurt, no mercy.'

'And the request?'

'I want to be close enough to watch.'

'Impossible! I work alone, always. I trust no one but myself.'

'Work alone, of course. I have a very fine pair of binoculars. I would be a hundred, two hundred metres away.'

'With half a dozen of your men around. It won't work.'

'Absolutely alone.'

'No. Perhaps it would be better if I went back to the hotel and get the first plane out.'

'Not a good idea.'

'Mister Rubai, are you threatening me?'

'I don't see it that way. Patrick Uchome, you met him in this very place. He is desperate to get back on a good footing with me. I look on him as a kind of insurance policy. Only a fool would not look to protect his investment.'

'Or I could shoot you right here and now. No, too noisy, but I never travel without my good friend, Mister James Bowie.'

Abel chuckled and held out his hand. 'At last, we speak the same language!'

Alfredo did not accept the handshake. Instead, he gazed directly into his boss's eyes. It did not make pleasant reading. Rubai had him cold and was enjoying the experience. Alfredo's instinct provided him with his best plan to ensure that he would leave the country still breathing and with his payout. The handshake was accepted.

'You African bastard. They warned me about crooks like you before I took this job on.'

'So I take it that you agree to my being a spectator.'

Alfredo leaned back into his armchair and contemplated the log fire that had been lit against the chill of the night. He was working his way through half a dozen possible scenarios while he was being scrutinised closely by his smiling employer. At that moment, life was very agreeable for Mister Abel Rubai, fixer in chief. He was about to get his wish to be present at the climax to his big project. An unexpected thought struck him. The raging anger that had been set off by a potent mix of grief, guilt and frustration had cooled. The thirst for revenge that had become an obsession that would not leave him alone was weakened. They were replaced by the excitement of anticipation. Thomas McCall and the rest of them would be part of history, he would be free with the bonus of being able to pick up the wreck of Londiani for a knock down price.

'So, when do you go in?'

'You insist on this, er, interference, then?'

'Don't let's waste our breath on that any more. Give me a day and a time, and name a place with a view.'

'Listen. When I'm ready, I will make a single brief call. Then it's up to you. To you this business may be some kind of crusade, but to me it's a job. I am a man who takes pride in his workmanship. I will deliver.'

* * *

Next morning, breakfast was late in the pink palace in Karen. Papa had slept on. Sometimes he was grouchy on the morning after. Today was different.

'Abel, bacon and eggs, all that toast, a whole pot of coffee, you must have had much success on the screens last night.'

'Woman, can't a man feel happy just to be with his family on a lovely morning?'

'Papa, it's raining.'

'Reuben, the fields will be happy, the trees will be happy, the animals will be happy. That makes me happy.'

He would have been even more pleased with life if he could have shared his news. Pembroke House, that ramshackle school, high up in the Rift Valley, the White Highlands, in that place a bad seed had been sown. That tiny seed had been big enough to carry a name: McCall. For years it had grown without him understanding the danger. When the truth of this ugly weed had revealed itself he had failed to cut it down in time to save his Julius. There was some regret that he had been obliged to bring in a stranger to finish the job, but soon …

'Sally, I'm thinking of going into the flower business. Perhaps we could be lucky. When a farmer has lost his crop and many of his workers, he might lose his interest in the land.'

'Londiani?'

'Sure, Reuben, and with you as the man for Nakuru South in parliament, we would have somebody on the spot to make sure everything was in order.'

'Abel, I don't like that idea. It would be like stealing.'

'Stealing! I would offer double what the place is worth. I would not make the first move. I would be doing them a favour.'

'I know those people better than you. They are tough. They

will make that farm better than ever.' Sally was staring out at the rain. When would her husband be able to shake off this imaginary burden? Her hope was being carried in her belly.

* * *

The crowd around the village fire at the rondavels was the biggest anyone could remember. It was also the quietest. You could actually hear the sound of the newly placed logs as they crackled and spluttered in the leaping tongues of flame. No one from the village had been taken by the fire down in the fields. Six of the young women sitting in that crowd owed their lives to Bwana Kamau.

When the family left the Kamau home, their entrance roused the villagers and their other well-wishers. They stood as one, cheering and applauding. Rebecca was used to such receptions on stage, but here, amongst her own people, with Jane and Martha leading the way and she and her mother flanking her father, the positive emotions were overwhelming.

The release of pent-up feelings burst around them, sending the waves of screaming and wailing out into the lake and up the empty hillside towards the dark ridge of the Escarpment. Stephen himself showed little emotion. How could anyone know the feelings of the heart of a man who had left the world and been restored to life? As he moved along, he was still deep in a sense of wonder. 'How can this be?' He had whispered these words a thousand times since he woke on a bed in that cool room and looked up into the eyes of those two smiling, weeping women. He had never experienced love of such intensity. The first word he mouthed was 'angels'. When his strength began to return, he recognised the white robed figures and chuckled, and felt a sharp prickle of pain across his chest and arms.

* * *

'Lazarus.' He did not want to get into that territory, but it was the name that Martha spoke just as they were cresting the ridge of the Escarpment.

'Papa, I have been thinking. You are just like him, aren't you? Do you think that Jesus was helping you after the fire? We have read that story so many times.'

Angela watched her husband's reaction carefully. She thought she detected some discomfort, even embarrassment, behind his patient smile.

'Child, you are asking me to claim a pretty big thing there.'

'But if we are in trouble, you say that Jesus will always be ready to help us.'

'That's true, Martha.' He nodded his head slowly, overwhelmed by the mystery that was still engulfing him. He drifted off into a long silence and peered down the long hillside as his beloved lake came into view. 'To tell the truth, I feel a little funny in the head. Now, no jokes, please! There's a kind of emptiness, coolness up there. I cannot get a good hold on it.' His tone changed and he reached for his wife's hand. 'Angela, why have I been spared? I've seen it over and over in my mind, the flames rushing along the tents like madmen, the screams of pain, smoke throttling the breath out of you. Next thing, everything goes quiet and I'm walking away, going home along a grassy path. And I feel so tired I take a little spell under an acacia.'

* * *

A wooden armchair, softened with blue cushions on the seat and back, is ready for Bwana, close to the heart of the gathering. Big-eyed children watch him pass along while their anxious parents, scarcely able to believe that their Stephen is back amongst them, stare and hope that all is really well and that this upright, dignified figure is restored in full. At last, his little family group reach the chair. Stephen grasps the back and looks around. After a brief pause, he begins to speak.

'Agnes Kibet, Antony Wakamba, Mary Macharia, David Dalon, Thomas Koskei, Rita Koskei ...' He continued to recite the names until the list was complete. His eyes were closed and he paused between each name. The deep baritone of his voice rang out like a heavy church bell. The long silence that followed was broken by the piping tones of little Sammy Koskei, youngest brother of the twins who had died as they searched for one another up and down the lines of different flower tents.

'Bwana, is there a story tonight?'

Stephen, unruffled, reached into the crowd to lift Sammy out. He sat on a blue cushion and placed the child on his lap. The boy felt no fear, hoping rather that his hero had singled him out for special treatment.

'How old are you, Sammy?'

'I am eight, Bwana. I am going to school now. Sometimes the teacher tells us a story, but we like your stories better.'

'I know that you are a very clever boy. Your brother told me, just a few days ago, that you told the people at home better stories than me.'

'Oh, that is a very big whopper, Bwana!' Sammy's face was beaming with a naughty boy grin.

'Yes!' Stephen reflected with a deep sigh. 'A story. Sammy, you know that I love telling you stories.'

'I know it. You tell a story and Rebecca sings to us. That is the best time for me.'

'And you know that I have been away from the village for a few days.'

'Thomas and Rita, they have gone away, too. On a long journey. Did you see them when you were away?'

'You know, Sammy, I think that I just did. We passed each other. I forget where it was now.'

'Mama said that you would. They have died, you know. Gone to be with Jesus, our teacher told us.'

'She is a very wise lady.'

'Mama said that things have changed. Papa and she were talking. What does it mean?'

Rebecca was standing behind her father. She began to sing, one of Toni Wajiru's songs and one of her favourites, 'Hope comes with the dawn'. The cheering and the excitement were far behind them all now. A mellow tranquillity had settled over the gathering. The physical beauty of the singer and the poignancy of the words she sang soothed the pain, made it more bearable. There was a golden edge to the heavy clouds hanging over the village. Sammy slipped from Stephen's lap and returned to his mother and father.

And what did Sammy's mother's words mean? All those friends were laid to earth and he had returned. But why? He saw clearly that it was a mystery and would stay so.

Soon the crowd dispersed, satisfied that they had seen that Stephan Kamau was with them and he was well.

Later Stephen himself with Angela, his firstborn and the young bwana took the path to the flower fields. In the half light, he saw that the vast garden where he spent his working day had been returned to an expanse of dark earth. He bent to pick up a handful of soil. He sifted it with his fingers and lifted it to his nose.

'Bwana, the land is ready for us again.'

* * *

Alfredo Rossi was brooding. This was a new experience for him and he did not enjoy it. The hotel room was everything he could ask for, but it had become just a comfortable prison cell. The best of it was the large window with a close view high above Uhuru Highway. He liked to look down on the traffic on the busiest road in the country. Not once did he step through the French window onto the balcony. He would not take the infinitesimal risk of being seen and recognised. He still had qualms about the night visit forced on him by his employer. The man was plain stupid and too used to being obeyed in his smallest whim.

On his normal jobs he made little contact with the particular rich person (he was popular with well-heeled widows) paying for the contract. He worked alone and was happy enough just to let his client know that his goods had been delivered and then fly out. No one ever took advantage of his absence to welsh on a payment. This time the vibes were bad. He saw himself as an artist. He was proud of the precision, the finesse he displayed. His studio was out of doors in a different location for every job, a factor that brought special problems, increased the risks. But this Rubai jerk was getting in his way. Alfredo was nervous, distracted. He needed to go to a good restaurant, have some conversation with intelligent people out there in the big world.

There was something else. He was in danger of allowing his emotions to interfere with his plans. When his parents decided to bring a touch of class to the Rossi family of New York, they worked it out that if they sent their smartest boy to the only fancy school in England that they had heard of, any rough edges in their son would be smoothed away. What they could not have foreseen was how hard it would be for him to settle in this alien environment. He was below average in size for a thirteen year old, he was not interested in the ancient Etonian traditions, his Brooklyn accent was a curiosity to his classmates. When one or two tried to imitate it, he was in with his fists to let them know that you did not make fun of a Rossi man. In time things worked out. In a matter of weeks, his speech was indistinguishable from the sophisticated patter of Dickie, the son and heir of some rich lord from the heartland of the aristocracy.

Eton toughened him up. He learned to distrust his emotions. He was pleased to learn that his favourite character in history was an Italian. Nicolo Machiavelli taught him that, more often than not, it pays to be something of a bastard. Calculate honestly and cut the sentimental crap. To be hard usually meant a satisfactory profit. So a career of eliminating the unwanted, doing the dirty work for the ultra rich suited him perfectly. 'Don't get involved'. That was his number one guideline.

Now this African Mister Big was rousing an uncharacteristic anger in him. That was one side of the problem. The other side had a greater potential for disaster and, this time, it was all his own fault. He had been too clever. Get to see his victims, use his visit to make his plan for the first strike. Smart move and the result was top-class. Anyone who watched the television saw that.

But, in spite of himself, he had got to like the people he was planning to send to glory. The McCalls had treated him with kindness. Normally such treatment was accepted but had no influence on his plans. He had dealt with many so-called nice people and moved on without a backward glance. He had spent time in his hotel room working on this problem. He had to understand it before he could root out its cause.

The conclusion he reached did not surprise him. But why Lydia Smith? He had heard some of her story and sympathised with her for the tough times she had endured. But she was not a part of the McCall tribe. Rubai had described her as an optional victim. He had steered clear of any involvement with women. Now this one had caught him unawares. He had enjoyed her company. He wasted time thinking about her. It was easy to rationalise that there was no future in such a relationship, even if she were interested. And there was not much chance of that. He was a midget Italian with a voice like an old-fashioned colonial bwana.

No, he would be able to cope. He was already beginning to squeeze her out of his consciousness. A small dose of body battering and he would be almost there, system clear and ready for action. He went through his routine of very hard physical exercise to the point where perspiration was dripping onto the thick pile of the carpet and followed it with a long soak in a hot bath.

The end of the job was close. That night he dined well and fell asleep with the best book ever written in his hand. He had read *Catcher in the Rye* at least a dozen times. He admired Holden Caufield for his free spirit and envied him that he had been lucky enough to have attended a boarding school within easy reach of his New York home.

He spent most of the next day checking and rechecking every detail of his plans. He shifted the desk close to the window. The light was better there and it gave him the chance to look down on life going on in the world below. He found the constant noise of the traffic comforting. It suggested energy and purpose. He was too far back to see the lines of cars, matatus, coaches and trucks easing their way along the dual carriageway in the warm morning sun. The red earth paths that crisscrossed the parklands opposite were alive with black shapes. Downtown Nairobi was on the move. He smiled. When he had accepted the job, he had inexplicably overlooked the people problem. A white man among thousands of black brothers and sisters would not make it easy to hide himself in a crowd.

He was excited, confident and the attack of broodiness was far behind him. The ice was back. The artist was ready to execute. At midnight he would leave the hotel through the back entrance, turn left and a hundred metres down the road slide behind the wheel of the black BMW waiting for him. It was time to travel north to make his final preparations for the climax of the exercise.

* * *

Not far away, in the suburb of Langata, two lawyer brothers were reading the national papers. *The Nation* and *The Standard* each carried almost identical headlines. 'Dead Man Rises From The Ashes' declared *The Nation.*

'So this is Rebecca's father?'

'Yep. Barnie, I wish I knew half of what is going on here.'

'You mean about the fire? How are the local cops getting on with finding the people behind that?'

'I'm not sure, but the Naivasha police have got some top-class officers. Yes, I know about the reputation about our men in blue. Inspector Caroline and her new sergeant, Hosea Kabari, would be an asset in any city force in the States.'

'Paul, I could get them a start in our precinct.'

'Our need is …'

'Okay, okay, only kidding.'

'Did you notice the name Maria Kabari in the report? She's Hosea's wife. Not much about her in the story, but ever heard of Maria Miller?'

'Our Maria? You know, I'd forgotten her married name. She never contacts us. I thought she lived in Western District.'

'Our Maria is quite a woman. Barnie, there's no doubt she has, well, healing gifts.'

'Faith healer? I remember, when we were kids, she was a dreamy sort of girl, sang weird songs. So it's Naivasha now. Three girls, isn't it?'

'They're all coming down next week. Family reunion.'

'Paul, who's this coming up the driveway? Carrying a briefcase. Not another lawyer? No. Can't be. He's not wearing a suit.'

Paul rose to meet his guest. 'Not a lawyer. Much cleverer than that.'

Jimmy Burgon, tall, with the long, slim legs of a middle-distance runner was smiling. Barnie noticed the expensive, fashionable clothes, especially the leather jacket which must have been tailor-made. Whatever this kid does for a living, there must be big profits.

'Paul, another set of pictures for you. A couple of puzzlers that may or may not be useful. That's your department.'

Paul explained to his brother. 'Barnie, technology has come to the Kenya legal system. Those last three words are in quotation marks, of course. Strictly speaking, what Jimmy and I do is not by the book, but it works. Electronic recording cameras, Jimmy makes them. See that pepper tree just there? What is it, ten metres away? See the camera on that low branch on the left?'

'Can't say that I do.'

'I'll show you later. What happens is that one of Jimmy's boys places one or maybe more in a place where it will take pictures.'

'I think I get it. A Mister Bad Guy appears in glowing colours in a place where he shouldn't be.'

'Robbery, corruption, wife cheating …'

'Do the courts allow these to be used in a case?'

'Sometimes. But, let's see the ones you've brought, Jimmy. What we do is look at my set and see what turns up.'

As Jimmy took out his folders of prints, Paul went on. 'No flash, no click and the lens swivels towards body heat. If we catch someone we're after on camera, we know we're on track. It gives us confidence.'

'Paul, here's the batch we took at the Rubai farm just outside the city, the one he thinks nobody knows about. You'll see that a lot of them are of Mister Big's heavies. But take a look at these.'

'Barnie, notice the quality of the prints. Superb clarity. Wow! That's Alex McCall. Must be the night when he was taken from the hospital. Did you hear about that?'

Before his brother could answer, Paul was yelping his surprise.

'Recognise her? It's our dear sister and Lydia on their rescue mission. Fantastic stuff, James.'

'Ah, this one is foxing me. Never seen this guy before. Doesn't look too happy.'

Barnie leaned forward and picked the print up for a closer look. 'I know this face. I saw it somewhere and recently as well.'

'You sure? You've only been back in the country a couple …'

'Yep. Got it and wasn't in Nairobi, not even in Kenya. Rebecca's concert. Name of Fred Ross. That's it. Fred Ross, from New York, or so he said. Unusual voice.'

'But what could he be doing over here?'

'At the Rubai place at two am. I must have missed something.'

'I think I could help out on this, if he's telling the truth about coming from New York.'

* * *

'Paul, this is what I've got. I think you'll be interested. Bob Hawkins said that, once he sorted out the name, it was a piece of cake.'

'What do you mean?'

'Fred Ross, better known as Alfredo Rossi, has form. A particularly nasty hit man, he does a lot of work outside the US. The description fits. Apparently the voice is a giveaway. Interpol know about him but can't nail him for anything.'

Paul put his hand to his forehead, deep in thought. He was rapidly confirming in his mind a terrifying implication. He shared his thinking.

'This Fred Ross dropped in on the McCalls, claiming to be some kind of scientist. They welcome him. He stays the night and before he leaves he wangles a tour 'round the farm. Stephen Kamau tells Alex that the young man who showed Ross around reported that the American bwana had been very interested in everything, even took notes. A couple of days later, well, you know about the fire. There were several fires, in fact, all connected to the farm's power points.'

Barnie took up the story with what he saw as a problem with the timing.

'But we saw him in Rebecca's concert, even before the fire. How come?'

'Easy. Delayed action. Fire bursts out and he's thousands

of miles away, making sure that he is seen. Great alibi. Three days later his face is captured on Jimmy's camera, visiting Abel Rubai's farm.'

'And this one, taken half an hour before ...'

Paul was horrified but not surprised by what he saw. 'Barnie, there's worse to come, and soon.'

'What's going on?'

'Rubai and Ross, Rossi, whatever. Do you remember a few months back Rubai's eldest son, Julius, killed on Muthaiga golf course?'

'Shot by his own gun. Read about in *The Globe*, tragic accident stuff.'

'That's not how Papa saw it. There was bad blood between Julius and Tom McCall. Trust me, the McCalls are in big danger. Rubai has tried twice already, using his local boys. They botched up so in comes a Yankee pro.'

'He's not going to hang about, Paul.'

'Fancy a trip up-country?'

'Like this minute? Bring it on. I hope the kids will understand about missing the trip into the park.'

'Don't worry. Miriam will take them. I'll phone ahead. Miriam!'

* * *

'That's the story, all of it.'

Paul and Barnie, sitting on the veranda wall at Londiani, looked around at the assembled gathering of family and friends. The silence was deep and solemn. There were as many takes on what they had just heard as there were people in the room. The only face that Barnie saw that seemed relaxed about the story was his own sister. He and she had barely had time for a hug and an exchange of greetings before the meeting got under way. Now she was sitting between Hosea and Inspector Caroline, studying the expressions of those close to her. She was a comforting sight.

First spoken reactions to the news focused on past events, specifically the fire and its aftermath. That was bad news that they could get their minds around.

'You mean that bastard Rubai was behind all this? Paying for some foreigner to come over here to murder our people?' Laurie Buckle was not finished. 'Paul, I know he's a slippery customer, but surely you can nail him for this!'

Tom was standing behind the long sofa, reaching down to Rebecca who was holding the arm of her mother. Angela, in turn, pressed her face, wet with tears, to her husband's cheek that was tense with the memory of his ordeal by fire. Tom asked Paul for confirmation of a technical point.

'And this could have been set up days before it went off?'

'Yes, it could, Tom.'

'And nobody noticed?'

'Tom, this man is very good at his work and he will rot in hell when the time comes. Our job is to make that time sooner rather than later.'

Maria raised her hand, wanting to speak. 'My heart is not made of stone, but I must say a hard thing. This town will grieve for many months to come. For some it will be a lifetime. Nothing can change the past, but the burden is big enough. We have the chance to change the future.'

'Can Abel Rubai hate us so much?'

'Maura, a crazy man can lose contact with reality.'

'But he is not crazy, Alex. He is so drunk with power, he knows that he can do what he likes and nobody in this country, nobody, will do a thing about it.'

Paul stood up from his place on the veranda wall and leaned forward aggressively. His eyes revealed the anger that was rising in him. 'Now it is my turn to say a hard thing. Maura, we can do something about it. Abel Rubai is many things. He is ruthless; he is angry; and, yes, he is heartbroken. But he's made a mistake and given us the chance to stop him in his tracks. A chance but not much of one. There is so much that we don't know. Caroline, you and Hosea are the experts. What's the best way of using what we've got?'

'Two quick points. All right, Inspector?'

'Go ahead, Hosea.'

'This house is the target and Rossi is in a hurry. This is the best evidence we have.' He paused. 'We could be sitting on a bomb, at this very moment. I'm scared and I would be a lot less scared if we moved over to 'Rusinga', like now!'

Two hours later there was a plan.

* * *

At ten o'clock on the following evening, Abel Rubai's mobile rang. He was in his screen room and the door was ajar. A mild shock made him shudder. At last!

'Rubai here.'

Mister Big was in a state of high excitement. For the hour he had been alone in his sacred room, he had been unable to focus on any of the information flashing up on his screens. Nor had he noticed that the door behind him was ajar.

Reuben had noticed on the three times he passed the forbidden room on his way to another part of the house. Through the open door he saw the green light coming from the screens, that and the electronic hum of machinery at work. This happened on the first two occasions that he passed. He assumed that his father had slipped out for some reason and left the equipment on.

On the third passing he heard his father's voice speak two words: 'Londiani' and 'Naivasha'. He pulled up sharp and listened. Whoever was on the other end of the line was dominating the exchanges. His father's voice was agitated in a way he had never heard before. His part in the conversation was a series of staccato replies to what seemed to be instructions: 'Yes, one am. I know that but where exactly? In the car? My car, but how did you know ...? Written directions and a map. Right. No, I remember. I won't move.'

There was no more conversation. Neither was there the sound of any movement inside the room. From where he stood, unsure of what he should do next, Reuben could not have suspected that Papa's mind was in a state of turmoil. For a few moments, Abel felt as though he was drowning in a wild confusion of random thoughts. The moment that he had been longing for was close by and his reaction was numbing fear. Irrelevant memories crowded in him, distracting him further. He made one audible reaction, a loud groan.

Reuben, ignoring the restraints that in normal circumstances would have kept him firmly rooted to the spot on the outside of that room, afraid of rousing his father's considerable bad temper, burst in.

'Papa, is everything all right? Are you feeling ill? Can I help you?'

Abel swung 'round, stunned with surprise. The world was going crazy all 'round him. For a few seconds, father and son stared at one another in disbelief. They had entered new territory in their relationship. Reuben had struck an unwitting blow against his father's domination. Abel felt not anger but relief at his son's intrusion. The sight of Reuben flashed up in Abel's mind, the memory of a smiling, confident, even arrogant Julius.

For a fleeting moment it was his dead son standing there in front of him.

The moment passed, but its afterglow acted like an electric charge on Abel. The doubt, the fear, the guilty hesitation vanished instantly. He had rediscovered his purpose, his drive, his determination to finish his task, gloriously. A minor regret came and went. He needed the help of a stranger to achieve the wonderful, shocking, cleansing revenge.

This stranger had ordered him to travel to Naivasha alone. But no, he would be his own man on this. Reuben would go with him.

'Reuben, go up to your room and put on your darkest clothes. Be at the lodge in twenty minutes. We're going on a journey together, perhaps the most important journey of our lives.'

Chapter Thirty-five

Go high enough into the night sky and look down. The Central Rift is a dark mass that, to the eyes of a stranger up here, is a plain broken in places by strings and pools of light. Nairobi to the south and Nakuru to the north glow with city brightness. Naivasha, directly below, has its straggling ribbons of white dots reaching out a short distance from its heart, itself pale except for two large rectangles on the shores of the lake where the flower farmers are at their work of fooling their plants by creating their best imitations of the power of the African sun.

Swoop down thousands of feet and your perception changes. Now you see the shadowy outlines of hills all around. On this moonlit night, the lake is an irregular stretch of grey plate, reflecting a cold light. From above, rings of security lamps define the home farms that snuggle along the shore. Londiani and Rusinga are silent from where we are.

At this late hour, hardly a vehicle passes up or down South Lake Road. A single black Mercedes carrying two men is moving steadily along the lower road from the Escarpment. The road is straight, cutting through a wide, barren plain with the craggy mass of Longonot looming to their left. It is a good time for letting the thoughts wander.

Darkness can be a friend, as it was on this night. Alfredo Rossi had set out as the brief Kenya dusk was turning into full night. He was well aware that this was a dangerous time to be travelling along even the A104, the busiest road in the country. But he was ready for any violent attempts to slow his progress. Two loaded pistols fitted with silencers lay on the seat beside him. They would see off any possible trouble.

He turned off South Lake Road at the entrance to the country club and parked close to the road but out of sight behind a pair of heavy-limbed pepper trees. It was just a short walk to Londiani and, after reluctantly phoning Rubai, as promised, he set off carrying the two black leather cases that held his equipment. He took his time, moving off the road every fifty metres or so to make certain that he had no company.

Once onto the McCall property, his first job was to check out the spot he had picked out for his paymaster. It would be very easy for Rubai to find although Alfredo had hopes that, at the last moment, the man himself would have a change of heart and not turn up.

After that it was a question of waiting and keeping a close lookout. For half an hour he lay on the ground motionless, enough time to make doubly sure that no one was close by. He had chosen a spot with direct, straight sightlines to the house. In the distance to his left he could see the open wood fire burning low at the heart of the village. Up ahead, less than thirty metres away he saw that there were lights on in three upstairs rooms in what the workers called Big House. At last he had his target in front of him and he was pleased to see that at least some of the family were about. He opened one of his cases, took out the rifle parts and assembled them. It was his backup, but he hoped he would have a chance to use it for the personal touch it brought to a job. He was ready.

He opened the second and smaller case. Through the

heavily filtered light of a headlamp, he peered down. He checked the circuits. All connected and neatly fitted. It was the tenth time he had used the system, passed on to him for a big fee from a military man. The hard part had been completed in the dead of night forty-eight hours before. Now it was a matter of pressing a single red button. Those inside who did not cop it in the explosion would find all exits from the house blocked, except for the one down the steps from the veranda. He had been a first-class marksman since his schooldays. They would feel virtually nothing.

The series of explosions was satisfactory and fire a billowing mass of red and gold. As he raised his rifle to his shoulder, he glanced across to his right. Rubai was on his feet, throwing one arm up in triumph.

'The bastard!'

Rossi had seen two where there should have been one. Never mind. He had a job to finish. He had his night sight trained on the veranda steps, unnecessarily. In the brightness of the blaze he could have picked out a black cat without straining his eyes. No one appeared. He unloaded and broke down the rifle into parts. In two hours he would be at the airport on his way back to civilisation. Nobody could have survived in that house. He was right.

His focus was fixed in the wrong direction. Rubai and son saw what he could not. A stream of people was racing towards Londiani from Rusinga. He recognised the rolling gait of Tom McCall and behind him his father. He had brought his own rifle hoping that, at last, he would be able to pull a trigger and finish some of his own dirty work.

'Watch out, Rossi! Over there!'

It was the American, not the rich African big man who panicked. All Rossi could think of was his own safety. He had been outwitted by a bunch of hick town deadbeats. He would find his way back to the car over the fields. Getting away from this jinxed place was the only thing that counted. He was off.

Abel ran forward. He could not resist one more scream of anger before he finished off at least one of his tormentors.

'Better late than never, McCall! Your turn to feel some pain!'

Tom stopped to peer into the darkness. He knew the voice too well. He was close enough to see the barrel pointing straight at him. As the rifle shot cracked the night sky he was diving for the ground. The pain in his shoulder came from his impact with the ground.

He looked up to see Bertie Briggs slowly remove his rifle from his shoulder and, further away, Reuben Rubai bent over a prostrate body.

Best-selling titles by Kerry B. Collison

SID HARTA PUBLISHERS

Readers are invited to visit our publishing websites at:
http://sidharta.com.au
http://publisher-guidelines.com/

Kerry B. Collison's home pages:
http://www.authorsden.com/visit/author.asp?AuthorID=2239
http://www.expat.or.id/sponsors/collison.html
email: author@sidharta.com.au